FINDING MR. JULY

Also by Anna E. Collins

Worst in Show

FINDING MR. JULY

Anna E. Collins

FOREVER

New York　Boston

This book is a work of fiction. Names, characters, places, and incidents are the product of the author's imagination or are used fictitiously. Any resemblance to actual events, locales, or persons, living or dead, is coincidental.

Copyright © 2025 by Anna E. Collins

Cover design and illustration by Sarah Kellogg
Cover copyright © 2025 by Hachette Book Group, Inc.

Hachette Book Group supports the right to free expression and the value of copyright. The purpose of copyright is to encourage writers and artists to produce the creative works that enrich our culture.

The scanning, uploading, and distribution of this book without permission is a theft of the author's intellectual property. If you would like permission to use material from the book (other than for review purposes), please contact permissions@hbgusa.com. Thank you for your support of the author's rights.

Forever
Hachette Book Group
1290 Avenue of the Americas, New York, NY 10104
read-forever.com
@readforeverpub

First Edition: July 2025

Forever is an imprint of Grand Central Publishing. The Forever name and logo are registered trademarks of Hachette Book Group, Inc.

The publisher is not responsible for websites (or their content) that are not owned by the publisher.

The Hachette Speakers Bureau provides a wide range of authors for speaking events. To find out more, go to hachettespeakersbureau.com or email HachetteSpeakers@hbgusa.com.

Forever books may be purchased in bulk for business, educational, or promotional use. For information, please contact your local bookseller or the Hachette Book Group Special Markets Department at special.markets@hbgusa.com.

Print book interior design by Taylor Navis

Library of Congress Cataloging-in-Publication Data

Names: Collins, Anna E., author.
Title: Finding Mr. July / Anna E. Collins. Other titles: Finding Mister July
Description: First edition. | New York : Forever, 2025.
Identifiers: LCCN 2025005741 | ISBN 9781538742310 (trade paperback) | ISBN 9781538742334 (ebook)
Subjects: LCGFT: Romance fiction. | Novels.
Classification: LCC PS3603.O4525 F56 2025 | DDC 813/.6—dc23/eng/20250210
LC record available at https://lccn.loc.gov/2025005741

ISBNs: 9781538742310 (trade paperback), 9781538742334 (ebook)

Printed in the United States of America

LSC-H

Printing 1, 2025

Starting over is hard.

This book is for all of those who've dared to leap from the safe to the unknown, and for those still looking for their nerve.

Beautiful things grow out of ashen ground.

1

There are pros and cons to getting stuck in the office pantry closet. Pros: It's calm and quiet, it smells like coffee beans, and challenging situations are good for exercising the mind. Cons: The "stuck" part. And possibly spiders.

I bang on the door with my palm again. "Hello? Anyone out there?" It's an optimistic move since it's only 6:50 in the morning, but you never know. Could be some other overachiever decided sleep was for losers and that an early start at the environmental nonprofit where we work was in order. Most likely not, but hope is the last thing that leaves us, or so I've heard.

Hope and dignity.

I fan myself and eye the vent cover in the ceiling, gauging how far I'd have to leap from the shelving unit to reach it. *No.* While I'm no stranger to facing challenges head-on, there are limits to how far out of my comfort zone I'm willing to push myself. Leave my job as a corporate attorney and accept an unpaid internship for a chance at a new start? Yes, I'll do that. Contort myself *Mission: Impossible* style to ensure everyone's morning coffee is brewed on time? I don't think so.

I sigh. This is quite the turn of events on a morning that started out great. I woke up before my alarm, got in a fifteen-minute yoga session to loosen my limbs, and enjoyed a nice, hot shower in my brother's guest suite where I'm currently living. Not only that, but for once, my shoulder-length hair also cooperated with me, and the bagels I'd ordered for the team were waiting for me at the shop on my way in.

It has to be said—I do love an empty office in the morning. To flick on the lights, hear my footfalls play a solo against the laminate wood flooring, open the blinds to take in the waking city outside, be the first to breathe life into the sleeping corners. It feels like walking in on a secret.

On a morning like that, I'd have expected the pantry door to cooperate, too. Instead, this.

There is exactly zero air circulation in here, so I unbutton my blouse while I sink onto a low step stool and glare at the treacherous door handle that refuses to budge. If only I had my phone, but no...I don't normally walk away from it, but in my defense, I was only intending to start the coffee maker and set out the bagels in the kitchen and then return to my desk. But then the filters needed restocking...

I fight off that insidious stinging behind my eyelids that threatens at the most inopportune times nowadays. The one that speaks of unfairness and bad luck. I don't have time for tears. "Channel it into action," I mumble to myself—a nugget of wisdom I've picked up from my brother. Not that there's much I can do about my situation at the moment. But maybe there's at least a lesson to be learned from my predicament.

My gaze sweeps past bales of paper towels, stacks of napkins, assorted tins of tea, tubs of party decorations, and other miscellany. What value does this situation bring to my experience here at Global Conservation League?

I've been here for nine months. HOLLY KING, INTERN, GCL,

FINDING MR. JULY 3

SEATTLE my badge reads, but if I play my cards right in the weeks to come, I'm hoping it will instead say, HOLLY KING, PROGRAM LIAISON, GCL, GLASGOW. Perhaps being stuck in this closet is meant to force some uninterrupted brainstorming time for how I might best approach the new role once it's mine. Or maybe it's a metaphor for my life, the need to break free?

I get up and pace the few feet available to help me think, but as much as I try to wring this particular lemon into a sweet-tart beverage, I'm unable to ignore the fact that soon my colleagues and bosses will arrive, and I will have failed at the most menial of tasks. The other four interns may not be as experienced in the workforce as I am, being almost a decade younger than me, but they sure as hell get their coffee duty right. I've got to get out of here. Now.

"Help!" I call, banging both fists against the door. "Help, I'm stuck!"

"Hello? Is someone in there?" A deep voice I don't recognize responds on the other side.

Finally! "Yes, hello. It's Holly. Can you help me out? The handle won't turn."

The knob rattles, presumably the man on the other side making sure I'm telling the truth.

"Oh jeez," I hear him huff. "Okay, hold on a sec. I'm going to..." His voice trails off.

I rest my forehead against the door. "Come on," I mumble.

Hurried footsteps return. "I can't find a key. Was it locked when you got here?" His voice is growing more urgent, and it's rubbing off on me. My pulse picks up.

"There's no key. I think it's the handle."

He rattles the knob again. "Damn it! How long have you been in there?"

Is this more serious than I thought? I look around the small space, but no obvious reason for his alarm stands out to me. "I don't know. Twenty minutes maybe."

"Twenty minutes? Um, okay...Just stay calm, and I'll..." A thud follows that sounds like he's slammed a shoulder into the door.

"Hey, don't hurt yourself."

"We've got to get you out!" Another thud and the door frame creaks. "Stand clear!"

I spin away from the door, but as I do, my half-open blouse snags on the offending handle, and the remaining buttons rip loose. I make it to the opposite wall right as the door swings inward with a snap of the door plate. Two rolls of paper towels come tumbling off the shelf above me.

"Are you all right?" A panting male figure dressed in black blocks the doorway with wide shoulders. To my surprise, I recognize him as one of the creatives. I think his name is Jonathan, but I've never heard him speak before. The other interns have nicknamed him "The Shadow," which sounds more menacing than it is. Mainly it's because he stays in the periphery in meetings, not engaging. Also, he's always in black. He's the last person I'd have guessed comes to work early. A lot of people here are zealous about the mission of the organization—something I'm working to emulate. Jonathan usually appears, for lack of a better way to describe it, the opposite.

At first his frantic eyes are on my face, but then they dip to my white lace camisole that's serving much more than its intended peekaboo look. A vague thrill at being caught out echoes through some dormant part of my belly, but I still hurry to wrap my open blouse around me and clutch it together with one hand while I pick up the box of coffee filters I came in here for. His features are unique: the long ridge of his nose kinked as if it's been broken at one point, the sharp jawline covered in intentional stubble, a fuller lower lip. The kind of face that reveals something new every time you see it, I think. Then I blink the odd thought away.

"I'm fine. Running late now, but courtesy of you, not everything is lost. Thanks for that." I gesture to the door frame with my elbow.

He takes a small step forward. "You're sure you don't need to sit down for a bit? That must have been..." He gives a small shudder but doesn't finish his sentence.

"Must have been what?" I ask.

There's a quick hint of a self-deprecating grimace. "I was going to say 'an ordeal.'"

I squint at him. Beneath his thick, dark eyebrows, his gaze is surprisingly soft. If I didn't know better, I'd think he's genuinely concerned. How odd. Being trapped was inconvenient, and I suppose I did lose my composure for a moment, but all things considered, this was only a small snafu in my book.

I look down at my disheveled appearance, and it occurs to me that that's what must be sparking his reaction. I do look like I've wrestled a couple of angry raccoons. "Well, I definitely need to go tidy myself up."

"Mmm." The syllable is short and noncommittal.

"You don't think so?"

At my question, his open expression shuts closed. "No, I do. But maybe it wouldn't be my first priority after something like this."

I raise an eyebrow at his curtness. "Some of us have to worry about stuff like that because I can't come off unprofessional unless I want to remain an intern. 'Ordeal' or not."

I can tell he doesn't like me throwing his choice of words back at him, but he checks his tone nonetheless. "Sorry. It just seemed an odd thing to focus on after this." He gestures to the closet.

Personally, I think the oddest thing about this is how big a deal he's making about it. What is he not saying? "The key word being 'after.' The door got stuck, and then you got it open. Time to get on with my day. I don't like to dwell."

He opens his mouth as if to rebut but stops himself. He looks away, lips pressed together. Takes a step back. "You should always prop doors like this open, you know. There's a stopper right there." He nods toward the gray rubber wedge resting against the baseboard trim, his cadence now matching the sulky air he normally gives off. "You're lucky I showed up when I did or who knows what might have happened."

I tilt my head. Patronizing much? "My guess is thirty more minutes of boredom for me and no coffee for the people. But like I said, I'm very grateful."

For a moment, we stare at each other, neither of us moving.

"Do you mind?" I nod to the open space behind him.

"Not at all." He walks off.

I scoff at his receding backside. What a weirdo.

By the time I get back to my desk, several other people have arrived.

"There's coffee and bagels in the kitchen," I say as I pass them.

"You're making the rest of us look bad," Callum, the youngest of the interns, tells me. "I didn't bring in food when it was my week."

"Moms got to 'mom,' right?" Letitia says from her desk, giving me a friendly smirk. The statuesque business grad is my fiercest competition for the program liaison job. She's mature, professional, and passionate about our cause here at GCL. I shouldn't like her, but unfortunately, she's also exceptionally personable.

"Still not your mother," I reply in a singsong voice. It's been a standing joke from week one that I'm the "mom" of the group because the rest of them have yet to turn twenty-five and I'm thirty-four.

"Oh, come on. It's a compliment, and you know it," Ashley says, setting her blinged-out travel mug down on her desk. "Where's Eric this morning?"

Eric rounds out our group of five, and I've suspected for a few weeks that he and Ashley have something going on. I'm about to make an insinuating comment, but then the glass door to the elevator vestibule swings open, and my former college roommate turned nonprofit mentor, Rachel, walks in. Time to get to work.

"How is your morning going? Mine is tip-top," she says when I join her in her office. She's in an orange and yellow floral blouse that makes her brown eyes pop and sparkle. It's impossible to be in a bad mood around Rachel Denofrio.

I tell her about the closet mishap while she unpacks her laptop and starts it up.

"Wait. Jonathan got you out?" she asks, pausing for a moment, power cord in hand. "Jonathan Summers?"

I shrug.

She leans back in her chair. "Well, color me baffled. He's always struck me more as the type who'd want to lock people in a closet. Preferably the whole office so he doesn't have to deal with us."

"Right?" My phone buzzes in my pocket. It's my brother texting me:

> Delay in a case this afternoon. Can you drive Ava to tennis practice?

"Hold on one sec," I tell Rachel as I type out my response: **Sure thing!**

My niece is pretty cool for an ornery teenager, so I don't mind spending time with her.

"Hot brother?" Rachel asks.

I glare at her. "Don't call him that."

She grins. "I bet you wish you'd never introduced us."

"Is that what I did? If my memory serves me right, he stopped by to pick me up, and you inserted yourself into our conversation."

"Details, details."

I flick a paper clip her way across the desk.

"So cheeky for an intern," she says, but the smile remains in place. "Where were we?"

"Let's go over the agenda for this week." I pull up the schedule on my laptop.

"Did he talk to you at all?" she asks.

"My brother?"

"No, Jonathan."

We're still on that topic? "Some, I guess."

"Really?" She leans forward. "Like what?"

"What's with the twenty questions? Like 'Help I'm stuck,' 'I'll get you out,' 'Thank you,' 'You're welcome.' Riveting stuff."

"That's it?"

"Oh, and he may also have insinuated I'm vain and careless, so there's that."

"Mmm, yeah, sounds more like it. Such a waste of a pretty face."

"His face is pretty, isn't it?" I agree. "Ugh. Anyway. You have a busy week, which means I have a busy week, so let's not waste it on grumpy web designers."

"Right." Rachel puts on her blue-framed readers and peers at her screen. "What's first?"

"The release on the Madagascar forest project needs to go out by Wednesday. It's almost done. Then we have the donor breakfast tomorrow." I scroll further into the week. "And Friday is Foundation Day, when I'll get my final assignment."

This will be the assignment that decides which intern will win the program liaison job in Glasgow. GCL is opening an office there to work specifically with the preservation of the Celtic rainforest, and since our office here in Washington and our Australian branch have had a lot of success with temperate rainforest work, Manny Gupta, our executive director, is sending staff from these two offices to get the new branch up to speed and train local staff. The assignment is for a year with a possibility for an extension, and it's a great opportunity to jump-start a new career. Manny is making a big deal out of the announcement of the assignment—a secret task— having saved it for the annual GCL birthday party on September 16.

"Are you nervous?" Rachel asks.

My knee-jerk reaction is to tell her no, that I've got it under control, but we've known each other long enough that I can afford honesty. "A little. I don't like not knowing what it is, but I feel ready."

"I've taught you well, my young Padawan." She puts her palms together and bows her head.

I smile. "That you have."

Rachel is the GCL communications manager in our office, and together with her team and counterparts in Copenhagen, Brasilia, and Canberra, she handles the flow of information for the organization. With her as my mentor, I've learned about everything from managing contacts for digital fundraising efforts and creating press releases, to strategizing internal training to make sure each global office stays consistent in their messaging and endeavors.

I've cycled through several different teams and seen other sides of GCL, too, in my nine months here, but I started with Rachel and will end with her as well. Her enthusiasm for her work has been a breath of fresh air. After slogging through the past few years of legal consultancy for Fortune 500 corporations that are more interested in finding loopholes than making a real difference, her passion for the world we live in and matching expertise are exactly what the doctor ordered. On days when I question my career switch, all it takes is a dose of Denofrio, and I remember why I'm here.

"Let's get to it, then." Rachel tucks an auburn curl behind her ear and rests her palms on her desk. "We'll need to follow up with our Aussie friends when they wake up over there. They should have compiled survey results for us. Remind me."

"I can get the stats from R&D for the press release if you want," I offer.

"Thanks. Yeah, if you can do that before the all-hands, that would be great."

And the day is off and running.

At 10:00, we head to the large conference room on the other

side of the elevator vestibule. GCL takes up a whole floor of this five-story building in downtown Seattle, and when they leased the space, they left the walls up that divide the floor into two separate offices. To get from one side to the other, you have to pass the elevator bank. In addition to meeting spaces and a rec room, the other side also houses HR and the creative team—event planning, web design, and such—so as we enter the room, I find myself looking for Jonathan. He's in his usual spot in the far corner opposite the windows, staring at his phone.

Typically, he stands, no doubt to facilitate a quicker exit once the meeting is done, but today he's pulled up a chair, and his left hand absentmindedly massages his right shoulder. Black Henley, black jeans, black leather cords around his right wrist, lips set in an impassive line. He's every emo kid at the back of my high school classroom in adult form. Above this. Uninterested. *Lost maybe?* The thought is there unprompted. His corner looks like a solitary bubble in contrast to everyone else milling about, abuzz with late summer revelry and speculations about the Foundation Day party on Friday. GCL always throws a nice bash, and this one comes with a dose of suspense because of the impending intern assignment.

"Do you think he looks more miserable than usual?" I ask Rachel under my breath. I hope he didn't hurt himself breaking down the door earlier.

"Who?"

I tilt my head in his direction.

She glances that way. "Nah. Same old."

I nod and look Jonathan's way again. He's put his phone down and crossed his arms, but his gaze is still locked downward. His left foot taps against the carpet.

"Happy Monday, everyone!" Manny calls, entering the room,

effectively hushing the noise. "Let's start off with a round of applause for Margot for getting such great visibility with her piece on our collaboration with the Nature Conservancy last week. Well done!"

Once the room quiets again, he goes on to announce on-track numbers for the third quarter, areas that need attention this week, and his excitement for a potential new corporate sponsor. It's short and sweet, like the man himself.

"And obviously I hope I'll see you all Friday evening," he says to wrap up before giving each of the team leads an opportunity to speak. Sometimes they use their time to acknowledge good work, other times it's to make requests for collaboration or to ask advice. When the design manager, DaVon, speaks up today, it's none of those.

"Just want to let everyone know I've alerted facilities of a safety issue," he says. "It's been brought to my attention that the pantry closet door can get stuck if you're not careful. Apparently, there was a close call recently. They should be replacing the hardware before end of day tomorrow."

Rachel nudges my side. "Is he talking about you?" she hisses.

He is. Startled, my gaze flicks once more toward the back corner, and this time, Jonathan is watching me. I don't know if I should be flattered that my "incident" has sparked this lingering worry in him or offended that he's somehow managed to insinuate again that I was careless. But despite my internal conflict, I'm still unable to look away. He's so frustratingly inscrutable.

"A close call?" Manny asks.

"Yeah." DaVon turns to Jonathan. "Did you want to elaborate?"

The question breaks our connection as Jonathan shifts and

huffs out a breath. "Not really," he says curtly. "I can fill Manny in later."

Judging by the whispers that follow, I know I'm not alone in today being the first time I've heard his voice. This is rare indeed.

Rachel grips my sleeve. "What is happening?" she asks under her breath. "Did you break him?"

As if stringing a few words together in public is a feat. Most of us do it on a daily basis. I am concerned about his shoulder, though. He's rubbing it again.

DaVon shrugs like "fair enough" before ceding the floor to the event team, and the meeting soon ends.

As usual, Jonathan is the first one out the door.

"Give me one sec," I tell Rachel, and hurry after him.

He's fast, but so am I, and I catch up to him before he rounds the corner to his office. "Hey!"

At first, I think he's about to ignore me, but when I call out a second time, he spins.

"Oh, it's you."

"Last I checked." I try a smile but get nothing back.

Over the years, I've sat across the table from countless clients, some posturing, others submissive, all needing my legal expertise for one reason or another, and if there's one thing I've always prided myself on, it's the ability to read people's eyes. Windows to the soul and all that. They may act confident, but their eyelids will twitch with suppressed nerves, or they'll assure me their paperwork is in order while refusing to look straight at me. Jonathan's eyes are a light gray with a pronounced darker outline around the iris, but where I expect to find more clues as to his state of mind—curiosity maybe, or irritation—there's nothing. His expression is utterly controlled. Like he's pulled down a shutter and padlocked it. It makes any words I'd planned on saying dissipate.

"Did you need something?" His hand goes to his shoulder again.

"Um." I swallow. "Yeah. Yes. I was just going to make sure you're not hurt?" I nod toward his arm.

Finally, a tiny double-blink. He drops his hand to his side. "I'm fine."

"Because if you're sore, I have this muscle cream that—"

He cuts me off. "Not necessary." He looks past me to where people are making their way down the hallway. "If that's it, I should get back to work."

I press my lips together. "Okay. Well, I'm sorry that I..." My voice trails off as he turns and walks away. Again. *What the?* "Have a nice day," I call after him to no reaction at all. "Or whatever," I mutter to myself as I set off back to my desk. "A miserable day works, too, if that's what you prefer."

Unreadable or not, at least I figured out one thing about incorrigible grump Jonathan Summers today. If I never have the misfortune to encounter him again, it will be too soon.

Sitting down to dinner that evening, I let go of cramped spaces and awkward conversations as I sip a glass of sauvignon blanc in my brother's airy kitchen. Jude and I are across from each other at his oval table while his fifteen-year-old daughter, Ava, busies herself by the fridge. Jude and I are both average cooks, but Ava is going through her high school's culinary arts electives as if her life depends on it and already has her sights set on a year at a French institute after she graduates in three years. That is, unless she gets a full ride to play college tennis somewhere. She's keeping her options open.

"It smells great, hon," Jude says, sitting back in his chair. The glow of a gorgeous September evening lights up the room from the window behind him. He closes his eyes and lets out a long sigh. "Man, what a day."

"Do I want to know about it?" I ask.

"Probably not."

"Contested paternity," Ava supplies from the stove where she's sticking a thermometer into a pork tenderloin. "Guy doesn't have a case."

"Oh, you know that, do you?" Jude asks.

"Come on, Dad. I saw them at the office when you dropped off paperwork the other week. The kid looks exactly like him."

He rolls his eyes in good humor. "Glad we've got that figured out, then. I'll tell the judge, shall I?"

"I'm just saying." Ava sets a coaster on the table and then the meat, which is fragrant with garlic and herbs. There's also jacket potatoes, carrots, and a red wine jus. Not shabby for a Monday night. Their goldendoodle, Morris, agrees, judging by his skidding entrance into the room. His tongue flops as he swings his head between the table and the kitchen as if unsure where it smells best.

"Go lie down, bud," Ava tells him.

His head tilts, one ear perked up, but then the message hits home, and he saunters to his bed in the corner and lies down with a dejected huff.

"Do I have to sign something so you get class credit for this?" Jude asks her.

"This isn't an assignment." She sits down at the head of the table. "I just wanted to try out this recipe."

"How do you have his genes?" I ask her.

"Hey." My brother gives me a pretend glare. "And here I thought you're a guest in my house."

"I offered to pay rent."

"With what money?"

I stick my tongue out at him even though he's right. Not that I need to be reminded of the events that led up to draining most of my savings and taking an unpaid internship.

"Too soon?" Jude mimics flicking food off his fork in my direction.

"I really feel for Grandma and Grandpa right now," Ava says. "Were you like this growing up, too?"

"Worse," I say.

"Great." Ava pushes the bowl of glazed carrots my way. "More eating, less talking, then. How is it?"

"Amazing. As always." Jude shoves another forkful into his mouth.

I try the meat, which melts in my mouth. "I never want to stop eating this."

Silverware clinks against ceramic plates as we let the flavors silence us, and for a while, only the house finches nesting outside the open window above the sink provide an additional soundtrack.

But once we're on to second helpings, Jude points at me with his fork. "Speaking of Mom and Dad—have you talked to them lately?"

I shake my head. "They're always so busy. And when they're not, I am."

They moved to Texas seven years ago and are living the good life with sun, golf, friends, and activities customized to their demographic.

"You know they're not upset with you any longer, right?" Jude studies me.

Why would you throw away half your life? is how Dad phrased his initial reaction to my news that I'd left the firm. I'd wanted to follow in his lawyerly footsteps for as long as I could remember, even before Jude announced it was his chosen path as well. Falling from grace had left a lasting bruise even though I knew there was much more to my story than simply quitting. "Yeah, I know. Did you talk to them?"

"Dad threw his back out again. It's been a bit of a hassle."

"Ouch."

"Yeah. Starting to wish they weren't so far away. They're not getting any younger."

Always the responsible older sibling. "They chose to leave," I say. "And I don't think any amount of convincing will get them back here."

Jude nods as he rummages his fork around in the potato for a last bite. "No, I know."

I rest my hands over my stomach. "Oof, I'm so full."

"Not too full, though, right? I'm trying out a dairy-free chocolate mousse for dessert." Ava gestures toward the fridge.

"Maybe give us a few minutes," Jude says. "At our age, we don't digest things like you."

"As someone six years your junior, I urge you to speak for yourself," I tell him, and we're off again. While we bicker, I help Ava clear the table.

I really do have the best big brother that a girl could wish for. When my ex, Chris, threw me under the bus at the law firm where we both worked, and I chose the quiet exit offered, I had to move out of my apartment to save what little money I had left. Jude offered his guest suite without questions asked and didn't once blame me for what happened. He knows firsthand that the legal world can be cutthroat and disillusioning, though he still gets energy from his cases and clients.

I sit back down again when we're done, but Ava gets a rapid burst of notifications on her phone and disappears into the living room. Jude glances after her. Then he leans across the table toward me and lowers his voice. "I don't want to say too much yet, but I've been thinking. If you get this job, you'll be moving to Scotland, right? Maybe it's time for us to make a move, too."

"Where to?" I distribute bowls and spoons to our place mats.

"Texas. Mom and Dad are going to be old in a few years, Hols. They'll need someone to help them with stuff, and if you're across the ocean, that leaves me."

"But you haven't talked to Ava about it?"

"It's too soon. I will, though."

We lapse into a silence punctuated by Ava's laughter in the next room. I can't help but wonder what she'll think of this idea. I scan the black-and-white photographs on the walls. This is the only place she's ever lived. The only place with a connection to her mom. Ava might not remember her, but this house still bears Jolene's fingerprints if you know where to look.

"What are your chances of landing this job?" Jude asks after a few minutes, interrupting my thoughts. "If you're going to be realistic."

"Well…" I adjust the spoon next to my bowl while I consider the past few months. I may not be the typical intern, but no one at GCL has ever made me feel that's a disadvantage. If anything, I think I bring a lot to the table from my previous career. Too bad I'm not the one doing the hiring. "I'd say one in three. I don't see either Callum or Ashley being top picks. Not saying they're bad at what they do, and they're both very nice, but if it was up to me—which I know it's not—I'd say they need a bit more experience under their belts for a job like the Glasgow one."

"Which leaves… was it Letitia?"

"Letitia and Eric. Any company would be lucky to have them. It's really going to come down to whatever this final task is. Who excels."

Jude nods. "Do you have a plan B?"

His question triggers that stupid lump in my throat again because I know I should have one. It's irresponsible not to. But I quit Heckles & Romer so suddenly that it spun my world off-kilter, and when Rachel hooked me up with the internship at GCL shortly after, it seemed like the perfect solution. Not only did she vouch for me with Manny to get around my lack of references—at that point no one at Heckles & Romer would have touched me with a ten-foot pole—but also GCL sounded like the complete antithesis to what I was leaving. That's to say it's people-centric, committed to lasting global change, and not-for-profit. And, best of all, the internship sounded like a fortuitous twofer for the future winner of the intern challenge—a fast-track ticket into a new career and the opportunity to help start an office far away from Washington State and the rumors of my disgrace.

Less than a month later, I did my intern orientation. There's been no time to stop to consider the possibility that this might not work out. It *has* to work out. I would have a lot of explaining to do if I tried to go back to law again, and I cannot stay in Seattle, where reminders of my past abound.

"I intend to win," I tell my brother, having swallowed away the intruding angst. "And like Dad always says, 'intention is half the battle.'" It helped me graduate high school at the top of my class, do my undergrad in three years, my grad in two, pass the bar on my first attempt, and land the first job I applied for. Granted that was years ago, and I haven't flexed my intention muscles in a while, but I'm sure it's like riding a bike.

"You can say that about a lot of things, though," Jude says. "Intention is half the battle, discipline is half the battle, intelligence is half the battle, hell, money is half the battle."

"You think Dad is full of it?"

"I think Dad started his own practice at thirty with the help of his dad's inheritance. Those were different times. But..." He holds up a finger to stop my rebuttal. "That said, I do think this change has been good for you, even though what happened to you was wrong. Last year this time, you were such a miserable curmudgeon. If anyone can do what they set their mind to, it's you." He raises his glass in salute and drinks.

I relax against the back of the chair and finish my glass of wine. "Thanks." His words help me remember a not-too-distant past when I was invincible. I can get there again. They also prompt an image of another curmudgeon I know. Is that what's going on? Is Jonathan just unhappy with the work we do?

"Hey, have you ever had a client that you couldn't read?" I ask Jude.

"Like if they were lying to me?"

"Yeah, that, and what their motivation was, what they were thinking."

Jude chuckles. "I don't ever know what my clients are thinking. That's beyond my pay grade and psychic ability. Why do you ask?"

I gnaw at my lower lip as I picture Jonathan retreating down the hallway. "No reason. It's someone I work with. I can't figure him out." I twirl the stem of my glass and peer toward the living room where Ava is pacing, still engaged in animated conversation.

"Hoo boy, I know that look," Jude says, interrupting the spinning wheels in my head.

"What look?"

"That look." He circles a finger in the direction of my face. "The 'Holly tackles a challenge' look. I pity the fool."

I ball up my napkin and toss it at him. "No need. This one is a lost cause, and I don't have time for any more challenges right now."

He smirks. Then he stands to get dessert out of the fridge because Ava sounds like she's finishing up. "Whatever you say, sis. Whatever you say."

"So today is the day," Rachel says as we prepare cups of coffee in the kitchen. After the rocky start, my caffeine duties have gone off without a hitch, and it seems everyone has appreciated the carb offerings I've brought in, too. It's a small win, but one I'm cherishing as the hours tick down to our final challenge being announced.

"And you really have no idea what it is?" I lean my hip against the counter as I stir in my milk and sweetener.

"Cross my heart." She makes a half-assed gesture near her chest.

"I just have this feeling Callum knows. He looked pretty smug yesterday at lunch."

"His mentor does have the office next to Manny's. I suppose he could have overheard. But don't worry. Callum is not your competition. And I've set this whole weekend aside so we can tackle whatever leadership throws your way."

I nudge her with my elbow as we make our way to our desks. "It means a lot to me that you'd do that."

"As long as we're done by five tomorrow. Me and the guys are going cruising."

Rachel owns three vintage muscle cars that she treats like

they're her babies. If she's not at work, she's in the garage doing whatever a car-obsessed person does in a garage or she's showing off the shiny lacquer in a rumbling procession down Pike Street with her dad and his buddies.

"I promise. Wouldn't dream of getting in the way of all that horsepower."

We set our mugs down, and Rachel pushes a stack of papers aside to access her laptop.

"So, knowing come Monday you'll be consumed with whatever Manny has in store, let's wrap up any other project you have and follow up with Brasilia on Paranoá today. Do you have other loose ends we need to handle?"

"Maybe checking with the Sounders on their in-kind intentions for the holiday auction?"

"Sounds good."

I know I'm not yet done at GCL, but her words make it feel final somehow. Whatever happens, I'll be leaving this office, leaving Rachel, soon. I'm supposed to be this calm, cool, and collected professional, but that thought is somewhere in the realm of terrifying. My time at GCL has been such a reprieve from where I was before that it's hard to fathom it coming to an end.

"You're looking a little pale all of a sudden," Rachel says, squinting at me. "You okay?"

I blink to drive back my emotions and put on a smile. "Yeah. Just eager for tonight."

GCL has rented out the swanky bar on the first floor of the building for the party. The space is lit with modern brass chandeliers that reflect off the intricately patterned ceiling, but the real star of the show is the illuminated glass shelves behind the bar with row after row of top-shelf booze. Two tall, steel-grilled windows frame the display.

There's already a steady buzz of conversation in the room as I enter, and everyone is dressed up.

"Holly!" Letitia and Ashley holler in chorus.

I wave and make my way to the table they've claimed. It sits right in front of a giant screen displaying a slide show of moments from the past year. A picture of Rachel shaking hands with some British philanthropist shuffles past. I scan the room, but she's not here yet.

"What are you drinking?" Eric asks me.

Letitia and Ashley both hold martini glasses with something translucent red inside.

"I'll have what they're having. Thanks."

He tips his beer to me and disappears to the bar.

"I'm nervous. Are you nervous?" Letitia asks.

"Nothing to be nervous about," Callum says with a poorly concealed smile.

Ashley elbows him. "You totally know, don't you?"

"Yeah, you do know," I say. "Spill."

Callum puts up his hands. "I may have heard little whispers, but that's it. Not my place to say. I could be wrong."

Letitia's eyes narrow. "Not cool, man."

Callum takes a swig of his beer. "We'll know in a few anyway. Besides, it is a competition. I'd be a fool for tipping my hand."

So that's how it's going to be? Letitia and I share a look that tells me she's of the same mind. But he's not wrong. Only one of us can get the job.

"Your drink, ma'am." Eric sets it down in front of me.

"'Ma'am' me again, and you'll be wearing it," I say sweetly.

"But thank you." I have a sip, and it hits every spot on its way down my gullet. As my shoulders relax, I realize I must be more on edge than I thought. Where the heck is Rachel? I nod toward the mingling people. "I'm going to do a lap."

I've ended up halfway through the room stuck in a conversation with Britt from accounting about software usability versus cost when a spark and crackle over the speakers saves me, followed by Rachel's voice.

"Hello, good people!"

The conversations stop, turning instead to widespread "yays," "hellos," and "woos" in response.

"I saw a microphone and thought it had my name on it, so here we go." Rachel grins, and the crowd chuckles. "Manny—the man." She points to Manny at the bar. "You don't mind, do you?"

He shakes his head and raises a glass of red to her. Wait, is that...? Yes, Jonathan is seated next to him. Still dressed in all black. I didn't expect him to show up.

"Cool, cool. Then I'd like to officially kick tonight off with a toast." Rachel mimics Manny's gesture with a tall ice-filled glass of something. "To GCL and the people who make it the best fucking place to work. Period."

The cheers grow louder.

"We're going to have fun tonight!" Rachel declares. "We're going to eat and drink, and then we're going to make life a whole lot more interesting for our *ah-ma-zing* interns." She finds me in the crowd, her eyes glittering.

She knows now, too, I realize. Manny must have told the mentors beforehand what our task will be.

"But I'm going to leave that to Mr. Manny Gupta, because doling out projects is his specialty. My specialty is, as you know..." She sidles to the DJ and says a couple of words off mic.

"Don't tell me she's going to sing," I say out loud to no one in particular. Nothing makes me more uncomfortable than spontaneous karaoke.

"She always sings," Britt says. "It's tradition."

The first guitar riffs to "Mustang Sally" flows from the speakers.

"Yeah!" a guy I don't recognize calls out.

And Rachel sings her heart out, hamming it up on the makeshift stage to the crowd's delight. When she finally joins me on the floor, her cheeks are flushed and her grin lights up the dim space.

"You're nuts," I tell her as we hug.

"I know. And it feels great." She chugs what's left in her glass before she grabs my sleeve and tugs me toward the bar. "I need another one." She looks me up and down as we wait for service. "Loving this." She points to my cap-sleeve black dress with a lace-trimmed neckline. "God, I wish I had your legs."

"It's the heels," I say. "I'll regret them tomorrow."

"And those earrings." She touches one of my dangly, silver lightning bolts and then points to the stage. "You should get up there."

"I'd rather eat glass and take a laxative."

"Pfft." She elbows me in the arm and mutters, "Definitely due for another drink."

"But that will be my last one. I'm not getting wasted at a work function."

Rachel shoves a glass of white wine into my hand. "It's. A. Party. Bottom's up. Try to have fun. Tomorrow the real work begins." She winks.

"Yeah, about that..."

"Nuh-uh. Drink first." She clinks her glass to mine, and I oblige. "That's better."

"Manny told you?" I ask.

She eyes me over the rim. "He did."

"And?"

"I'm not at liberty to say."

I take another sip for strength. "Do I have a chance? Will I win?"

"I'm not a fortune teller."

"Come on. You know what I mean."

Rachel's expression sobers. "You're kidding, right? Don't you already know that you'd have a chance no matter what you're assigned? You rule. Best intern ever."

A burst of affection explodes in my chest. "Really?"

"Really, really." She glances over my shoulder and nods at the stage. "Come on. It's time."

I turn to see Manny making his way through the crowd. My heart does its best imitation of a bongo drum.

"Is everyone having fun?" Manny shouts into the microphone.

A wave of enthusiastic assent flows through the room.

"Good, good." He tips back on his heels. "Another year, another few steps forward for our environment—thanks to all of you." He raises his glass. Lots of toasts tonight. "But I'm not going to be long-winded. Tonight is not only about celebrating what's past, but also about looking forward. Can I have Letitia, Ashley, Holly, Callum, and Eric come up here, please?"

"Sounds like you do have to get up on that stage after all," Rachel whispers.

The five of us make our way forward. Several people pat me on the shoulder as I pass with sporadic "good luck" wishes interspersed.

"Let's give it up fooooor...our interns!" Manny tucks the microphone under his arm and leads the applause.

"Oof, so nervous," Ashley whispers next to me.

"May the best man win," Eric says.

"Or woman," Letitia adds.

"Naturally." Eric grins.

I'm used to being the center of attention in a room. As an attorney, you need to be comfortable "holding the floor," whether that's a small conference room or a large courtroom, so all these faces turned my way don't bother me. But there is one face missing. Over at the bar, Jonathan's profile stands out like a sore emo thumb, like he's determined not to engage with the rest of us. The light from the backlit bar sharpens his jawline with well-placed shadows and makes his dark hair appear almost black. He's scrolling on his phone, I think. The sight makes the rapid drumming in my chest slow to a more ominous gong. But just as I'm about to think more ungenerous thoughts about how he's checked out even here, he looks up and straight at me as if he's heard my thoughts through the room.

Thankfully, Manny's voice booms through the mic again, forcing my attention back to the stage.

"You all know these five hotshots. They've become part of our GCL family. But after tonight, the countdown begins." He pauses for dramatic effect and then continues close to the mic so he sounds like a movie voice-over. "Only one will remain standing in the end."

Sporadic laughter and cheers sound from the floor.

"Are you ready?" Manny asks us.

We nod. Here we go.

"Over the next six weeks, each of you will plan and execute a fundraiser for GCL."

Letitia stirs next to me and lets out an excited noise.

"You will have access to a limited budget, your mentors' advice, and the option to team up with an in-house creative for promos, et cetera, but that's it. The rest is up to you. All of the net proceeds will go either to our temperate rainforest conservation work or a GCL cause of your choice, and the person who runs the most successful fundraiser wins. That person will join two of our Australian team members, as well as Fred from our office, in Glasgow as a program liaison to get the work off the ground."

Fred, our lead conservationist, stands up and waves. "Can't wait for the haggis," he shouts with a grin.

"Ah, ha, ha. Better you than me, buddy," Manny responds before facing us again. "So there you have it. Think outside the box and make sure that whatever event, service, or product you come up with is done before the deadline on October 28. 'May the odds be ever in your favor.' The clock"—he raises his hand and lets it fall—"starts now."

4

In a wild scramble, the other four rush off the stage and into the crowd. I have no idea why they're running. It doesn't strike me like that type of assignment.

A fundraiser. I can do that.

I blink at the lights beating down on me as my brain sparks with flashes of ideas.

"Holly?" Manny asks next to me. "Did you have something you wanted to say?" His kind brown eyes rest on me.

The noise around me comes back in full force. "Um, what?"

"Did you have a question or…" He gestures to the room. A suggestion that I also get going.

I force a smile, trying to make it natural. Way to make a bad impression. I should have run off to tackle the task with the others. "Got to think before you act," I say, like I'm some kind of low-budget Yoda. To make things worse, I tap a finger against my temple.

There's a pause, and then Manny smiles. "You're right. And you're going to do great."

Phew.

"Thank you," I say. Then, finally, I get off the stage.

"So?" Rachel asks when I join her on the floor. "Totally doable, right? Any immediate thoughts?"

My palms are clammy. Maybe I'm not as chill about this as I'd like. "Several. But first I want to see if I can find Jacques and get him on our team." Someone like him, with a good eye and client focus, will elevate whatever I settle on doing for this project.

"I like the way you think."

I spot the preppy UX designer lounging in a booth by the windows. The only thing that betrays he's a few drinks in is the fact that he's pushed his horn-rimmed glasses up onto his head. Other than that, he's as sartorially put together as he is in the office. He's talking to someone I can't see because of a tall plant, his hands gesturing in wide circles, and I have time to think that that's exactly the kind of energy I need for this task.

Then I round the plant, and my step falters. Jacques is talking to Letitia.

She spots me and puts up a hand to silence Jacques. "Hey, what's up?"

I can't think of a good lie, so I go with the truth. "I was going to ask Jacques to team up, but I see you beat me to it. Good for you."

"Nice to be in demand." Jacques leans back and grins. There's a small gap between his two front teeth, adding to his boyish appearance.

"Do you already know what you're doing?" I ask Letitia.

A secretive smile. "I have a few ideas."

"Nice." I nod and then look to my left and right. "Then I suppose I should..." I let my sentence trail off and merge backward into the crowd. I think I saw DaVon by the bar.

But DaVon has already committed his services to Eric. Pippa, who does social media graphics, has teamed up with Ashley, and Callum is deep in conversation with the creative writer on the team. That one is no surprise. He and Biggie are basically the same person, and their families know each other.

I return to Rachel, dragging my feet and with welling panic pulling my esophagus tight. I can't believe the creatives I might have worked with are already spoken for. How is it possible that I'm already behind? *Get it together, Holly!*

When I share this development with Rachel, I make sure to downplay any concerns and infuse my voice with faux confidence. Faking it till you make it is an underestimated method for success.

"I'm not worried," I say, twisting the stem of my empty wineglass on the table. "We can do this anyway, right? I'm not the most artistic person, but you can handle yourself."

She scrunches up her nose. "Of course. But... I'll still have my job to do. The mentors are mainly supposed to lend moral support." She glances past me toward the bar. "There is one other person you might ask."

I follow her line of vision. Jonathan is talking to the bartender now. It makes him come alive a tad. He's sitting up straighter, almost smiling.

The spark of optimism that just flared fades instantly. "No way."

"Why not? You are one of the few people in the office he's talked to. That basically makes you besties."

"If by 'bestie' you mean 'person you plan on avoiding forever,' then sure."

"No matter what fundraiser you come up with, you'll need someone to help with promo and graphics."

I don't know about that. I have social media—maybe I can figure the creative bit out on my own.

Rachel raises an eyebrow. "This won't be like posting to Insta. And you don't even understand the filters there."

Gah. She knows me too well. I hate it when she's right. "But I don't want to work with him." An unbecoming whine edges its way into my voice.

"I know." Rachel finishes her drink. "But maybe you got off on the wrong foot. Look, the bartender just got busy—this is your chance. You must have schmoozed a thousand difficult people in your previous job. I believe in you."

I glance over my shoulder. Jonathan cradles what looks like a glass of water with one hand, the other hand rubbing his cheek as if easing a tense jaw. "Hardly a thousand," I say. But again, she's right. I used to pride myself on not shying away from difficult clientele. With wits, charm, and projected self-assurance, you can crack the hardest nuts. Why would Jonathan Summers be any different?

"You want to win, right?" Rachel asks. "Can't hurt to ask."

I do. More than anything. I let out a sharp breath. "Fine."

"That's my girl. I'll be over by the finger foods if you need me. Break a leg." She gives me a double thumbs-up and leaves.

I spin around. Straighten my dress. I *need* to win.

"Hi there." I sit down in the chair next to Jonathan and rest my elbows on the bar counter.

"Hello."

I forgot how unexpected his voice is. Not that it doesn't suit him—it's more the fact that he has a voice at all. And a pleasant one at that.

"Having fun?" My voice is too chipper. I can tell by the weight of his eyelids that he thinks so, too. But behind them is a hint of something I haven't seen before. Something lifelike. Maybe the drink he had earlier picked at the padlock of his shutters.

"It's all right," he says after a beat.

"Didn't expect to see you here."

"Didn't realize you'd be looking."

My eyes widen. *What?* "I meant..." I'm not sure how to finish my sentence.

He puts up a hand as if to spare me the effort. "I know Manny likes everyone to show up to these things. He's a good friend."

"Oh. You know each other outside of work?"

Jonathan nods. Drinks.

I wave the bartender over. I need something to hold, and I have a feeling Jonathan will be more amenable to my ask if he gets something stronger in front of him than water.

I order a gin and tonic. Then I turn to Jonathan. "You?"

Again he pauses. It's as if he's unaccustomed to the normal rhythm of a conversation.

"I'll have the same," he says finally. "Thanks."

Something moves in my peripheral view. I glance that way to see Rachel nodding encouragement from the small dance floor. I roll my eyes.

We get our drinks and have a sip. The zesty tang invigorates.

"So, how do you know Manny?" I try to sound casual. Making small talk. I have no agenda here, no sirree.

The ice in his glass clinks together. "We've played together a fair bit over the years."

"Played?" While Manny's whole being screams physical energy, I can't picture Jonathan running after any kind of ball if his life depended on it.

"He's an excellent trumpet player."

The sports scenario in my head tilts ninety degrees as I try to fit a trumpet into it. "So like...a marching band?"

It's his turn to look confused. "What? No. Blues."

The coin drops. "Ah. You play music."

"The piano." His fingers do a drumming motion against the bar as he says it.

My mind conjures sultry nightclubs, evocative tunes, dexterous hands...

Hot.

The instinctive thought is there before I can stop it. I have another swig of my G & T to hide a flush, and then I clear my throat. "So you're in a band together?"

"Occasionally."

"Which means?"

He tilts his head. "Do you always ask so many questions?"

"Are you always this economical with your responses?"

The corner of his mouth quirks up. "I can see why you were a lawyer."

That gives me a momentary pause. "I didn't realize you knew that."

He shrugs. "By 'occasionally,' I mean that many part-time musicians play where there's opportunity. At one point, we were on the same quartet for six months, but we've also gone a year or more without crossing paths. We've always stayed in touch, though, and he got me the job here, so..."

"So, you owe him?"

"No." He huffs and turns more firmly toward me. "That's not..."

"Come on," I tease. "You can't tell me this is what you would have chosen to do with your evening if it was up to you."

His gaze skates down to my dress and then off to the side into the crowd. He finishes his drink. "Maybe not. But I'm having a good enough time."

"Ouch." I chuckle, ignoring the slight thrill at his brief attention. I need to get out more.

He shakes his head and smirks. "Think you have me figured out, then?"

Nothing could be further from the truth. "You tell me."

"I think..." He dips his chin down and leans closer. Looks up at me from beneath dark lashes.

His gray irises are like magnets, and though I'm suddenly very aware of our proximity, I don't retreat. "What?" My voice sounds breathy.

For a long moment, his gaze doesn't let me go. The lights around us play new shadow games across his face. A cave of secrets beneath his left brow. A hidden trail from his nose to the corner of his mouth. It's the most interesting face.

Abruptly, he leans back in his chair and crosses his arms. "I think you want to win this fundraiser, and you're only talking to me because you need my skills on your team."

My lungs deflate like a popped balloon. My first instinct is to object, but I'm a little dizzy, and nothing comes out.

"Admit it," he says.

"I..." I lift my glass. Set it down again. Oh, what the hell. "Fine. I do need a creative on my team, and Rachel suggested I ask you."

"Because everyone else is spoken for."

Again, I want to object, but it's possible he's got me figured out better than I have him. "You just don't seem to like me very much," I blurt. "It has nothing to do with your skills."

"I don't know you enough to have formed an opinion."

"First impressions don't count?"

He lets his arms relax in his lap and then bends his head as if stretching out his right trapezius. "Maybe we can agree that neither of us was at our best Monday morning."

I consider this and decide it's fair. "Then you'll do it?"

Jonathan's mouth opens, but before he can respond, the bartender interrupts to ask if we need anything else. We both decline.

"The other interns have full teams already," I say once we're alone again. "Please."

Jonathan sucks in a breath. "No."

"No?"

"That's what I said. Not interested. I do my forty hours a week, and that's it. Got a full slate. In fact, I can think of nothing I want less than adding another group project to my schedule. No thank you."

I blink at his blatant refusal, heat flaring at my neck. This is not at all going the way I planned. I scramble for another angle. Maybe some light flirting…

He laughs. "And don't give me that look. I am way too sober for that to work."

Well, fuck. "Bartender!" I call. "I changed my mind."

"What are you doing?"

"Fixing your susceptibility issue." I glance his way before ordering. "Can we get six shots of tequila, please?"

"I'm not doing shots." He reaches behind him for the lightweight bomber jacket draped over the backrest.

No, no, no. He can't leave. I put my hand on the soft fabric to stop him. "Are you afraid I'll drink you under the table?"

"Ha!" It's a gruff exclamation, but he sits forward again. "You couldn't if you tried."

"Oh yeah? Clearly you have no idea what goes on in law school."

He puts one elbow on the counter, his eyes narrowing. I don't look away. If I do, he'll go, and somewhere behind us, Rachel is trusting me to seal this deal.

"That a fact?" he asks. There's a faint hint of a drawl in his voice when he's more relaxed like this. Like he's spent some time in the South. It softens his edges.

The bartender sets six shot glasses, limes, and a saltshaker in front of us. I push one of the glasses Jonathan's way. "Tell you what," I say, taking hold of my own shot. "If I cave first, you're off the hook, but if I can outdrink you, you'll help me win this contest using whatever magical, design-y skills you have. And you'll do it with a smile." I demonstrate to him what that would look like.

"A drinking contest?" he clarifies, skeptical.

"Unless you're chicken." I flap my elbows at my side.

His face cracks open with amusement, transforming his whole person, and my stomach does something I haven't felt since I was little and got so high on the swing in our tree that I thought I was flying. Now he has lips that might tell jokes and cheeks I'm sure his grandmother used to squeeze.

I barely have time to collect myself before he reaches for a slice of lime and holds it up between us. "Oh, you're on."

Gray light filters through my closed eyelids as a buzzing sound from someplace far away pierces my unconscious. I don't move, willing sleep to return. No matter what time it is, I know on a visceral level I'm not ready to be alive yet.

I exhale through parted lips and catch a whiff of my own breath against the firm pillow beneath my cheek. *Ugh, gross.* It's enough to have me swear off tequila forever. Little glimpses of the evening make themselves known: Manny onstage, DaVon and Eric breakdancing, the fundraising challenge, doing shots with...

The buzzing noise comes closer. I want to yell at Jude for vacuuming this early on a Saturday morning, but I don't have the energy. Besides, it could be noon already. The thought pulls me closer to the surface. If that's the case, I should rally. I know I have plans today—except it's hard to remember exactly what they are.

Before the swirling thoughts in my head can settle, the buzzing retreats again. It's almost soothing. Maybe I'll sleep a little longer after all.

I attempt to turn my face into the pillow, but it doesn't give, and when I run my palm across it, the feeling jogs something in my memory. Something significant. My foggy mind starts clearing, becoming more aware each moment. The wall behind me is softer than usual, the ever-noisy finches silent, and—this is where I firmly leave sleep behind—the light is coming from the wrong direction. There's no window opposite the bed in my room.

Then my mattress moves. It's subtle, but there's no mistaking my palm rising and falling. With the movement, a rush of familiar but misplaced scents washes over me—whiteboard marker, lemon cleaner, dusty fabric, and, more immediately, the musky floral hints of cologne.

Instantly, my brain summons a visual memory that hits low in my belly. No warning, just *zing*: a bare chest and firm hands caressing my hips.

My eyes fly open, and a split second later, I'm pushing myself up and off what I now realize is the couch in the GCL rec room. The one facing the windows with a view of South Lake Union. The commotion disturbs my "mattress," aka Jonathan, who, still asleep, lifts his hands to his head and arches his back off the cushions in a stretch. His black shirt is unbuttoned to his navel. A faint smattering of hair decorates his defined pecs.

"Nooo..." I groan as I will my head to stop spinning. "No, no, no, no, no." Behind me, the vacuuming noise approaches again. The cleaning staff. They're here for their weekend sweep. I flick Jonathan's foot and hiss, "Wake up."

"Huh?" he grunts, still not opening his eyes. His lips part on a deep breath, and as his full lower lip moves, I know by how my mouth waters that I've tasted it. The memory forces a stop to my tense movements.

"*This is a very nice dress,*" *he'd said, running his fingertips along my collarbones through the lacy fabric at my neck. His touch had been reverent and goose bumps–inducing. I'd straddled him here on this couch with my hands on his shoulders as I leaned down to kiss him.*

The hair at my nape rises with the echoes of his touch. Did we...?

I run my hands down my body and then up over my shoulder in a quick inventory. Clothes are still on and in their right places, thank God, but the zipper is open. I try and fail to reach the pull tab between my shoulder blades.

"Hey," I say a little louder. "Jonathan. Wake up."

"What is it?" he mumbles, but then he finally squints at me, and I see exactly when the situation registers with him. His eyes fly open, and with a distressed "wha," he's up and seated as far from me on the couch as possible. He runs a hand through his hair, his unfocused gaze cutting between me and the window, me again, and then the interior of the rec room. "How did we...? Why are you...? What happened? Fuck, my head." He leans forward and buries his face into his palms.

"I was hoping you could tell me." I scan the floor for my shoes, but they're nowhere to be found. I frown as another image appears of me holding on to his arm and taking them off. In the stairwell? Why didn't we take the elevator up?

He cracks his neck and rubs the back of his hand across his mouth. "Did we both sleep...here?" He touches the couch.

I glance over my shoulder. The cleaning staff will be here soon. "Seems like it."

He shakes his head as if to rattle loose the memories. Looks down. And at the sight of his bare chest, something does hit him. He stands abruptly and yanks his shirt closed. "Did we...?" He frowns as if searching his brain for an answer. One of his palms strokes the top of his abs, mimicking a move I'm pretty sure I was responsible for last night. When his hand stills, a disbelieving smile tugs at the corner of his mouth. "You tried to seduce me."

If I was still in heels, I'd stumble backward. No way am I letting him take the narrative in that direction. "Excuse me? Isn't it much more likely that you tried to seduce me?"

"Why? Because I'm a man?"

"Well, yeah."

He matches up the first button with the wrong hole. "If I remember right, you're the one who suggested a drinking contest. For all I know, this is what you had in mind the whole time." *Gotcha*, his expression says.

I push down the possibility that he's right and laugh. "Don't flatter yourself. I get that women fawning over you is probably a regular occurrence, but what I was after was a team to win the fundraiser."

"And yet here we are." He's finally figured out the buttoning sequence and starts tucking the shirt into his jeans.

My fingers through his belt hoops, pulling him closer. His lips against my throat.

I shrug off the memory. "Exactly—which is why I think this was your doing."

He crosses his arms. "I would never."

"Neither would I."

Is it just me or might we both need to work on delivering our lines with more conviction?

We stare at each other as the rising sun separates us with shafts of light through the half-drawn blinds. I almost have time to forget what we're arguing about. It's tricky holding on to arguments in the state I'm in. We're in. I need water and ibuprofen. Stat.

He doesn't break eye contact until we hear the rattling of

garbage cans being emptied somewhere nearby. Then his shoulders slump as he lets his arms drop. "We should get out of here," he says, looking around for something. "Did I have a jacket?"

"I don't know if you brought it up here. Everything's kind of foggy."

That elicits half a smile from him. "We probably should have known better than to dive deep into that bottle of tequila, huh?"

I nod. What was I thinking? As I do, my mind catches up— *His shoulders solid beneath my palms as I push the jacket off him*— only the location of that particular interaction is still a haze.

"Do you have everything?" he asks, approaching the door.

I look down at my bare feet. "Yeah, I think maybe my shoes are in—"

"The stairwell." His eyes widen with the realization.

So he does remember some of it. "Don't ask me why."

A tense silence settles between us as he holds the door open to the vestibule. The tile is cool beneath my feet.

"Hold on. Your dress." He makes me stop and comes up behind me.

I'd forgotten about the zipper.

Gently, he takes hold of the pull tab. His other hand holds the two sides together. With every tooth closed, I'm finding it harder and harder to breathe normally, and when his fingertips inevitably make contact with my skin to brush my hair aside, there's a ripple beneath the surface that makes me step away as soon as he's done.

"Thanks." I roll my shoulders back and pretend I'm busy smoothing down my skirt.

"No problem." His voice has softened in contrast to our squabble a few minutes ago.

There are more memories echoing off the concrete walls and

steps in the stairwell. He'd made me laugh, causing our walk up the four flights to take longer than it should have. And over there, in the corner by the fire extinguisher on the third landing, he'd pushed me up against the wall (or is that where I pulled him to me?). That was the first kiss, I think. The tip of his nose had been warm next to mine, his smile alive against my cheek.

I clear my throat and make sure to stay a step ahead of him, so he can't tell what I'm thinking. With any luck, he won't remember. One floor down and there are my heels carelessly discarded. I pick them up but don't put them on. I don't trust that my equilibrium and this descent will be a good combo this morning.

"Why did you say that earlier?" he asks suddenly. "About women fawning over me?"

I pause halfway down the last set of stairs. "Um...because of how you look."

"And how is that?" His expression is searching, curious, not fishing for compliments.

I wave my hand up and down in front of him. "Like this. All mysterious and..." I swallow the next word. He has a big enough head without me calling him *hot*.

"Oh." His eyebrows jump.

We keep walking.

"Thanks, I guess?" he says, making it sound like a question. "They don't, though. Women, I mean."

"Just me when I'm drunk, then." I instantly regret the comment and bite down on my cheek.

A warm chuckle. "If you say so."

I want to object, but my head isn't clear enough to reason myself out of that semantic labyrinth.

"Speaking of drunk," he says, "who do you reckon won?"

I hold the door for him this time, put on my shoes, and then we step out into the lobby of the building.

"Won?"

"The shot contest."

Even in my current state, I know there's more to his question than simply calling it in favor of one or the other. The dynamic between us has shifted. I don't know much more about him than I did yesterday, and he doesn't know me, yet we can no longer claim to be strangers. The question then becomes, will I still insist on us working together after last night? Will he still insist we don't?

But also, if I'm being completely honest, it does seem like I remember more of the night than he does, and surely that should count in my favor.

"Pretty sure I won," I say as we step outside, and the sun hits our faces.

Maybe I'm imagining it, but for a split second, it looks like he's sucking in the corner of his lip to stifle a smile. "Is that so?"

We face each other, ready to go our separate ways. A truck rumbles by next to us. The fact that it's alone must mean it's still early.

"Uh-huh." I force my chin up. *Confidence is half the battle.*

He scratches his temple, his gray eyes finding mine again. He nods slowly. "Guess I'll take your word for it."

6

"Where did you run off to last night?" Rachel asks when I pick her up from her West Seattle condo that afternoon. "One minute you were at the bar with Jonathan, and then I couldn't find you."

After a shower, a change of clothes, and a couple of leftover pierogies courtesy of Ava, I am renewed. I've even worked out a cover story. "I realized I'd forgotten something in the office, so I went to get it and got stuck upstairs thinking about the fundraiser. I thought I texted you, but I must have forgotten to hit SEND. Did you have fun?" I ask before she can question me for details.

She folds down the visor to check her hair in the mirror. "Tons of fun. You missed the dancing."

I stop for a red arrow before turning right. "No, I saw it." Through a Reposado haze, but still.

"I definitely need coffee, though."

She doesn't have to wait long. We find a table at our favorite café on Alki Beach, and after letting the caffeine hit our bloodstream, we both sigh in relief. I pull out a notepad and pencil but allow a few more idle minutes to pass. The café is hopping, and the boardwalk offers a steady stream of good people watching.

Finally, Rachel puts her mug down and faces me. "So, are we going to do this or what?"

Brainstorming is on the agenda, so I pick up the pencil and give a firm nod. This is it. The beginning. I'm ready.

"By the way, did you ask Jonathan about working with us?" Rachel's question is offhanded but sends my momentum veering right off the paved track. For the purpose of a clear mind that might generate winning ideas, I'd rather forget all about him.

His hands buried in my hair, his breath hot against my lips.

"What's that look?" Rachel asks. "Don't tell me you didn't talk to him about it."

"No, I did. And he will." I hide behind another mouthful of my latte.

Rachel lights up. "That's great! Phew." She relaxes in her wooden chair. "Okay. Then how do you want to do this?"

We take ten minutes to generate as many ideas as we can without qualifications as to their merits. We're left with a mix of big and small concepts—from a bake sale to a concert—and a few of them feel promising.

"I should tell you I texted with the other mentors this morning, so some of these are already taken," Rachel says with an apologetic grimace. "We could double up, but then you run the risk of splitting the target audience."

"Yeah, I don't want that," I agree. "Which ones are out?"

Rachel takes my pencil and crosses out *social media* first. "Ashley has that one in the bag," she says. "I'm not sure exactly what she's doing, but you don't have much of a following anyway. And since Callum's parents run one of the wineries in Woodinville, he's doing some sort of raffle to benefit our riverbank vegetation projects along the Columbia River." She crosses out both wine tasting and raffle from our list. *Damn it.*

"Must be nice to have connections," I grumble. "What about something like a parade or a race, then?" I point to that item on the list.

Rachel shakes her head. "Letitia is planning on a walk-a-thon, and she's reached out to the Plant-A-Tree foundation to partner."

"Already?" I slump. "Did our brains work like that in our twenties, too? Just..." I make a quick chopping motion with my hand.

"It could fall through. Fast doesn't necessarily mean good."

She's right. One of the benefits of having more experience is knowing that often the tortoise will win over the hare.

"I'm going to get a cookie. You want one?" Rachel gets up.

"Please."

While she's in line, I add *flower delivery* and *used book sale* to the list.

The chocolate chip pastries are still warm, and we take a moment to savor them before returning to the list.

"I like the idea of going big," I say, pointing to the fourth line on the paper. "If I could pull off a concert, that would be something. There are so many local bands in this city."

"Except..." Rachel draws a line through *concert*. "Eric is throwing a 'green party'—green because of the temperate rainforests—and he's getting a band to headline. DaVon is really excited about it."

"No, really? What the hell?"

"But you still have..." She checks the list. "Eh, maybe not flower delivery since it'll be late October by the end of this." She crosses it out. "And definitely not a bake sale post-pandemic."

I take my notepad back. "Which leaves dog walking and used books. Thrilling." I roll my eyes. "There's got to be something better."

We've finished our coffees, and since other patrons are waiting for tables, we gather our things and head down the boardwalk. It's a warm enough September day that a handful of children play at the water's edge, but the beach is nowhere near as crowded as during the height of summer. Only two of the seven beach volleyball courts are busy. We find a bench with a view and make it ours.

"Hey, don't stress," Rachel says. "You'll figure it out. You're going to win this, remember? Have faith in the process."

"Ha!"

"Too cheesy?"

"Cheddar explosion."

She bumps me with her elbow. "You know what I mean."

I shield my eyes and gaze across the glittering waters of Elliott Bay. Overhead, seagulls swoop and caw, and in the distance, the Seattle skyline does its best to match the blue-gray waves. *Come on, ideas!*

Loud cheering pierces the air from the volleyball court closest to us. A group of shirtless guys calls for the ball, diving and jostling and sending sand spraying. A beautiful boxer circles them, barking happily to cheer on his non-canine buddies.

"Look at the dog," I say. "Thinks he can play volleyball, too."

"He'd be better at it than me," Rachel says. "I have two left feet and zero hand-eye coordination. If it doesn't have an engine, I don't engage."

One of the teams scores, and the guy who slams the ball down does a victory lap, the dog on his heels.

"Woo-hoo," Rachel hollers, clapping her hands.

The guy spots us and grins—white teeth against tan skin. As the game continues, he looks our way whenever there's a break.

"I think you got his attention," I tell Rachel. "You should go talk to him."

She waves me off. "Nah. Sports bros are better at a distance." She puts her hands behind her head and winks at me. "Nothing wrong with the view, though. Bare skin, muscles, action, nature. Plus, we know they're pet-friendly. You could charge almost any woman in the world for a view like this any day of the year." She sighs blissfully.

Something happens inside my head at her words. The joyous hollers from the game continue, the boxer keeps barking, the sun keeps beating down on us, and the bay still sparkles, but each component becomes a fragment of a greater equation that spins and spins until, finally, it settles.

"Rachel, that's it," I say, clutching her forearm. "Remember that firefighter calendar Joanne has on the wall behind her in the video meetings?"

"Canberra Joanne?"

"Yeah."

"Vaguely."

"What if we do that, but instead of firefighters with koalas and kittens, we'll do hot, outdoorsy guys with dogs?" As I process verbally what my mind is doing, more and more pieces fall into place. "If we do outdoor photos, we'll hit on the environmental aspect, and we can sell it all over the country, not just locally. Online orders, national reach." I realize I'm still holding on to her, so I release my grip and wait for a reaction.

She's quiet for a beat before she nods, her expression brightening by the moment. "I like that. And it's completely different from what the others are doing. Only Ashley will have a similar reach with her social media thing, but what you're proposing is a product, something tangible." Her brow furrows. "You'll have less time, though. You'll want at least the last three of the six weeks for sales, which means your timeline just shrunk by a lot."

"I can be very efficient."

"Oh, I know. But do you already know a bunch of attractive guys with dogs to ask?"

"I'm sure between the two of us, we'll think of a few. And Jonathan might have friends to ask, too."

"Aren't you the optimist all of a sudden."

"It'll work. I know it." I plead with her silently to get on board. I'm decent at taking pictures, Jonathan can do the layout, and Rachel can liaise with the North Carolina office for help with marketing on the East Coast.

Finally, she nods. "It's a good idea," she concedes. She pulls out her phone and types something in. "My Monday is completely packed, but I'll set up a meeting Tuesday for the three of us to meet. How about you talk to Jonathan before that and get him up to speed?"

"Sounds good." I'll also need him to promise not to mention last night to anyone. In the midst of the awkwardness this morning, I completely forgot about that. Not that he seems like the type to kiss and tell.

Rachel bends her neck and hides her face behind one hand. "Shit, he's coming over. What do I do?"

I glance the way she's indicating, and the volleyball guy is indeed striding toward us, the dog in tow.

"Act normal," Rachel whispers before she straightens and smiles.

"Hey," the guy says.

"Hi there." Rachel squints up at him. "Good game?"

"Pretty good. I saw you watching."

I suppress a chuckle. Flirting can be so awkward. But good for him for putting himself out there.

"This is Bo, by the way." He pats the dog's shoulder. "I'm Nick."

"Rachel. And this is my friend Holly."

"Cool. So listen...any chance you'd be up for grabbing a cup of coffee or something?"

Wow—he's really going for it.

"Um..." Rachel wrinkles her nose. "I'm kind of with my girl here, so..."

"Oh. Right." He digs his bare toes into the sand.

I nudge Rachel as discreetly as I can, hoping to convey she should not let a polite go-getter like this slip through her fingers. It works.

"But how about you give me your number, and I'll text you later?" she asks.

Nick lights up. "Very cool."

As he returns to his friends, Rachel puts her phone away and then looks at me. "I can ask him if he has a friend who's available if you want. Make it a double date? You haven't so much as flirted with a guy since being at GCL, and you should. If I looked like the long-lost twin of what's her face? That actress—*Edge of Tomorrow*, um, *A Quiet Place*..." She snaps her fingers to remember.

"Emily Blunt?"

"Emily freaking Blunt. Yes. If I looked like that"—she waves her finger in the general direction of my face—"I'd strut my stuff every weekend."

"I don't look at all like her."

"Sure you do. Oh, she did *Mary Poppins Returns*, too."

"You think I look like Mary Poppins?"

"Don't twist my words. It's a compliment."

I let out a vague huff and pretend to have something in my shoe. Last night was a long time coming, but she doesn't need to know that. "Thanks, but I'm good. I don't have time for that, and if I can make this calendar thing work, I'll be moving to Scotland soon anyway."

"That's true."

We make sure we have our garbage and our bags. Then we set off toward my car. Rachel can have all the dating fun. I'm going home, making a pot of coffee, and tackling this calendar idea. By the time Monday morning rolls around, I intend to have a detailed plan to share with Jonathan so we can get started on the actual work.

The sky looks a little bluer, the people in the streets a little happier, and my future a little brighter as I navigate my way through North Admiral back toward Rachel's place.

What a difference a few hours can make.

7

The atmosphere in the office between the five of us has changed over the weekend. The only interns who interact ongoingly through the day are Ashley and Eric. Everyone else keeps to themselves, hunched over keyboards or on their phones in a corner somewhere. It's not hostile—we still say hi in the lunchroom—but if there was ever any doubt about it, we're in the competitive homestretch of our time here, and we feel it.

I make lists and timelines. What I'll need, when each step has to be completed, people to talk to, projected expenses. I'm giving myself this first week to recruit models, and then two weeks for the photo shoots. The rules of the contest state that we can only fundraise at our events, when a service is provided, or with a finished product, but if I start marketing and registering interest as soon as I have a couple of pictures, I'll at least have a list of sales leads for when the calendar is done.

I also stay far away from the rec room, doing my best to pretend Friday night didn't happen. Rachel is in meetings all day, but she DMs me after lunch to tell me that Jonathan hasn't accepted her meeting request for tomorrow yet, which means I can't delay seeking him out any longer.

He has his back to me when I approach the office he shares with Jacques, who I spotted with Letitia in one of the conference rooms on the way over, looking deep into planning mode.

I knock lightly on the doorpost, suppressing the nervous flicker in my belly at how his shoulders tense at the sound. "Hello?"

"Oh hi," he says after he turns around, almost sounding friendly. His fingers curl into his palms in his lap.

First small obstacle cleared.

"Getting a lot done?" I ask, stepping into the room.

"You know." He gestures to his desk but doesn't say anything else.

His space is tidy, with two monitors lined up in front of him. There's a plant in a white pot adding ambiance in one corner, and a cup with a swirling piano key motif holding a handful of pens in another. To-go mug, orderly stack of papers, and a framed photo of him and an older man by the pyramids of Giza, and that's it. On the wall to his left are two framed black-and-white photo prints that look like aerial shots of mountains. Like his own face, his workspace doesn't reveal nearly enough about him.

I force myself to stop my visual snooping. "To be honest, this department is probably the one I know the least about," I say. "What exactly do you do?"

"Um." He glances at his monitors where a document labeled "GCL Design Style Guide" sits open. He clicks his mouse, and the screen goes black. "Nothing interesting. Did you want something?" His tone suggests curiosity despite the brash question.

"Rachel sent you an invite for tomorrow to talk about my fundraiser. Are you free?"

"What time?" He spins back to his computer and opens his calendar. "Never mind. I see it. Yeah, that should work."

"Cool."

His hands flash across the keyboard.

Soft fingertips dancing over the pounding pulse on my neck.

I swallow hard. "And so you know—I mean, so we're clear—I haven't told her or anything. About... you know."

He clears his throat. "Ah."

"I was hoping we could agree to keep it to ourselves?"

"Of course."

"My judgment has never been great on tequila." I give him a self-deprecating frown.

He watches me for a moment. Then he nods. "Yeah, no. Me neither."

"Which is why I usually stay away from it."

"Mmm."

He's still intent on me, and it makes me want to keep talking for the sake of it. I bite down on my tongue.

"So, how was your weekend?" he asks after the silence stretches.

"Good. Fairly productive. Rachel and I brainstormed an idea we're excited about, actually." He looks interested so I volunteer what we have so far about the calendar idea. "Basically dogs, hot guys, and nature," I summarize. "What's not to like?"

If I had paid closer attention to him while talking, I might have ended on a less chipper note because his eyebrows have lowered into a scowl.

"And let me guess—you assume I'll take the pictures for this calendar?"

I'm not sure why he suddenly sounds so irritated, but I decide to ignore it. "I don't know who'll do what yet. My phone has a good camera, so I figured I'd use that."

"A phone camera for a professional print product?" His jaw is tense.

"No?"

"Well..." He stands. "As it turns out, that will be up to you. I've changed my mind. Photos of 'hot guys'?" He does air quotation marks. "I'm too busy for a stunt like that. You'll have to find someone else to help you." He opens the door and ushers me out in front of him.

I think he's going to shut me out of his office, but instead he starts walking as if physically wanting to get away from me.

"Why?" I follow him down the hallway. "Did you not hear the part where we plan on selling them all over the country? It's a great idea."

"Says who?" He opens the door to the elevator vestibule.

"It will raise a lot of money for GCL, I know it will." He reaches for the handle to the stairwell door, but I'm faster and block his way. "You know there's no one else I can ask, and we made a deal."

"It's a cheap attention grab, and I don't want anything to do with it. No offense." Not able to get past me, he eyes the elevator button for a moment before pressing it. "And we don't know that you won the deal, do we?"

"I remember more of the night than you."

"Oh yeah? Care to share?"

Just then, the elevator doors open, and he hurries inside. We look at each other through the doors.

"Didn't think so," he says.

Last second, I jump inside with him. The doors close behind me.

"You're wasting your time," he says.

I block the button panel so he can't press one and cross my arms.

"Bottom floor, please." His nostrils flare with each determined breath.

"Not until you explain why. Where are you going anyway? Cutting out early?"

"If you must know, I'm going to check if I left my jacket downstairs. The bar just opened."

Oh.

"And it's because I have standards. A pinup calendar? No."

I let out a sharp laugh. "Now you're a prude? Come on."

"Please push the button or move." He shifts his weight as his eyes bore into me.

Maybe it's the enclosed space and how its limited air supply has become infused with our clashing energies, but as the seconds tick, the temperature seems to increase by a couple of degrees. I blame every sexy movie elevator scene I've ever seen for my surging heart rate as I hear him exhale and feel the weight of his gaze on me. Is this what happened Friday at the bar? Is this how it began? I don't like how my body has started to betray me since then.

I inhale the thickening air, the traces of his familiar cologne curling my toes. "Not until you agree to be at the meeting tomorrow."

"Holly, I'm not joking," he growls. "I need to get downstairs."

That voice triggers a thrill in the pit of my stomach. Without thinking, I press my palm to it. His gaze follows my movement, his fingers tightening on the handrail he's holding on to. Maybe he's about to cave. I can drag this out all day.

"What's the hurry? They'll be open until midnight."

"Oh, for fuck's sake." He takes hold of my shoulders, moves me aside, and then hammers the ground floor button with his fist before leaning his forehead against the wall.

I stare at him as we start descending. I've missed something here—something beneath the surface. "Are you okay?"

He looks at me out of the corner of his eye. "Do I look okay?"

Now that he mentions it, his complexion is sort of pasty. "What's going on?"

He turns to face me, his jaw working. "If you must know, I'm claustrophobic."

The word takes a second to compute, but then several pieces fall into place. Why we took the stairs up here Friday night. Why he had such a strong reaction to me being stuck in the pantry closet.

"Then why are you in an elevator?" I ask.

"Because you blocked the stairs." Exasperation tinges his voice.

That's right, I did. "Sorry," I say, my voice small. "Why didn't you tell me?"

He runs a hand through his hair and mutters something.

"Sorry what?" The elevator passes the second floor. Almost there.

"It fucked up my last job," he says. "So I prefer not to talk about it."

"How?" But I'm too late. The doors open to the lobby, and Jonathan is out of the elevator before I have a chance to react. "Hey, I'm sorry," I call after him. "Please come to the meeting tomorrow."

He doesn't acknowledge me, and at this point, I'm not sure I blame him. *Crap*. Did I screw this up before it even began? (And by "this," I mean the fundraiser. Just to clarify.)

As I ride back up to the fifth floor, my so-recently runaway pulse settles into a sheepish patter. I'm going to have to change tactics and start over because I definitely need a designer to create a calendar.

I sit down at my desk and take stock of what I know, my churning thoughts accompanied by the tapping of my pencil against the wood. Jonathan hates small spaces and thinks my hot-guys-with-dogs calendar is crude. He prefers black clothing and reposado tequila, which lowers his inhibitions. Judging by the picture on his desk, he might be close with his dad. Something happened at his old job, whatever that was.

I spin a full circle in my chair, scanning the workspaces around me. All this tells me is that I still have countless questions left to answer. I simply don't know enough about Jonathan to know what might convince him my calendar is a good idea, which means I'll have research to do tonight when I get home. Some might call it snooping, but in the legal world, the preferred term is *data gathering*.

After driving Ava to a friend's house and scarfing down a spaghetti dinner, I nestle into the pillows on my bed and open my laptop. I've had hours to justify what I'm about to do, but I'm still contemplating locking my door like I'm seventeen again and about to try my first (and last) cigarette.

I type *Jonathan Sommers* into the search engine. A slew of random social media links pop up along with Wiki info on an Australian singer. I click on a Facebook link, but it's not the right person. That's also when I spot my spelling error, so I change the *o* to a *u* in his last name and add *design* as a tag.

This time, his face is the first one I see along with headline after headline that further underscores how little I know about him.

Award-winning photographer arrested! Picture not perfect—the truth behind Jonathan Summers's fall from grace! National Geographic cuts ties with Summers!

I scan the text of the first article. The accompanying photo shows a man with a jacket over his head being led away from a plane by police. A few words stand out—"drunk and disorderly... held on bail... the end of an illustrious career..."—but I'm still having a hard time reconciling what I'm reading with the reticent GCL web designer I'm trying to convince to do a fundraiser with me.

Do you know if Jonathan used to be a photographer? I text Rachel.

She responds right away. **I forgot about that, but yeah. Hey!!! That's PERFECT!** 😊

I shake my head. So that's why Jonathan assumed I'd want him to take the pictures. More pieces fall into place. Why does he have to be such a puzzle?

The rabbit hole takes me deeper and deeper into his past career. He really did win awards for his photos. Many of them are available online, so I can see why. Buried several pages into the search results is a photo from a local bar of a band playing. I recognize a younger Manny right away, and off to the side in the picture is a dark figure bent over a piano, eyes half closed, fingers splayed, his mouth curled into an introspective smile. I suppress the urge to reach out and touch the screen.

"What happened to you?" I whisper.

Then, finally, I close the laptop and add these new pieces of information to my list: photographer, involuntary career change, music makes him happy. The question is—how does that help me convince him my fundraiser is a worthy cause?

The answer comes to me while I brush my teeth. I can't convince him, but there is someone who knows him better who could. Someone who shares his happy place.

A quick email to Manny later, and I go to sleep confident I've set us on the right path again.

8

Rachel has booked us a conference room for our meeting. I still don't know if Jonathan will show, so I keep an eye out for him as I pass the design offices. He's not at his desk, but when I get to Manny's office, I spot him through the window. Jonathan has his back to me, but the way he gestures as if to underscore the point offers a good idea what the topic du jour is. Manny, on the other hand, looks as calm as a proverbial cucumber. Unfortunately, there's no way to determine who has the upper hand in the two seconds it takes me to walk by.

My mentor is already waiting when I enter the room. She's set out notepads on the table and is pouring herself a glass of water from the cooler by the door.

"It might only be us," I tell her as I take a seat. "Jonathan doesn't love the calendar idea. We'll see what Manny can do."

"Manny?"

"I may have enlisted him for our cause." When Rachel still looks confused, I add, "They're friends—I barely know him. Maybe Jonathan will listen to him."

"Smart."

"In the meantime, let's get started." I place my palms on the table for a moment to center myself before opening my laptop.

"The deadline is October 28, so according to my timeline, we have until October 7 to make this calendar happen in order to allow three weeks for the sales campaign. Today is September 20, which leaves us less than three weeks. First order of business—where to find guys and dogs for the calendar. Without models, everything else is moot. Also printers. I'm talking to several different ones today."

Rachel sits back, looking amused. "Oooh, boss lady. I'm liking this side of you."

I do, too, judging by this surge of energy traveling up my spine. It feels good to take charge of something again. "Well, this is it, right? This is how I steer my life back on track."

"Sure is. Are you keeping the temperate rainforests as your cause?"

I tell her that's my intent. Ashley and Eric are doing the same. It seems like the best option considering that's the focus of the job we're vying for.

"Okay, so what have you got?" she asks.

Time to make it rain men. "I'm thinking of asking the barista around the corner. The one with the golden retriever. He's cute, right? And there must be someone at your gym."

"My first thought was your brother."

My momentum sputters to a halt. "What about Jude?"

"Asking him to pose for the calendar. He's hot, he has a dog…" Rachel's eyes are wide and innocent.

"Absolutely not. And stop calling him hot."

"Not to mention he's single." A salacious smile spreads across her lips. "I picture him with—"

"Nuh-uh. Time-out." I T-up my hands to interrupt her before my ears fall off. "No family members. New rule."

"You're no fun." Rachel pouts. "Fine," she says with a sigh.

"I can ask Dennis at the gym. He's always going on about his Chihuahua."

"He's good-looking?"

"Very. And Dennis isn't too bad either."

"Haha."

"What?" She smiles. "It's obvious you need me here for laughs. Gotta make sure boss lady doesn't get too serious."

I toss a pencil her way. "Is that better?"

"Much." She beams. "Who else?"

"I'm going to stop by the police station after work to see if there's a K-9 unit willing to pose, I have calls out to three different veterinarians, and then there's that agility club on Mercer Island." I hesitate. "I also had this one idea, but it's kind of out there."

"Here for it."

I type in the URL on my laptop and spin it so she can see. "It's this local dating website I came across—Pawsome Partners. For pet owners. Maybe we can find people there."

She's about to respond when the door whooshes open and Jonathan steps inside.

"Not cool," he says, pointing at me. Then he sits down one chair away, arms crossed, legs stretched long.

"Good to see you, too," Rachel says. "Having a rough morning?"

"I've been informed that my participation in this situation"—he gestures across the table—"isn't optional. So here I am. Guess we're making a pinup calendar." He glances at me. A brief but accusatory *This is your fault.*

"A classy pinup calendar," Rachel amends. "For a good cause. Do you even know how few temperate rainforests remain? Do you care?" Her teacher voice has the desired effect, and there's no response. "Yeah, I didn't think so."

"I'm not going to apologize," I say, forcing Jonathan to look me in the eye. "This fundraiser will benefit GCL, and I assume, since you're here, you believe in the company enough to want to keep your job." I soften my tone a smidge. "Can't you look at it as a means to an end? With your skills, we can make the calendar beautiful. Those photos you took in the Serengeti blew my mind."

There's a brief widening of his eyes. "You looked me up."

My cheeks heat. "Maybe."

"See, I knew that's what you were after. But I don't photograph people."

It's my turn to cross my arms. "I wasn't after anything. When I asked you to team up, I didn't know about your old job, but then what you said in the elevator... I wanted to—"

Rachel leans forward on the other side of the table. "Elevator?" The word ends higher than it started.

"You're not exactly forthcoming," I continue. "I was curious. Sue me."

"I would never, Ms. King County Bar Association Award winner. See I also know how to use a search engine. That professional headshot was *mwah*." He kisses his fingertips.

Unfortunately, I know exactly what picture he's referring to. I have no idea what I was thinking at the time—probably that a bronze tie-neck blouse would make my colleagues and clients take me more seriously as a new attorney. Instead, I look like I'm playing dress-up in an eighties Glamour Shots costume closet. All that's missing is blue eyeshadow and Aqua Net hair. I was stuck with that headshot for five long years, and it certainly didn't ease my uphill battle with being taken seriously as a woman in corporate law.

An ick-triggered shudder runs through me as a cavalcade

of the disrespectful nicknames I've been called by those who were supposed to be my professional peers echoes in my mind. I scramble for recourse and cling to the first thing that pops into my head. "Tell me—what happened on that plane?"

To my satisfaction, the smirk on his face disappears.

"What plane?" Rachel's gaze ping-pongs between us.

Jonathan scoffs and stands. "You know what, I change my mind again. Enough of this shit."

His tone finally snaps me back to my senses. What am I doing? He was here ready to work, and now I've driven him to leave.

"I'm sorry," I say in a rush. "I withdraw the question. I mean, that was unnecessary. Please don't go."

"I'm so confused," Rachel mutters.

Jonathan hesitates. He looks toward the door and then back at me. Tilts his face to the ceiling. A world-weary sigh escapes him as he sits back down. "Fine. Whatever."

Rachel and I exchange a look of relief. Close call.

"Let's get this over with so I can go back to my actual job. What exactly are we doing here?"

Rachel must sense that I need a moment because she hurries to summarize our timeline and our first objective. "We were about to get Holly on a dating site when you were kind enough to join us."

His attention flicks to me. "A dating site? Why?"

I catch him up to where Rachel and I left off. "It might be a good way to meet local guys with dogs."

"But dating?" Jonathan frowns. "I guess I didn't...Are you, like, looking?"

"For?" I squint at him.

"You know. A guy."

"Oh." I sit back. "No. No, no. Definitely not. Nope. Last thing I need."

"That's a whole lot of nos right there," Rachel says to the table.

I award her an icy glare. "It's purely for the calendar. If they fit what we're looking for, I'll tell them about the project when we meet and, you know, let them down easy."

"Why not just reach out and ask them online?"

"Yeah because 'Hey, stranger, can I interest you in this modeling opportunity?' sounds totally legit and not like a scam at all."

"Point taken."

Rachel cracks her knuckles. "Let's do it, then. One dating profile for Holly, coming up. Believe me, I know all the best tricks."

"Is that why you're still single?" I ask her.

"Yikes." Jonathan winces, but that rare smile of his flashes at the same time.

I return the favor, and finally the tension eases in the room.

"Oh, I see," Rachel says. "This is how it's going to be? He's rubbing off on you."

I can tell she's not really upset, but I play along. "I'm sorry, low blow." I reach for her hand over the table. "And no one's going to be rubbing off anything on anyone."

Is it my imagination or is there an almost inaudible "shame" coming from my left? I glance at Jonathan, but he gives nothing away.

"I forgive you." Rachel squeezes my hand before refocusing on the keyboard. "Are we doing this or what?"

Over the next ten minutes, we answer an uncalled-for number of questions about me and what I'm looking for.

"Interests?" Rachel asks after we've tackled *favorite city? favorite food? favorite music?*

"Um, I don't know. Reading?"

"No, like, what do you do for fun?" Rachel waits, hands perched above the keys.

"You know that's what I do. I don't have a lot of time."

Rachel and Jonathan look at each other, a silent understanding passing between them.

"Since it's not a real dating profile, maybe make something up?" Jonathan suggests.

"Wouldn't that be lying?"

"You're already bending the truth by not looking for a date, aren't you?"

"True." I consider possible extracurriculars, but nothing solidifies.

"What did you do in high school? College?" Jonathan asks. "There must have been something other than books and work."

The unexpected rush of spraying snow hitting my face comes at me from deep in my memory. It brings a smile to my lips. "I was a great alpine skier. Ranked in high school." I haven't thought about this in so long that it feels like someone else's past. "And Jude and I both did archery."

When I look back up, Rachel and Jonathan are both staring at me.

"Let me get this straight," Rachel says. "You, Holly King, were once involved in the badass Bond-esque pursuits of skiing and archery?"

I nod. "Yup."

"How did I not know about this?"

"It was before I met you, and I guess it never came up."

"That's wild." She shakes her head before tapping the keys in a frenzy.

"Yeah, that's neat," Jonathan concedes, and I admit some small part of me warms at his approval. "Though I fail to see what it has to do with double-oh-seven."

Rachel pauses her typing. *"The Spy Who Loved Me? For Your Eyes Only?* Come on—the skiing scenes only cemented Roger Moore as the best Bond."

Jonathan glances at me, clearly not used to Rachel's hot takes on popular culture. "If you say so."

"I do."

"Yeah, well, it was a long time ago," I cut in to wrap up the topic. "What have you got so far?"

Rachel consults the monitor. "You are now Holly Saint Bernard—figured that would draw the dog lovers—a fiend on the slopes, frequenter of Greece, connoisseur of sushi."

"I sincerely hope that's not how you've worded it."

"I'm paraphrasing, okay? Chill." She reads us the rest of my profile, and when we don't have anything else to add, she pauses with the pointer above the PUBLISH button. "Ready to meet your match?" she asks.

Beside me, Jonathan shifts in his seat. For the briefest moment, our eyes meet.

"Ready."

"Aaaand posted." Rachel closes her laptop. "Ah! All in a day's work."

"And now what?" I ask.

"Now you wait for a bunch of complete strangers to approve or disapprove of you as a human being based on these few superficial traits," Jonathan says.

Rachel smirks. "Someone knows his way around dating apps."

"Do not." He glares at her.

"You already have someone special in your life, then?" she asks.

I kick her under the table. "You don't have to answer that," I tell Jonathan. Among the articles I read last night, there were several mentions of a messy divorce on the tail end of the messy career implosion.

"I don't," he tells Rachel, ignoring me. "And that's how I like it. If there's nothing else, I'd like to get back to my real job, please." He stands.

"But you'll be my photographer?" I get up, too. "As soon as we've got a few guys lined up, we should scout locations and get started."

Rachel joins us on our side of the table.

"Yes, all right." Jonathan rolls his shoulders back, about to say something else, but just then the door opens, and Manny sticks his head in. "Hey, hey." He enters, eyeing Jonathan. "Checking to see how things are going. Is this one behaving himself?"

Jonathan scowls.

"Rocky start, but we're cruising now," Rachel says. "Wrapping up, actually."

"Great." He steps closer to Jonathan and hands him a jacket. The missing one. From Friday. "Hey, the cleaning crew found this below the foosball table in the rec room on Saturday. It's yours, right?"

"It is." Jonathan does a decent imitation of someone who has no idea how that might have happened, but I don't miss the miniscule start at the mention of the rec room. He takes the garment and puts it on, shoving his hands into the pockets.

"So, Holly, are you feeling on track?" Manny asks me. "Jon tells me you're producing a calendar. I think that's a fantastic idea—if you can get it done in time. Remember you need time to sell the product before the deadline."

Out of the corner of my eye, I register Jonathan's hand in his pocket, moving around and grasping something.

"We'll be done in time," I tell Manny. "The plan is set in motion. I'm lining up a printer today, so I'm not worried."

As Rachel launches into her excitement about the project, Jonathan fishes whatever he's found out of the pocket and looks at it. It's an earring shaped like a lightning bolt. My earring.

"Well, all three of you are highly competent people," Manny is saying as Jonathan hands me the piece of jewelry.

It kept getting tangled in my hair, beneath his fingers. Getting in the way of his lips. He'd plucked it out of my ear so gently and tucked it into his pocket "for safekeeping."

Our fingers graze over the cool silver, sending a jolt up my arm. The exchange is over quickly—Manny is still talking—but my breathing has quickened, and Jonathan's eyes have gone more vivid. *He remembers, too.*

I shove the delicate jewelry into my own pocket and ignore the curious flicker of Rachel's gaze cutting between me and Jonathan. There's a tiny crease between her brows.

"Keep me posted," Manny says, nudging my elbow. "I look forward to seeing what you come up with."

I step back from our little circle and clear my throat. "Thanks, I will."

As Manny leaves, Jonathan calls after him, "I think I'll join you. Got plans for lunch?"

They both disappear out the door, and I go to grab my things from the table. Rachel remains in her spot.

The silence in the room grows like an avalanche until she finally asks, "What was that?"

I move my tongue to try and remedy its arid state. "What do you mean?"

She starts tucking her laptop into her bag. "Why did Jonathan have your earring in his pocket?"

Crap.

"Um, it was bothering me on Friday. I took it out at the bar, and he offered to keep it for me." I venture to meet her querying gaze. "No pockets on that dress."

"What about your bag?"

"Didn't have one." I point to my chest. "Credit card. Bra."

"Keys?"

"In my jacket in the coat check."

Her eyes narrow, but after another moment passes, she relaxes. "Yeah, I guess that makes sense."

To my great relief, she's back to talking about the fundraiser as we head down the hallway to the elevators. On Tuesdays, there's a taco lunch special across the street. "Did I tell you Eric is looking to book the Chihuly Glass Museum for his green party?"

I pause my stride. "Wow. That's..."

"Ambitious? Ballsy? Wildly expensive?"

"I was going to say 'hard to compete with.'"

Rachel presses the elevator button. "I wouldn't worry. I'm sure it's booked up months if not years."

"What about Letitia and Ashley? Have you heard anything more about their projects?"

"No." As if sensing my upped anxiety, she taps my foot with

hers. "You're the one with the award-winning photographer on your team, remember. I can't believe that slipped my mind."

"Yes, that was impressive," I agree. "Or concerning."

We both smile, but then silence engulfs us again, lingering until we step onto the elevator.

Rachel presses the button but then cocks her head as if analyzing the lit-up LL. "Sorry, just so I'm clear. You said Jonathan had your earring because it was bothering you at the bar on Friday and you had no place to put it?"

I suck in a breath. "Mm-hmm."

We pass the third floor, the second.

The profile of her forehead is set in concentration. "But his jacket wasn't at the bar. It was in the rec room," she says quietly. "Left in the rec room Friday night..."

A second later, her eyes jolt to mine, the spinning wheels behind them stopping with a clank. She reaches out a fist and pounds the emergency stop button. We thump to a halt.

"You and Jonathan were both up here Friday night," she says, triumph in her voice. "You didn't leave the bar to work. You came upstairs to..." She gasps. "You had sex, didn't you?"

"No!" I try to reach the button behind her, but she won't let me. What irony that I was in a similar position yesterday with Jonathan. "I would never!"

"Then what?" She raises her chin.

"Then nothing. I could have been in the office working while he was in the rec room without running into him."

"Except, now that I think about it, you both disappeared from the bar at the same time."

"I don't know what you're talking about."

She puts her hands on her hips. "We have security cameras,

and I happen to know that the guy who runs them really likes muffins."

Damn, I didn't think about the cameras.

Rachel's curly hair frames her like a halo. She won't back down. "I'm going to ask you one more time. Did you, or did you not, tap that fine Summers ass Friday night?"

"Charming." I shuffle my feet while scanning the shiny walls of the tiny space as if there's a secret portal somewhere.

"Holly..." Rachel says, the warning clear in her voice. "Don't make me bake muffins. You know I'm unreliable near ovens."

I huff out the air in my lungs until my mind goes blank. I know when I'm beat.

Rachel's text pings as soon as I get in the door that evening. We've been apart less than an hour, but her incredulity knows no bounds. I wait to look until I'm in my room because it sounds like Jude and Ava are arguing in the kitchen.

> I cannot believe you made out with him in the office!!! 🏢😼😸

I sink onto my bed and lean against the cushions as my phone keeps pinging.

> *Ping!* I know you said you don't want to talk about it...
> *Ping!* But this is a big deal...
> *Ping!* And I'm a really good listener.
> *Ping!* And I won't tell a soul.

I scrub a hand across my forehead. I knew it was a mistake to tell her. She's always on about how I need to get out more, so she'll never shut up about this.

But also, she's my best friend, and she means well. It's not like I don't understand the universal appeal of juicy gossip.

I sit back up, crossing my legs.

Ping! **At least tell me if it was any good.**

The offending earring rests on my nightstand. I reach out to straighten it. As I do, the echoing sensation of him carefully lifting it out of my ear reverberates through me. Such a small move, but the delicate touch, the withdrawal of the cool metal, and the soft, warm pressure of his lips in its place replay in my mind, drawing my fingertips to the spot. I shiver. Yes, it was fucking good.

Let's just say it wasn't bad, I text her.

Ping! **Knew it. Do you want to kiss him again?**

Well, that's a no-brainer. **Absolutely not,** I type. I have a full plate without adding that sort of complication to my life. I'm about to check responses to my dating profile, and at some point before bed, I also want to email info to the veterinarian who left me a message earlier saying he'd be interested in learning more about the calendar. Not to mention how dating someone from work backfired last time I gave it a go.

When two doors slam closed downstairs in rapid succession, I add to my list a possible need to mediate between my brother and niece. What on earth are they fighting about?

I pull my laptop out of my workbag and log into Pawsome Partners. To my surprise, I have five matches already. Two are old enough to be my dad, so I decline those. I know I'm not looking to date these men, but it would still feel weird. The third one's username is FelineFiend, so I reject him, too, before accepting the "connect" requests from the remaining guys. I'll have to respond to them before calling it a night. Since one of the printers I spoke to earlier can get me scheduled for October 10 with a five-day production timeline—the closest option to my original plan—I plan on signing their contract as soon as they send it over. The time crunch is now real.

Ping! Do you think he wants to do it again?

I stare at the words on my phone. Does he? Jonathan's attentive eyes flash before me, causing a flutter in my belly. No. He doesn't appear to remember much from our night together.

I start peeling my socks off, and once my feet are free, I wiggle my toes.

But what if he did want to? If he initiated something, would I decline?

My mind labors over this hypothetical situation while I change into a pair of yoga pants.

We are coworkers—teammates as of hours ago—so there's that. I plan on leaving Washington for good, hopefully soon and through GCL, though he knows that already. And if that's not enough, we also have nothing at all in common, and neither one of us is looking for a partner. Not that anyone said anything about dating.

I shrug out of my bra and into a tank top before reaching for a soft crewneck sweater.

But I suppose, with that in mind, if he did suggest an openness to an encore, maybe that wouldn't be the worst situa—

Ping! Hello?

My thoughts come to a screeching halt. What is wrong with me? Surely I'm not seriously entertaining the idea of unbuttoning buttoned-up Jonathan Summers again. Even if I didn't have personal reasons to avoid entanglement, he barely tolerates me.

I can say with certainty that he doesn't, I text Rachel. **Sorry to disappoint.**

I tell her about the two hits on Holly Saint Bernard's profile and promise to share my responses with her in the morning. Then I give in to my growling stomach and set course for the kitchen since whatever war was being waged down there is now at a ceasefire.

I've almost finished making myself a sandwich when Jude pushes open the door from the foyer and enters, Morris on his heels. It's started raining outside, and the goldendoodle shakes off a few droplets before coming up to sniff my knees.

"There you are," Jude says. "I thought you were working late, but then I saw your car in the driveway." He grabs a slice of cheese from the pack I have out and tears it in two before offering one half to his eager companion. "Good boy."

"I didn't want to get in the way," I say, raising an eyebrow.

"You heard that, huh?" My brother sinks onto one of the counter stools.

"Everything okay?"

He runs a hand through his dirty-blond strands. "Depends on who you ask. I thought I had exciting news to share when I got home today. Ava thinks I'm ruining her life." He reaches for another slice of cheese.

"Want me to make you one of these?" I ask, indicating my sandwich.

He nods.

"What happened?" I ask as I smear one slice of multigrain with mayo and another with mustard.

"I was able to get a couple of interviews lined up in Texas. Figured I'd tell her about the plans."

I put the knife down and rest my hands against the cool marble. "And is that how you said it? 'Hi, sweetie, guess what? I'm interviewing for a job in Texas, and we'll be moving. Thought you should know.'"

He tuts. "Of course not. I told her it will likely take several months. I'm only starting to look."

"Oh my God."

"What?"

"Do you know your daughter at all?" I tuck a wad of turkey and some lettuce between the two slices of bread and push the plate his way. "She's a teenage girl with ambitious plans. A move would be a huge deal for her."

"I know that. She'll miss her friends and her tennis cohort and whatnot, but she'll meet new ones there. And we'll be close to Mom and Dad, so she'll have grandparents around."

"She doesn't care about that. She's fifteen."

"Oh, come on. She loves them."

"Of course she does. But you're nuts if you think they would replace her friends."

Jude takes a big bite of his sandwich and chews it carefully. "So what am I supposed to do, then? Not move? Stagnate in my career? Let Mom and Dad figure things out as best as they can, fingers crossed?"

A drumroll of footsteps thunders down the stairs, and Ava

appears in the doorway. "You're supposed to talk to me first," she yells. "You're supposed to care what I have to say, and you're not supposed to move us to fucking Gilead."

"Language, please," Jude says. "And I don't know of any Gilead in Texas. The jobs I'm looking at are in Austin near your grandma and grandpa. I already told you that."

Ava lets out a frustrated growl before she stomps back upstairs and slams the door to her room.

I eye Jude as he takes another bite of his sandwich.

"What?" he asks.

"I take it you didn't read *The Handmaid's Tale* in high school. Margaret Atwood?"

His forehead creases. "Don't think so. Why?"

I explain to him as briefly as I can that Gilead refers to a fictional, misogynistic, dystopian society. "Honestly, it's a valid concern. With women's and reproductive rights under siege in this country, I don't think you can dismiss it outright. Some states are safer than others."

"Oh." He looks decently chastised. "Didn't think about that. But she's likely going to college elsewhere anyway. It would only be for a couple of years."

"Sure. But talk to her about it. She's not a kid anymore."

"I know." He brings the sandwich toward him as if about to take another bite but stops. "I don't like it."

I chuckle as I put the condiments back in the fridge. Artwork Ava made in elementary school still adorns the door, held up by magnets. Stick figure milestones. It wasn't that long ago, and yet it feels like another lifetime. If I move to Glasgow (correction—*when* I move to Glasgow), what more will I miss? I run my fingers over the yellowed paper.

"It's times like these I wonder what Jolene would have done,"

Jude says. "I bet she'd have known exactly the right thing to say."

My brother has that faraway gaze in his eyes that's reserved for memories of his late wife. He doesn't talk about her often, but it's clear she's still very much with him.

"It would be her first time parenting a teenager, too," I tell him. "So I'm not so sure about that."

"Mmm." Jude turns his plate ninety degrees, still somewhere else in thought.

I study him, my big brother. He wears his hair longer nowadays, almost long enough to stay behind his ears when he tries to tuck it. His jaw is intentionally stubbled, he keeps himself in shape, and he has the most contagious smile. It's a shame he has no one to appreciate him.

"Hey, can I ask you something?"

He smirks. "Since when do you need permission?"

Around us, the house is quiet except for the faint music coming from Ava's room. Everything is orderly, the counters clean. In the family room off the kitchen, a tray on the coffee table is home to a candle, a stack of books, and the remotes. A gray blanket lies folded over the armrest of the couch. There could be so much more life here, I think. And once I move out, it'll be even worse. "Do you ever think about getting out there again?" I ask. "Finding someone?"

Jude taps his fingers against the marble top. "Sure."

"But?"

"Between work and Ava, there's not much time, is there? And Morris," he adds when the doodle lifts his head off his paws at Jude's feet. "Can't forget about you, bud." Jude scratches Morris's ears.

"I don't think Jolene would have wanted you to be alone."

He sighs. "I know that."

"So why not do something about it?"

He watches me for a moment. "Since when are you pro-relationship? You're like the poster child for putting work first. Did something happen?"

"No." It comes out too fast.

Jude sits up straighter. "Who?"

"No one." I grab his plate and put it in the sink. "Nothing." I force a smile before I turn back to him. "Just looking out for you." It's not a lie, I tell myself. I don't want him to spend the rest of his life alone. I'm legitimately busy, and this thing with Jonathan is a complete nothing-burger. Rachel's words must be messing with my head. "And I joined a dating site to find guys for the calendar—that's probably what got me thinking."

Jude's eyes remain narrowed, but thankfully the new topic distracts him. "Really? What's that like?"

Phew.

I tell him about it and my other plans to find models while I do the dishes, and by the time I finish up, we've gotten far enough from the relationship topic to move safely into the evening. Still, I vow not to drop the issue of his singlehood entirely. Jude needs some fun in his life, and if he's unwilling to put himself out there, maybe I can help now that I'm soon to be a dating site pro. At the very least, I could set him up on a few dates so that when he gets to Texas, he'll already know how to go about it. It will be less intimidating that way, and then Texas can be the fresh start he needs, as much as Scotland is for me. I know better than most that it's hard to see new possibilities when you're still surrounded by the past.

Days until printer deadline: 18

The model search is off to a slower start than I'd hoped, and the next few days bring several disappointments. My K-9 idea is a bust, as there's too much red tape for officers to be able to pose in a commercial product, and the agility place is closed for renovation based on their voice mail. I leave a message, but since their recorded greeting ends with "see you again after Thanksgiving," I won't hold my breath. I'm not letting these setbacks get me down, though. The vet I've been emailing with is still interested, and I'm hoping to lock him in for a date and time soon. I've also been messaging back and forth with one guy on Pawsome Partners.

But ultimately, it's Rachel who comes through for me first.

"I've got our first model!" she announces after lunch on Thursday. She's holding her phone in the air as she marches up to my desk with a triumphant smile.

Finally! I close my laptop, where I've just accepted contact requests from two more guys on the dating site. "Who?"

"Dennis from the gym. Remember I told you about him and his Chihuahua?" She shows me a picture of a tan guy with a bright smile and muscles that threaten to pop his T-shirt. In his arms is a scrawny, short-haired little dog with perky ears and large brown eyes. They're the most mismatched owner and pet duo I've ever seen except their heads are both tilted a smidge to the right as if they've moved in synchrony.

"That's great. Can you text that to me so I can show it to Jonathan? When is Dennis available? And you told him we can't pay, right? That it's for a good cause?"

Rachel smiles. "Deep breaths. Yes, he knows that. And he's free Sunday if we can make that happen."

"We're going to have to."

My phone pings with the image, and I waste no time setting course toward Jonathan's office.

I haven't seen him since our meeting Tuesday, so I don't know if his attitude has improved or deteriorated since, but because Rachel has set this next phase in motion, I can't afford to care about that. No matter the reason, he said he's in, so I'm going to take him at his word.

I stick my head through the doorway into the office where he and Jacques are working. "Hey."

His usual scowl is surprisingly absent today when he responds in kind. "Hey, what's up?"

So far, so good. I glance at Jacques. For all intents and purposes, he's teamed up with the enemy, so I gesture for Jonathan to come outside. "Do you have a minute?"

He catches on and joins me in the hallway.

As he closes the office door behind him, the draft sweeps a hint of his scent past me. Goose bumps rise on the back of my arms. If only I'd had more tequila that night so I wouldn't remember quite so much. Knowing I've slept with my cheek against this man's bare chest remains a tad distracting.

I clear my throat and show him the picture. "Ready and willing," I say.

His eyes cut to mine, an amused glint beneath his brow.

My neck warms when I hear what that must have sounded like. "I mean, Rachel has found our first guy who is ready and willing to model for the calendar."

"Yeah, you scared me there for a moment."

"Haha. You free Sunday?"

He checks the calendar on his phone. "That works. Where?"

Yes! So far so good on my timeline holding up. "I thought maybe we could discuss that together?"

Something passes across his face. "Really?"

"You're the creative genius. It would be foolish of me not to take advantage of your vision when I've lured you over to the dark side." When he doesn't immediately respond, I backtrack with a shrug. "Or I could tell you what to do and when to do it."

That hits a nerve. "No, no. I know some good spots."

I award him a smile. "That's what I was hoping. Any immediate thoughts on a good one for Dennis and his tiny pup?"

Jonathan takes my phone, his forehead creasing as he considers my question. "Let's do the Seattle skyline with them. At Kerry Park. Five thirty p.m." He clicks something on my screen, and then his fingers move. "I'm giving you my number so we can reach each other. Sending..." His phone beeps in his pocket. "There. Now I've got yours, too." He hands the device back.

The metal is warm from his touch. "Thanks."

"Uh-huh." He looks at me expectantly, as if waiting for more.

"Um..." I stare at the screen where he's typed **Holly's number** in a text to himself. Something about seeing my name written by him feels...intimate. It shouldn't. We're coworkers. Rachel has me in her phone, too. But Rachel is also my friend.

Maybe Jonathan and I can be friends.

The thought is there from nowhere. Or from seeing my name backlit in matter-of-fact sans serif.

"Got any other fun plans this weekend?" I ask.

He flinches. "Plans? Why?"

On second thought, maybe friendship is better off not begun with drunken canoodling.

"Never mind. Just making conversation. I'll check with Dennis and get back to you. Do I need to bring anything to the shoot?"

He shakes his head. "I've got everything I need."

"Great." I start backing away.

Jonathan reaches for the door handle but pauses. "He's going to wear clothes, right? In the photo? We're not going to get cited for public indecency or anything?"

Is that what he pictures? An actual full-frontal pinup situation? I decide to have some fun with him. "Oh no," I say. "It's nature-themed, remember? And what's more natural than the human body, dicks and all? It'll depend on the model's comfort level, of course. Buns are fine, too." I draw a line in the air with my whole hand as if painting the picture. "Man and Mother Earth in perfect harmony."

At first he stares at me, but after a long moment, he purses his pretty mouth. "You're yanking my chain."

"Yup, I totally am." I wink at him. "Don't worry, they won't be naked. At least not completely."

"What do you mean by 'completely'?" he calls after me as I set off down the hallway.

"See you Sunday," I call back.

That evening, I set my plan in motion to help my brother find a date. He's an easy guy to talk up, so his Pawsome Partners profile basically writes itself. Who wouldn't want to meet an attractive, well-groomed, six-foot attorney who is a great dad, a dog lover, a decent cook, and an avid hiker? I select "casual dates" in the drop-down menu for what he's looking for (as opposed to "long-term commitment"), and then I submit it and cross my fingers. I should have done this a long time ago. Then again, I've been somewhat preoccupied by my own life drama for the past couple of years. Well, that changes now.

I stare at the screen for a moment where a pawprint in the shape of a heart announces, "Your purr-fect match awaits!" and then I open my work email for a final check before bed. The printer still hasn't emailed me the contract I need to sign, and while they did say it might take a couple of days, I don't like anything being left to chance. For peace of mind, I shoot off a nudge, keeping my tone upbeat and understanding. Better safe than sorry.

"T's crossed and i's dotted," I mumble as I crawl under the covers. That's how you make things happen.

Days until printer deadline: 15

Kerry Park is one of Seattle's premier spots for skyline photography and consequently it's often overrun by tourists. But late on a Sunday afternoon like this, we only share the spot with a handful of others when we arrive for our photo shoot. I've brought Rachel along since she knows Dennis, and I don't know who's more excited—she or Dennis's petite Chihuahua, Tank.

As soon as Tank gets out of their car, he jumps up and down at Dennis's feet, which, considering he's leashed, gives an uncanny impression of a yo-yo. Dennis scoops him up with one hand and joins the rest of us at one of the benches where Jonathan has set down his equipment bags. Behind him, the Space Needle glows at the summit of the skyline, which peaks like a man-made imitation of Mount Rainier in the background. The mountain is out in full force today, appearing superimposed against the blue September sky.

Rachel makes introductions, but it's hard to hear her over the Chihuahua's sharp bark, which for some reason seems aimed at me.

"Tank, hush," Dennis tells the irate pup, but when that

doesn't work, he covers Tanks eyes with a giant hand and twists his face into an apologetic expression. "It's your hoodie," he tells me. "Tank doesn't like zippers."

I stare at him blankly. "I'm sorry. What?"

"Yeah, it's a thing. Can't stand them. Right, T?" He scratches Tank's neck. "I've had to throw out half my closet. Can only do pullovers."

I make eye contact with Rachel and Jonathan, who look as bewildered as I am.

"Okay, maybe I'll hang back, then," I say. "Give Tank some space?"

"No." Dennis scratches his temple. "You see, he knows you're here now. Part of the group. With the zipper. He'll sense it."

Jonathan tuts. "Come on, that's—"

I stop him. "It's fine." It's our first shoot—let's not end it before it's begun. "What if I take it off and lock it in the car? Would that work?"

Dennis considers this. "We can try."

"Great." I give him a tight smile before I hurry to the car to shrug out of the offending garment. I only have a cropped workout top on underneath, having planned on a jog through Queen Anne once we're done here, and the light breeze of the cooling day draws goose bumps across my skin. But I've said it before. I'll do whatever it takes to get this calendar right.

While away from the group, I also quickly check my email. The printer got back to me on Friday and promised I'd have the contract before Monday, but still nothing. I take a deep breath to placate the stirring unease inside me. Yes, the weekend is almost over, but they're a reputable place so I'm sure they'll make good on their word. Worst case, I'll call them tomorrow and have them send it while I'm on the phone.

"It'll be fine," I whisper to myself. Then I force my brow to smooth out and tuck my phone away.

"There," I say when I return sans hoodie. "Better?"

Jonathan's gaze sweeps past my bare midsection once, then again in a double take. I pretend I don't notice either that or the way it makes my stomach dip, but it does help me refocus on the present company.

Dennis removes his hand from Tank's eyes, and the Chihuahua blinks at the light.

"Hi, Tank," I try. "Who's a good boy?"

This time, his tongue flops out of his mouth as he yawns. No bark.

"Great." Jonathan taps his thighs. "Then we can get started."

Rachel and Dennis take Tank for a stroll so he can get his zoomies out before the shoot while Jonathan heads to his gear.

"Can I do anything?" I ask him. He's extending the legs of a collapsible tripod, working fast with an impassive expression on his face. The sleeves of his black Henley are pushed up to his elbows, and the muscles of his forearms play beneath the skin in the late afternoon sun.

"Nope, just want to get this ridiculousness over with." Next, he squats down by the bench to go through his lenses, his fingers skimming each one almost reverently. He pauses by one, glances toward Dennis, mutters something to himself, and moves on.

His tone nags at me, but I'm determined not to take it personally. As long as he's here doing his job, he doesn't have to like it. And one glance down at my top tells me he's not completely wrong. There are aspects of the ridiculous at play here. Even so, it would be more pleasant for everyone else if he could get over himself.

"Thank you for doing this," I say, hoping to kill the grump with kindness. "I hope you know how much I appreciate it."

He stands, the chosen lens in his hand. "You do what you got to do." He scans the ground around him while scratching his head. "On second thought, can you get the reflectors from my car? Two soft cases in the trunk." He tosses me the keys.

"Sure." I count the request as a win. The car unlocks with a click, but the moment I touch the handle of the trunk, a violent beeping ruptures the stillness. I jump back and aim the key fob at the trunk, pressing the button over and over. "I don't know what I did," I holler over my shoulder as Jonathan comes jogging over. "I swear I unlocked it."

He takes the key from me and wields it like a magic wand in front of him. Finally, the alarm stops. "Sorry, I've been meaning to fix this. I think it's the key fob battery or something. Not your fault." He reaches past me and hauls out the cases, handing me one so he can lock up again.

"It's always something, right?" I say, going for common ground. "My trunk has recently decided it's analog and only opens with the actual key. Cars..."

He makes a humming noise in response, nothing else.

We head back to the other equipment in silence, but when we pull out several shiny, circular screens from the cases, I venture another question, determined not to give up that easily. "How long has it been since you did this?"

Jonathan stops what he's doing and looks up. "This?" He gestures toward Dennis and Tank.

"Not this specifically. I know my inspired vision here is not your jam." I smirk. "I mean photography in general."

His lips press together. "It's been a while."

"Should I not ask about it?"

FINDING MR. JULY 93

"You can always ask. Can't promise I'll answer."

"Smartass."

I almost miss it—his teeth flashing bright with unguarded humor as he turns away from me. When he looks up next, his expression is once again composed.

I'm about to restate my question when Rachel hollers, "Are we doing this or what?"

Jonathan hoists his camera in one hand and a stool in the other and makes his escape. "Over here," he calls to Rachel. "Let's do it."

Typical. Just when I was getting somewhere.

Dennis has his shirt off before he reaches us. "Pants too?" he asks Jonathan, fingers perched in the elastic of his joggers.

Jonathan levels me with a pointed glare.

"Pants stay on," I hurry to say. "Thanks, though."

While Jonathan arranges Dennis and Tank on the stool in front of the view, Rachel and I hang to the side. The sun is setting, gilding everything and everyone, and I have to give credit to Rachel for her pick. Dennis's physique is impressive, if too bulky for me, and I can already tell this will make a great opening image in the calendar. Hello, Mr. January.

I tell Rachel as much while Jonathan starts shooting.

"Dennis might have a friend he can ask for us, too," she says. "If we need more people."

Jonathan has Dennis hoist Tank higher in the crook of his arm and look off toward Puget Sound. As he snaps pictures, something shifts in his posture. Gone are the restrained movements and the stony brow, instead replaced by swiftness and presence.

"Hello? Did you hear me?" Rachel nudges my arm.

"What?" I force my attention away from this new version of Jonathan. "Oh yeah. That's good. We'll need anyone we can get.

Pawsome Partners isn't off to a great start judging by the guy I met up with yesterday."

"I thought he canceled?"

Jonathan straightens. "You went on a date?"

"He did cancel, but then he changed his mind. It should have been the first red flag."

Jonathan edges a step closer to us. "Why? What happened? I hope you met him somewhere public at least."

"Someone ca-ares," Rachel singsongs under her breath so only I can hear.

"Does not," I hiss through my teeth. To Jonathan I say, "Yeah, at a café. He opened with 'I typically go for brunettes, but you're not bad for a blonde,' then went on to forget his clearly make-believe dog's name in the first ten minutes. I excused myself after that."

"Yeesh." Jonathan grimaces.

Rachel concurs. "I'm telling you. It's rough out there."

"Fingers crossed for the guys I'm meeting this week. Surely one notch down on the creep scale can't be too much to ask." Though maybe that's karma working her magic since I'm not being completely up front myself. The thought has started to gnaw at me.

"What do you think of something like this?" Dennis asks Jonathan. He's put Tank on his shoulder to balance like a tiny cheerleading flyer.

With some reluctance, Jonathan leaves our date conversation and returns to his models. "Oh yay, tricks," he says, his tone clashing with his words. Nevertheless, he picks his camera back up.

"Hey," Rachel whispers to me after a minute, "I think he's kind of into you."

I paste on a smile and start walking toward the railing that prevents tourists from taking a tumble down the slope beneath the overlook. "I hope you're talking about Tank," I whisper back.

"Very funny. Didn't you notice how he got all protective when you mentioned the bad date?"

I did notice, but... "You're imagining things." I lean against the railing and follow the dark outline of the islands against the water in the distance. "And even if you weren't, I'm not interested. He's not my type."

Rachel rests her back against the metal. "Yes, hot, brooding photographer who can't take his eyes off you. Bah-humbug."

I glance over my shoulder. There is something about a man in his element. Jonathan has Dennis seated on the railing with Tank in his lap. It does not look safe by a long shot, but Dennis is all smiles, so I stay out of it. He's signed our legal forms anyway, releasing us from any obligations regarding potential risks as well as compensation for use of the images. They're far enough away that I can't hear the instructions Jonathan gives Dennis, but at one point, there are gestures and conversation before Dennis lifts one arm and flexes his huge bicep. I smile to myself—could it be Jonathan is getting into it more than he thought he would?

"I rest my case," Rachel says to my right.

"I'm enjoying watching him work, that's all."

"But he's 'not your type.'" She air quotes my words.

"It's the whole right brain, creative-type thing he's got going. I like planning, logic, efficiency."

"Sooo fun."

I push at her shoulder. "Stop. I'm serious."

"I know. Which is why you should be with someone like that. Plus, honestly, by your own admission, you don't actually know what he's like at all. You're making assumptions based on his job."

I want to object, but being who I am, I know better than to push when opposing counsel has a stronger argument. "Maybe," I concede.

"Thank you. And for the record, that right brain, left brain stuff has been debunked. People are more complex than that. Including you."

As I let that settle, Dennis jumps off the railing and sets Tank on the ground.

"All done?" Rachel calls.

"Done," Jonathan confirms with a wave. He says something to Dennis, and the two of them laugh.

I really like his laugh.

"Everything go okay?" I ask when we reach them.

"Yeah, we're good." Jonathan still wears a smile as he tucks the camera away into its bag.

"I'll send you a link, man," Dennis tells him. "I'm not kidding—it's the best thing I've ever done."

"Cool." Jonathan returns Dennis's fist bump. "See ya."

"Done what?" I ask. I've never seen him like this before.

"He was telling me about the shelter in Arizona where he found Tank."

"Ah," I say as if that explains everything. I look to Rachel for help, but she's walking Dennis and Tank to their car.

The tripod disassembled and packed away, Jonathan turns back to me. "I was thinking I'd do a light edit on the top contenders and send those to you. It'll be faster than going through all of them together. Then you can pick your favorite. Thoughts?"

Thoughts? Planning, logic, and efficiency are a few that come to mind. *Damn.* "That's a good idea."

He flashes me another smile and hoists the bags onto his shoulders. "Cool. I'll see you tomorrow, then."

"Tomorrow," I say to his receding back, the word fluttering to the ground as Rachel returns to my side.

"You look like you're doing a crossword puzzle in your head," she says.

I start walking, fighting the urge to turn and watch the dip in the road where his car disappeared. "Um, yeah. Something like that."

A gust of wind zips past us, making me shiver, and that finally snaps me out of whatever strange place I just visited. I pull out my phone to check my email again.

"Still want to go for a run?" Rachel asks.

I stop. Finally, the printer has sent the contract. "Hold on a sec," I tell her while I open the attachment and skim it. Everything looks good. Except... My eyes snag on the production time clause. *Fifteen days.* "No, it's supposed to say 'five.'"

"What is?"

I show her the screen. "There's a typo in the contract. Damn it, now I'll have to wait for them to fix it."

"So you'll call them in the morning." Rachel shrugs. "It's a two-second fix. Now, come on. Let's race." She starts jogging in place.

She's right. And a run is exactly what I need. It always helps me focus.

"Not sure about racing, but you're on for a jog," I say. A run, a shower, dinner, and a good night's sleep. Then I'll be back to work and have better things to think about than Jonathan Summers and how there might be so much more to him than I'd originally thought.

Days until printer deadline: ~~14~~ *18*

"What do you mean the contract is correct?" I ask the printing company rep at 8:01 Monday morning. "I was quoted five days for production last week."

"I don't know what to tell you," the rep says. "It's always fifteen. You must have misheard."

"I must have…" I rest my forehead against my fingertips and count to five slowly—incidentally the number the contract should say. "Is there anything at all we can do?" I ask. "I don't have fifteen days."

"Well, we could do a rush order."

"Okay."

"For a cost, of course."

I suppress a groan. "Right. Yeah, I don't have much wiggle room there."

The rep is silent.

I'm silent.

The wall clock above my desk says 8:05, just to rub in the number.

"Morning," Rachel says behind me.

I turn toward her and shake my head.

"What?" she whispers.

"The printer," I mouth. "Production time." I show her a thumbs-down.

"Ma'am?" the rep says. "Are you still there?"

"Yeah." I spin back around. "There's really nothing you can do? Six days? Seven days?"

"Unfortunately not. A submission to us on the tenth means delivery on the twenty-eighth."

I sigh. "I guess you'll have to take me off your schedule, then. Thanks anyway." I hang up. *Damn.*

Rachel is at my side instantly. "What happened?"

I relay the information. "I know what I heard. They said five days."

"I believe you. So now what?"

I spread my hands on my desk and roll my shoulders back. While I had hoped for a better outcome this morning, I've already mentally prepared a swerve to avoid the roadblock. "The local printers are booked, so I'll have to look farther away. Maybe even down in Oregon."

She crosses her fingers, and I do the same.

An hour and a half later, I have a new printer lined up. Portland for the win. They can't fit me in until the fourteenth, which is not ideal, but they do offer an actual five-day production timeline, and they have an integrated sales platform for online orders, plus the production cost is slightly less. All in all, it could be worse, and I have no choice but to sign on the dotted line. Which I do. The contract is in my inbox less than thirty minutes after ending the call, and I'm free to go back to regularly scheduled business.

I've never been the kind of person who enjoys swimming in the dating pool, so the week ahead of me is daunting to say the least even without printer mishaps. I have five meetups scheduled with guys from Pawsome Partners that feel more like grueling chores than fun social happenings, and the first one hangs over my head all day.

Come late afternoon, I've dragged my feet to the point that I'm about to be late to it unless the elevator shows up soon.

Rachel sticks her head through the door into the vestibule where I'm repeatedly stabbing the call button. "Text me after, okay? Be safe and good luck."

I wave at her as the doors finally open and I'm whisked downstairs.

I'm meeting Garrett at a coffee shop two blocks away. All I know about him is that he's a house painter from Canada and that he has a beautiful Newfoundland appropriately named Bear. He knows I'm Holly, that I work at GCL, and based on my profile picture, he probably thinks Morris is my dog. My plan is to address this minor deception as soon as I've established rapport.

Garrett stands and smiles at me as soon as I enter the coffee shop, and wow, his profile picture did not do him justice. He's a redhead with an even redder beard emphasizing his angular jaw, and he has the bluest eyes I've ever seen on a human.

"You must be Holly," he says, offering me his hand. I appreciate the formality of a handshake considering it's a date I have no intention to make a date.

He already has a coffee in front of him, so I go get mine—a double shot latte—from the girl behind the counter before I join him at the small rectangular table by the window.

FINDING MR. JULY

"So," he says, "how did you hear about Pawsome Partners?"

I immediately can't do this. Garrett seems like a nice guy. He's here on time, he has a non-creepy greeting, and so far, he's refrained from any and all insulting comments about my appearance. His vibe is genuine, which makes me a phony.

"Funny story, actually," I say. Then I launch into an explanation about the fundraiser.

When I'm done, his alpine-lake eyes have widened, and he's stroking his beard in that way I can only assume they teach men to stroke beards in beard school. "So, if I understand things right, you are not looking to meet someone?" he asks. *Stroke, stroke, stroke.*

"Right."

"You're in a relationship already, then?" *Stroke, twist, stroke.*

"Um, no."

He lets his hand drop to the table. "Aha. So, technically, we could still have coffee and see if we hit it off. I mean, we're already here." A wide grin bursts forth from the red jungle.

It's contagious and helps the knot at the pit of my stomach ease. "I don't understand. You're not upset? I basically tricked you."

"Nah." He waves off my concern. "I've been on some really... interesting... dates lately. The last woman asked if she could call me 'Daddy' before we got our first drink. This is different, I'll give you that, but you strike me as normal enough."

I chuckle. "Thanks, I guess. Right back at you."

He toasts me with his coffee cup, and we drink.

I'm not about to string him along past basic compliments, though, and he seems to read that into my silence.

"But I take it you're serious about this not being a date?" he asks.

I nod. "I am. Sorry. We need models for the calendar. I totally understand if you're not interested, and you can take your time to think about it, but we'd love to have you and Bear featured. He's a gorgeous guy."

"That he is."

"And it's for a good cause. All proceeds go to the preservation of temperate rainforests."

"True."

I dig through my bag and find a business card that I hand to him. "My number. Just let me know."

"Holly King?" he asks. "Not 'Saint Bernard,' then?"

I press my lips together. "Right. That was my colleague's idea. Because of the dogs."

"Good thinking." He flips my card over twice. "I'll do it."

His words are unexpected. "You will?"

"Hell yeah. I'm approaching forty. It's not every day a bona fide modeling opportunity like this falls in your lap. I get to keep the photos, right?"

"I'm sure we can work something out."

After Garrett checks his availability for the week and gives me his number, he takes off, hopefully with better dates on the horizon.

I text Rachel, **He said yes!** and then, because I suspect this might constitute a turning of the tides, I stop in at the other café around the corner from the office and ask the barista with the golden retriever if he'd be interested in modeling for us, too.

And that's how it's done. Two yeses in one fell swoop.

Tuesday is rougher. I get one polite but firm no at lunch and one "I might do it if you sweeten the deal, sugar" at happy hour. Yuck.

"You've got to kiss some frogs," Rachel says when I complain to her over the phone that evening. "Besides, you already have two shoots lined up this week."

"That's not enough. I need more guys."

"*She's a man-eater*," Rachel sings.

"Man-repeller is more like it. I really thought it would be easier to find models, but not only do they have to be attractive and have dogs, they also have to say yes. Did I tell you that veterinarian still hasn't given me his availability?"

"He will. So that's three, plus Dennis is asking his friend—so one more."

"Good." I sigh, leaning against my headboard. My fingers find the fringe on one of the throw pillows to comb through. The repetitive motion is soothing.

"And..." Rachel pauses on the line. "I suppose I could ask Nick."

My pinkie snags on a knot. "Who's Nick?"

"You know—beach volleyball guy. He's taking me out Friday."

I sit back up again. "You have a date? Also, yes. Please ask him."

"Can't let you have all the fun."

"Is that what you call it?"

"You know what I mean."

She tells me more about her date plans, and then we hang up. I have emails to read still, and then I need a good night's sleep. In addition to attending a 7:30 meeting Rachel is hosting with our Copenhagen office tomorrow, I also have a photo shoot with Jonathan and Oliver the barista at the Alki Point lighthouse at sunset. In other words, there's a long day ahead.

Days until printer deadline: 16

Silence permeates the air in Jonathan's car as we pull out of the parking garage late the next afternoon. I blame Rachel. When Jonathan stopped by our desks earlier to confirm times, my meddling mentor suggested he and I take only one car since parking is notoriously difficult near Alki. I'm onto her. Clearly this is some sort of misguided matchmaking attempt, but it's not like I could say no in front of him when he was on board. Plus, Rachel does have a point about the parking.

So here I am, no more than a foot away from the guy who's living rent-free in my head lately against my wishes. His car smells good—it's not a new car smell, but a warmer, more comforting scent I can't put my finger on. The tight space intensifies it. Which begs the question...

"How are you able to drive a car when you have claustrophobia?" I blurt.

He glances my way before stopping at a light. "It's fine as long as I'm driving. And I'm okay in the passenger seat with the window down. Back seats, not so much, especially if it's a two-door car. Something about cramped leg room and nowhere to go."

Like on a plane. I'm about to ask if that's what caused the issues with his old job, but he's not done talking.

"And sometimes it's unpredictable. I once successfully rode an open-air Ferris wheel, for example, while I've been close to a panic attack on a crowded escalator."

"Sounds difficult."

He shifts his grip on the steering wheel. "It can be."

Outside the window, the tall buildings rush by as Jonathan navigates the obstacle course that is downtown Seattle. The sky is still a mottled blue with some heavier clouds moving in for predicted overnight rain. By the art museum, the leaves on the trees are starting to turn.

I hold my breath when we pass my old law offices. The mere sight of the building makes my muscles tense. The cronyism, the greed, the thankless hours I put in only to be blamed for Chris's mistake—everything comes rushing back. Jonathan doesn't notice, but when he speaks again, his voice reminds me that as long as I win this thing, I'll soon be far away from that chapter of my life, and that helps me relax again.

"You asked about the plane incident, and yeah, in a way, my claustrophobia made me lose my job," Jonathan continues as if he read my mind earlier.

"You don't have to share if you don't want to. Like you said, I ask a lot of questions."

His lips quirk up. "I don't really mind." Another glance. Dancing gray eyes. "It's sort of refreshing."

"Okay." I turn more fully toward him. "So what happened?"

He starts a right turn but pauses to let a mom with a stroller cross. "I had to fly a lot in my old job. All over the world. Not ideal if you're me, but I'd worked so hard to get there, to be afforded those opportunities, that there was no way I was going to turn them down. In the beginning, I made sure to get on red-eye flights so I could sleep through it, but the busier I got, the less I was in control of my schedule. So I'd drink instead. A breakfast whiskey in the airport lounge, a couple of beers, and more on the plane. It was the only thing that worked."

"You were an alcoholic?" I give myself a mental slap for challenging him to a shot-drinking contest of all things.

"No." The protest is definite. "No, that's not it. I didn't drink at all the rest of the time—only when I had to travel. It was more like self-medicating."

Oh. "You couldn't get an actual prescription for something?"

"Would have, could have, should have. I was a proud idiot."

"So you got drunk on a plane. Don't people do that all the time?"

He scrunches up his face and taps the steering wheel. "I got drunk on a plane and tried to fly it."

Despite the seriousness of what he's telling me, a snort escapes me. "Oh my God."

"I know. Like I said, I do better in the driver's seat."

We've left downtown and are passing the sports arenas on one side and the industrial cranes that resemble giant *Star Wars* walkers on the other. In between stacks of shipping containers, glimpses of the water dazzle through my window.

"Anyway, they restrained me until they could do an emergency landing. Then I was arrested, fined, and put on a no-fly list, where I remain to this day. I lost my job and all other gigs I had lined up—no one wants to gamble on a loose cannon like that—and a few months later, my wife had had enough of my miserable ass and left. The end."

"Holy wow." I shake my head. "I'm really sorry."

"Aren't you glad you asked?"

I study his profile before responding. His eyes are firmly on the road, dark eyelashes sweeping down with each blink, but the tension in his jaw betrays his casual question. "I am," I say, putting as much sincerity into my voice as I can. I didn't expect him to be this honest, and the peek into his mind makes his blurry contours sharpen. "Thanks for telling me."

I consider his story as we navigate the residential streets closer to Alki in search of a parking space. I know something about low points, too, and about what it's like being forced out of a profession you excel at. And here I used to think we were so different.

"Good thing you had Manny," I say. The same way I had Rachel.

Jonathan nods. "Thankful every day for him giving a screwup a chance."

I wait until he's parked and we're out of the car to continue. "Even though you hate the job?" I squint at him.

He frowns. "What do you mean?"

"Come on. It's obvious to every single person at GCL that you don't want to be there."

Instead of answering, he opens the trunk. When I join him, he's still surveying its contents. "I don't hate it," he says before facing me. "It's complicated. Web design is..."

"Not your passion?" I supply.

"More than that." He reaches for his tripod and hands it to me. "It's a daily reminder that I failed. I had everything. Now I have a paycheck." His eyes flash with suppressed emotion.

I reach for his arm and grasp it gently above his elbow. His muscles tense beneath my touch—a familiar sensation that reverberates through me. Still, I don't release him right away. Not until he says my name.

"Holly." It sounds like it should be followed by something more, but instead it trails into nothing.

I step back. "Sorry. About all of it." I gesture to the trunk. "Can I carry something else?"

For a while, the unloading of equipment provides a welcome respite. We're a few blocks from our destination, and with each house we pass, each turn we get closer to the water, the air gets easier to breathe, the tension subsiding. But seeing him carrying his camera equipment, I can't help but wonder if my project is bringing his regrets to the surface, reopening the wounds.

I'm looking for the right words to apologize for that, too, when we emerge from between buildings and an unencumbered view of the water is before us.

"The clouds will work to our advantage," Jonathan says, face tipped upward. "They'll make for a dramatic sunset. Where did you say we're meeting them?"

He's switched to photographer mode. A seamless transition that I'm not sure he's aware of. But I'm not about to get in the way of it, so I put a pin in our earlier conversation and point him instead toward the beach near the lighthouse. We're not allowed on the actual lighthouse property since that belongs to the US Coast Guard.

"That's them," I tell him as we make our way along the stony shoreline toward the spot where Oliver and his dog are playing catch. "Hi there!" I call out to Oliver.

"Lucy, go fetch." He throws the ball our way, and his golden comes running, her coat shiny in the low sunlight.

Jonathan drops to his knees and puts the camera to his face on instinct. *Click, click, click* goes the shutter. As Lucy returns to Oliver, Jonathan checks the screen. "Yup, should be good," he says to himself. He holds the camera out for me to see. It's an action shot where Lucy is just about to catch the ball. Pure energy in a snapshot.

"Nice." I smile at him.

He looks at it again. "Wouldn't win any awards, but…" He shrugs.

"So modest." I bump his arm with mine. Our eyes meet, and for a moment, I'm sucked in, almost tripping on a piece of driftwood in our path.

"Whoa there." He catches me by the shoulder and prevents a tumble.

"Hello," Oliver calls out. He approaches and introduces himself to Jonathan. "And this is Lucy." The dog is sitting pretty at his side, panting.

Jonathan drops his hand from my shoulder. It's instantly colder. "She's gorgeous," he says.

"So," Oliver says, extending his hands to encompass the rocky beach. "Where do you want us? I've never been in front of a camera like this."

A gust of wind sweeps past us, making me shiver. It ruffles Jonathan's dark strands. His hair has gotten longer since the night of poor decisions. *There'd be more to grip now.*

I turn away from them, right as Jonathan asks Oliver, "How would you feel about getting in the water?"

I can't believe Oliver agrees, but he signs our paperwork without questions asked, and maybe it's not so bad since Jonathan is a professional and takes care to be quick with the shoot. Lucy is also a professional, posing exactly as the men tell her to, nose to the horizon, the wind rippling through her coat. In the background, the sky is shifting pink and purple with darker clouds lined in bright orange. I don't have to look at the photos to know they'll come out well.

While Jonathan packs up, Oliver dries off with a small hand towel that was wrapped around one of the lenses before. I wait until he's pulled on his jeans and shirt before I approach.

"Thanks for being a good sport. I'm sure that wasn't pleasant."

He grins. "Refreshing." The blue tint around his lips tells a different story, but who knows? There are people who enjoy that sort of thing. "Do you think you got what you need?"

I assure him that we did.

The sun is slowly disappearing, trailing remnants of color on the far sky that cast the low clouds in ominous relief. The rain will be here within the hour, so we'd do best to start moving.

"See the sky?" I ask Jonathan.

"Almost done." He shoves a reflector into its bag.

Oliver pulls on his sneakers and gives a sharp whistle to get Lucy to come. "Hey, I was wondering," he says to me after leashing her. "I've seen you around at the café, and I've been meaning to ask. Would you be interested in grabbing drinks at some point? Maybe this weekend?"

I glance at Jonathan, who's finished packing up and is standing stock-still with his back to us. "You're asking me on a date?"

Oliver smiles. "I am." He cuts his gaze between me and Jonathan. "Unless you two are... Ah shit, did I step in it?"

"No, no, not at all," I hurry to say. "It's just that I'm completely immersed in this project right now. Between work and the photo shoots, there's no time." That's a valid excuse, right?

But Oliver isn't so easily deterred. "Maybe when you're done, then? With the calendar, I mean." He wears the exact same expression as Morris does when he's hoping for a treat.

"Maybe," I say, unable to cut him down outright.

"Cool." He grins. "See you around. Come on, Lucy."

"See ya."

"Later, man." Jonathan lifts his hand in goodbye, making it clear he's heard the whole conversation. "Nice guy," he tells me when Oliver is out of earshot.

I yank one of the bags onto my shoulder and set off in the direction we came from. "Yeah, you think I should have said yes?"

"I'm surprised you didn't say no. I thought a guy was 'the last thing you need.'"

"I did turn him down."

"You said maybe."

I stop to face him. "The guy sat in like fifty-five-degree water off and on for twenty minutes for us. I didn't want to be rude." I walk a few more steps but then stop again. "But you know what is rude? Eavesdropping."

He lets me take the lead over boulders and slippery pebbles, trailing several yards behind me with his heavier load.

"You're not going to go on a date with him, then?" he asks after a while.

I sigh, trudging on. "I'm hopefully moving soon, remember? What would be the point?"

He's quiet for a beat. "Right."

I slow and let him catch up on the concrete ramp leading to the street, slightly out of breath from the rock-strewn trek. "Besides, in case you missed it, I'm currently in the midst of an up-close-and-personal field trip into the world of online dating, and I can't say it's leaving me wanting more."

We walk shoulder to shoulder past a few old single-family homes and a condominium, and we've just passed a cute stick library for dogs when the first raindrop hits me square on the nose.

"You don't miss having someone, then?" he asks suddenly.

It's such a direct question that every ready-to-go, hating-on-dating response flies out the window. Because of course I do. I'm human. Which is probably why our little misstep has played on repeat in my mind since it happened. But I can't tell him that.

"Do you?"

"I asked first."

I huff at his insistence. "Fine. To be honest, it's been so long that I'm not sure I remember what I'm supposed to be missing. That said, I believe there can be purpose to aloneness, too. Like, right now, I need to get the other parts of my life in order. Not being attached frees up my time."

We reach the car, and he pulls the key out but remains standing with his hand on the hatch for a moment. "Huh," he says. "Interesting. As if choosing it makes it noble instead of sad. I might have to steal that when my dad tries to set me up with his friends' daughters."

Before I can decide whether to object or probe further, the quiet of the evening erupts in light and noise as his car alarm goes off again.

Days until printer deadline: 15

Another day, another hour wasted on a date that led nowhere. I'm beginning to think joining Pawsome Partners was a bad move, if for no other reason than it's probably ruining my dating karma forever. My happy hour date today was a nice enough guy but clearly disapproving of my ulterior motive. And he wasn't wrong. Most guys I've communicated with are only after casual hookups, but the few looking for something real—those are the ones compelling me to look elsewhere for models. I have one more date tomorrow, and after that, I'm shutting it down.

I drown my guilt in a glass of wine and one of Ava's homemade chocolate cupcakes when I get home. Jude is working late, and Ava is at tennis, so it's just me and Morris, who's snoozing on his back on the couch, not a care in the world. My plan is to go through the Pawsome Partners profiles that have matched with Jude, but as soon as I spot a new email from Jonathan waiting for me, that plan goes out the window. Since I have yet to broach the topic of dating with Jude again anyway, I suppose I can save that for later.

Like after the first shoot, Jonathan has sent me a handful of favorites from yesterday. I download the zip file and open it up.

"Holy wow," I mumble, flipping through the images. Morris rolls onto his side next to me and blinks a sleepy eye my way.

I pull out my phone and send a message to Jonathan. **The pics are incredible. Could def win awards.**

Somehow, he's caught the way the wind makes Lucy's coat look as liquid as the water, and Oliver's skin is a radiant bronze in the low light reflected off the surface. He's a merman and Lucy his trusted aquatic guide. A mer-dog.

Thanks, I'm happy with them, he responds.

I can't help myself. **Bet you never thought you'd say that when we started the project.**

You know me too well.

I snort. **Pretty sure I don't know you at all.**

His response takes longer this time. Long enough for me to wonder if he took offense. But when my phone finally dings, the words on the screen warm my core. **Are you saying you want to?**

Maybe it's the wine and the cozy quiet of the house, or maybe my dating debacles have lowered my inhibitions, but before I can analyze whether engaging with him like this is a good idea, I've already sent my response: **Yes.**

We'll be spending enough time together, I think. We could be friends. Friends share.

What do you want to know? he asks.

Where do I start? I have spent way too much time mulling over his comment about his dad setting him up on dates, but I need to be smart about how to ask about that. Hmm... Eventually I settle for **Are you close with your parents?**

Dad, yes. Mom, no.

Elaborate pls.

Dad lives nearby. He has glaucoma and can't drive anymore so I'm his chauffeur. I see him all the time. Mom left when I was ten. New family.

Reading his matter-of-fact words triggers a pang inside me on behalf of the boy he once was, but before I can respond, another message pops up. Can I ask about you too? Or is that against the rules?

I shrug off the jolt of pity and allow a smile in its place. If there are rules, we're already in the process of bending them. Go ahead.

Three moving dots, and then, You've had your heart broken. I inhale sharply. That's not a question.

What happened?

I rest my phone against my thigh while I think. If I'm going to be able to ask about his ex-wife at some point, I can't dodge this. I burrow deeper into the pillows. He was someone I worked with. In the end work was more important to him than loyalty to me.

How so?

I sigh. He's not going to let this go without details. I had a chance to make partner. He took credit for my work. Now he's partner instead. Plus some other stuff.

Asshole. Is that why you left?

I smile. "Asshole" is putting it mildly, but I appreciate the sentiment nonetheless. I should have, but no. Sometimes I wish I could go back in time and slap some sense into old Holly. Where was my pride? I stayed on for another year and a half after that. Ridiculous.

Then why did you?

I decide to throw his own words back at him. Do you always ask so many questions?
He responds with a grinning emoji.
My turn, I type. How long have you been divorced?

It'll be five years in December.

Do you still talk to your ex-wife?

No. She lives in Italy now. Married up.

Hey—no self-deprecation allowed. You know you're a catch.

Oooh, a compliment. Thank you kindly, but I'm not so sure about that. It's been a while since I was at the top of my game.

Sounds familiar. That makes me curious. When were you?
Peru, ten years ago, comes his quick response.

That's very specific.

Well...

A photo pops up in the thread of a younger Jonathan posing with two other men against a colorful, mountainous backdrop. His white shirt is unbuttoned, and the sleeves rolled up, revealing a tan chest and strong forearms, and there's a sheen of light perspiration across his brow that brings to mind all kinds of vigorous activity. He grins at the camera with the kind of careless joy you get from big adventures with friends.

It was my bachelor trip. Good times. Lots of possibilities ahead, he texts.

I agree—he does look like he's on top of the world in the picture, literally and figuratively, and I tell him as much, adding the caveat, **You do know the world is still full of possibilities, right?** To avoid veering too serious, I throw in, **Good-looking guy with your talents,** more as an objective truth than a personal opinion. Though if you ask me, he wasn't any less attractive yesterday at Alki than in this photo. Quite the opposite. I prefer the complexity the past decade has added to his features.

The typing dots appear and then disappear a few times. Then **Are you flirting with me?**

What? I toss my phone onto the couch as if it's stung me. Squeeze my eyes shut for a count of ten. Then, carefully, I pick it back up and stare at his question. Am I? Eventually, I decide I can play this one of two ways. Either I shut it down with a firm "no" right this minute or...

Or I allow this bubbling feeling in my chest some leeway. It's been a long time. And I did just come out in favor of possibilities.

I inhale deeply and type, Do you want me to be flirting with you?

His Maybe makes my insides simmer.

Let me guess, he texts. You had some tequila and got nostalgic.

Wow. He's really going there. I bite my lip to stifle a smile. Nostalgic for...?

You know.

I do. But I thought your memory was hazy at best.

I remember enough.

Okay, then. I press my right hand to my belly to settle the fizz. What is happening?

He's typing again. Probably shouldn't do that again though. So unprofessional of us.

I read the lines several times. Stupid texting. How am I supposed to know if he means it or if he's being facetious?

Right, I type as the front door handle rattles and Morris shoots off the couch with a happy bark. Someone's home.

"Hello!" Ava calls from the foyer.

I'm going to take that as being off the hook. Sorry niece is home. Gotta go. I hit SEND and head toward the kitchen. He probably did mean it. And it was unprofessional—not to mention lacking judgment in general. Was it fun? I mean, yes. Of course. Could I theoretically see myself kissing him again? Sure. But should I?

Now, that's the million-dollar question.

Days until printer deadline: 14

Jonathan is out of the office Friday without explanation. You'd think he might have mentioned a dentist appointment or feeling under the weather, but no. My phone burns a hole in my desk next to me as I create my first marketing blast for the calendar ("Sign up here to be notified when it drops!") using a cute snap from the first shoot, but I'm committed to not texting him. After last night, who knows what unfiltered truths might escape my fingertips? Besides, he was the one who brought up professionalism this time. Finally, we're in agreement about something.

I'm dying for a glass of wine by the time I enter the bar downstairs after work. Another day, another date. This guy actually is a model, which is the only reason I've agreed to meet him. His personality has left a lot to be desired so far. Mikael is a Swedish giant at six foot seven, stereotypically blond and blue-eyed, and he's already drawn the attention of two other women at the bar when I enter. It doesn't escape me that they hand him a note while I order. In a smooth move, he tucks it into his pocket while simultaneously escorting me by the elbow to one of the round two-tops by the window.

The space is less than half full of people, and the early hour makes it feel like a completely different venue from when I was here last. Still, the ambiance is lazy and casual, the lights dim but helped by the afternoon sun outside, and when the pinot grigio hits my bloodstream, the stress and tension of the day melt away, leaving a pleasantly warm gooiness behind.

I blame that for allowing the conversation to go longer than I'd planned. Mikael can talk. Mostly about himself and how he's been to LA, Toronto, and London in the past two weeks ("You're lucky I could squeeze you in," *wink wink*), but also about food. This guy loves his food. I finish my wine, tuning in and out of what he's saying when he gets to how smoked salmon goes with capers, but only a specific kind of capers, preferably on freshly made bagels from a particular bakery in New York. They ship, in case I'm interested. Something about his accent puts me in an almost trance-like state.

This is why, when he suddenly suggests we go back to his place, it takes me a moment to catch up. I thought we were only talking—or he was—but he thinks we've hit it off and reached the time for the main event.

"I don't live far," he says, signaling for the check. "A few blocks. Do you want to walk or call a car?"

I blink at him. Those are my only two options, huh? "Um, I actually need to head home soon. Sorry."

His face turns into a question mark.

"I should have said something sooner, but I'm not looking for a hookup. The real reason I'm here is because I'm looking for models for a project. Models with dogs, to be specific. You do have a dog, right?"

"Cujo, yeah. But wait... Are you telling me that I've spent"—he checks his expensive-looking watch—"forty-five minutes on this conversation, and you were never going to come back to mine?"

"Like I said, I apologize. I should have been clear from the start."

"You think? I turned down several other females for you."

O-kay, so total douche canoe. I grind my teeth together and stand. "The night is still young. I'm sure they'll be ecstatic when you call. Thanks for your time." I turn but don't get far before he calls my name. Or he calls "Molly," but close enough.

"What's the modeling gig?" he asks.

And so, while the ick factor is high, I do arrive home with a commitment from Mikael to pose for the calendar. It's a dubious score, but a score all the same. Especially since it's his job, and he knows I can't pay him.

I haven't been home long before it is clear that padding around in my sweats without plans on this Friday night poses a risk of the phone-related kind. No word from Jonathan means my imagination is running amok, conjuring alternating scenarios of him injured and amnesia-riddled in some hospital with less dramatic ones where last night made him not want to talk to me ever again. Neither is reasonable, of course, but too much time on one's hands can be a real mindfuck.

To distract myself, I trail Jude around the house as he does his weekly cleaning. He puts a dust rag in my hand and points to places where I might wipe, but I don't think he's happy with my work because he goes over everything a second time.

"How pathetic are we that we're at home cleaning on a Friday night," I complain.

"Not pathetic. Hygienic." Jude pulls out the vacuum from the closet. "And if you're so bored, why don't you call Rachel? She's usually up for going out."

"She's on a date."

That makes him stop what he's doing. "Really. Who's the guy?"

"That beach volleyball player we met at Alki."

"The one who inspired the calendar."

I nod.

"Huh." He untangles the cord and plugs in the machine.

"Which means I can't call her. So I'm still bored."

"Maybe you should have gone home with what's his name after all."

"Mikael. Ugh, no. I'd rather be bored forever."

Jude laughs. "Tell you what. Morris is almost out of food, so I've got to swing by the pet store when I'm done here. Come with me, and we can grab dinner, too."

My spirits lift instantly. I can always count on Jude to come through for me. Hopefully I can repay the favor soon.

"You had me at 'dinner,' but as so happens, visiting pet stores is actually on my to-do list for this weekend, too."

Jude pauses what he's doing. "Why? Do you have a secret hamster squirreled away in your room? A cockatoo I don't know about?"

I play along. "What? I didn't tell you about Frank and Beans, my flatulent ferrets?"

Jude's eyes narrow. "That's awfully specific. Should I be concerned?"

"Only if you're allergic to ferrets."

He rolls his eyes. "Hols..."

"Fine. It's because of the photo shoots. Surely some attractive men work in pet stores?"

"At Marla's? Unlikely."

Marla was once a client of Dad's, so we're on a first-name

basis with the shop owner and have a standing 10 percent discount at her store.

"Yeah, maybe not. But I'll come either way." If nothing else, Jude's company should prevent me from dwelling on the Jonathan situation, which in itself is a win.

"If you wipe down the countertops, we'll get out of here faster," Jude says.

I scowl at him. "This feels very twenty-five years ago except, back then, you paid me to do your chores for you."

"No regrets. First drink is on me." The vacuum roars to life.

"Deal," I say, but he can no longer hear me, which, judging by his gleeful smile, he's only too happy about. I toss the dust rag at him before I go to make the already-tidy kitchen cleaner.

We grab seats at the bar at Facinelli's and get shoestring fries to share while waiting for our pasta. It's food before errands, and I'm enjoying my (blessedly Swede-free) glass of wine when Jude runs a hand through his too-long strands in a move I've seen many a time. He's either about to ask for a favor or lay a hard truth on me.

"Uh-oh," I say. "What's going on?"

He takes a sip of his Manhattan, puts the glass down, and rests his palms together as if taking a moment. "I had a second interview yesterday. That's why I was late home."

Truth it is. "And?"

"And it went great. I think they'll make an offer."

I lean against the low backrest and let this sink in. "Well, shit."

He frowns. "You think it's a bad idea."

"I didn't say that. It's just happening pretty quickly. When will you know for sure?"

"Sometime next week. I'm still in talks with two other firms, too. Who knows what'll happen?" He takes a big swallow of his drink.

"Have you told Mom and Dad?"

"No. I'll wait until it's official."

"Mom will lose her mind."

He chuckles. "She will, won't she?"

"But in a good way." I toss several fries into my mouth and chew. "Ava, on the other hand..."

"I know." He falls serious, his gaze locking someplace far away.

I hesitate. "Look, I totally understand why you want to move, and I'm all for pursuing new opportunities—obviously—but does it have to be now? No one wants to move in the middle of high school."

"Hols, I..." He sighs. "It could be great for my career. It *would* be great for Mom and Dad. And lately I've just felt like I need something to happen, you know? Anything."

This is my chance. "What if I told you that you could shake things up here?"

"Meaning?"

I steel myself and lean forward. "Okay, don't be mad." I tell him about the dating profile I created for him and that there are two responses that seem promising. "Regardless of where your career takes you, this could be good practice. Sort of easing into it." I move my hand forward in a smooth move to illustrate. "What do you think?"

He drains his drink before responding, which doesn't bode well. "What do I think?" he asks finally. "I think you mean well, but you've lost your marbles. I'm talking about moving to another state. The last thing I want is to date someone here."

"It's one date. Not a commitment. Even if you do move—which is not yet set in stone, mind you—having a date or two under your belt can't hurt."

"I love you, but the answer is no. Absolutely not."

"But—"

"Nope."

"But I just—"

"Nuh-uh-uh."

My shoulders slump. I've known him long enough to know there's no point arguing when he gets like this. "Fine."

"Good."

Jeez. It's just a meal. Or a drink even. A drink with a woman who might make him smile. But okay. I'll let him think he's won. For now. I decide to extend an olive branch to mollify the situation. "So, tell me more about this job, then."

He relaxes again. "You really want to know?"

"Of course. I'm sorry."

While we finish our food, he describes the firm and the conversations he's had with the partners. It's more money, a better career track, and Austin has over three hundred sunny days per year. By the time our plates are empty, it's easy even for me to picture him relaxing in a sun-soaked backyard. As big of a change as this is, I have to admit it could be good for him. But that still doesn't mean it has to happen now.

As an added bonus on top of a nice dinner, my misgivings for the pet store visit also turn out to be unfounded. For a Friday night, it's hopping with customers, and when we reach the back shelves, we learn why. Most of the other customers are lined up against the window facing the administrative offices because the owner's beagle has had puppies that will soon be put up for adoption.

"Please remind me that Morris wouldn't do well with a sibling," Jude says, his eyes heart-shaped at the seven sets of tiny floppy ears before us.

I do, and I'm about to add that a puppy would make an interstate move all the more stressful, but then a good-looking guy enters the puppy room with food, and new hope infuses my mission for the visit.

"Hold that thought," I say, and backtrack to the service desk where I spotted Marla earlier.

Ten minutes later, I've been introduced to Marla's nephew, Theo, who's working for her until the end of the year, and Jude's gotten to hold a puppy. I drew the longest straw, though, because while Jude leaves the store without a puppy, I leave it with a tentative photo shoot scheduled for Sunday. Theo and the puppies will make a great November spread.

Days until printer deadline: 13

I rarely sleep past 8:30 on weekends anymore, but I'm up extra early today. It's the day of the Garrett and Bear photo shoot—so far my only positive dating site experience—and since Jonathan suggested a waterfall backdrop when I told him Garrett said yes, we're meeting at the Coal Creek Falls trail at 10:00, ready to hike. For the occasion, I've dug up my barely used hiking boots, a beanie, and some gloves. It's the first day of October, and the temperature dropped below forty-five last night for the first time this season.

Jonathan is running late, but I don't mind. The crisp air is heady with earth and cedar at the trailhead, and Garrett and Bear show up only five minutes after I do.

"He's restless," Garrett says about his giant dog as he straps on his backpack. "This is his favorite thing in the whole world, and I swear he knows we're about to head out as soon as he wakes up. You don't mind if we get a head start, do you? Meet you at the falls?"

I tell him that's fine by me if I can just get his signature on our paperwork first—Jonathan should be here soon anyway if his text is anything to go by. ETA 10:19, he messaged five minutes ago. It's now 10:15.

We're not the only ones vying for the outdoors this Saturday. A steady trickle of cars arrives at the gravel lot, unloading other hikers. I get a few curious looks where I stand by my lonesome near the information boards, but I ignore them and focus instead on stretching. I skipped the morning yoga to get out the door, but what do you know? Jonathan's tardiness has given me a chance to rectify that.

He pulls in a few minutes later in a pair of aviators that at a first glance makes him look a lot more *Top Gun* than *Into the Wild*. As soon as he's out of the car, though, it's clear he's done this before. He's in well-worn boots, gray pants, a red-and-black checkered flannel, and some sort of weather-safe jacket. It's the first time I've seen him in something other than black, and I say as much in greeting.

"What do you mean?" he asks, looking down.

"This," I say, taking the collar of his flannel between my thumb and index finger. "Color. Didn't know you had it in you." Then, because getting handsy with his shirt has put me in rather close proximity to him, I let him go and step back.

"It's my dad's," he says after a beat, his gaze inscrutable.

I can't tell if he's joking or not, so I roll with it. "That explains it. It suits you, though. Not that the black doesn't, but it's good to see you...um...branching out." I gesture to the trees around us, and my mission is accomplished. He smiles.

"I like your smile," I blurt. *Good Lord, Holly.* "Um, I mean, need any help carrying stuff?"

The glimpse of his teeth disappears, but his lips still tug up at the corners. "No, I'm good," he says, reaching for the hatch. "And thanks. I like your smile, too."

A sudden need to retie my boots makes me dip below the bumper out of sight. When I stand again, he's aiming the key fob at the car. "Brace yourself—they should have fixed the alarm issue yesterday, but you never know."

Yesterday… "Is that where you were? When you weren't at work, I mean."

He shoulders his equipment pack, which today is in one large bundle instead of several small bags. "Yeah, I took a personal day to take care of some errands. Car maintenance was one. Dad had a couple of appointments, too, so it worked out."

"Ah."

"Don't tell me you missed me." He gives me a look of feigned horror.

We start up the trail, now a solid fifteen minutes behind Garrett and Bear.

I roll my eyes, hoping it will hide how close to the truth he is. "You wish."

He shrugs and then grins again. "Maybe I do." He slows to let me get in front when the trail narrows.

Does he? We walk in silence for a few minutes, my thoughts refusing to come to a conclusion. When counting pine cones no longer serves as a distraction, I switch topics and tell him about my pet store outing. "Are you free tomorrow for another shoot? I know it's last minute, but the puppies are getting adopted this coming week, so it's our only chance."

He groans lightly. "But then I have to cancel my Sunday plans."

Darn, I knew it seemed to come together too smoothly. "Well, maybe I…"

Jonathan reaches out and touches my shoulder. "I'm joking, Holly. I can totally do it tomorrow."

Such a comedian today. I turn and keep walking backward. "You're weird in the woods," I say.

"Good weird?" He looks hopeful.

"I haven't decided yet."

"I guess I forgot how much I love hiking." There's definitely something about it—the surrounding growth still and green yet bursting with quiet energy. It suffuses the air and seeps into your pores, its ongoing creation so filled with possibility that it could ease the most wearying burden.

"But how come you were with your brother?" Jonathan asks as we pass a couple taking selfies in front of an ancient, moss-covered tree. "I thought you had a date. Another bad one?"

"Depends on your definition of a bad date." I pick up a long, straight branch from the ground that could serve as a suitable walking stick. "Did he assume I was going to have sex with him after forty-five minutes? Yes. Did I reject him and get an earful? Sure did. Still on board for the calendar, though, so..." I imitate the two pans of a scale with my hands, almost poking him with the stick in the process. "Oops, sorry." I toss it back into the woods.

"I see. Still sounds like a crappy date to me."

"Yup. Just thankful I'm not truly in the game. But I'm not going to use Pawsome Partners anymore. I'm canceling my account tomorrow. At some point in my life, I hope to have time for real dating again, and I'm afraid that it'll put me off men forever if I do any more of these."

Jonathan nods but doesn't respond, and soon we fall into the meditative rhythm of footfalls and breathing, making our way to our destination.

The main waterfall is too crowded, but Jonathan knows of

a hidden one off-trail, not far away, so that's where we head for the shoot.

Bear is the biggest ham I've ever seen. As soon as Jonathan puts the camera to his eye, the huge Newfoundland swings his head in the direction of the lens. Pose, click. Pose, click. A catwalk model has nothing on him. I've brought a Davy Crockett–like hat for Garrett, and with his shirt off and Bear at his side, he looks every bit the woodsy thirst trap I was hoping for. We get shots of them scouting the far side of the stream, perching on slick rocks, and peeking out from behind a tree trunk the width of a small car.

We're nearly finished when Jonathan puts his camera down and mutters, "Now who's this jamoke?"

Another hiker has walked into the shot with his pretty Dalmatian.

"You certainly don't see this every day," the guy says with an Irish accent, nodding to Garrett. He's about our age with a groomed hipster beard and a large frame.

"Hey," Garrett responds. And then, because Bear is padding toward the Dalmatian, he asks, "Okay if they say hi?"

"Of course." Irish guy steps closer. "Is this a fashion shoot or something?"

The two dogs circle and sniff each other, but when that's done, they go their separate ways. No soulmates in the woods today. Womp, womp.

"Sort of," I say. "It's for a fundraising calendar."

"Oh really?" Irish guy nods. "Well, good on you. I'm fresh off the Charity Challenge Hike myself. What's the cause?"

"Temperate rainforest conservation," I tell him. "We're with an environmental nonprofit." I look at Jonathan and raise an eyebrow in question. Is he thinking what I'm thinking?

He gives a small nod. "We're still scouting for models. I don't suppose you and your dog would be interested?"

Irish guy makes wide eyes at us. "Me? Oh, I'm hardly built for it."

"What's your name?" I ask.

"Pete. This is Nala."

"Pete, he's an award-winning photographer." I gesture at Jonathan. "And you two would be perfect. Nala's white-and-black coat against the green? Striking."

"It's a cool experience, dude," Garrett says, proving again to be the only good thing to come out of Pawsome Partners.

Pete seems to think it over. He puts his hand on Nala's flank. The Dalmatian looks up at him. "I can keep my shirt on?" he asks.

"Of course," I assure him. I'm sure Jonathan can work some magic with that beard and rolled up sleeves.

"Fine, then. Let's give it a lash."

Jonathan and I linger as Garrett, Pete, and their dogs continue on forty minutes later. Two-for-one is not bad for a Saturday, and the shots of the Dalmatian and her Irish handler are beautiful. Jonathan managed to time a ray of sun so that it cut through the trees just right and hit the two where they were resting against a tree trunk on the mossy forest floor. With Pete's bedroom eyes and come-hither smolders, I predict his spread will be one of our most popular.

"Ready to head back?" Jonathan asks after packing up.

"Ready." I slide off the log I've been sitting on, but no sooner is the word out of my mouth than my foot disappears through the moss where the ground meets the log. "Ah," I yelp, tumbling to my hands and knees.

"Are you okay?"

I take stock. The ground is soft enough. "My knees are wet, but that's about it." I wiggle my foot to get it out of the hole. *Huh.* I try to turn my ankle and pull. Nothing. "I think I'm stuck, though. The stupid shoe."

Jonathan's legs come into view. "If it went in, it should come out," he says.

"That's what she said," I quip under my breath.

"Very funny. But seriously. Pull."

I do, trying to leverage my body weight against the pit of doom devouring my limb. "I can't."

"Okay. Hold on." Jonathan sets his pack on the ground and crouches down behind me. "It's a root. I'm going to..." He grips my calf with one hand and reaches into the hole with the other, bending my foot and twisting the boot at the same time. "Now try."

I do, and with a squelch, I'm face down in the moss. "Oof."

"There we go. How does it feel?"

I sit up and move my foot gingerly. "Okay, I think."

He wipes his hands on his pants. "Let me see. If it's twisted, I'll have to wrap it before we head back."

He unlaces the boot and pulls it off my foot along with the sock. His fingers are warm and gentle as they prod and bend, sending goose bumps up my leg.

"Thanks," I say. "You saved me. Again."

"You got stuck. Again." He winks, putting my boot back on. "I think you're all right. Want to try to stand on it?"

I nod, and he hauls me to my feet. He overestimates the effort, though, because I go flying forward, only stopping myself from crashing into him with a hand against his chest. I've been here before, inches in front of him, my hands against his warm body. Here and closer...

The water from the falls burbles in the background, and little winged things swirl about our heads. But I only see his chest rising and falling, a movement that's matched by the rush of blood in my ears. His proximity is intoxicating out here in the wild.

"Does it hurt?" he asks, his voice a low rumble in his chest.

I shake my head and let go of him. "No, I'm fine." I force myself to look up. His gaze is searching, intense. *Eyes to drown in.* But that would be a mistake. I've mixed business with pleasure before and that did not work out. Not to mention my impending emigration when he can't fly. But I'm getting ahead of myself.

Mustering whatever self-control I have left, I back up a step.

Jonathan clears his throat as he reaches for his backpack.

We start walking without another word.

But the thing about the woods is that it's difficult to hold on to the awkward and the untimely. With our muted footfalls below and the swooshing of branches above, we soon fall back into easy conversation. We'll need to make the beagle photo shoot an indoor one, but Jonathan has an idea for a setup that might still give the impression of being outside.

We're closing in on the parking lot when he glances at me over his shoulder and then slows until we're side by side. He scratches his neck. Pauses. "So, I was thinking."

"Congrats."

His lips press together. "These bad dates you've had to go on...It's a shame...I mean, it would be a shame if..." He sighs, his hands fidgeting with the straps of his pack. "Look, I don't want that to put you off dating for good. So why don't you let me take you out? I promise not to be a creep like the others."

My stomach somersaults, and my lips part in surprise. That was the last thing I expected him to say. "Out?" I ask stupidly. "Like on a date?"

"On a date," he confirms. "A good one for a change. Um, hopefully. Are you doing anything tonight?"

I would play it cool, but the muscles in my cheeks have a different idea. I haven't been on a real date in forever, and the prospect of Jonathan being the one to break the hiatus is more than appealing. It doesn't have to mean anything. Maybe he feels bad about how his fellow men have treated me lately.

We've come to a full stop at the trailhead. "I have no plans. As per uzhe," I say. "And I'd love to go on a date."

Maybe the sun was already on him, but I swear his face gets brighter at my words. "Cool," he says, tempering a smile in vain. "I'm filling in at a happy hour gig from four to six at Red's Blues in Ballard. You want to meet there at six, and I'll take you to dinner?"

I nod. "I do."

For a long moment, neither of us looks away. It's not a loaded silence as much as it is one filled with something buoyant and optimistic.

When he finally breaks away to take his pack off, I'm already mentally in my closet, thinking about what to wear.

Days until printer deadline: Still 13

I cheat. I know Jonathan said 6:00, but he also said he'd be playing beforehand, and there's no way I'm missing a glimpse of that. Consequently, I'm circling the neighborhood in search of parking a little after 5:00, and shortly thereafter, I step into the muted light of Red's Blues—a dive bar that's been a staple in the area forever. I haven't been inside before, but I've passed the oversized red-and-blue neon sign a million times.

Lamenting notes wash over me when I open the door. The space is deep and rectangular with a small stage at the far end. One wall is brick, the others dark gray with brass sconces. The ductwork above is exposed. Most of the small round tables are occupied, but I find one in the back and pull off my black leather jacket. After much debating, I'd settled on a white, V-neck wrap blouse and distressed black jeans for tonight. The jacket gives the look an edge. Of course, I'm also wearing the silver lightning bolt earrings.

A waitress comes by, and I order a glass of house white, too preoccupied with the stage to browse a drink menu. Jonathan is at the piano, back in black. He's joined onstage by a drummer, a bass player, and a guy at the mic with a trumpet in hand and a guitar at his side. I don't recognize the tune, but the music envelopes me until it feels like part of my bones.

I look only at Jonathan. I'm too far away to see the expression on his face or the way his hands move across the keys, but I can tell from how he rocks into the instrument that whatever notes he's playing originate someplace deep within him. Melancholy low notes beneath hopeful high ones. More facets of him showing in the reflections of the spinning disco globe above the stage. On instinct, I pick up my phone, zoom in, and snap a picture.

It's over too soon. I get forty-five minutes that feel like ten before the musicians leave the stage. I should have gotten here sooner. *Next time.*

Jonathan spots me halfway through the room. I stand and wait for him, indulging the butterflies in my stomach that flutter in circles at his approach.

"Sneaky," he says with a smile.

I shrug. "I couldn't pass up the opportunity. You're very good."

He glances back at the piano. "Thanks. It was my first love before photography." He gestures toward the door. "Shall we?"

I have a final sip of my wine. "Yeah, let's."

My nerve endings jump at his light touch against my back when he guides me outside. Up until this point, I've allowed myself to be excited about this date with the caveat that it will be a platonic one. Just a fun night out with a colleague to offset the bad taste in my mouth left by the other dates this week. Now I'm wondering if my body has ulterior motives.

"You look amazing," he says when we reach the sidewalk.

The appreciation in his eyes as he takes in my getup makes heat pool low in my stomach. His gaze snags on my earrings, and I swear his pupils go darker. "Good choice," he murmurs. "Are you hungry?"

My inhale is shakier than I'd like for it to be. "I could eat."

He's scored a table for two at Stoneburner on Ballard Avenue—a place I've been to and enjoyed many times before. We get a booth near the bar with a good view of the restaurant, and before long we have drinks in front of us (tequila-free) and food on the way.

"Did you take piano lessons as a kid or are you self-taught?" I ask after a hearty sip on my elderflower cocktail.

"Lessons. Classical at first, but I got bored with that as I got older. It was too neat."

"So that was improvised?" I indicate the general direction of the blues club.

"Some of it, yeah. I have a pattern and a chord progression to guide me. Playing with a band is symbiotic, a give and take. Sometimes you follow and sometimes you lead. No two gigs are exactly the same. That's what I love about it."

I have another sip of my drink, letting it relax me.

"So, is this your MO for dates?" I ask, emboldened by the ambient sound of conversation around us that lets me pretend us being here is normal. "Some music, a compliment or two, a bite to eat? How does Jonathan Summers date?"

He chuckles. "I don't have an MO I'm afraid. Sorry to disappoint. And I've already told you I don't really date anymore. This is an exception."

"Because of your divorce?"

"Because I've been a miserable grouch since I blew up my career."

I nudge him with my foot under the table. "You admit it, then."

"Yes." He puts both palms on the table and leans forward. "I'm a grouch. Sue me."

And *whew* do I want to kiss him again when he looks at me like that. With a challenge, with a twinkle in his eye, with his hidden layers visible only to me.

I resist the urge to fan cool air onto my burning skin. "I think you're coming around," I say, trying to keep my tone light. "Slowly, but you're making progress."

He smirks. "Thanks." Considering me over the rim of his glass, he says, "But you—you didn't let it get to you. Your career transition, I mean. It's like nothing fazes you."

He fazes me. "Nothing could be further from the truth."

"No." He states the objection as if he knows something I don't and then adjusts his position to rest an elbow on the table. "You left a lucrative career, decided to take this internship to win a job in Glasgow, and once that's in the bag, I'm sure you'll"—he points forward with his whole hand—"move on toward the next goal. I've never met anyone like that. I'll be honest—it's put my own moping in perspective. I wish I had your drive. Kind of makes me want to do better."

"Really?"

"It's true."

I ignore the fact that he seems to think my career change was completely by choice because learning that I inspire him in any way makes it positively sweltering in here.

The waitress brings our food. We've decided to share a few things, and I'm about to stuff a slice of honeyed pepperoni pizza into my mouth when the door to the restaurant opens and who walks in but Chris, a gorgeous brunette on his arm. I haven't seen him in almost a year, but of course he's here tonight of all nights. This city is too damn small.

My eyes narrow, and had I been in less sophisticated company, a growl might have spilled out of me. That's what seeing Chris still does to me—I'm right back at the firm with security holding me back by the sleeves to keep me from throttling him.

"What's that look?" Jonathan asks, glancing over his shoulder. "You know those people?"

I realize the pizza is still halfway into my mouth, so I bite it off and chew while sinking deeper into my seat. The seconds it takes for the food to go down helps me regain composure. I could make up an excuse, but Jonathan is being so genuine tonight that I simply can't. "My ex," I say, moving the small floral table decoration as if that can hide me.

"The disloyal one?"

"Yup."

Chris and his date sit down next to each other at a table by the windows. They're huddled together. Handsy. He only has to shift his head right and he'll see me.

"Hey, look here instead," Jonathan says, pointing to his eyes. "Take it from me—grudges are bad."

"I know."

"So will you tell me why you left, then? You said it wasn't the partner stuff."

Chris is whispering something in the brunette's ear. She's giggling.

"Holly." Jonathan's fingers brush across mine on the table.

"Sorry. Um, yes, I... Oh shit, he's coming over."

If this wooden seat would only swallow me whole. I grasp the napkin in my lap and press my back to the backrest while plastering on a smile as Chris approaches. This is where I need to rise above.

"Holly? Hey, I thought it was you." His teeth are so white that it makes him look like a Ken doll. Did he get veneers?

"Chris." My cheeks protest the upward motion I'm forcing them to do. "Hi."

My ex puts his hands on his hips in his signature power pose that I, at one point, somehow, must have found attractive. "How have you been?" His gaze dips to my cleavage. "Broken any more priceless works of art lately? Hahaha. No, but seriously, you look great. But is it true you're an intern?" He says it like it tastes bad.

Jonathan's foot touches mine under the table. I breathe in. "This is my colleague, Jonathan Summers," I say. "Jonathan, this is Chris Dirk."

"Chris Dork?" Jonathan deadpans.

"Dirk. It's Dirk, man. Nice to meet you." He looks back at me. "Colleague, huh? Working dinner on a Saturday? All business and no pleasure. Sounds like my Holly. Hahaha."

"So funny." I'm about to go off about how I most certainly am not his and that I'd be more than happy to give his date a heads-up about his ability to bring pleasure into the equation, but beneath the table, Jonathan is tapping gently against the side of my foot, and that stops me. I don't want to cause a scene. "Everything is great," I say instead, smiling sweetly. "How about yourself? Found any new coworkers to blame your professional inadequacies on now that I've moved on? Or maybe that's a question for your date."

My words must hit their intended mark because Chris's cocky facade wobbles at the edges. He runs a hand over his slicked-back hair and licks his lips. "We're still on that, then?" He huffs. Shifts his stance. "Just wanted to be the bigger man and say hello. I'm gonna..." He hooks a thumb in the direction of his date, backing away with a croaked, "You take care."

My head is buzzing and not in a good way. "I know," I say before Jonathan can comment on younger Holly's lack of judgment. Then I finish my drink. Better get this over with. "So about why I left... I already told you about the partner stuff and the breakup, and I should have known it was a bad move to stay, but landing a job at Heckles and Romer was a dream come true. Or so I thought anyway."

"Even I know who they are. That's like—you've made it."

"Right. Except for the Big Bad Wolf–type cases they started to take on toward the end—like the Snake River Pesticide thing where they represented the agrofarm responsible for the leak. I was having qualms about that."

"Almost poetic that you work for GCL now, then."

"Exactly. But anyway, Chris and I were working a case, and I have to be deliberately vague about all the specifics here, but he bungled some paperwork that made us look like amateurs and blamed the whole thing on me. When I went to tell my boss, Chris had already whispered lies in his ear, and I lost it."

Jonathan frowns. "What do you mean 'lost it'?"

I press my lips together and hesitate. "I threw a stapler at him across the office."

A surprised huff escapes Jonathan. "You did not."

"Unfortunately, I missed, and instead the stapler knocked over a very expensive glass bust of Remy Romer Senior, shattering it—and my legal career—in a thousand pieces."

"No."

"Mm-hmm."

"Oh, so that's what he meant about priceless art?"

I nod. "I was given the choice to pay for the damage and

resign or have charges pressed, so...here we are. Turns out you're not the only one who's left scandal in their wake."

"Damn." Jonathan's eyes are wide. "And here I thought you were this flawless professional. You just don't strike me as the stapler-throwing kind."

"Push the right buttons enough times..."

"But why not go to a different firm? Why GCL?"

I sigh. If I had a quarter for every time someone's asked me that. "Lawyers are the biggest gossips. There's not a firm this side of the Cascades that hasn't heard about my 'vicious attack.'" I roll my eyes. "Plus, I can't exactly use Heckles and Romer as a reference, can I? It was time for a change anyway. Like I said, I'd already started questioning some things. I got into law to make a difference. The actual work gradually felt more and more like the opposite. So when Rachel told me about the internship..."

"Another thing we have in common. Saved by a friend." Jonathan shakes his head. "Unbelievable."

"Yup. She squared things with Manny about my lack of references, and since GCL seemed respectable and matched my values, not to mention it came with a possibility of relocating as far away from the rumor mill as possible..." I flip my palms up.

"Here you are."

"Here I am." I pick up another slice of pizza and nudge it in my ex's direction. "And there he is. Still in bed with the devil and, if I was to guess, yet another one of the paralegals."

Jonathan finishes his plate of chèvre-topped roasted beets, regarding me with that enigmatic expression of his. "Want to make him jealous?" he asks, gesturing to the waitress for a refill of our drinks.

He says it so casually that, at first, I think I mishear him. But I'd recognize that drawly cadence of his voice anywhere. A while back, in a different bar, he used it to ask me if I wanted to go upstairs. His words may have been somewhat slurred that time, but tonight they are well-articulated by anyone's standards. Still, I need to be sure.

"You know it's pretty frustrating not being able to tell if what you say and what you mean are the same things," I say. "You were doing it in the woods earlier, too, insinuating you wanted me to have missed you when you were out yesterday."

"If it helps, I always mean what I say. I did like the idea of you looking for me when I wasn't there."

Oh. "Why?"

"Why?" he repeats. "Because I'd look for you if you weren't in the office. Because as much as I wanted out of this project, I'm not too proud to say it's brought a welcome change. And because... well, I like you. Even more after what you told me tonight."

My breathing hitches at his declaration. I swallow with a gulp, mesmerized by his charged attention. "I like you, too," I finally say. "But—"

"Nuh-uh." His gaze grows more intense. "We don't have to figure everything out right this minute. Have a bit of fun. Do you want to make that loser jealous?"

I really do, especially if that means what I think it means. I nod.

Without hesitating, Jonathan reaches across the table, letting his fingertips push against mine until, joint by joint, our hands meet and our fingers braid together. His palm is warm and dry, and as his thumb strokes the base of mine, my nipples pucker against the lace of my bra.

It makes me braver, so I lean forward and ask, "Now what?"

A devilish glint enters his eyes. "Is he looking?"

I glance Chris's way. "No." But just then, he does, and he raises his glass to me when he sees he has my attention. "Oh wait. Quick, come over here." I tug my hand free and scoot in to give Jonathan room on the seat next to me.

He doesn't hesitate. He even makes it look natural, shrugging out of his jacket (*the* jacket) and draping it across his old seat before sliding in next to me.

The moment the warmth radiating off Jonathan seeps through my clothes, I forget that we're doing this for show. We're thigh to thigh, hip to hip, and then he reclaims my hand in one suave move, bringing it to his lips. The damp heat of his breath against my skin makes my toes curl. I want it against my neck again, against my lips. I'm not a PDA sort of person, but I almost don't care that there are people around. Almost. No matter how much my body craves getting even closer to him, decorum wins out.

"Hey, pretend to whisper something in my ear," I murmur.

Jonathan glances Chris's way, flashes me a smirk that says we've been noticed, and then he reaches up and pushes my hair back. His touch lingers against the shell of my ear, tracing it down to the lobe where he gives the smallest tug at my lightning bolt earring. I shiver, the sensation rippling down my spine to a central pulse point that thrums with a need for relief. I squeeze my thighs together, but that accomplishes nothing but a magnification of the emptiness inside.

Jonathan lets go of the earring and leans in slowly until his lips are almost at my jaw.

"I may not remember everything," he whispers, "but I do remember your skin tasting of coconut and your tongue of lime."

And every time I've seen you since, I've wondered what other flavors I missed out on because we were too drunk off that fucking tequila."

The curse is a jolt to my senses that makes my head slump and my eyelids fall closed. I register that he retreats a fraction, but other than that, I'm absorbed by the sparkling whirlpool he's set off inside me and the knowledge that I'm completely unprepared for this. For him.

When I finally meet his gaze again, he tightens his grip on my hand and cocks his head, a hint of danger beneath those dark brows. "How's that for pretend?"

"Highly convincing," I manage. "Almost like it wasn't pretend at all."

The cheery waitress picks that moment to sidle up to us to ask if we're interested in dessert. "The brownie bar is a favorite, as is the coconut lime pie."

Jonathan gives a short laugh next to me and presses his thigh to mine. "I bet. I was just saying how much I enjoy those particular flavors." He turns to me. "What do you think?"

I think I'm thrilled I'm not the only one with vivid memories from that night. I think I'm so horny that one more food reference might make me combust. And I also think I want to get out of here. "I'm good," I say. "Just the check, please."

I note absently that Chris and his date are gone when we make our way outside into the cool evening. Jonathan is still holding my hand, but we're not talking. It's as if going from the din of the restaurant to the hushed expanse of clear night air requires more caution. Still, the energy flowing through our grip has me on edge. I shouldn't want more, but I do.

I stop beneath a tree that we've meandered toward, tugging on his hand to spin him to me. The streetlights streak his dark hair with gold but leave shadows that hide what he's thinking. I reach for his jaw as if that will tell me. He covers my hand with his, stepping into my space. His other hand goes to my waist and snakes under my jacket and around to my back, pressing me to him. I've dreamed of this feeling, about the unyielding expanse of his chest, the rise and fall of his breathing, and his scent engulfing me. More than once, I've woken up from a dream at night just short of ecstasy with these exact sensations drifting away like a spectral fog. But now here he is.

"I don't remember being nervous last time," he murmurs next to my temple. "But I like this better."

"We're sober. Ish. Do you think I still taste the same?"

He makes a gruff sound in his throat at my question and draws his head back. "Only one way to find out."

I haven't told him that I remember the sweet spice on his lips from that night, too, but one soft brush of his mouth against mine and I'm like a poor, shipwrecked soul offered food for the first time in weeks. I open for the soft stroke of his tongue and meet it with mine. His lips are plump and satiny, contrasted by the rasp of the surrounding stubble, and I lose myself in the sensation.

Hunger builds as he draws his teeth against my lower lip, and I allow my hands to roam up his arms and into his hair, settling at his nape. He steadies me with a firm grip on my ribs, his thumbs resting below the cups of my bra. I want him to slide them up and under. Free me. I want his mouth on my bare skin, and mine on his.

As he kisses a hot trail along my jaw and down my throat, I grasp his jacket and clamber closer. But standing upright like this, I can't get enough leverage to satisfy the throbbing need inside me. Something akin to a sob escapes my throat.

"Get a room you two," a voice says, passing us. "Jeez."

We finally come apart, both breathing hard.

"Fuck," Jonathan says. "I almost forgot where we were."

I touch two fingers to my swollen lips and nod. "Me too." The couple that passed us are out of earshot now. I tip my head their way. "Maybe they were onto something?" I say, hope unabashedly tinging my voice. When Jonathan doesn't immediately agree, I add, "Or you know, not. It's whatever."

He takes my hand again, squeezing it tight. "It's not whatever." After a harsh exhale, he tilts his head back.

I know I'm not reading too much into this—no one fakes a kiss like that—yet something's going on. "But?"

I swear his heart jumps beneath my touch. "Oh God, you're so…" His mouth slants over mine again like he'll perish without one more morsel. Long, lush strokes of his tongue lay siege to me, leaving me dizzy. But then he retreats, apologizing. "I shouldn't have. I…Look, this is kind of complicated right? For several reasons. I don't want you to do something that you'll regret tomorrow."

I start shaking my head but the movement falters. He's right. What am I thinking? I have no business doing this. Not when stopping feels this difficult. I hold his gaze. Dig deep for willpower.

"To be clear, it's not what I want," he says. "But it's what's smart, and you know it."

I nod. Disappointment floods my system, inviting the night chill in to settle. *Damn.* I sigh. "So maybe you'll walk me to my car and we'll leave it at that?"

"I'll still see you tomorrow for the puppy shoot."

I suck in a deep gulp of cold air and force myself to put a few feet between us. Better do it before I change my mind.

Tomorrow's Holly had better be more grateful for this decision than the current version of me.

I'm parked around the corner, so it doesn't take us long to get there. He opens the door for me. I get in. He watches me leave.

Driving home is like leaving a dream behind. I know it's real, though. All I have to do is lick my lips to know he's been there. Pepper and cabernet.

I've just pulled into the driveway and turned off the car when my phone dings with a message. Jonathan has sent me a text. As I read it, warmth blooms from my belly to my face.

So what do you think? he asks. **Still swearing off dating?**

Days until printer deadline: 12

The first thing I do after waking up the next morning is check my messages, and finally, Robert the veterinarian has committed to a day for the shoot.

I'm free Wednesday at 7:45 a.m. if we stick to the Eastside, his text reads, and that's guy number eight scheduled. I pat myself on the back.

The second thing I do is log into my Pawsome Partners account to cancel it. There's one nice guy I've been messaging with a few times, so to preserve whatever dating karma I have left, I send him one more message where I tell the truth. After detailing my model search, I apologize profusely and wish him the best on his quest for true love, and to my surprise, a response pings in my inbox before I have a chance to close the account.

> **Xanderful:** I appreciate you letting me know.
> Sounds like a good cause, and I'm flattered that you considered me. Are you set on models then? I'd be happy to help.

See, I knew he was a good guy. What the heck—if he's volunteering...

> **Holly St.Bernard:** No, still looking. Are you saying you're interested? We can't pay.
>
> **Xanderful:** I figured. Yeah, for sure I'm interested. I only have one condition.
>
> **Holly St.Bernard:** Which is?
>
> **Xanderful:** I have a prosthetic leg. Car accident in college. I'd like it to show in the photo, cuz it's something you never see. Ok?
>
> **Holly St.Bernard:** Definitely! It's a great idea.
>
> **Xanderful:** ☺
>
> **Holly St.Bernard:** And your dog is on board too?
>
> **Xanderful:** Milton is jazzed for anything that'll land him a treat.
>
> **Holly St.Bernard:** Note taken.

I give him my number, and he gives me his, and then I finally leave Pawsome Partners behind for good. I also revise my earlier count. Only three guys to go. Piece of cake!

Jude is alone in the kitchen when I enter. He's putting chili ingredients into a slow cooker to bring to his Sunday night poker game later, but when he hears my stomach growl, he promises to leave a bowl for me.

"Nothing for Ava?"

"She's at Makenna's. Hating my guts." He makes a sour face.

I steal a pinch of grated carrots off his cutting board. "I take it you told her things are progressing in Texas, then?"

He nods. "Maybe you could talk to her? She won't hear me out."

"And you think she'll listen to me? I'm not even sure that I completely disagree with her. Just give her some time. She could come around."

"In a few years?" Jude dumps the carrots into the Crock-Pot and stirs. "I'm serious. I can't stand the doomsday atmosphere around here. Please. I'll give you fifty bucks."

"Ha!" I pour myself some leftover coffee and sit down at the counter.

"A hundred?"

I'm about to decline when a brilliant idea strikes. "You're pretty desperate, huh? Fine. I'll talk to her"—I put up a finger to stop him from thanking me yet—"*if* you agree to see one of the women from the dating site. Just one teeny, tiny date."

Jude crosses his arms. "Come on."

"Those are my terms. Take 'em or leave 'em."

He grunts, lips tight. "Oh, all right. One date."

"Plus the hundred bucks."

"I'm going to give it to you in coins."

I laugh. "So testy. Who knows, you might even have a good time."

"Don't hold your breath."

Jude opens the fridge and takes out the ground beef, then sprays a pan with oil. We don't speak while it heats. I know when to back off and celebrate my victory in silence. But after he's added the meat to the pan, he switches topics on me.

"You were out late yesterday," he says, glancing my way. "Is that why you're so obsessed with me going on this date?"

My fingertips instinctively go to my lips. After a dream-filled night's sleep, I'm inclined to concede that Jonathan and I were wise to stop things when we did. Not because I don't want more, but because it's taking quite a bit of brainpower to process even the little bit that did take place. We're two date-adverse people with no future together, yet last night was the best time I've had in a very long time, and I'm counting the hours until the photo shoot later today. How do I make sense of that?

"I was," I say, ignoring the second half of his question. I bring the cup of dark brew to my lips but quickly set it down again as the burnt smell of reheating reaches my nostrils.

Jude turns, one hand still stirring the beef. "Care to elaborate?"

I hesitate, but Jude knows me better than anyone, and I don't feel like lying. Besides, I have a feeling he'd like Jonathan. "Jonathan took me out to make up for the grueling model search dates."

"And did he?" He moves the spatula absent-mindedly. "Make up for it?"

I screw up my lips in a failed attempt to keep a neutral face. "He might have," I say, hiding the breadth of my smile behind the coffee cup but regretting it instantly as I once more choke on the fumes. "Ugh, get this thing away from me. Is this coffee from yesterday?"

Jude switches off the burner and turns more fully toward me. "You like this guy," he says.

I blink at him, momentarily stumped. "It's not really like

that. I'm not..." I sigh and stare at the wall filled with pictures of Jolene with Jude and Ava. "What I mean is, there's no 'potential' if that's what you're suggesting."

"Hmm." Jude nods slowly. "Because of work."

This is one of my favorite things about my brother—that he gets me. "Right. And because I plan on being far away from here real soon."

He looks thoughtful for another moment, but then his face brightens with a cheery "okay" before he turns back to the cutting board. For the next minute, he chops garlic like a line cook, and he only stops when something outside the window catches his eye.

"Someone's here," he says. "Oh, it's your friend—Rachel."

I join him at the window. Rachel is here?

I beat her to the door, holding it open as she marches right in and spins on me in the middle of the foyer, hands on her hips.

"You didn't call me," she says. "Didn't text. Nothing."

"Um, I...didn't know I was supposed to?" I phrase it like a question because that's what her presence feels like to me.

She stares at me, dumbfounded. "Wow, you really are bad at this stuff. Holly, it's implied. If you say, 'I have a date with this guy at work I'm thirsting for,' any girlfriend worth her mettle will finish that sentence in her head with 'and I'm gonna call you right after with the deets.' Come on."

I close the front door carefully. "Thirsting?"

"You know." She does a crude motion with her hands. Then she stops abruptly to sniff the air. "Mmm. Something smells good."

I roll my eyes but gesture for her to come inside. "Sorry, I didn't realize I would be held accountable for things you thought I implied."

As we step into the kitchen, Jude raises his hand in greeting, which stops Rachel in her tracks. "Oh shit, I forgot you live here," she says.

Jude gives her his megawatt smile. "It would be weird if I didn't since it's my house." He points to the slow cooker. "Making chili. Don't mind me."

"You cook, too?" Rachel turns to me and mouths, "He cooks, too," her eyes going heart-shaped.

I don't reward that with an answer, but is it just me or does Jude suddenly start cooking with a touch more flair knowing he has an audience? Because Rachel is definitely paying attention.

But this could work out for me. She appears to have forgotten why she's here, so maybe if I'm quiet, I can slip up to my...

"Hey!" Rachel catches on when I'm almost to the threshold. "Sit your skinny butt down and spill."

"In front of my brother?"

Her eyes widen. "Stuff happened?"

"O-kay," Jude says, voice starting out about an octave higher than normal, then dropping down. "I'm basically done, only need to..." He dumps a series of spices into the pot, covers it with a lid, wipes his hands, and gives us both a curt smile. "All yours. Nice to see you again, Rachel."

"Bye, Jude," Rachel calls out after he's disappeared. To me, she whispers, "I can't believe you won't ask him to be in the calendar. Robbing women all over the country of that treasure."

"Keep it in your pants, will you? Gross."

"Only if you tell me about your shenanigans with Mr. Summers."

There's a twinge inside my rib cage at his name, his voice ringing in my ears. *This is kind of complicated, right?* Complicated and exhilarating. Hard to describe. Personal.

"We ran into my ex," I say. "Can you believe it?"

Her face falls. "What? No way."

"Yup. With his most recent girl."

"Ugh." Rachel screws up her face. "Fucking Chris. What a buzzkill. I take it any mood was assassinated by his presence? Damn it!"

I chuckle at her expletive. "You know you are way too invested in this, right?"

"Define 'too.'"

"Why are you, though? Aren't you busy with beach volleyball Nick?"

Rachel looks away. "Can't a friend want a friend to be happy?"

"Sure, but that's not what's going on here." I waggle a finger between us.

"Yes, it is. Mostly."

"Mm-hmm..." I stare at her until she continues.

"I do want you to have some fun," she says. "And ever since I figured out what you two got up to the night of the announcement, I feel...involved. Responsible. It's bringing out the facilitator in me."

"That's ridiculous."

"Hey, don't knock my skills. My high school bestie is married to the man of her dreams thanks to me."

"Who said anything about marriage? I'm banking on moving soon."

"I know!" Rachel grimaces and mumbles something at the countertop.

"What?" I ask.

"I said, maybe I'm not looking forward to that so much." She peers up at me. "And if you and Jonathan hit it off..."

So that's what's going on. "If we hit it off, you think I might reconsider leaving."

She shrugs. "Worth a shot."

Back in freshman year of college, Rachel and I may have been tight like Bonnie and Clyde from day one (except less focused on criminal endeavors and more on global warming), but our friendship has never been touchy-feely. Seeing her like this—vulnerable and tender—tugs at my heartstrings more than I expect. "You forget I haven't won yet."

She *tsk*s. "You will, and you know it."

"All I know is I'll do my very best." I decide to throw her a bone. "No matter how great the date was last night."

Her head jerks up. "But I thought you said—"

"You assumed," I say, cutting her off. "Because I brought up Chris. Sorry I didn't call. I honestly don't know how to talk about it."

"But it was good?" Excitement tinges her voice. "Did you...?"

"No." But that's for the best, I remind myself.

She frowns, but to her credit, she drops any further questions about my potential sexcapades. "So, what happens now?" she asks instead.

The question deflates something inside me. With the topic reaching a dead end, so does the thrill that's run amok inside me since last night. "Probably nothing," I say with a lift of one shoulder. The words taste bitter and real. "Like you said, I'm on my way away. What good would it do?"

She studies me for a long moment, and then she echoes what Jude said not even an hour ago. "You *like him* like him, don't you?"

And damn it all to hell if they're not both right.

Days until printer deadline: 12

Laughter is the first thing I hear walking into the pet store Sunday evening. Low masculine notes of joy resonate through the air, interspersed with quiet conversation. Or maybe it isn't conversation—I only hear one voice, and it's Jonathan's.

I expect to find him on the phone or setting up camera equipment—images already ingrained in my mind. I do not expect to walk in on him sprawled like a starfish on the floor covered in beagle puppies. Yet here we are.

I pause in the doorway to take in the scene. We've had to improvise this indoor setup so there's fake grass on the floor and fake plants scattered about. Theo will be in a sleeping bag with the puppies around him, and then Jonathan will do his photo editing magic and superimpose a campfire in the foreground. He's assured me it will look like they're ready for a night beneath the stars.

Jonathan laughs again as he tries to protect his face from puppy slobber. Two of them have paws on his shoulders, the other five are doing their best to pin the rest of him down like he's Gulliver.

"Come on, guys," Jonathan chuckles. "You've got to let me sit up. We talked about this. There's only one of me and seven of you." He lifts the one closest to his face straight up in the air with one hand. I think he's going to move it away from him, but instead he puts the tiny tail-wagger down on top of his chest. For all his protestations, it's obvious he's loving his current predicament.

I watch for another minute, my heart turning progressively gooier at the sight. Is this the monosyllabic, people-repellant man who rescued me from the pantry three weeks ago? This man who wrestles with puppies and offers to make exes jealous in the best of ways? I dig my teeth into my bottom lip at the thought. My plan until this moment has been not to bring up last night. To pretend it didn't happen. But seeing him like this, my convictions are on shaky ground.

To avoid dwelling, I step into the room. Jonathan has finally made it up to sitting, but the puppies are still climbing all over him, tugging on his gray fleece and nipping playfully at his fingers.

"Hi there," I say when he doesn't notice me.

His gaze flies to mine. "Holly. Hey." He grins but doesn't make a move to get up.

I set my bag on a chair along the wall. "Having fun?"

"I fucking love puppies."

He says it with such gusto that I have to laugh. "Could have fooled me."

He lifts one of the squirming creatures into his lap. "This one is Elvis. I had a beagle growing up. Milo. They're the best dogs." He pats the floor next to him. "Here, come sit."

I hesitate. The invite is tempting, especially when expressed in that warm cadence that speaks of a certain familiarity. The idea of being close to him again hasn't left me alone since we parted last night. "Where are Marla and Theo?" I ask.

"Right here." Marla appears in the doorway to the back office, effectively shutting down any such ideas. "Theo forgot the sleeping bag at home. He should be back soon. Are you all set?"

"Pretty much," Jonathan says.

A small puppy who keeps circling me gets bolder when I squat down to her level. "Hi, little one," I coo.

"That's Dolly. She's the runt." Marla steps closer. "I think she likes you."

No sooner has she said this than Dolly digs her tiny teeth into the bottom hem of my jeans leg. I gently free it from her jaws. "Oh no, you don't. I don't care how cute you are."

"That's puppies for you." Marla smiles. "I'll be right back. I'm going to get some puppy pads to put down."

"Did you ever have a dog?" Jonathan asks once Marla is gone.

I shake my head, keeping a careful eye on Dolly at my feet. "My parents wouldn't let us." Another bolder puppy puts his paws on my knees as if he wants me to lift him up. I settle for scratching his ears. "But you had Milo? How old were you when you got him?"

"Seven." He pets Elvis on his lap. "He was my best bud. Slept in my bed and everything. Man, I still miss that dog."

"How old did he get to be?"

"About twelve. I think." Something shifts in his voice, going from nostalgia to something rawer. "Mom took him with her when she left, so I only got three years with him." He shrugs, but within that movement is contained much more than indifference.

I gape at him. "She took your dog?"

"Technically, he was her dog. She did all the work. But yeah."

I finally sit down next to him and am instantly attacked by three new wiggling mischief-makers. Jonathan points to each of them in turn. "That's Lennon, Cash, and Joplin. Cash is the alpha."

"How do you already know their names?"

"I may have gotten here early." His eyes crinkle.

For a while, we direct our attention only toward the dogs, sitting in companionable silence. But our proximity reminds me of the unspoken things between us, and I've never been particularly good at feigning ignorance. With a glance in the direction Marla disappeared, I put my hand on Jonathan's knee. Just a light stroke of the thumb. "I'm sorry you lost Milo like that. It must have made your mom leaving even harder. I can't believe she did that."

He watches my hand. "That she left or that she took Milo?"

"Both. But taking your dog almost seems crueler in a way. Maybe that's weird."

"No. I missed them both, but now, decades later, it's Milo I think about the most." With the stealthy move of someone trying to catch fireflies and ladybugs, his hand covers mine. Warm skin against my cooler.

I swallow hard. Turn my palm up so our fingers can interlace.

"All right, he's parking." Marla marches back into the room oblivious to the echoes of last night reverberating against every flat surface of the room.

I pull my hand away and stand. Run it against my jeans.

Jonathan follows. He rolls his shoulders and his neck out before stepping up to the camera waiting on its tripod and taking hold of it as if in need of support.

"Let's put some of these down so we avoid more accidents." Marla places puppy pads outside our faux turf area and calls for the puppies to join her, tempting them with small treats.

Theo enters the room, carrying a sleeping bag and a big boulder that's either fake or proof he's the Hulk. "I figured this might work in the background," he says, setting his cargo down. "Where do you want me?"

Jonathan consults the viewfinder. "Try a couple of steps forward from where you are. Head over there, feet there." He points before facing me. "Holly, come have a look."

Me? He's never wanted my input before. Nevertheless, I join him and put my eye to the camera. He's standing so close that my left shoulder almost touches his chest, and in this huddle of him and me and the camera, the rest of the room is reduced to miniature movements through the lens. I'm instantly more aware of every intake and exhale of air (mine) and every shift of muscle (his). It's impossible to concentrate with him right there, and it doesn't get easier when he shows me how to adjust focus. As I twist the lens, his fingers brush against my knuckles in featherlight guidance.

"Good?" he asks, his voice a low murmur.

A full-body shiver skates through me. "Mm-hmm."

Marla steps into view in the foreground of the mini-image, making me jerk back. She's carrying two of the puppies. "Okay, let's get this going before chaos descends," she says. "Where do you want Joplin and Cash?"

Jonathan's departure is too abrupt for my liking as he moves into the scene we've set up, but it's impressive how quickly he switches to professional mode. "Theo, if you can get into the sleeping bag. Rest your arm on the ground like so. Good." He returns to my side and adjusts a ground spotlight that illuminates Theo's face in an approximation of glow from a fire.

"Shirt off, too," I say as a reminder.

Jonathan smiles up at me. "Mine or his?"

My lips part as something between a hiccup and a chuckle escapes me. "Um..." What's the right answer here? "I'll settle for his," I say. "For now."

His eyes darken as his smile extends into a wolfish grin. Then he nods once.

It's at that moment I realize that, for him, slowing things down last night was *only* a slowing down. Not a full stop. Lord have mercy.

Somehow we get through the shoot. Marla and I tag-team to corral the puppies while simultaneously doing our best to stay out of the shot. It's like whack-a-mole but with less whacking and fewer moles. When one puppy obeys, another finds an interesting piece of lint off-camera.

Theo poses like a pro, though, and by the end of it, Jonathan is happy.

"These edits will take a little longer to get to you," he says. "But you won't be disappointed."

"I already know that," I say, which earns me another flash of his pearly whites.

Once we're packed up, I help him carry equipment to the car. We take several trips since we have extra props, so Theo beats us to leaving, the fake boulder strapped to his flatbed truck. On our final turn to the car, the parking lot is dark and quiet, only illuminated by two yellow streetlights. The last box doesn't fit in the trunk, so Jonathan loads it into the back seat, and then he comes around to the back where I'm standing.

"That was fun," he says, cocking his head toward the building while not taking his eyes off my face. He's stopped three feet away from me, but after an hour of circling each other in the presence of other people, I'm tired of resisting.

"You're very good with dogs," I say, moving into his space as subtly as I can. "And I don't mean just tonight."

He bridges the last foot between us, forcing me to tilt my head back. I steady myself with a hold on his jacket that awards me a faint hum from deep in his chest.

"Last night was also fun," I say, diving in. "Did I say thank you for the date?"

He taps a finger against his fuller lower lip. "I'm not sure. Did you?"

"If I didn't—thank you. And also for being a gentleman."

"Yeah?" His hands find their way to my hips, pulling me closer.

I shrug. "Pacing is good. You were right."

"Yet here we are." He looks up at the moon, and I'm overcome with the impulse to kiss the slight protrusion of his Adam's apple.

I regain control only by tipping my head to his chest.

The tenderness of his lips against my hair sends a befuddling wave of warmth rushing down my spine. What the heck is this? I've never been so torn between wanting to curl up in someone's embrace and jumping his bones. My indecision only gets worse when he tucks me close, like he's protecting me from the world, which also reveals how unmistakably excited his body is at having me there. Which begs the question…

"Are you also confused?" I ask into his chest.

He's quiet for a beat. "Very," he says finally.

I'm about to ask him to elaborate when his phone rings in his pocket. The twangy chorus to "You Can't Always Get What You Want" grows in volume as he pulls the phone out. "My dad," he says. "Sorry. Hold on."

To my surprise, he stays close to me as he takes the call. I can't hear the other side of the conversation, but Jonathan's short "mm-hmm," "no worries," and "yeah, not long" tell me enough. This is it for tonight.

And sure enough. "Sorry, I'm late getting Dad from his container gardening class. He's patient to a point, but I'm afraid I'm way past that. I've got to go."

"Fitting ringtone, then," I say with a smirk. "Rolling Stones," I clarify when he squints at me.

"Oh. Yeah. It's sort of an inside joke. But you're right. Fitting."

With a low groan, I push him away from me to make it easier to let go. "Guess I'll see you at work tomorrow."

"Maybe I'll run into you in the rec room." He winks.

And while I know we'd never do anything in the office when there's people around, the insinuation alone increases my need for a cold shower tenfold.

"Go," I say. "Get your dad. Good work tonight."

There's a beat of inertia where I think he might stay, say "to hell with Dad," but then he backs away and opens the driver's door.

I shiver at a chill in the air I hadn't noticed until now and wrap my arms around myself. If this were a normal situation, I'd take matters into my own hands at this point and ask him on a second date to move things along. I've never been one for waiting around for the guy. But this isn't normal. I'm not planning on being here for much longer, so asking him out wouldn't be fair. And he's a smart guy—he probably realizes that. Hence his comment about things being "complicated." The date last night was an anomaly.

No, I need to be fine with the status quo, I think as I walk to my car. Then I head home with new resolve to keep it in my pants until the other pieces of my life are settled.

Days until printer deadline: 10

As it turns out, I don't see Jonathan in the office Monday. I don't know why this surprises me. Before the fundraiser contest, I saw him so rarely that someone could have told me he was an occasional contractor and I would have believed them. Only his attendance at the weekly meeting gave away that he was an employee.

It doesn't mean I'm not keeping an eye out, though, and when Rachel invites me to tag along to a conference on environmental sustainability at Microsoft on Tuesday morning—something I'd normally have enjoyed—my first thought is of the distance that puts between Jonathan and me.

Rachel must sense my hesitation because she plays the mentor card and tells me it's not optional. "I want to introduce you to the people from Climate Solutions. They'll be valuable connections for you to have." Then she lowers her voice. "Besides, you have another photo shoot with him later anyway."

I scan our surroundings to ensure no one else is there to catch her insinuating tone, but everyone is at their desks across the room. Eric didn't land the Chihuly museum venue, so I know he's been scrambling to find another space, and Ashley spends most of her time on the creative side of the elevators with her social media maven, Pippa. Only Letitia appears both in control of her fundraiser and still engaged in the day-to-day work of her internship. She's currently on the phone with our Brasilia office, impressively peppering the conversation with Portuguese phrases she's "picked up." I'm not going to lie—I sometimes miss the steel-trap brain I had in my twenties.

At least Manny isn't playing favorites, and I take it as a positive sign that he wants me involved in the grants process for our Save the Reef efforts in Australia. For days, he's been sending me articles to read so I'll be able to keep up at the meeting next week. If only I could find the time to do so.

I wish I could say I take full advantage of my opportunity to mingle at the environmental conference. I try, but mentally I'm already at Discovery Park where I'm meeting Jonathan later. As much as I know I'd be better off not getting involved with him, at this point we might just have to knock boots if for no other reason than to clear the air. I'm too pent-up to think straight.

I park at the south lot of Discovery Park a whole twenty minutes before the photo shoot thanks to the conference ending early to allow for happy hour. It's a sunny October day, but the air has that unmistakable crisp tinge of fall that always serves as a reminder to locate tucked-away scarves and sweaters. Because I'm early, I text Jonathan to meet me by the old chapel and set course toward the wide, sloped expanse of the park. The canopy is yellowing but still thick enough to feel like a secret passage separating the park from the city, an illusion made more magical by several white bunnies scurrying into the thicket, likely descendants of pets released into the wild.

I take my time, enjoying the peace after a day of intense socializing. I'm not alone in reveling at this urban lung and its beautiful view of Puget Sound. There are plenty of joggers, hikers, and dog walkers about. I move to the side to let two women with golden retrievers pass in matching yoga pants (the women, not the dogs). One of them waves to a guy in the distance who's walking a beautiful white floof. A Samoyed, I think. I only know that because my eighth-grade PE teacher had one.

Seeing the two goldens and the Samoyed together forces me to take stock of my fundraiser progress. I have a week and a half until the finished calendar goes to the printer and so far, only five photo shoots are done. If not for the fact that I have three other guys scheduled, I'd feel a lot more anxious. For the four spots that remain, I have a verbal promise from Rachel that Nick is game, Dennis's gym buddy is one more good lead, and I have calls out to both North Seattle Fly Dogs and a poster up at the local dog run. That's decent progress by any standards, I think.

Except, I've never been one to settle for good enough, and my goal is twelve photos not nine. So while the three strangers and their dogs congregate, I linger out of earshot from them and pull out my phone. Using the camera, I zoom to get a better look at the guy. He has long hair under his beanie and is shorter than both of the women, but when one of them says something funny, his smile radiates through my screen. He's cute in a hemp-sweater, granola sort of way, and considering my stint as a virtual catfisher, surely it's not beneath me to approach men in parks, too.

I wait until the women leave before I follow the guy and his dog down a trail to the left of the chapel. They move in sync, the dog frequently looking up at its owner, and the more I watch them interact, the more convinced I am that they'd make an excellent addition to the calendar. All I have to do is figure out the best way to approach them.

After a few minutes, the guy veers off the paved path, cutting across the hilly meadows where dirt trails meander this way and that. At one point, he stops and glances my way, so I quicky feign interest in the yellowed grass at my feet. Then I scan the horizon on my left for good measure before continuing after him.

We're going uphill now, and he's faster than I am, so by the time I reach the crest where a paved path intersects, I'm breaking a sweat. A gust of wind sweeps past, blowing hair into my eyes, and when I've forced the strands into place behind my ears, the guy and his dog are gone, swallowed by the earth. *What the hell?* I rest one hand on my head and do a three-sixty turn that yields nothing, and I'm about to give up when the two of them step out from behind a large bush, startling me.

"Why are you following me?" the guy asks. "Did Kiera send you?"

Whoa. I back up a step. "Um, I don't know a Kiera."

"Because I've told her a million times, I'm not seeing anyone else. But I can't not walk Sam, can I?"

Sam the Samoyed. How original. "I wasn't following you. Not for that reason any—"

"Yeah, you were. You were filming, too. Those two women

are friends of my sister's, nothing else. If you're going to show her the footage, at least tell her that."

I frown. What kind of noir plot have I stepped into? "Tell who? Look, I'm sorry—I didn't mean to scare you. But again, I don't know a Kiera. She sounds fun, though."

The guy stares at me. "If you're not with Kiera, then why are you stalking me?"

"I wouldn't call it stalking as much as—"

He interrupts again. It's almost enough to make me feel for this Kiera person. "From all the way up there"—he points—"over the field and back here. I'd call that stalking. So what gives?"

When he puts it like that… "I thought your dog was pretty," I say meekly, flushing hot with embarrassment.

He tightens his grip on the leash. "You're after Sam?" He steps forward and points at me. "Over my dead body. I'll scream. There are people about."

Am I really that scary? "No, no, no. I'm not going to steal your dog. I'm looking for models," I hurry to say before he can cut me off again.

He balks. "Like a sex thing?"

Oh jeez. "No, of course not."

"Then what? You have thirty seconds."

In my peripheral vision, a tall figure comes hurrying down the slope on my left. Jonathan.

"Everything okay here?" He stops a yard away from me but positions himself between me and the guy.

"He thinks I'm a stalker," I say under my breath.

Jonathan spins toward me. "Why?"

"Are you a cop?" the guy asks. "This woman has been following me for the past ten minutes. She says she wants my dog."

I huff out a breath and cross my arms. "I did not say that. I said I'm looking for models for a calendar." I take a step forward, which makes the guy retreat. "I'm sorry I followed you, but I promise I mean no harm." To Jonathan I say, "I was waiting for a good opportunity to approach. Don't you think they'd be perfect?"

"Perfect for what?" The guy looks horrified.

"Okay, why don't we back up a few?" Jonathan asks. "Get some facts straight."

"Maybe I should wait up there?" I ask, indicating the chapel.

"Might make this easier," Jonathan agrees.

"Sorry again," I tell the guy as I back away. "Didn't mean to freak anyone out." With that, I head up the hill with my fingers crossed that Jonathan can clean up my mess.

He joins me five minutes later, waving a piece of paper in the air. "He'll do it," he says. "I showed him the other photos, and he came around. Said he's big on fishing, so we'll find a good place for that."

"Is he available this week?"

"Yeah, but..." Jonathan scratches his temple and scrunches up his nose. "You can't be there. It's his one request."

I scoff. "I really wasn't being creepy. I promise."

"Be that as it may."

I scan the slope to see the Samoyed's white tail disappear into the trees. He'd make model number nine. Or ten, actually, if I count Nick, even though he still needs to get scheduled. "Fine. I trust you."

"You do?"

I do, I realize. "You've come a long way from accusing me of producing soft porn. Just don't let it get to your pretty head."

He looks at me with amusement. "Pretty head?"

"You know what you look like. You have a mirror." I start walking, and he follows.

"It's an odd choice of words, though. Not 'handsome'? Or 'chiseled'?"

That awards him a cheeky smile. "I said what I said." I check my phone for the time. "Where is this guy? Didn't we say five?"

We lap the chapel, but there's no sign of our model, and considering this is Mikael the giant Swede from bad date number umpteen, he should be easy enough to spot.

"I'll set up while we wait. He could be caught in traffic," Jonathan says.

I sit down on the low stone wall separating the chapel grounds from the grassy slopes. The setting sun is still warm enough on my skin that I turn my face to it, letting it paint golden swirls on the inside of my eyelids. Soon enough, the rains will come.

When ten minutes have passed, I text Mikael to make sure he's not at one of the other sections of the park. **Let me know your ETA. See you in a bit.** I put the phone away and turn back to the sun. Of all the places to be kept waiting, this isn't the worst.

Click!

My eyes fly open, and there's Jonathan, the camera to his face. "Sorry, you looked so peaceful." *Click, click.*

I put a hand up to stop him. "Come on. I'm not..."

He lowers the camera. "Not what?"

My phone beeps in my pocket. Perfect timing. "One sec," I say. Mikael has texted back, but I have to read the message several times to understand it.

Doesn't feel so good to have a date not work out, does it?

"What's going on?" Jonathan asks.

I hold up the phone, and he comes closer to read. "What the?"

"He never meant to show. It's payback for me not putting out on Friday."

Jonathan's jaw drops. "Holy shit. This is what women have to deal with?"

I shrug. "It's on the pettier side." I tip my head back and close my eyes again. "Fuck," I mutter. I'm right back to nine models, and now I've wasted Jonathan's time, too.

Click.

"I told you to stop that," I say, still not opening my eyes.

"Holly." His voice is cajoling.

"No."

"Can I please take your picture?"

"No."

"But the light is perfect, and I've got everything set up."

I finally look. He's pointing to the chapel wall where a reflector stand and the tripod are waiting.

"You like the photos I've taken so far, right?" he asks. "You might be pleasantly surprised. If they don't turn out, I'll delete them." He holds out a hand for me to take.

I hesitate. "I need to brush my hair."

"You don't."

"And I'm still in my work clothes."

"You can always take them off."

His unexpected quip cuts through my resolve, and a small laugh finds its way up my throat.

"Ha! Made you smile." He grins at me. "Now, come on. Don't be scared. I am a professional, after all. Award-winning, even."

"Fine." I take his hand, and he hoists me off the stone wall. I expect him to let go once I'm on my feet, but he doesn't. Instead, his fingers wrap around mine in a confident grip as he leads me to the chapel and the protected spot he's found that's aglow with the setting sun.

As I survey the space, Jonathan lifts his camera again. "You don't have to look at me. Do whatever."

Do whatever... Well, since my body wants to mimic a concrete block at the moment, I guess I'll stay right where I am.

He starts snapping pictures, moving around me, and occasionally checking his screen. "A little to the left. Good." Jonathan waves his fingers toward the wall. "Over there maybe?"

"So not whatever?"

He looks up. "What?"

"You said I could do whatever, but now you want me over there. Which is it?"

"Am I being bossy?" *Click, click.* "Turn your back to me."

I do, looking over my shoulder. "A bit."

He crouches low. "You don't mind?"

To be honest, it's a relief not to have to be in charge for once. "Not really. Like you said, you're the expert here."

He stands, considering me. "Would you lose the jacket? It's too formal."

I do without argument. I'm wearing a thin blue blouse underneath that I know flatters my coloring. The cooling air seeps through the fabric, making the hairs on my arms rise.

"Against the wall over there." Jonathan points.

His words are innocent enough, but his undivided attention and commanding tone stir something deep inside me and expand the gooseflesh to my sides and down my legs. I know I'm blushing as I lean my back to the white wood, and the tight peaks of my nipples are probably visible through the blouse, but I force myself to look straight at the lens this time.

Jonathan snaps a few shots, but then he lowers the camera. His gaze roams up and down my body, his throat moving as he swallows hard. "Eyes to the left," he says in a low voice, taking two steps toward me. *Click, click, click.* "Turn around. Face this way. Place your hands on the wall on either side of your head."

My breathing grows shallower as I sense him closing in. His movements stir the air, little caresses against my barely protected skin. I rest my right temple to the chapel wall and hold still as the camera comes into view.

"Move your hand closer," Jonathan says. When I try but get it wrong, he reaches out and nudges it toward my cheekbone. "There." Then, as if he can't help himself, he lets the back of his fingers trail along my jaw. "Good."

My eyes fall closed at his praise.

"No, look at me."

I expect to see the dark circle of the lens trained on me, but instead I'm met by his gray eyes. The low light dances within them, telling a story I'm not sure I've heard before. He presses the shutter once, though the camera remains below his chin.

"How am I doing compared to the other models?" I ask under my breath.

"Holding your own," he says. "Except I never had the urge to kiss any of them."

"But you do now?"

Click. "I thought that was apparent."

I push off the wall and turn toward him, at the same time extending my left hand to block the lens. "Put that thing away."

In one swift move, he's hooked the camera over his shoulder so it's hanging safely at his back and taken the one long stride necessary to grab hold of my waist. He leans in until we're forehead to forehead. "I really didn't want to leave the other night," he says. "I need you to know that. And that stupid song. You'll be happy to know I've switched the ringtone."

I lift my chin and steal a kiss. Only a peck, but how can I not?

"Bold," he murmurs, approval in his voice.

"Maybe I can't get everything I want, but I can still take what little I can get."

His fingers flex against me. "Oh, I'm sure you can have more than that," he says. Then he kisses me in earnest.

His lips are hungry and lush as he fits them against mine, first softly and then coaxing entry for a deeper savoring that steals my breath. My hands fist in the material of his shirt, and he takes the hint, maneuvering us back a step so I'm once again up against the wall. This is a far superior version of that pose, with his body pressed against mine, his hands roaming from my hair, my neck, my jaw, and down my arms, my sides, my hips. I don't immediately notice him untucking my blouse from my pants, but when his fingers make contact with the sensitive skin at my waist, painting trails of heat to the small of my back, I gasp, open-mouthed, against his lips.

"You like that," he says, repeating the move.

I'm a tightly wound bow, ready to spring, yet I manage a nod.

He kisses me again, his thumbs digging under my waistband

and tracing the ridge of my hip bones. I cling to him, the feel of his hair between my fingers exactly like I remember it from that first night, soft and infinitely tuggable. He groans when I do.

"I'm tired of being confused," he breathes between nips and licks. "We're both adults. Please tell me it wouldn't be a bad idea. I want you so much."

And quite frankly, it's probably not only a bad idea but also a terrible one, but all I can do as he trails kisses down my throat is move one of his hands up to my breast and grind into him until we're both panting.

He retreats a few inches and looks down at me. Then he glances over his shoulder to make sure we're alone. His fingers go to the top button of my blouse.

"What are you doing?" I ask, my voice raspy with need as I watch him undo it.

"I just want a tiny bit more. A new flavor." The pad of his thumb brushes over my covered nipple, but then he stills, waiting, watching me.

I make double sure no one can see us and nod quickly. "Yes." I arch my back into his touch. "But hurry."

He needs no urging. He makes swift business of another two buttons before he dives for the swell of my chest, inhaling deeply where black satin meets skin.

My head tips back against the wall when his mouth makes contact. His lips lavish hot kisses along the lacy edge while his hands hold me steady. A gentle nip of teeth followed by a soothing lick, and then he shifts his body so that one of his legs slides between mine. In my current state, I'm not sure if it's a fortuitous accident or intentional, but I take full advantage, grinding into him like we're teenagers in the back seat of someone's minivan.

I hold on to his head, clasping it to my chest as I shamelessly ride his thigh. Weeks of built-up tension unfurl low in my stomach, building the electrical current through my limbs until I'm certain I won't be able to stay upright much longer. "Oh God," I mumble. "I need…"

He pushes one cup of my bra down with a grunt, and a split second later, heat envelops my nipple as he sucks it into his mouth.

My orgasm hits like a lightning strike, linking every point of me in contact with him. It's quick and intense, over before I really have time to grasp what's happened. I don't know who's more surprised, Jonathan or me.

"Did you just…?" he asks with a devilish grin as he straightens.

I don't know what's gotten into me. We're out in the open for Pete's sake. And I never come that easily. My face flushes, and I adjust my clothes. He's going to think I'm easy. Or desperate. Or both. "Sorry. I got… That was really, um…"

"No, hey." He tilts my face up to his. "Why are you apologizing? It was fucking hot."

Hot. Yes, that's the word.

"You're hot," he continues. "And you taste so damn good."

"But I don't usually…" I nudge my head downward.

"Come?" he asks, the word sexier on his lips than it has a right to be.

"Not like that."

"Hmm." The sound comes from deep in his chest as he braces my face in his palms. His thumbs stroke along my jaw. "Maybe you do now." He kisses me softly, an unhurried depression of our lips. "Want to get out of here?"

My whole body lights up again at what his question might imply. "Yes."

He folds up the tripod on autopilot and tucks it into his pack. "Will you grab the reflector?"

I do, and a few minutes later, we've made sure nothing is left behind. The trek back is a silent one between lengthening shadows, but as far as I'm concerned, I'm completely safe with Jonathan at my side, and that feels different than what happened mere minutes ago. A tangled mess I can't reason my way out of.

It seems he's right there with me because, as we approach the parking lot, he suddenly says, "I meant what I said, by the way. I'm tired of overthinking this. Of worrying about how complicated it might be." He pauses to retrieve his car keys from his pocket. "But that's me. If you feel differently, I'll respect that."

"I don't," I say quickly, tuning out whatever alarms are blaring "danger" inside my head. I want this. Want him. Even if it is temporary.

He stops. A wave of something that looks like relief washes over him. "We could pick up food. Eat at my place?"

I'm about to let out another "yes," but something he said triggers my mental calendar. Food, dinnertime... It's Tuesday. "Oh, damn it." I grimace. "You have no idea how much I want that, but I can't tonight. Jude has a date, so I told Ava I'd catch the end of her tournament in Kirkland and take her to dinner after."

Jonathan's shoulder slump matches exactly how I feel. "Our families aren't making this easy, are they?"

"Needy people." I smile. "But I promised Ava burgers and milkshakes." It's also the best opportunity I'll get to bring up the move, so I need to take it since Jude's keeping his end of the bargain.

"Yeah. Can't go back on that."

I wrap my arms around his waist. "Another rain check," I say into his chest. "The last one. I'm free this weekend."

"Friday," he confirms. "My place. Seven o'clock. Dads, nieces, and brothers not invited. Phones on mute."

It's a(nother) date.

Days until printer deadline: 10

Ava takes second place in her tournament and is still recapping match balls she's particularly happy with when we enter the restaurant. Her cheeks are flushed from the game, and she's radiating energy, but once she gets a malted chocolate milkshake in front of her, she finally falls silent.

"They have the best milkshakes here, don't they?" I ask as I watch her drain half of her glass in one go.

She nods and sets it down. "So good. I haven't had one in forever."

I consider my options. We can chitchat about school and friends, eat and be merry, and then I can ruin the mood by bringing up Texas at the end of our meal. Or I can rip off the Band-Aid right now and have time to turn the mood around before we get home to Jude. I decide to rip.

"Didn't your dad use to take you here every first day of school or something?" I ask.

"Yeah." A shadow passes across her face, but she doesn't say anything else. She puts her straw back between her lips, but this time, she just nibbles on it.

"You're pretty upset with him, huh?"

"Duh."

"Do you want to talk about it?"

She spins her glass and then drags a finger through the condensation ring on the table before she looks up at me. The light in her eyes has dimmed, and I hate that I'm the cause of it. In my book, she has every right to be upset, but I promised Jude I'd try to mediate.

"There's not much to talk about, is there?" She pouts. "Dad's just being an asshole."

"Aw, come on now. That's my brother you're talking about."

"You already know, then." One corner of her mouth quirks up.

I smile. "Girl…" Maybe not all is lost here if she can still joke about him.

She sits back. "I just don't get why he needs to move now. Things are fine here. I'm happy here. Doesn't that matter?"

"It should," I say before I can stop myself. "I mean, he knows that. But maybe he thinks you'd be even happier there."

She scoffs. "I really don't think he cares. This is only about what he wants to do. It's just not fair."

"Right." I clasp my hands together on the edge of the table and then unclasp them again. I need a new angle here.

The waitress comes to my rescue with our food right then, which gives me a moment to regroup. Once she's left and Ava has dug into her fries, I try again.

"Okay. I'm not saying you don't have reason to be upset, and I'm not taking sides. But as a thought experiment, walk me through what you think it will be like to move."

She waves a fry in the air. "It's going to suck."

"Because…" I take a bite of my burger, which is topped with chèvre and bacon jam.

"My friends are here, I know where everything is, all the trees, I like the rain..."

I cock my head. "You do not like the rain. Do you know how many mornings I wake up to you stomping down the stairs because, and I quote, 'this fricking rain will ruin my hair again'?"

Ava rolls her eyes. "Fine. Not the rain thing, then. But my tennis team, and my school, and my house."

I nod. "There are a lot of good memories here. And I totally get that you'll miss your friends. But you would still be connected on social media, and you're old enough to travel back to visit on your own."

Ava grumbles something inaudible in response.

"What about good things?" I ask. "There must be something."

"Nope." She balls up a napkin and reaches for another. Her burger comes with pineapple, and it's juicy.

"Come on. What about tennis? I'm sure sunny Texas is prime, all-year-round tennis heaven."

Ava presses her lips together before she concedes. "Maybe."

"And your grandma and grandpa are there. You can swing by anytime."

She pulls the bamboo skewer out of the second half of her burger. "I do miss seeing them." She nibbles on her lip. "But it's just... Texas! Of all places."

"I get it, believe me."

"Like, how would you feel if you had to move somewhere against your will?"

"Not great," I admit.

"Right. But because I'm 'a child'"—she puts bunny ears around the word—"I'm supposed to just smile and go along with it?"

"I don't think that's what your dad is expecting at all. I think he wants to talk about it." I lean forward to catch her eye. "But it's kind of hard to talk to someone who's giving you the silent treatment, no?"

She has nothing to say to that, so I back off and take another bite of my burger. Hopefully, I've at least planted a seed.

"So when's the next tournament?" I ask after I've allowed a few minutes of quiet reflection. Time to undo this tension.

Ava licks off her finger, her shoulders visibly lowering. "Next weekend in Olympia. Coach wants me to get as much match play in as possible this year, so I have a better chance of being scouted as a junior."

"I don't doubt colleges will be fighting over you."

A grin lights up her face. "Fingers crossed!"

Jude is already home when we get back, feet on the couch, reading. He does not look like someone who's just had his first date in over a decade, but I wait until Ava has disappeared upstairs before I launch an inquisition. As usual, she doesn't even say hi to him, but hopefully that's because she's desperate to shower and get her homework done, not because my talk failed. If Jude notices, he doesn't let on.

"So," I say, balancing on the armrest of the couch, "tell me everything."

Jude looks at me over the frames of his readers. "About?"

I shuck a throw pillow at him, which dislodges his grip on the book. "Don't be cute."

He smiles and takes off his glasses. "Oh, you want to know about my evening? The date you set up? The one you blackmailed me into going on?"

"Blackmail?" I huff. "Aren't you a lawyer? I suggested a mutually agreeable proposal. Now, spill."

He swings his legs over the edge and sits up straighter. Morris lifts his head next to the couch. "Fine. We had drinks. A few appetizers. She works in IT, grew up in New Mexico, married once."

"And?" I spin my finger to encourage more details.

"And..." Jude runs a hand through his hair and inhales deeply. "I don't know. Her name is Mona. The food was decent."

"But did you have a good time? Are you going to see her again?"

"It was fine, I guess."

"Oof. Not great praise."

"Yeah, we didn't make plans if that's what you mean. She was just very"—he wiggles his head as if searching for the right words—"factual."

Not what I was expecting. "She seemed cool in her profile."

Jude raises an eyebrow. "Maybe she, too, had a meddling sibling create one for her." He leans down to scratch Morris's ear. "I'm not saying it was bad. It just lacked a bit of, I don't know, fun, maybe? Energy. Like, you know, when Rachel came by the other day. How vibrant and positive she is. It's kind of contagious, right?"

I nod in agreement, though I have no idea how Rachel has suddenly become a part of this conversation.

"Mona was the opposite of that. Very nice, sure. But not for me."

"Noted. I'll make sure the next one is a better fit."

"Next one?" He pushes off the couch. "No, no, no. This was a one and done. No more. Have you talked to Ava?" He turns to

Morris, who's now on his feet, tail wagging. "Are we going outside, bud? Are we? Yes, let's go."

I stand, too. It's never a good idea to be the only person sitting during a conversation like this. "As a matter of fact, I have. And I think you'll find her more amenable to a conversation now."

"Then good." Jude extends a hand to me. "Deal, done."

I shake it. "Fine. Then I'm going to bed." I grab my bag from the floor, intending to make a smooth exit, but then I remember I have an early morning photo shoot, and darn it if I didn't forget to stop at the store.

Jude and Morris are already on their way to the door when I call out, "You didn't happen to pick up more cereal bars, did you?"

My brother watches me for a moment, his lawyer persona still at the surface, but then his features soften and he smiles. "Two boxes. Milk and eggs, too."

Like I said—the best brother.

Unfortunately, no amount of breakfast foods is enough to prepare me for Robert the vet who shows up to our morning shoot without a dog.

"I didn't realize you wanted one in the photo," he says. "I thought it only mattered that I work with them."

I make Jonathan look at our email exchange to verify that yes, the subject line of all our emails was always "guys and dogs photo shoot" and I'm not losing my mind. Then we reschedule for Robert's next available day, which is the twelfth after work.

"And I can bring any pet?" he asks as we part ways.

Jonathan puts a hand on my shoulder as if he senses I'm about to blow a gasket. "I've got this," he says to me before setting Robert straight.

"A dog," he says. "Please bring a dog."

Days until printer deadline: 7

"Whoa, Aunt Holly. You look great!" Ava gives me an appreciative scan as I enter the kitchen Friday evening.

"Thanks." I set my bag on the counter and open the fridge. I need something to drink. Nerves have turned my mouth into a desert.

"Do you have a hot date or something?"

I'm in a long-sleeved, black shirt with a deep V-neck and woven-in metallic accents, and my favorite knee-length, black skirt. It's a confidence booster of a getup, and one I've not worn in a long time. I run my hands over the skirt and tweak the seams so they align with my hips.

I open a bottle of water and lean against the counter. I'm not sure I want to talk about Jonathan with my niece. "It's a meeting to go over the photos we have for the calendar so far, tweaking edits, that sort of thing." I almost canceled. With two photo shoots going bust this week, I don't know that I've earned a night off, but Jonathan promised we can brainstorm more model recruitment over dinner, and to be honest, I need to see him.

"A work thing?" Ava frowns.

Before I can respond, Jude joins us, carrying a dirty mug from the den, and Ava turns away. It's official. He's got a job offer from a Texas firm, and consequently, she's stopped speaking to him altogether. Which means Jude is barely speaking to me. Something about "doing more harm than good" in talking to her. Apparently, her only takeaway from our conversation was that I agree Jude is being unfair. Go figure.

I wait for Ava to probe further, but to my relief, she's found the snacks she needs and has already moved on. "Have fun," she says, disappearing up the stairs. No acknowledgment of her dad's presence.

"Whew, arctic," I note when she's gone.

"Getting used to it," Jude says. "Sooner or later, she'll need something from me." He grabs a handful of grapes from the fridge and studies me for a long moment as he chews. "I think the more important topic here is, who is coming to this meeting of yours."

Now he wants to talk? "I thought you weren't speaking to me?"

He shrugs. "I'm bored, and you're dressed for a date. Sue me."

"Fine, it's not *not* a date."

"Just you and Jonathan?"

I nod. *Finally.*

"Your top is inside out."

"What?" I look down so fast I almost pull a muscle in my neck.

Jude chuckles. "Gotcha."

"Dick." I throw a forgotten, balled-up receipt at him, but I can't help but smile. At least some of the tension gripping me evaporates in the presence of brotherly antagonism.

"So what are you kids up to?" He opens the fridge again for more grapes. "Is he picking you up?"

"Maybe you should make some real food instead," I suggest. "I'm going over to his place."

Jude's eyes jump to mine. "Really?"

"Yeah. Why?"

"I hate to tell you, but that's a date-date. And I thought you were set against that considering the fundraiser and Scotland and everything."

I check my phone for the time. "Thanks for reminding me."

"No, no." He comes around to my side of the counter. "I'm all for this. I'm just surprised."

"And besides, we're working, too." In addition to more model searching, I've requested that Jonathan mock up the layouts for me since we only have one week until the printer deadline.

"You don't have to explain, Hols. It's your life."

I know that. But maybe I need to explain it to myself.

I inhale deeply. "Okay, here I go. Keys, phone, wallet, gum." I also have a pack of condoms in my bag because a girl can hope, but Jude doesn't need to know that.

"Drive safely." He picks up the kitchen towel and waves it in the air in farewell, making me smile again. What would I do without him?

"Have some real food," I say. "And don't wait up."

Jonathan lives in a tall, narrow house in the Crown Hill neighborhood of Seattle. The square footage is moderate, he's warned me, but it has a garage and is close to everything, which makes up for its other deficiencies. It's also around the corner from his dad's place, which was a key factor when he and his ex bought the property almost a decade ago. Or so he's told me.

I don't allow myself to hesitate in the driveway. As soon as I've turned off the car, I get out and march to the front door. One shaky breath in and I ring the doorbell.

Continuing his new experimentation with color, Jonathan is in a maroon crewneck and fitted black pants. The fine knit of the sweater outlines every scrumptious ridge of his chest and arms, and I can't help but ogle him as I step inside.

He does the same to me. "You always look good, but that top is something special," he says, helping me out of my jacket. His eyes linger an extra beat on the serpentine pendant that's resting between my breasts before he snaps to it. "Come on in. Want a tour?"

We're in a narrow foyer that leads past a set of stairs to a closed door beyond. Jonathan pauses with his hand on the railing. "That's the laundry room. Everything else is upstairs."

I follow him, taking care not to let my heels trip me up. He's telling me about the neighborhood when my eyes snag on his right hand where his thumb keeps worrying the wide silver band he always wears on his index finger. That knot of nerves that made me speed on the way here eases a bit. He's anxious, too.

We go all the way up to the third floor, where he shows me a small sitting area lined with full bookcases that leads onto a large, partially covered deck with views of endless rooftops, mature trees, and the occasional church. Somewhere in the distance is Puget Sound, and beyond that, the Olympic Range. "Putting this roof here was the best decision I ever made," he says. "The only time I'm not out here is when it's too cold for the heaters to make it comfortable. Other than that—rain, wind, sun, hail—this is my spot. Sometimes I even sleep out here in the summer."

"Over here?" I ask, sitting down in an upholstered lounge chair.

"Yup."

I stretch my legs out and try to picture him moon-gazing at night, sipping his coffee in the morning, and taking in the uneven roofline of the neighborhood. "Your love for open spaces—is that because of the claustrophobia?"

"Nah, I just like perspective and air."

I nod. I've always lived in places where the horizon was obstructed, but I could get used to a view like this. "It's lovely."

Back inside again, he points to the only other door on this floor. "My bedroom," he says, but then he heads toward the stairs.

"I can't see it?" I ask.

He turns, one foot on the step below. "It's not very interesting."

"Why don't you let me be the judge of that?"

He lets out an amused noise but then gestures toward the door. "Be my guest."

He's right behind me when I push the door open and turn on the light. The room is painted white, but most of the space on the wall behind his queen bed is taken up by black-and-white photographs in pewter frames. The bedding is also white, except for a loosely knit, multicolored throw at the foot of the bed that brings warmth to the masculine space.

"Like I said, not very interesting," he says, his hands snaking around my waist in a stealthy hug from behind.

It's our first physical contact since I got here, and paired with the amplified scent of him in this room, it takes effort not to drag him to bed this instant. "I beg to differ," I say, covering his hands with mine. "Did you take these pictures?" I free myself from the embrace out of pure self-preservation but hold on to his hand as I move deeper into the room.

"I did."

I take my time studying each and every one. Foggy forests, snowy tundra, stony mountains, a herd of elephants. "No people," I point out.

"Like I said."

I release his hand and go to examine his nightstand instead. He has two books in progress if the bookmarks are anything to go by—one about the UW rowing team in the 1930s Olympic Games and the other a memoir by a photographer I've never heard of. I pick it up and leaf through it. "You're a better photographer than her," I say as I put it down.

He chuckles. "I'm objectively not."

I run my palm over the colorful blanket on my way back to the door before doing another full turn of the room. "I subjectively disagree."

He pauses with his hand on the light switch. "Seen enough?"

Not nearly enough, but all in good time. I give him a cheeky smile as I pass him. "For now."

He doesn't miss a beat. "Came here with an agenda, did you?"

"I'm not the one who put clean sheets on my bed today."

"Ha! Fair point." He follows me down a flight of stairs.

"So let me guess," I say, standing at the landing. "If downstairs is for car and laundry, and upstairs is for sleeping and reading, this must be where you work, eat, and play."

"Excellent deductive reasoning, Ms. Watson." Jonathan opens a door to a room above the garage. "Office slash guest room." Then he points to a closed door in the hallway. "Bathroom." Rejoining me, he puts a hand to my back and steers me into the open kitchen and living room. "And I'm sure this is fairly self-explanatory."

I stop at the two-level island and put my bag down before proceeding into the living room where a grand piano takes up a quarter of the space. There's also a plush-looking couch, a media stand with a large TV, a vintage armchair in worn leather, and a coffee table. Again, the walls are full of photographs, but here, they're interspersed with other artwork.

I do a full lap while he watches me from his perch on a counter stool. The far wall has two large windows and a sliding door that leads to another deck that fits a small table and chairs and a grill that's currently smoking hot.

"I don't cook a ton in here, but I can do almost anything on the grill," he says. "Comes in handy when you're on assignment away from civilization. I hope you like salmon."

"Salmon is great." I throw him a quick smile before continuing my exploration. He has several large plants on the windowsills, meticulously cared for. I can't even keep a cactus alive, but he doesn't need to know that. I pick up a small frame with a photo of Jonathan and his dad laughing. His dad is in a uniform of some sort.

"What's your dad's name again?" I ask.

"Wayne."

"Wayne." I nod. "You look like him."

"Weathered and balding?"

"Why, yes, I thought that's what we agreed you see when you look in the mirror. Where's this taken?"

"Dad's retirement ceremony. He was a park ranger."

"So that's where you got your love for the outdoors." I set the frame down. "Are you just going to sit over there and stare at me? It could make a girl self-conscious, you know."

"Sorry, but I'm quite enjoying myself," he says, staying seated. "I haven't had guests in a long time."

"By guests do you mean women callers?" I stop at the piano and rest my hand on the lid. "Will you play for me later?"

"Any guests," he clarifies. "And yes, if you want me to."

"Good." I browse the prints on the final wall as I return to him, this time walking right up to where he's sitting, in between his knees. I rest my hands on his shoulders as his gaze roams my face. "I love your house," I say. "It's very..." For a moment, I struggle to find the right word. The space oozes comfort and style, but more than that, it's lived in and cared for. "Calming maybe? Welcoming."

He pulls me closer, his hands caressing my sides. "Thank you. Makes me wonder what you were expecting."

"A month ago, I might have said a dark cave. Blinds drawn round the clock. A dartboard with the faces of people who have wronged you above your bed."

He lets out a deep guffaw. "That's very specific. Though, to be fair, there are probably still a few people at work who'd say the same."

I shake my head and reach out to push back a wavy strand at his temple. "No, you're different now. And not just with me."

He captures my hand and brings it to his lips. The softness against my knuckles is mesmerizing. How the sensation expands up my arm. He hums a low note before he moves to get up. "I'd better put the food on the grill before it's too late."

I don't need to ask what he means.

Reluctantly, I get out of his way to allow him passage to the fridge, from which he produces several foil-wrapped parcels. He sets them on a tray. "Hold on, let me get my laptop, and you can look through the photos from yesterday while I take care of this."

Yesterday was the Samoyed photo shoot. The one I was banned from.

"Did everything go okay?" I call after him as he disappears into his office.

He returns with his laptop bag. "Oh yeah. Easy. I think you'll like them. The guy's name was Samuel, by the way. Samuel, not Sam. I got several reminders."

"Because his dog is Sam." I roll my eyes. "Way to make things confusing, guy."

"Here you go." Jonathan turns the screen my way and puts a folded paper next to it. "His form. I'll be back in a few."

"Great." I tuck it into my bag so I won't forget and then turn my attention to the screen.

It's soon apparent that Jonathan has outdone himself with this photo shoot. It rained most of the day yesterday, but luckily, they must have found a brief reprieve. Against a backdrop of dark green pines and the still waters of a lake that breathes wisps of fog straight out of a fairy tale, Sam's white coat stands out in stark contrast to the gray rocks at the water's edge. Samuel is in the water behind him, dressed in fisherman's pants that go to his waist and are held up by suspenders, and nothing else. The whole series of photos is remarkable. The way the Samoyed's attention moves between his owner and the water, Samuel's muscles shifting as he adjusts the fishing pole—it's a vignette of Pacific Northwest solitude. A true tribute to man's relationship with nature.

Which is good for me because now that Jude is for sure

moving, I'll soon be out a place to stay whether I get the new job or not. Now, more than ever, I need to win this thing!

I'm still staring at my favorite in the series when Jonathan returns, tray held aloft.

"I think that's the best one," he says. "You like?"

I close the laptop and watch as he opens the steaming foil packs with quick fingers to skirt the heat. "Remind me again why you don't do this full-time?"

He looks up. "Cook?"

"Take pictures. You're so good. The world is missing out."

"The world?" A glint of amusement beneath that serious brow.

"It's been years," I say, careful not to step in it. "Surely there must be other opportunities out there by now. You don't want to do web design, and this"—I tap the laptop—"is your fricking calling."

Jonathan turns to get two plates out of a cabinet. "Tell you a secret," he says as he plates our food. Salmon with slices of lemon, and skewers with tiny onions, mushrooms, and other veggies I can't immediately identify. He hands me a bottle of Viognier and two glasses. "You take these. I thought we'd eat outside. The grill warms the deck."

I follow him through the living room. "That's the secret?"

"No." He sets his cargo down on the small table and then gestures for me to sit before he pours the wine. "The secret is that, before you came along and 'forced' this project on me, I hadn't picked up my camera since everything went to shit. And I thought I never would. It was collecting dust in my office closet."

I could feign surprise or ask why, but I think I already know, so instead I say, "That's a long time."

"I told myself I didn't miss it."

"And now?"

He gestures to my plate. "Now we eat, and you have permission to gloat about being the one who reminded me that I'm still a photographer at heart."

"Oh, come on. I'm not going to gloat." I pick up my fork and dig into salmon so tender and flaky I already know it will melt in my mouth. "At least not much. Can't help that I'm good at not taking no for an answer."

"Yes, you are very determined." Beneath the table, his foot comes to rest against mine.

"I doubt you mind." I extend my leg so my bare calf meets the smooth fabric of his jeans.

"Never said I do."

His burning gaze challenges me, a continuation of our verbal sparring that makes me forget how to eat. The forkful that was on its way to my mouth halts in the air and then lowers back to my plate.

"You need to stop looking at me like that," I mumble, averting my gaze. "Or you will have cooked for nothing."

"What way?" He lifts his glass, feigning innocence.

"Like I'm the meal."

"Maybe I can't help it."

As if he's a magnet, my attention snaps back to his face. His pupils are dilated, his lips slightly parted. For a long moment, the unspoken promise of more to come hovers between us, until he picks up his cutlery again and uses them to point to my plate. "But fair enough, you should eat. Omega-3 is good for you."

"So thoughtful." I take a big bite of salmon and bell peppers to settle my smile.

The rest of the meal we chat about his first piano performance (he was eight and the sheet music fell off the stand), my first slalom competition (I was seven and nerves made me forget to turn), and family in general.

"Wayne sounds like a great dad," I say after Jonathan has regaled me with stories of their adventures together. After Wayne retired and before his eyes got bad, he'd sometimes accompany Jonathan on assignments.

"He is." Jonathan finishes the wine in his glass. The sun has set, but the light from inside illuminates his earnest aspect when he asks, "Is it weird that I'd like him to meet you?"

It should be. I dated Chris for two years and never once met his parents. But haven't I also entertained the idea of Jude and Jonathan getting along? Yes, it's futile and whatnot. In a few months, none of us will be in the same place, but still... "Not that weird. I'd like to meet him, too."

"Maybe we'll make it happen." He leans forward as he stands and gathers his plate and silverware. "Head inside?"

"Sure." I follow his example. "I believe I was promised musical entertainment."

"No dessert?"

"I'm sure we can fit that in, too. Dinner was delicious, by the way. Thank you."

He glances at me over his shoulder, a flash of delight brightening his face as if he's not used to such compliments. "You're welcome."

While he tidies up in the kitchen, I kick off my heels and sit down on his comfortable couch. He moves differently here than at work. Nothing is hurried, yet every motion is fluid and intentional. Efficient. I scold myself again for having misjudged him in the beginning.

"Coffee?" he asks. "Or more wine?"

"Coffee, please." I fully intend to stay on the sober side tonight. No more half-assed recollections. If he takes that maroon sweater off at some point, I'm going to memorize every swoop of muscle, every smattering of hair, and exactly what parts of him respond best to my touch.

"Um, maybe you should stop looking at me that way," he says from the kitchen.

I grin. Stealing my words, is he? "Or what?"

He turns on the coffee maker. "Or I might be too busy hiking you over my shoulder and carrying you upstairs to play for you."

My stomach clenches deliciously at this promise disguised as a threat. "Oh no," I say. "I'd better be careful, then."

He opens the fridge to get creamer, which he sets on the counter. "You're still looking."

I flip my hair with a coy tip of the head. "That's me. Living on the edge."

He laughs as he rounds the counter and walks past me. "Nice try." Finally, he sits down on the piano bench and rolls his shoulders back. His eyes rest on me above the body of the beautiful instrument. "So, what do you want me to play? Do you have any favorites?"

I nestle deeper into the cushions. "I'd rather hear your favorites."

There's no hesitation before a tranquil chord rings out, followed by a complex trill at the high register of the piano. I let the notes carry me as the music swells and dips. His hands chase each other across the keys, one moment in a rhythmical flurry, another in soothing repose. I don't recognize the tune, so when the final rise and fall fades and Jonathan comes back to reality, I ask him the name of the song.

"It doesn't have a name," he says. "It's just something I've been working on lately."

I gape at him. "You made it up?"

He shrugs. "Sometimes I find it easier to express myself through music. It makes whatever goes on here"—he touches his temple—"more tangible."

I get up and walk over to him. Press a key down so a low note gongs from inside the piano. "Give me an example."

He plays a high key that corresponds to mine, glancing up at me with a smile. "Like after I lost my job, I played a lot of stuff like…" He hammers down the keys in a few measures of a familiar classical tune. "Really anything—I'm happy, I'm sad, I'm tired. There are melodies for everything. I sit down, I play, and when I get up again, I've put it all out there. Does that make sense?"

"Each song is a piece of you," I say, moving behind him to rest my hands on his shoulders. "What would a song about me sound like?" I ask, my thumbs idle on either side of his spine.

He leans into my touch. "You're putting me on the spot?"

"Mm-hmm."

He runs a hand through his hair before patting the narrow space on the bench next to him. "Come sit."

I do, and I like that we're pressed shoulder to shoulder, my arm, hip, and leg lighting up with awareness of him.

"A song about Holly," he says in a low voice. He lets one finger drag across the fabric of my skirt from my knee to my hip almost absent-mindedly as he lifts his hands to the keys.

My breath snags on an intake.

The first chord is bright but with a rumbling, deep undertone. Jonathan looks at me as if waiting for a reaction. I hold his gaze as he moves into the next chord and the next. Then he hits his stride, and his eyelids fall shut.

This melody is contradicting and wholly different than the other song he played. Pulsing rhythms drive a sometimes uplifting, sometimes contemplative tune that I feel from my toes to the top of my head. Goose bumps break out on my arms, my pulse quickens, and when the song reaches its crescendo, my hand comes down in a tight grip on Jonathan's thigh with no conscious intention.

His playing ends abruptly, and before I have a chance to say anything about it, he's spun me up to stand in front of him, his knees framing my legs, his hands at my waist. He looks up at me, his chest rising and falling as if struggling with what comes next even though we both know what's about to happen. We knew it before he invited me over here tonight.

It's time to finish what we started in that deserted office rec room.

Days until printer deadline: 7

With a firm grip on my waist, Jonathan pushes me back toward the piano keys, a move that lets out a dissonant jumble of notes. He buries his face against my stomach, his breath hot through my top. My fingers are already nestled in his hair, and when he starts kissing his way up to where the V neckline meets my sternum and reaches bare skin, I tug at it out of pure elation.

He looks up at me, his gaze hooded with want. I caress the side of his face and his jaw, keeping his head tilted back so I can commit every angle and curve of his features to memory the way I've promised myself I would.

He strokes down my hips and thighs, hooking his fingers under the hem of my skirt and yanking it upward to more atonal accompaniment. I gasp and then wiggle to allow the fabric's ascent up my legs.

"Was this part of the song?" I ask, my voice breathy but steadier than I thought it would be.

He looks down, letting his whole palm caress the inside of my bare thigh from where my legs meet down toward my knee.

He kneads the skin there briefly before running his knuckles up my other thigh, stopping short of where a flood of warmth is currently making it difficult for me to stay still.

"No, I've decided to add a new verse. It's goes like this." His thumbnail traces the hemline of my panties up toward my hip, and then he stands, molding himself to me as his hand grips my bunched skirt.

I push off the keys as best I can to reach his mouth, devouring it in a frantic kiss that I hope reflects exactly what I think about his improvisation skills. Such a gifted musician.

He slides a palm under the fabric covering my ass to press us even closer. Hikes my leg up for a moment. He's hard and straining against his jeans, and I grind against him without shame while sucking his lower lip in between my teeth. This has been a long time coming. No pun intended.

"Phones on mute, right?" Jonathan murmurs against my neck. His touch is growing greedier by the second, roaming anywhere and everywhere all at once. Leave it to a piano player to span every octave of my body in less than a count of four.

"I turned mine off on the way here," I pant as he caresses my top off my shoulders and down my arms, sending it to join my skirt at my waist.

"Smart," he says, leaning back in seeming confusion. "No bra?"

"It would show under this top."

Satisfied with the answer, he returns his full attention to my chest, grazing soft thumb pads across my nipples. He grunts deep in his throat when they tighten further. When he ends with a cheeky pinch, it sends a flash of lightning straight to my sex that makes my hips jerk toward him. I try to kiss him again, but he captures my face in his hands and holds me still, scanning my flushed skin as if searching for something hidden beneath it.

"Are you sure about this?" he asks. "If it makes things too complicated, I…"

"I can handle complicated," I say in a rush. "We need this. Or at least I do."

My assurance settles it.

"Hell yeah, we do." His lips crash to mine as he lifts me up.

I wrap my legs around him and cling to his shoulders as he maneuvers us out from the tight space between the piano and bench and toward the stairs. This need is new to me, an edgy seasoning to a dish that's already appetizing. I can't get enough.

Jonathan makes as if he's about to carry me upstairs, but I have no patience for that.

"I'll walk. It's faster," I say in a rush as I release the grip my thighs have on him and slide off his body. In response to his approving grin, I grip the front of his sweater and pull him forward and up in a stumbling dash to get to his bedroom.

We're both breathing heavily as he spins my back to the wall outside his door. He dives for my breasts, licking and stroking, before coming up for another breathless helping of my lips.

I tug at his sweater in an attempt to get it over his head. He retreats only long enough to help, and then he's on me again. His skin is a hot novelty against mine, and I can't help but dig my nails into his back to get him closer.

"I need to taste you," he murmurs near my ear as one of his hands finds its way down between my legs. "All of you. Please."

I jolt at his touch, my head tipping back. "Yes," I breathe. "Yes, please."

He picks me up again, and seconds later, I'm surrounded by

pillows on his bed. I try to sit up, reaching for his belt, but he prompts me back down and undoes it himself. His jeans and boxers are soon around his ankles and...there he is. Jonathan Summers in the nude.

I prop myself up on my elbows for a front-row seat to the show as he kicks his clothes to the side and prowls closer. Everything about him is mouthwatering, from the trim muscles to the dark hair smattered across his chest and down the middle of his abdomen to his eager dick.

"Let's get these off," he says, crawling over me to pull my shirt up and my skirt down. His hard length drags along the outside of my thigh, making promises I sure hope it can keep.

Once my belly is free of fabric, he runs his palm across it and down over the lace of my panties. I'm ready for him right now, but he has other ideas as he follows with his mouth and nose, nuzzling into the crook of my hip. The onslaught of desire coursing through me makes it impossible to stay balanced on my arms any longer, so I collapse onto the bed, closing my eyes to the overwhelming sensation of his breath right where I want it most.

"Fuck," I moan as he moves my panties to the side and his tongue makes contact. "Stop, I'm going to come. I don't want to yet." It's infuriating how trigger-happy he makes me.

He doesn't share my concern, though. He lifts his head and looks up at me, his eyes dark and yearning. "Why not? I want you to feel good." His strong hands dig into my hips before sliding up to my waist and back. He kisses the inside of my thigh and then nips the skin with his teeth. "Don't you want more?" He runs the back of his finger down my slick crease, pausing there for consent.

My body approves before I have a chance to say anything,

my hips moving up to meet his touch. "Yes," I hiss as his finger enters me and his mouth joins the cause again.

I'm a writhing mess beneath his touch, and soon, I'm too far gone to stop the wave of pleasure crashing over me. He rides out the tremors with me, murmuring encouraging sentiments against my skin that prolong the ride. This makes two times he's gotten me off without asking for anything for himself. Time for me to make this good for him, too.

"I need you," I whisper, beckoning him up to me.

He pulls off my panties and covers my body with his, rolling us until I'm on top and he can squeeze my ass to his heart's content. He's so hard against my belly that, to my surprise, a fresh wave of desire makes my core clench. I push myself up to sitting and look down at him sprawled against the white bedding. My hands drag across his ribs, up his chest, to his shoulders, and down his arms. Then I lean down and take his lips in a gentler kiss than what we've clambered for so far. I trace the seam of his mouth, satisfied at the huff of air that escapes him when I do. He opens for me, inviting me in, and together we tangle in a succulent dance of lips, tongues, and teeth until our bodies start moving of their own accord, wanting more.

"I need to be inside you," Jonathan pants when I sit back up. "You're so..." He grasps his shaft and tilts his head back. "There are condoms in the nightstand. Please."

Thank goodness since I left my bag downstairs. I find one and return to my perch within seconds, my body thrumming with unexpected, renewed appetite. I bat his hands away and grip his length to roll on the prophylactic, satisfied with how he twitches and strains toward me as I do. As soon as it's on, I move up his body, and, supporting myself on his chest, guide him to my opening.

His hands roam from my waist to my breasts and back down as if not sure if he wants to speed this up or enjoy the scenery. Right then our eyes catch. We're sweaty, ruffled, and out of breath, but in that moment, something, maybe some intangible connection between us, makes us both smile. It's a sort of calm before the storm as he reaches for my cheek, and I kiss his palm.

Then I start to lower myself onto him, and any composure we have left crumbles.

I've made do with vibrators for a good long time, so Jonathan inside me is a revelation. Breathing hard, I pause at the base to allow my body to adjust. Jonathan's fingers dig into my thighs, and I can feel him throbbing inside me.

"Sorry in advance. This will probably be fast and furious," he grunts. "Damn, you feel good."

Encouraged by his enthusiasm, I rise up a little and then sit back down. My chin falls to my chest as the tension starts building again. This is very unlike me.

"I'm not kidding, Holly," Jonathan says, taking hold of my hips to encourage more movement. "I don't think I've ever been this turned on."

"How about now?" I ask, rising all the way up and coming down fast.

"Ah," he moans. "Yes. More."

I repeat the move, and it's not long before my own need for rhythm takes over any desire to tease, and I begin to ride him in earnest.

"Holy shit," I pant. "I'm going to come again."

"Yes, do it," he says as my body starts trembling. He holds me seated on top of him, leveraging his hips to keep the motion up as I fall apart for the second time tonight. But this time, he's right there with me, grunting out his own climax as I clench and quiver around him. In a head-spinning move, he flips me onto my back and drives into me once, twice, three more times as if to ensure there'll be no craving left to satisfy, and then he collapses on top of me, his heart hammering against my chest.

As the aftershocks subside, I gradually become aware of the rumble of the furnace kicking in, the light pattering of raindrops on the roof above us, and the spring-like scent of the sheets surrounding us, mixing with that of warm, satiated bodies. I run ghosting nails up and down Jonathan's back that make him shiver and nip at my throat, which is where he currently rests his head.

I giggle but don't open my eyes, aware that this dreamy state we're in will be easier to hold on to if I don't move, don't look, don't speak. I don't even mind his weight crushing me into the mattress. I just want to stay here, in this perfect contentment.

But apparently, Jonathan is a gentleman who prefers his partners being able to breathe, so after a minute, he rolls off me and flips the comforter over our legs. I shift so we're facing each other and rest my cheek against my hands. He reaches for me, tracing the outlines of my features with the tip of his finger while his gaze delves deep into mine.

He exhales with a deep "phew," his teeth digging into his lower lip. Then he kisses me gently as if wanting to balance the frenzy from before. As soon as the tip of his tongue touches mine, I'm warm all over again, but this time I don't act on it.

"Are you good?" he asks, tucking his hands under his head, too.

I smile at him. "So good. You?"

He nods. "Will you stay over?"

There's a sizzle and pop in my belly. "If you want me to."

He wraps his left arm around my shoulder and pulls me close to his warm body. "Oh, I want you to. If you're not careful, I might never let you go." He kisses me on the forehead.

His choice of words causes a brief but sharp sting somewhere in the vicinity of my heart, but I choose to push it aside for now. Instead, I nuzzle my cheek to his chest and close my eyes again. We might need a few hours of sleep, but there will definitely be an encore at some point tonight.

Days until printer deadline: 6

I'm alone in bed when I wake up the next morning. Whiffs of something sweet and comforting drift through the half-open doorway, making my stomach rumble. I flip to my back and blink at the ceiling, every muscle in my body protesting in the best of ways. I had at least four orgasms last night. That's a new personal record. Granted, I had a couple of years to make up for.

I yawn and stretch like a cat, arching my back off the bed. Then I sit up and rub my eyes. Now that my senses are waking up, I make out faint notes of music coming from downstairs and the clanging of pans. A glance at my phone tells me it's almost ten o'clock. I also have a missed text from Jude: **Have you been kidnapped or was the date that good?**

I smile to myself. I should have texted him when I decided to stay over. I send him a brief, **The latter. I'm fine**, and then I pad across the floor to the bathroom as I pull my hair up in a messy bun.

My clothes from last night sit folded in a neat pile on a stool outside the shower, but what's even better are the sweatpants and T-shirt Jonathan has set out on top of them as an option. I take a quick shower, get dressed in his clothes, and head downstairs to investigate the lovely smell.

"Good morning." Jonathan greets me with a wide grin as he flips something in a pan on the stove. "I was about to come get you. I hope you like French toast."

"Love it." I go to him and nestle into his arms. "When did you get up?"

"Couple of hours ago."

"You should have woken me up."

He pushes a strand of hair that's escaped my bun off my temple and hums. "You looked so peaceful; I didn't want to disturb you. Plus, you definitely earned your rest last night." His mouth pulls sideways as his eyes glitter. "That was..."

"Amazing," I fill in, tipping my face up to his. Merely thinking of it makes my body alert again.

After a leisurely kiss, he untwines from our embrace. "Gotta flip these," he says. "Grab a plate. There's orange juice in the fridge, and I'll grab the coffee in a minute."

I do and sit down next to where his laptop is open on the counter. "You've been working?" I ask as he serves me two thick slices of gooey, cinnamon-dusted toast.

He sits and moves the syrup bottle within my reach. "I want to show you the images we have so far, see if you want any more tweaks. And don't hesitate to tell me if you do. I know you want the calendar to be as perfect as it can be." He doesn't look at me when he says it.

I watch his profile for a moment. "That's not a problem, right?" I ask. "That I want it to be perfect because I need to win this job?" Maybe it's a blunt question in light of the night we just shared, but it has to be asked. We both agreed we could handle "complicated," but I don't want either of us hurt. Whatever this is, it has an expiration date in the not-too-distant future, and we can't forget about that.

He looks up from the screen. "Of course not. Don't tell anyone, but I'm proud of these photos, and I've never been one to settle for less than perfection myself."

I search his expression for signs of something other than earnestness but find none. "Okay," I say. "Sorry, I didn't mean to kill the mood."

He leans his shoulder to mine. "That would take a lot more than fundraiser talk. I'm pretty sure this"—he waggles his finger between us—"is an unkillable mood, and if you let me know the minute you're done with breakfast, I will carry you to the couch over there and prove it to you."

His words fan the embers in my belly. "Yeah?"

"Oh yeah. We're good. But maybe we agree not to go there with, um, the rest of the stuff."

"Okay. Good. I like that." I have a bite of French toast, relishing how the cinnamon and maple syrup mix on my tongue. There has to be a way for us to enjoy whatever temporary thing this is. Maybe if we both are adults about it and say what's on our minds? I decide to give it a go. "Honestly, I just want to be with you while I can. Have some fun."

He nods. "Me too. No need to overanalyze and get all serious." His nose wrinkles.

"Right." I mimic his expression automatically, eager to move on from this corner of the conversation. I know I said it first, but there is a small part of me that still recognizes that his words don't go down as smoothly as I want them to.

Thankfully, that notion gets easier to ignore when he says, "And as promised, there is something we could do today to find more models. If you're free," he hurries to add. He types something on the computer and hits ENTER, but nothing happens. All we get is a spinning color wheel.

"Not again," he grunts. "Hold on, I need to reboot the router." He disappears into the office, returning moments later. "Sorry. It'll be a minute. My internet leaves a lot to be desired at times."

"No worries."

Finally, the page loads, and he shows me the screen.

"Bellevue dog adoption fair," I read out loud. "That's perfect."

"Yeah, I figured, since this week was stressful and we still have spots to fill before Friday."

As in, time is running out. As in, I'll hopefully be leaving Washington soon. Even though this isn't news, the realization sits jagged in my throat for a moment before I gulp it down. "Let's do it," I say, taking care to make my voice upbeat.

But first I want to see the photos. I have, of course, seen them before as part of his editing reels, but this is the first time I'm seeing them laid out as calendar pages. We've decided on a template to use that comes with the major holidays already listed, and with the professional images in place, my project comes to life.

Jonathan steps aside to let me flip between the pages, but his hand rests against my back as if to let me know he's still there. "I know you haven't decided which photo will be used for what month yet, so that's something that will change." He points.

But here they all are: Tank the Chihuahua at Kerry Park, Lucy the golden glowing at the beach at sunset, the bearlike Newfoundland in the woods, and the bonus Dalmatian, the beagle puppies that wrapped Jonathan around their tiny paws, and most recently the fishing Samoyed. Each image is stunning, and I keep clicking back and forth between them to choose a favorite.

"It's impossible," I say eventually. "I can't pick one. They're all so good." I tilt my face up to find him looking down at me.

He kisses my forehead. "Then I've done my job."

Jonathan gives me a head start so I can stop at home to change into my own clothes. Then he picks me up, and we head east across the bridge to Bellevue.

The adoption fair is sponsored by one of the big eastside shelters, and a crowd of people has already gathered in the parking lot of the church that's hosting it.

"So how many more do we need?" Jonathan asks as he parks. "I mean, I know we have six photographs so far, but you had some other guys lined up, too, right?"

"Yeah, Xander from the dating site is tomorrow, I rescheduled the vet for Wednesday after work, and then there's Nick the volleyball guy. I've not been able to confirm Dennis's gym buddy yet, but that will most likely also be Wednesday but during the day. That leaves another two."

"We're cutting it close."

"I know." I unbuckle my seat belt and look at him. "But thanks for saying 'we.'"

He reaches for the handle. "I guess we'll have to make today count."

He comes around to my side of the car, and together we approach the crates, kennels, and pens set up beneath white party canopies all around. The adoptions are already in progress with excited prospective owners being interviewed and signing forms. There are dogs of all ages, colors, demeanors, and sizes. Something for everyone.

We've barely entered the fray when Jonathan grabs my hand and squeezes. It could be to ensure that we don't get separated, but I prefer to think he does it on impulse simply because he wants to. It's different than being at his place because here I can see us reflected in the other people milling about us. Can see what they see. To them, we're no different than any other couple browsing for new family members on this overcast October Saturday.

What if you were? my brain asks unprompted. *Would that be so bad?*

The vision appears fully formed before I can stop it. Jonathan and I waking up together on some future weekend morning in tangled sheets, except it's my place, too. My books in his bookcase, my clothes in his closet. Our closet. We'd roll out of bed, have breakfast, read a bit maybe, or go back to bed. We'd go for walks at Alki holding hands, and at some point, there might be a smaller version of him or me swinging between us or searching for shells on the beach. I see family dinners, vacations, celebrations, funny inside jokes, deep conversations, fights and makeups. A life.

"Holly?" Jonathan tugs on my hand to make me stop. "Where did you go just now?"

I blink the vision away, glad to see it dissipate. It must be the lack of sleep playing tricks on me because I know that's not in the cards for us. That it's not the path I'm on now. I need to get as far away from Washington and my past as I can to start afresh without the implosion of my legal career weighing me down, and this GCL opportunity is the solution. This is my lucky break, and I'd be foolish to jeopardize that. "What?" I ask.

"I said, look at that one." He nods to a crate where a large dog sits observing the passersby with big, droopy brown eyes. "He kind of looks like my dad. Poor buddy." Jonathan releases my hand and crouches by the crate. Instantly, the dog sidles up as if pleading for pets. "What's your name, bud?" Jonathan asks. "Aw, you're a good one, aren't you? Just want some ear scratches."

"I see you've met Sir Leonard," an older woman says on the other side of the crate. "He's our senior boy, part Leonberger, part Lab we think."

Jonathan offers her a smile as he stands. "So sweet. I'm not really looking, though."

"Maybe your wife can convince you?" She winks at me, and there's that vision again.

"Oh, we're not married," I say, mentally shrugging off an image of Jonathan and me opening gifts in front of a Christmas tree. *What the heck?*

"Sorry. Girlfriend, then." She beams at me while offering Sir Leonard a treat.

Jonathan peers at me with an amused twinkle in his eyes, unbothered by the woman's mistake. "Thanks for the look," he tells her. "But we should keep moving."

"Unless..." I say. "You don't happen to know anyone here who might want to model for a good cause?" I explain the calendar to her. "We could even mention the shelter in the caption if it worked out." I look to Jonathan for confirmation that would be okay, and he nods.

The woman's forehead creases as she thinks. "The only one I can think of is Shawn. He's over there by the Aussie puppies." She points toward the fence at the back of the lot.

"Great." I start walking, but Jonathan lingers, making me turn.

He gives Sir Leonard a final pet. "I hope he finds a home," he says.

The woman shrugs. "You know how it is. These older dogs... It's hard."

"Yeah." He backs away. "Sorry."

The Aussie pen is a circus when we get there. A toddler has found the hinged gate and crawled inside, and his mother is chasing him around, a feat that is greatly impaired by six adorable fluff balls circling her feet for attention. All the while, the man I assume is Shawn narrates the show as if he's the ringmaster and the woman and toddler the clowns being bested by ferocious(-ly cute) beasts.

"I know we run the most *pup*-ular show in town," he yells into a pretend microphone that upon closer inspection is a tall energy drink can—which explains a lot. "Are you all catching this *paw*-some *paw*-ty?"

The crowd cheers, and the woman inside the pen laughs, a good sport in a situation where many would be flustered. I'm sure it helps that her kid wears the expression of someone who's found the gold at the end of the rainbow or whatever the toddler equivalent of that is.

"We have to let the pups rest, honey," she cajoles. "Come on, let's get you a snack."

The kid evades her and giggles, dodging left and right between the puppies.

"Those two are going through some *ruff* times, don't you think?" Shawn continues. "What do you say, should I help them?"

"Please," the woman huffs through a smile, two puppies gnawing at her pants.

"I guess that's it, folks." Shawn sets down the can and steps inside the pen. It takes him ten seconds to scoop up the puppies so that the woman can do the same to her now-incensed kid. "I hope you've had a *fur*-iously fun time. If you're interested in bringing one of these cuties home, come see one of our staff members in the back."

Jonathan leans close to me and whispers, "If I ever start talking like that, please smother me in my sleep."

Ignoring the fact that "ever" suggests a long time into the future, I quip, "Yeah, you'd be in the *doghouse* for sure."

He gapes at me and groans. "Not you too."

I seize the opportunity granted by his proximity and give him a quick kiss on the lips. "That's the only one I've got. Promise. Come on, let's go talk to the pun man."

It's a lengthy wait until the prospective dog owners drawn in by the show have had their turn, but when we're finally up, Shawn shoots us down before we've even had a chance to explain the cause benefiting from the calendar.

"No can do," he says. "Traumatic yearbook experiences. I'm not ever giving anyone another public chance at drawing mustaches on this." He indicates his face. "Next!"

Jonathan and I move to the side to allow others to approach.

"So much for that," Jonathan says. "Sorry."

But then a sixty-plus guy with a full, silver beard and Sean Connery vibes comes up behind Jonathan. "Excuse me," he says. "Are people like me welcome in this calendar of yours? I've just adopted the mama of those little ones, and I'd be interested in learning more if you'd have me. I was the face of Sterling Jumpsuits back in the eighties if you believe it, so I know something about being in front of a camera. Met my wife that way and everything." His bright blue eyes gleam at what must be a fond memory.

Jonathan and I look at each other, a silent agreement passing between us.

"As long as you're available this week, we'd be happy to have you," I say. "I'm Holly, and this is Jonathan, the photographer."

"George." He extends his hand, and we shake, with me ticking another model box in my mind with a flourish. Only one to go.

And while George and Pepper turn out to be our only successful recruits when the fair is said and done, that still puts me one step closer to finishing this thing.

One step closer to kilts and haggis.

Days until printer deadline: 5

"It's raining."

I wake to Jonathan's whispered weather report against my shoulder, his finger tracing the vertebrae of my neck.

"All the more reason to sleep in," I mumble into the pillow even as my body comes alive at his touch.

"We did sleep in. It's almost eleven o'clock."

"It is?" I flip to my back.

He's smiling down at me. "No, it's nine thirty, but I know you don't like sleeping the day away so... good morning."

I grunt at this unfortunate truth. Jonathan's bed is so comfortable, and the steady patter of rain outside could relax the most highly strung type A person, but tomorrow is Monday, which means my alarm will go off at 5:55, and we have photo shoot number seven this afternoon. I really shouldn't linger.

"You've closed your eyes again," he says somewhere nearby. "Does that mean we can stay in bed?"

"No." I reach for him without looking and pull him to me. He doesn't object as he rests his cheek against my shoulder and huffs out a small laugh.

The rain increases in intensity, creating an incessant *whoosh* against the siding of the house that surely will forgive another indulgent half hour. His wayward morning hair tickles my nose, so I smooth it away, my hand coming to rest on his shoulder. The weight of him anchors me to the soft mattress so that only my mind is free to drift.

"Hey. Sleepyhead." This time Jonathan's voice is right near my ear.

"Mm-hmm."

"It's ten fifteen. We should get up."

"What?" I open my eyes, yawn, and stretch. The rain is still pouring down outside, but the sliver of light visible between the curtain and the wall is brighter than before. "Is your bed some sort of wormhole in the time-space continuum?"

"Yup." He pushes off the bed, jostling me in the process. Wearing nothing but black boxer briefs, he rounds the bed and peeks out the window. "Ugh. What time is the photo shoot?"

I sit up and reach for my phone on the nightstand. "I think we said three. Do we need to reschedule?" We're meeting Xander and his dog in Green Lake Park for a shoot, but if the weather isn't cooperating…

"Maybe. Does it say when the rain will stop?" Jonathan sits down on my side of the bed and puts one of my legs in his lap.

I open the weather app to check as I hook both legs around his waist and try to pull him closer to me. He obliges until he's close enough that we can both see the screen.

"It says it'll end around three. I'll text him and see if we can move it to four."

Jonathan waits while I do. Then he takes my phone from me. "Does that mean we can stay in bed another couple of hours?"

"You're not done sleeping? It's almost ten thirty."

He runs his hands up my thighs. "Who said anything about sleeping?"

"I think rain is my new favorite weather," I tell Jonathan hours later as I maneuver around bicyclists and construction trucks on our way east toward Green Lake. The afternoon sun is bravely breaking through the receding rain clouds, making the changing leaves above sparkle like jewels, but the street gutters are still overflowing after the deluge.

Jonathan glances at me from the passenger seat, the window open behind him. "Let me guess. It's because the air smells incredible afterward. Or wait, I know—it's because you like plants, and plants need water."

I slap him lightly on the leg. "Like you don't know it's because of all those things we just did in your bed. And in the shower."

"Oh that." He braids our fingers together. "Yeah. You're right. That was better than plants." His grin is wide enough that I catch it out of the corner of my eye. "And you know what else is great? We're in the Pacific Northwest—the rainiest corner of the US of A. How lucky is that?"

I laugh. Lucky indeed. At least for a little longer. I squeeze his hand tighter.

Say what you want about rain, but the aftermath has the potential for spectacular footage. With the canopy above us shimmering gold and bronze, and the lake in the background a perfect mirror, we start setting up. Since Xander wants his prosthetic leg in the picture, we've decided on an action shot with him running on his blade. He and Milton both seem pumped when they show up. High energy. Smiles all around.

FINDING MR. JULY

After Jonathan has done a few light tests, he calls Xander over for a rundown of what needs to happen. Milton sits patiently at Xander's feet while they talk, his ears flopping up and down with a life of their own as if he, too, is taking directions. Starting over there? Left ear up, right ear down. Run to that boulder? Both ears up, head cocked left. Pause, then run back the other way? Left ear down, head cocked right.

"Does he understand what we're saying?" I ask Xander. "His expressions are so human."

"Who knows?" Xander smiles. "He's certainly smarter than many people I know."

We're about to start the shoot when a group of senior power walkers approaches, and since we're taking up a bit of the paved path, we're forced to wait until they pass.

While we do so, Jonathan explains to me what he does differently for motion and still shoots, so initially, we don't notice one of the walkers separating from the group and approaching us.

I look up first and greet the older man with a questioning smile. To my surprise, he puts a finger to his lips and sets aim for Jonathan, hunching his tall frame.

I'm about to call out a warning when the man jumps in front of the lens Jonathan is looking through, making him startle.

"Haha! Got you there, son," the man says with a smug grin. He has deep crow's feet behind his round glasses and a neat, silver-heavy beard.

Son?

Jonathan blinks a few times. "Dad?" He looks around. "What the heck are you doing here?"

"I'm with my walking group. It's Sunday."

This seems to compute for Jonathan. "Ah, that's right. But you usually walk in the mornings."

"Too wet today." He looks at me and then asks Jonathan, "Are you going to introduce us or what?"

Jonathan blinks another few times before getting it together. "Right. Sorry, Dad this is my Hol— I mean my colleague Holly King. Holly, this is my dad, Wayne."

Wayne extends his hand, and we shake.

"Very nice to meet you," I say.

Wayne gives his son a pointed look. "And you as well, my dear. I believe I've heard your name mentioned once or twice." Another smile pulls at the corner of his mouth.

Jonathan's eyes widen. "Dad..."

"So tetchy, that one." Wayne hikes his thumb toward Jonathan. "'Artistic sensibilities' they said when he was little."

"Oh really?" I grin at Jonathan, who rolls his eyes. "Why am I not surprised?"

Wayne nods. "Once he cried because the color of the sky wasn't the same as the crayon in his box."

"Okay, okay." Jonathan puts his hands up. "This has been fun, but we're working here so..."

"So I should get going?" Wayne asks. "Nah, I'd love to see one of these calendar shoots. Ruthie!" he calls to the group. "You all go on without me. It's my son." He points to Jonathan. "I'll see you later!" He shoves his hands into the pockets of his navy jacket and rocks back on his heels, looking from his son to me. "So, what are you all doing here?"

Jonathan has no other choice than to proceed as planned. To help, I take Wayne aside so Jonathan can focus.

Xander and Milton do run after run in front of the camera, never losing steam. Jonathan tweaks little things each time—if Milton should be to the left or right of Xander. How far forward Xander should extend his arms. Their speed.

We've been watching in silence for ten minutes when Wayne turns to me. "I want you to know that I'm very grateful you made him do this," he says. "This man…" He nudges a finger toward Jonathan. "I haven't seen him in a very long time. I've missed him."

His words stump me for a moment.

"Now try one where you're running toward me," Jonathan tells Xander.

"Honestly?" I keep my eyes on Jonathan while addressing Wayne. "It was purely selfish. I needed him for this project."

"To win the fundraiser—yes, I know." Wayne pulls off his Seahawks beanie and runs a palm over his closely cropped gray hair before putting it back on. "And I'm telling you that doesn't matter. His hand needed to be forced. You're the one who did the forcing. Credit where credit is due."

Ten yards away, Jonathan yells, "And go!" snapping away as Xander and Milton jog toward him. "That was great," he says with a smile. "Again."

"That smile…I'd forgotten what he looked like happy. I'm not joking, dear. And you'll have to forgive an old man for oversharing. I'm sure Jon would have my head if he heard me."

"I won't tell." I give Jonathan a thumbs-up from afar. "And I'm glad," I tell Wayne.

"You see the change, too, right?"

"I do."

Finally, Jonathan is satisfied and returns to us, flipping through the images. "Want to see?" he asks me.

"Always."

"How did we do?" Xander asks as they join us.

Jonathan shows him, too.

We agree our favorite photo is one where Milton looks like

he's flying. His tongue is flopping out the side of his mouth, his ears stand straight up, and all four of his paws are off the ground. Next to Xander's running blade, it has a futuristic feel that's artsier than the other photos. We won't put it in the calendar because those photos need to match in tone, but I promise to send him this one so he can blow it up and frame it.

Once they're gone and we start packing up, Wayne still holds on to the camera.

"They're really rather spectacular, son," he says. "Glad to see it's still in you."

"Thanks, Dad."

"The calendar is coming together, then?" Wayne asks me.

"Better than I hoped."

"She'll win for sure," Jonathan says.

"And then you'll be gone." Wayne eyes me carefully.

I force a smile. "That's the plan."

Wayne is quiet for a moment. "And then what?" he asks no one in particular.

Jonathan and I both stop what we're doing.

"What do you mean?" Jonathan asks.

Wayne tuts. "I may be old, but I'm not daft. You like each other, yes?"

My face flushes as I meet Jonathan's eyes.

"Let's not go there, Dad," Jonathan says, a warning edge to his voice.

Wayne draws himself up to his full height, which is only fractionally shorter than his son's. "Why not?"

"Because it's complicated," I offer.

"We know what we're doing," Jonathan says. "And it's no one's business but Holly's and mine. She'll win, and she'll move away. We know this. We're both adults."

Wayne stares at him. "And you're fine with that?"

Jonathan runs a hand across his forehead. "Why are we even talking about this? People leave all the time. I'm kind of used to it by now if you didn't know."

I flinch at the bitterness in his voice, and he notices.

"Sorry," he says. "I didn't mean..."

"It's okay." I force a reassuring smile as much for myself as it is for him. Maybe we do need to talk about this more because I have no intention of being lumped in with his mom and ex.

"It's not like there's anything major holding you to this job," Wayne mutters.

"No?" Jonathan frowns. "How are you getting home from here? Oh, that's right. I'll drive you. Like I do basically any time you need to go places. Happily. You need me here."

"I got a ride with Ruthie earlier."

"Not to mention I still can't travel. I'd say that's a solid reason to stay put."

"There are things you could—"

Jonathan puts his hand up. "Please stop." Then in a softer voice, he says, "I know you mean well, but Holly and I aren't worried about these things, so you shouldn't be either. We're fine."

All I can think as I'm watching their argument is that I'm undeniably not fine. I want to be fine. And I feel like I should be fine. Jonathan is right—he and I have agreed to make this as uncomplicated as it can be. And yet, is it so much to ask that he would entertain possibilities if only for a minute? Think about what could be? The speed with which he jumps at settling for the status quo makes my chest constrict.

But I also know I'm not being fair. The place we're in won't stand for demands, and I know that. If anything, he needs me on his side right now, so I make sure we're shoulder to shoulder physically at least when I smile at Wayne.

"We only just met," I tell him. "We're working well together, and we're enjoying getting to know each other. Sometimes it's nice not to dwell too much on the past or the future. I wasn't always good at that. That's why I'm gunning for this new start, a more worthwhile purpose to focus on."

"But what gives life more meaning than—"

"Dad!"

Wayne's lips remain parted as if he wants to say more, but one look at Jonathan and he clamps them shut. "Sorry," he says instead. "I'm out of line. I'll be quiet."

Jonathan relents. "No harm done, old man. Right, Holly?"

"Of course," I say. "Why don't we pack up, and I'll drive you guys home?"

"See, I'm not reliant on you driving me," Wayne quips to Jonathan as we start walking to the car. "There are plenty of chauffeurs in the sea."

I don't point out that his argument is flawed since this particular chauffeur soon won't be available. Instead, I take Jonathan's hand across the console and try hard to live up to my earlier aspirations of being present in the moment.

Days until printer deadline: 4

A front rolls in overnight, bringing unseasonably warm temperatures and predicted thunderstorms for later. The clouds are low and gray, the air dense and charged around me as I drive to work with the windows down, and at first, I blame that for the sense of unease nagging at me.

I sit down at my desk and open my laptop. According to my schedule, I'm with Rachel in one of her educational conference calls today where she's teleconferencing in as a guest lecturer at UC Berkeley. That should still give me plenty of time to get the data entry on my plate done and to tweak the copy about my fundraiser for the back of the calendars.

Jonathan is going to handle the photo shoot with George from the adoption fair tonight since I have to take Ava to tennis practice. Or, I don't have to—I've volunteered with the ulterior motive of asking her coach if he'll pose for the calendar. Apparently, he has two bulldogs. But if he says no and I still can't reach Dennis's friend, I could be in a bind. Is that what's bothering me?

I go make myself a cup of coffee, telling myself I've got

everything under control. Stir in sweetener, add a new stack of napkins from the cabinet to the counter because it's running low, wander over to the window, and take a sip. The first big raindrop lands on the glass with a splat, then another. No, there's something else churning inside me. Something I can't put my finger on.

"What are you looking at?" Rachel says, joining me to peer out across the gloomy city.

"Nothing." I turn around and lean against the windowsill. "Spacing out. I'm trying to remember... something."

"My birthday is not until December."

I smile. "Noted."

"I booked a room for the call at nine thirty. See you there in a bit."

Watching her walk away makes me realize I do have one more person I could ask about the calendar. Her first choice, and my last. I pull out my phone and open my thread with Jude. Maybe it's time to get over myself.

I have a big favor to ask, I type. **Still need a couple more models. Will you please be one of them?**

His response is immediate. **Is my daughter speaking to me?**

I grimace. **Still holding a grudge. Please.**

No. But ballsy to ask for my help. 👍

Well, it was worth a shot.

Staying busy helps take my mind off the proverbial red bow around my finger. Rachel's call is both interesting and valuable for my (possible) future role, so I take a lot of notes, and my copy for the calendar only needs a few revisions before I'm satisfied.

Just before lunch, I'm making my way through the data entry when a shadow falls across my desk. At the same moment I look up, there's a sharp crack outside as the first flash of lightning hits somewhere over the water. I jump as much from that as from Manny's unexpected company.

"Hey, Holly, you ready?" he asks. He's in a suit and carrying a manila folder.

I have no idea what he's talking about. Another flash, and thunder echoes between the buildings of South Lake Union. My pulse picks up. I know without knowing that the red bow is coming undone.

"Um, give me a second," I say, stalling. Since he can't see my screen, I pull up my schedule again to see what I might have missed. Nothing. Email then?

"You could totally smell the storm this morning," Manny says. He looks at his watch. "Almost done?"

"Mm-hmm." I scan the contents of my inbox from this morning, Friday, Thursday, all the way back to the beginning of last week for "sender: Manny Gupta."

Then I see it. Subject: **Re: Save the Reef symposium**

I never accepted the invite, which is why it's not in my calendar. And what's worse, the email has three attachments—articles I was supposed to have read by today. Articles I put off reading last week with the intent of doing it over the weekend. And did I? No, because I was with Jonathan.

I can feel the color draining from my face, but fortunately for me, Manny is looking at his phone. Another crack echoes between the buildings and the rain picks up outside. How could I be so stupid? Work comes first. Always. It's not that I regret spending time with Jonathan, or blame him; it's that I know better. Jonathan and I are temporary. That's the deal. This should have taken precedence, but instead I let myself get distracted and ugh... this is so embarrassing.

"Something the matter?" Manny asks.

"No. Nothing." I stand to gather my things. Maybe I can scan the articles while our counterparts present.

"I hope you found those studies I sent you interesting," he says as we start walking. "The discourse around ocean chemistry is perhaps more complex than one of them suggests, but it's a good place to start. Feel free to jump in at any time with your observations."

Oh shit. My step falters. What do I do? I can come clean and invite his disapproval now or I can try faking it and risk looking like an idiot in front of the senior global team.

Manny squints at me. "Holly?"

"I didn't read them," I blurt out. "I meant to, but I forgot."

Manny switches the folder from his right to his left hand. "But I sent them a week ago."

"I know. It's so unprofessional, especially since I really appreciate you inviting me on this call. I'm so sorry."

He looks at me a long moment. "That's unexpected," he says eventually. "Is there a reason?"

A brief flash of Jonathan's naked body sprawled out beneath me comes to mind. "Some of the calendar work has taken up more time than I expected. It slipped my mind."

"There'll be a lot more balls to keep in the air as program liaison, you know."

My stomach drops. "I know. And I promise I'm usually more on top of things."

Finally, his expression softens. "I know you are." He taps the folder against his thigh. "Tell you what—watch and learn today, and we'll say nothing more about it. Still read the articles, though."

"I'll do it tonight. Promise."

"Sounds good." He gestures for me to lead the way toward the conference room block, and we set off again.

On the way there, we pass Jonathan's office. As if he can sense me, he spins around in his chair and lifts his hand in greeting.

"Is he staying on his best behavior?" Manny asks, waving back. "No more tantrums?"

"No, he's come around," I say. *Way around…* "The photos are perfect."

"Excellent." Manny opens the door to conference room C and hooks up his laptop to the overhead monitor. We're about to start.

As member after member of the global team joins the call and Manny introduces me, I count every lucky star at my disposal that my temporary slip didn't end up with worse consequences. But one thing's for sure—I can't do this again. There's so little time left, and I need to keep my eye on the prize. No more behaviors allowed that might knock my chances of winning.

I'm halfway through the second article Manny sent me when Jonathan texts that evening. It's a photo of George and his Aussie stargazing. I'm about to comment on the impressive clarity of the night sky when he adds:

> The Milky Way is courtesy of editing software. We had to get creative because of the cloud cover.

It's still a strong picture, and plenty real looking. George's face is in partial profile, his beard gleaming silver in the supposed moonlight.

Love it, I say. We'll have to get creative tomorrow too. Ava's coach said yes—he and his partner will both be in it. I think it'll be good variation to have a photo with two guys.

Good thinking. Ideas for the shoot? It's supposed to keep raining.

It's a real bummer the PNW chose this week to live up to its reputation. All the photos must be done by Friday for the printer, and I'd have preferred them to be outdoors. But oh well. Getting them done is more important than crossing off the wish list. Plus, at this point, I know Jonathan can work his magic like the best of them. In more ways than one.

So indoor shoot it is. My gaze sweeps around Jude's living room as I think. Ava is upstairs, and Jude has gone to bed. They're still not talking. When I asked Ava about it on the way home from tennis, her only response was something that sounded like a literary quote—"A woman's place is in the resistance"—so maybe her English teacher is doing his job at least. Unless it's from *Star Wars*, which, come to think of it, might be more likely. Either way, I see no signs of her standing down, and Jude is flying out to meet the partners next week. Anything could happen.

As my mind wanders past the photos on the windowsill, my attention is caught by one of Ava with Santa Claus when she was seven years old. She was stubborn back then, too, and that year, she would only wear summer dresses. I smile at the memory.

Then inspiration strikes, and I text Jonathan.

What if we do a Santa shoot? The guys can both be Santas, and we can put antlers on the dogs. Presents, a tree, fake snow maybe?

He responds right away. I like it. Where?

I tap my lips as I think. With such short notice, our options are nonexistent. **Jude's garage is big. We can hang sheets as screens. Plus his Xmas tree is already put together in a corner. He never disassembles it.**

Efficient, comes Jonathan's judgment. It'll have to do.

It's decided. Looks like a trip to the craft store has been added to tomorrow's agenda.

My phone buzzes in my hands again. **Any chance I can persuade you to come over? I missed you today.**

A burst of warmth spreads through my limbs.

And I have a surprise, he continues.

I groan at my laptop where the article sits open, half-read. A surprise sounds so much more fun.

No. I straighten in my seat. I can't. Business before pleasure—that's what I committed to earlier today.

Sorry, I'm swamped, I type. **Tomorrow. After the photo shoot.** By then I should be done with this reading.

Can't wait, is his response.

Days until printer deadline: 3

With Ava's help, I set out to transform Jude's third garage bay into a Christmas wonderland. It's always been her favorite holiday, so when I ask her to lend a hand, she's in the attic space pulling out tubs of decorations before I can say "Santa Claus." She even offers to bake gingerbread cookies, and who am I to say no to that?

It's only October, but the spicy-sweet scents from the oven do lend an air of authenticity to the scene as we're seated on a white comforter ("snow") on the concrete garage floor, wrapping random empty boxes as presents.

"I'm going to hold on to these for actual Christmas," Ava says. "That's all Dad will get this year. Air."

I glance at her face, set in concentration as she curls another ribbon. As much as I understand her position, I need to get her talking to Jude again. For all our sakes. "And will that make you feel better?"

"Maybe." She continues wrapping.

I put my scissors down and throw a stick-on bow her way. "Hey."

She looks up.

"He's not doing this to spite you, you know."

"Yeah, I know."

I pause for another moment. "Why do you think your dad wants to move?"

Ava cuts a square of wrapping paper with a loud *wrrrichhh*. "For Grandma and Grandpa."

"Sure. Any other reasons?" I push off the floor to put the stack of presents we've wrapped under the tree. When I sit back down, Ava has stopped wrapping.

"I know he's still sad," she says. "But he has me. And I thought we were a team." She looks up, the anger no longer as obvious in her eyes.

"He only has you for a couple more years, though. You'll go off to college, and he'll... what? Work more? What kind of life is that?"

"That's what you do."

"Ouch. And also that's different. I'm at a crossroads, and that demands my full attention."

She rolls her eyes again.

"Ava..." I wait until I have her attention. "I think you know he needs to move on. That he deserves to move on."

Ava's gaze travels to the far garage bay where her mom's old Corolla still sits beneath a tarp, awaiting the day she turns sixteen. "You're saying he can't do that here."

"I'm saying he's been holding steady all this time for you. He's ready for a change. And maybe part of him needs that change to happen on his terms, before you leave. Before he's completely on his own."

She flips the present in her hands around. Views it from all sides. "I wasn't thinking of it like that."

"Which is fine. I get it. I'm not saying you can't be sad and upset. Change is scary."

"Are flights to Scotland shorter from Texas?" she asks. "In case you win." She starts digging around in the paper bag that holds Jude's Santa costume. Jonathan is bringing a second one from Wayne so that both our models can dress up.

"In case?" I pretend to be offended. "Do you not see the magic we're creating here?" I gesture around us. "But seriously. Talk to your dad. Please."

She hooks the Santa beard over her ears and says in a deep voice, "Ho, ho, ho. Have you been a good girl this year, Aunt Holly?"

I play along. "So good. May I please have a new job in Glasgow for Christmas, Santa?"

"A job? Are you sure you wouldn't rather have a new car or a trip to Hawaii? Or maybe a diamond ring from a certain handsome photographer?" She hugs a large, felted gnome to her chest and makes kissing noises.

Suddenly, the spirit of the season sticks in my throat because, the truth is, there are moments when I'm no longer sure I don't want that. When that vision I had of a life with Jonathan threatens to overwhelm all my other wants. It's terrifying.

"Very funny," I say, getting off the floor again so she can't see my face. "I think that's enough wrapping, don't you? What else?" I go through the list in my head. Snowballs, presents, tree, decorations, cookies, stockings, the sled from the lawn decor for the dogs... "The ladder," I say. "I'll need it to make it snow."

Once that's set up, we're ready to roll.

Jonathan, Ava's coach Marcus, and his partner Naveem are impressed with our holiday display when they arrive.

Ever so subtly, Jonathan sidles up to me and rests his hand at the small of my back. "Nice work."

"This will almost make up for the mall Santa photos my parents never let me take," Naveem says, tapping one of the fake snowballs with his shoe.

Marcus lifts an empty box and shakes it. "You've got presents and everything."

"Careful. Don't ruin Jude's gift," I say, winking at Ava. Hopefully after tonight's conversation, my brother will get something better than air under the tree this year.

"Here are the costumes, Coach," Ava says. "You can change in the bathroom over here."

Sensing Marcus's hesitation, I suggest Ava make herself scarce while we work. I do want the guys without their shirts on, after all. "The fewer people the better. For the dogs," I add.

"Speaking of which, I'll go get them from the car. We're almost ready, right?" Marcus looks to Jonathan for an answer.

"Yup. Just a few minutes."

The bulldogs are bonded sisters but could not have more different personalities. Bee acts as if it really is Christmas morning as soon as she's let in. She runs from person to person, her little stump wagging at the attention and the commotion, burrows her head into the fluffy comforter on the floor, and rolls over for belly scratches. And when Marcus asks her to come sit so she can try on the reindeer antlers, she does so without a fuss.

Lou, on the other hand, remains in the doorway watching the whole spectacle unfold, her nose turned up in seeming dismay.

"Come on, Lulu," Naveem cajoles. "You get to be in a picture. You like pictures."

Lou huffs as if that's preposterous, but when Bee starts pushing one of the gifts around with her nose, Lou lets out a low whine and sets one tentative foot on the step leading into the garage.

"Does she want a treat?" Jonathan asks, searching his pocket.

"Since when do you carry around dog treats?" I ask, adjusting the ladder so that it won't be in the picture. Once we're ready, I'll be at the top of it, throwing handfuls of "flakes" onto the Christmassy scene.

"Um." Jonathan looks from the treat in his hand to me. "Must have been from the dog fair." He crosses the floor and offers it to Lou.

Thankfully the treat works, and Lou descends the steps, but only to stop once more when she reaches the concrete floor.

"What now?" Jonathan asks in a soft voice. He squats in front of her and scratches her ear.

"She doesn't like hard floors," Marcus says behind her. He's wearing Jude's Santa pants held up by suspenders, dark boots, and the classic red hat. And man, tennis players are fit. "Your turn to change," he tells Naveem.

"You don't like hard floors?" Jonathan coos to Lou.

In response, she lifts one of her front paws and glares at the concrete.

"Let's go over here, Lou." Marcus passes her and reaches the spread-out comforter. "You'll like this better."

"Does she need to be carried?" Jonathan asks.

Marcus laughs. "She wishes. She can walk on it fine; she's just being a diva. Come on, Lulu."

Finally, Lou takes another step in our direction, then another, but she does it in a slow, tiptoed version of the passage movement horses do in dressage competitions. Each of her paws only touches the ground briefly as she bounces up and down, shuffling toward her sister.

"We had to install carpet in most of downstairs," Marcus says. "You're such a spoiled lady, aren't you?" He praises Lou once she gets to the comforter and starts walking like a normal dog.

Naveem joins us, now also dressed in red and white. Wayne's old suit doesn't have suspenders, but the pants have a wide belt holding them up. "What are we thinking? Jacket? No jacket?" He flashes open the oversized coat.

"Your call, Holly." Jonathan gestures for Naveem to get closer to Marcus and tells him where to stand so he can check the light.

The two men don't look at all like traditional Santas with their toned torsos and beardless jawlines, but then again, Bee and Lou are no reindeer either.

I join Jonathan by the camera to see how he's framing the shot. "I say keep it on, but open," I tell Naveem. "Maybe put your hands in your pockets."

Once Jonathan is done with his prep work and all forms are signed, I climb the ladder with my bag of fake snow.

"Let's do a few without snow first." Jonathan snaps his fingers to get the dogs to look his way. He captures the scene in a series of shots but pauses to look up at me. "And please don't fall off that thing."

While I wait for my turn to shine, I turn on a Christmas playlist. Soon, Frank Sinatra, Johnny Mathis, and the other greats croon about winter wonderlands and jingle bells, setting the tone. Marcus and Naveem aren't natural models, but gradually, they come around to making this yuletide photo shoot gay all the way.

"And now with snow," Jonathan says to me. "Only a pinch at a time. Marcus and Naveem, feel free to react to the snowflakes like you would if they were real. Lou and Bee, great job. Keep doing what you're doing."

Lou huffs another one of her signature snorts but stays where she is. Her antlers are tipped jauntily to the side, adding to the festive feel.

I take on my responsibility as snow machine with gusto, flinging handful after handful over the models below. Unlike real snow, these flakes don't melt on the tongue, so we get a few sputtered takes before Jonathan is happy and calls it a wrap.

Everyone gathers around the camera to have a look except Lou, who paces the edge of the comforter as if the floor really is lava. Then she barks once and plops down with a huff to wait for rescue from the scary, unyielding terrain.

"Is it just me or are the snow ones better?" I ask.

Jonathan smirks at me. "You did demonstrate superior snowflake action."

"It's in the wrist, baby."

After looking through the photos, we send the guys on their way with a promise to email them the whole series as they want to use one of the funny ones for their holiday card.

"Isn't it weird how everyone wants the bloopers?" I ask Jonathan as we start packing up.

He picks up a wrapped box with a chewed-off corner courtesy of Bee and shrugs. "It's where they look most like themselves. Usually, people don't get high-quality candids."

I fold up the comforter and then push the Christmas tree back into its corner, while Jonathan moves a stack of gift boxes off the floor.

"Watch out for the spiderweb," he says as I'm covering the tree back up with its sheet.

I freeze. "Where?"

"By the air duct."

Still not moving, I glance upward. It's not there—almost as if someone's walked through it already. "Jonathan," I say, my throat tight.

"Yeah?" He stacks another several boxes along the wall.

"I think it's on me." I close my eyes. Is that crawling I'm feeling on top of my head? "The spider," I whisper. "Help."

Finally, he stops what he's doing and comes over. "Where?"

"In my hair." I lean forward so he can check.

"I don't see anything."

It's probably nesting somewhere deep in my strands. A chill moves through me. "That doesn't mean it's not there," I say through clenched teeth.

"Maybe—"

He doesn't have time for more because that "maybe" makes it sound like he's found it, and that sets off the panic. "Get it off me," I cry, shaking my head. "Do you see it? Did you get it?"

"Holly, stop. There's no spider."

"Ouch!" My hair has snagged on something. Then I realize what he said. No spider? "Are you sure?"

"I'm sure. But my watch is stuck. Hold still."

"I thought I felt it crawling," I say in a small voice.

Jonathan shuffles his feet to my side. "I can't reach. Come over here. Can you sit?" He taps his foot against a kid-sized stool.

My head bobs back and forth as he tries to untangle my head from his wrist, and that's what Jude sees as he finds us a moment later.

"Oh fu— Sorry!" he sputters upon entering. "Damn it, Holly, there are kids in the house."

Realizing what this must look like since Jonathan has his back to the door, I hurry to explain. "I got stuck in his watch. My hair, I mean. Really, there's no funny business going on."

As soon as Jonathan manages to break free, I stand, brushing my tangles back.

Jude studies us through narrowed eyes but seems to conclude that I'm telling the truth. "Okay fine. I was going to ask if you wanted dinner. We ate already, but there's more."

I put another few feet between me and Jonathan. "Thanks, but we have to finish packing up, and then I'm helping him bring this back to his place."

"Gotcha. No worries, then." Jude raises a hand in an awkward salute.

"No 'funny business'?" Jonathan asks when we're alone again. Humor plays in his eyes. What about some 'canoodling' or 'hanky-panky'?"

"Shut up." I laugh as he saunters toward me. "And what's wrong with 'canoodling'?"

"Nothing. I could go for any of those." His hands settle against my waist. "I was almost getting nostalgic there—you stuck, me coming to the rescue."

"Is that so?" I fling my arms over his shoulders, my adrenaline finally simmering down.

"Mm-hmm." He leans in and runs his nose up the side of mine.

"As tempting as that is, let's not forget my family is on the other side of that wall. How about we finish up and get out of here? I'm ready for it to be just us the rest of tonight."

He doesn't argue, and before long, we're in his driveway getting ready to unload the equipment into his garage. But once there, he hesitates before turning off the car. "Hey, Holly?"

I pause with my hand on the door handle. "Yeah?"

His face scrunches into an expression of great conflict. "Remember when you said you were looking forward to some one-on-one time tonight?"

I smile, my guard naively down. "You mean fifteen minutes ago?"

"Yeah." He runs a hand through his hair. "So about that..."

Days until printer deadline: 3

"You got a dog?" I'm frozen in Jonathan's doorway as he squats to greet his newest family member.

"But look at these eyes." Jonathan accepts slobbered kisses as he tries to wrestle the beast into facing me. "I couldn't just leave Sir Leonard at the shelter. He deserves a home."

"A home with you," I clarify.

Sir Leonard lumbers over to me and boops my leg until I place a hand on his head. This big guy knows exactly how to get his way.

Jonathan gets off the floor. "See, he likes you."

"I like him, too, but...How? When?" Despite my shock, I find myself digging my fingers deeper into Sir Leonard's thick coat until he yawns with delight. Such a sweet old boy.

"Yesterday. I went back to the shelter after I photographed George. He convinced me it was the right choice."

"Good ol' George."

"You're not happy about it?" Jonathan studies me as I take off my shoes and set down my bag.

"No, that's not it." I go to him and rest my forehead against his chest. "If you're happy, I'm happy."

"But?" He takes me by the hand and leads me upstairs. Sir Leonard follows.

But now he's even more stuck here. Sir Leonard's noble name notwithstanding, a trip to Scotland is now basically out of the question. Not that it was a real option before, and not that I should want it to be, but... but...

Fuck.

"I'm surprised is all. It's a big responsibility."

"Well..." Jonathan backs me up to the kitchen counter. "Maybe this past month has taught me that focusing only on myself and my misfortunes got me nowhere." He reaches for my hands. "Much thanks to you."

I should be thrilled about this. Thrilled that my career aspirations—and forcing him to be part of them—have led to such an epiphany. Except I won't be here to enjoy the benefits of it. But Sir Leonard will.

Wait—am I jealous of a dog?

"I think he's jealous of you," Jonathan says in a startling echo of my thoughts. "Look."

The Leonberger mix has his head on his paws on the floor, eyeing us with large, soulful eyes.

"He should be," I grumble. "I was here first."

Jonathan's eyes twinkle. "Is that so?"

"Uh-huh." I pull him closer, reveling in the promise of his warm embrace.

He makes a gruff noise in the back of his throat as his mouth slants over mine. His strong arms wrap around my back, almost lifting me to him as our lips have their fill.

When we come apart, I pull my sweater over my head and toss it on the stool next to us. He's quick to follow, shedding both his graphite crewneck and the white T-shirt he has on underneath. His black jeans are slung low on his hips, and I can't help myself—I run my palm from his sternum down across his flat abdomen as if needing to make sure he's real.

"You're pretty hot, you know," I say. "Beneath that gruff facade."

He hooks his thumbs under my bra straps. "I'm not gruff. You're gruff."

He lowers first one strap and then the other. His bare chest rises and falls on slow and steady breaths as he reaches behind me and undoes the hooks. The bra drops to the floor, and for a moment, he merely looks at me, lips parted.

"I'll miss you when I leave." The words spill out of me before I can stop them.

His gaze joins mine, holding there. "I thought we decided not to talk about that."

My mouth has gone dry, so I swallow hard. I'm not sure what's gotten into me. "We did. Sorry." I'm not sorry. I should be, but what I said is the truth. I'll miss him more than I want to.

He reaches for my cheek and runs his thumb along my jaw. There's a storm raging in the gray of his irises. I rest my head against his palm for a moment but lift it again when he slides his hand into my hair and tugs lightly.

"Say it again," he mumbles against my skin before placing a kiss below my ear.

"I'll miss you," I say, grabbing hold of his belt to stay upright as he lavishes kisses along my throat and clavicle. "Do you hear me? I'll miss you so much."

As if this is the fuel he needs, he pulls back and lifts me onto the counter. His hands roam from my waist down my thighs and up as he crowds between my legs and clutches me tight.

"I'll miss you more," he says. Then he carries me upstairs, blocking the stairs with a gate so Sir Leonard can't follow.

I wake up before dawn, tangled in rumpled sheets that serve as a reminder of how good we are at cherishing what little time we have left together.

The plan for the day is to wrap up the final photo shoots. Dennis's gym buddy, Aroon, and Nick are scheduled for the Japanese garden later this morning, and then we have round two with Robert the vet after work. With two days left until the photos need to be at the printer, it's down to the wire, but layout and design are set, I've written the copy, and I've got my social media promos and email list ready, as well as tables booked at all the fall markets I've been able to find within the Greater Seattle area.

I glance at Jonathan's naked form next to me, tempted to lure him out of sleep to celebrate everything coming together but decide against it. Our alarm will go off soon anyway. Instead, I turn on my phone, which instantly buzzes with messages.

The first one is from Rachel: **Nick wants to know if he should bring his cowboy hat?**

They're still dating casually, and Rachel has asked to be at the shoot later.

A cowboy hat in the Japanese garden? My instinct tells me no, but who knows what opportunities might present themselves. **Sure, why not?** I text back. We don't have any cowboys in the calendar so far.

I scroll past a few spam messages, but then one message catches my eye that jolts me upright. It's a selfie of Robert by the Statue of Liberty with the text, **Sry forgot I had a conference in NY this week. Rain check?**

"Jonathan, wake up." I shake his shoulder as I type, **When will you be back?** to Robert.

"What?" Jonathan grunts into his pillow.

"Robert canceled."

"Who's Robert?"

"The vet. Our twelfth guy."

His eyes blink open. "You're joking."

I jump out of bed. So much for feeling on top of things. "I'm afraid not." I check my messages, but Robert has left me on read. I let out a small growl and toss my phone on the bed before collecting my clothes off the floor.

"What are you going to do?" Jonathan asks.

"So now it's me instead of us?" I snap before I can stop myself. I hear it before he can react and backtrack. "Sorry. I'm just freaking out. It's not your fault."

"Hey." Jonathan pats the bed. "Come here."

But even though I know he means well, that only furthers my irritation. "I don't have time." I finish pulling on my jeans and look at him. "I'm just going to go in to work and make a few phone calls before everyone gets there. I'll see you at the shoot later."

He calls my name as I leave the room, but I don't stop.

Nick and I are first on location, along with his boxer Bo, who is as energetic as I remember him from the beach, and I do my best to put on a composed facade for them. I've left messages with a guide dog training place, several pet stores, and two more vet offices, so at the moment, all I can do is focus on the task at hand and hope someone will return my call. Bo is a welcome distraction to the unrest swirling in my stomach. If he wasn't on a leash, I'm convinced he'd dive straight into the pond to chase the ducks paddling about.

Midmorning on a Wednesday, there aren't many people around, so we stroll the paths deeper into the garden while we wait. Nick tells me about the brewery he's opening with a few friends (I check, but none of them have dogs), and I tell him what he can expect from the photo shoot and ask him if he'd like his social media handles below his calendar image.

"You might get more DMs than you're comfortable with, though," I tell him. "We'll be selling it nationally."

"Could be good for the business," he says, and I appreciate that he's not immediately seeing it as a potential dating pool. Maybe he and Rachel are getting more serious. "By the way, I brought the cowboy hat." He pats his backpack.

"You're really into the cowboy theme, huh?"

He stops walking and lowers his voice. "Okay, don't tell anyone I told you this, but it's a childhood dream of mine."

"To be a cowboy?"

"Clint Eastwood, specifically. I was obsessed with his Westerns when I was little. I was thinking I could lean over the railing of that bridge over there, looking out." He gestures across the pond. "Maybe chew on a blade of grass, Bo at my side."

"Wow, you've really thought about this." I fight a smile.

He shrugs. "We live in Seattle. When else will I ever get a chance to don the hat and boots?"

He makes a good point. "I'll run it by Jonathan—see what he thinks."

"Is that him?" Nick nods toward the garden entrance. "If so, he's already in character as my sheriff nemesis."

Sure enough, there's Jonathan, back in all black and with his tripod across his shoulder like a rifle. He eyes me and Nick with a furrowed brow as he approaches at speed.

I go to meet him. He never responded to my message apologizing for how I left this morning. "Everything okay? Did you hit traffic?"

"I left my tripod at the office," he says. "Had to make a pit-stop."

I watch as he unloads his bags with more snap than necessary. "This is Nick, by the way. Nick, Jonathan."

Nick smiles. "I've heard a lot about you. Anything I can help with?"

Jonathan doesn't look up. "Is that so? No, I'm good."

What the hell?

Nick's smile falters. "O-kay."

I offer him an apologetic grimace. "We're going to set up. Maybe take Bo around the pond while you wait."

As soon as he's gone, I turn to Jonathan, my hands on my hips. "That was rude," I say.

He straightens. "What was?"

I gesture to Nick and Bo. "He was making conversation, and you completely shot him down. Are you mad at me or what's going on?"

"No. Nothing." He shoves his hands into his pockets. "I just didn't realize you two knew each other."

"We don't. And even if we did, what's the issue?"

"Then how does he 'know all about me'?"

There's a flash of something behind his rigid stance, and as I stare at him it crystallizes not into the anger it looks like at first glance, but something softer—worry. Nick worries him. *Oh my God, he's jealous.* I go to him as this dawns on me. "From Rachel. Because they're dating," I say. "That's where he's heard of you. I've only met him once."

Jonathan's forehead smooths out. "Rachel," he says, understanding dawning.

"Did I hear my name?" The woman in question comes around the path using a colorful umbrella as a walking stick.

"Hey, friend." I give her a smile and point. "Nick's over there. We'll be set up in a few. When is Aroon getting here?"

"I told him eleven since you said ten thirty for Nick."

"Perfect."

Rachel goes off to join her guy, and I turn back to Jonathan, who is looking a bit sheepish.

"Before you say anything—" he starts, but I'm faster.

"What exactly went through your head when you saw me and Nick talking?" I try to keep a serious face, but I'm sure the smugness I'm feeling shines through.

"It wasn't like that," Jonathan says. "I was..." He scratches his hair and looks off toward the bridge.

"Jealous," I fill in, helpful that I am.

"No." Jonathan's protest comes fast but without a convincing delivery.

I cock an eyebrow to encourage him to rephrase.

He stares at me for a long moment. "Look, since I know we're not supposed to be, I'm sticking with no for the sake of...you know." He reaches for my hand. "It was stupid. *I* was being stupid. I'm sorry. I think how we left things this morning set me on edge, and I saw red. I'm usually not like that."

I glance over my shoulder to where Nick and Rachel are walking close together in conversation. They're in their own world, so I take the opportunity to sneak into Jonathan's arms. "It's okay," I tell him. "You get one pass."

"I know I have no right to feel that way, just so you know." He kisses my hair. "I'll do better."

"Okay." I hug him tight despite having no business feeling good that some small part of him had a proprietary urge about me. I need to do better, too. Stay the course. This is not the time to blur the lines.

"Get on with the shoot?" he asks.

I free myself and nod. "Let's. After you apologize to Nick, too."

Jonathan does so with no hard feelings, and while he instructs Cowboy Nick on how to pose, Rachel and I watch from a bench off to the side.

"He was so excited about his getup," Rachel says. "It's cute, but…"

My mind wanders. For almost four weeks, I've done my best to make this happen. I've been proactive, organized…

"But?" I say absent-mindedly. I've adapted when things didn't go my way. And I've come too far to give up now. But what if no one returns my calls today?

"…the same thing out of life right now, you know." Rachel looks at me as if expecting an answer.

"Right." I nod.

"You have no idea what I just said, do you?" She purses her lips.

She knows me too well. "Sorry. Got distracted. You were saying?"

Her eyes narrow. "That's not like you."

I tell her about Robert canceling. "So I've got a lot on my mind."

"I see."

We watch Nick and Jonathan for a minute. Nick is striking every farmstead pose he can think of—elbows on the bridge railing, boot heel against a tree trunk. He even attempts to lie down on his back on the grass with his hat covering his face but jumps up quickly as the damp seeps in.

"I know you're against it," Rachel says quietly next to me, "but there's always your brother. Desperate times..."

I'm about to inform her that he's already said no, but a memory from last night stops me. He and Ava did eat dinner together after I talked to her, and if I helped, then maybe Jude won't be mad at me anymore. And if he's not mad at me anymore...

Rachel's right. He's my last chance. I swipe open my phone.

"What? You're actually doing it? He's going to be in the calendar?"

"Let's see, shall we? But before you get all excited, let me remind you that you are dating Nick." I nod in the direction of the men.

"Very casually. We're not exclusive."

I send the question off to him. **Please, please, please,** I end it. **I'd owe you big-time.**

"Nick is fun, but he's a boy," Rachel continues.

I chuckle. "Last I checked, Jude was also a boy."

"No. Jude is a man." Rachel's eyes glitter. "There's a difference."

I don't deign to answer that, but watching Jonathan's intense focus and the way he moves with the camera to get Bo's attention—especially knowing what it was like to have that camera aimed at me, the way it made me feel seen—I know she's right. There is a difference.

"Get one of Bo holding the hat," I call to him.

Jonathan flashes me a smile and a thumbs-up.

"Speaking of men," Rachel says at my side, "be real with me—what are you actually doing with him?"

"What do you mean?"

"You two looked real cozy earlier."

My cheeks heat. "So?"

"So, he's into you, and you're leaving soon. Do you see it going anywhere other than down heartbreak highway?"

I let out a sputtered protest. "As much as we lo—um, like each other, we both know it's temporary. That the timing is wrong. We're on the same page."

"Uh-huh."

"And even if that wasn't the case, he's stuck here. He's not allowed to fly, his dad depends on him a lot for getting around, his job is here, and now he's adopted a dog."

She startles at the last bit. "A dog? No, let's put a pin in that. But really, the rest are only excuses." She starts counting on her fingers. "His job, you say? The one he doesn't like? Not a sticking point. People get off the no-fly list all the time. Is there a process? Maybe, but it's not impossible. And his dad—ever heard of rideshare?"

"You sound just like him," I say. "Wayne, I mean. Jonathan's dad. He said something similar."

Rachel's eyes widen. "You've met his dad?"

"By chance. Calm down."

But as Jonathan and Nick wrap up, it does occur to me that maybe, just maybe, the reasons why Jonathan and I have decided to live solely in the present aren't as strong as we think they are, and that, as a logical conclusion, maybe there are possibilities we are overlooking. If we wanted to see possibilities, that is. Is there a chance there's a future where the two of us work out?

The question percolates as Aroon and his mutt, Cricket, replace Nick and Bo. Aroon is a huge guy with roots in Norway and Thailand, who starts by apologizing for being out of shape despite muscles that would make a prized bull jealous.

"I'm between bodybuilding competitions," he says. "Bad timing."

I assure him that he'll do just fine for the calendar and make small talk about how he knows Dennis while Jonathan decides on a new spot to set up.

"So when will the calendar be out?" Aroon asks. "Before Christmas? It would help with shopping for sure."

"If all goes well, orders will be up next week," I tell him.

"That soon? Cool."

"Yeah, you're one of our last guys. The project is almost done."

"Okay, let's roll," Jonathan says, interrupting. Despite Nick and Rachel having left together, he still seems off today, like there's something else bothering him. That surly reticence from a month ago is creeping back into his demeanor little by little. He insists nothing is wrong, but he's only been shooting for five minutes when he gestures for me to come over. Without a word, he points to the screen, indicating for me to have a look.

It's a series of maybe twenty images, half with Aroon flexing and Cricket at his feet and the other half of Aroon doing push-ups with Cricket on his back.

"What the heck is he...?" I lean closer to the screen. In every one of the pictures, Aroon looks great, but Cricket has his tongue plastered to either Aroon's leg or his head while making eye contact with the camera. It's like he's been captured in flagrante by paparazzi, and now the evidence of his degeneracy is on display for all to see.

"How am I supposed to work with this?" Jonathan asks.

"Maybe Aroon uses delicious lotions?" I suggest. "Try something else."

Jonathan mutters a quiet tirade about it being impossible.

"That's never been a problem before." I stare at him a moment. "What's going on with you today? If you're still in your feels about Nick, I'll have a problem with that."

He balks. "Of course not."

I place a hand on his arm. "Then please make this work. We're running out of time."

"You don't think I know that?"

My lips part in surprise at his tone, and he must notice because he backtracks immediately. "Sorry, that was unnecessary," he says, voice softer. "It's just hard to…" His jaw clams up. "Never mind."

"What's hard? Talk to me."

He looks away. "It's just a lot." He gestures vaguely to our surroundings. "But of course I'll make it work."

I search his cadence for something disingenuous but find only sincerity. "Okay," I say. Then, because I still feel like I've swallowed something jagged, "It's not us, right? We're fine?"

He nods several times. "Of course. Let's just get through this, okay? I'll shake it off."

He returns to the shoot, and I decide everyone is allowed a bad day. Thankfully, before I can dwell further, my phone buzzes with a message from Jude. It's a bulleted list in three parts:

- Deep clean the fridge/freezer
- Scoop out the gutters
- Sort and pack up the attic

I stare at the message with a frown. **Your to-do list for this weekend?**

His response is immediate: **What you owe me if I do this.**

Oh.

Well, it's not like I have a choice. **Deal. Thanks, big brother.** Then I add, **It'll have to be tomorrow. Get a haircut.**

You can't hear me, but I'm grumbling, comes his response.

I smile, victorious, and let out a long breath. Twelfth guy booked. Like so many times before, Jude has come to my rescue.

Days until printer deadline: 1

At least when I met Wayne, it wasn't planned so there was no time to be nervous. As I wait for Jonathan to show up to photograph Jude, my stomach is in knots. I don't know if I want the two men to like each other or not. I mean, I do—I've pictured them getting along before—but wouldn't it also be easier if Jude saw the merits of Jonathan's and my decision to not make a big deal of our fling? If he thinks Jonathan is a stand-up sort of bloke, I'll never hear the end of how I deserve to be happy and how, where there's a will, there's a way.

I jump when the doorbell rings and run my hands down the front of my jeans. Here we go.

But it's not Jonathan. It's Rachel. She sashays into the kitchen carrying a tray full of cookies.

"Um, what are you doing here?" I ask.

"Hello to you, too." She points to the tray. "Sustenance."

Oh no, she can't fool me. "Wearing a sheer blouse and skinny jeans? That's your date outfit."

"Can't a friend get dolled up visiting another friend?"

"They could, but I doubt that's what's going on here. Exclusive or not, does Nick not mind you coming here to gawk at another guy?"

"Doubtful."

"Aha! So you are here to"—I lower my voice to a whisper—"gawk at my brother."

Rachel stuffs half a cookie into her mouth and says around the crumbs, "I practically orchestrated this whole event." She gestures around the room while she chews and swallows. "You're welcome, by the way, since I believe your deadline is tomorrow." Then she cocks her head and gives me a once-over. "You're looking pretty dolled up yourself. A skirt?"

"I just got home from work."

"A different skirt than the one you wore to work."

Before I can respond, the doorbell rings again, and this time it is Jonathan. He was completely normal today when I saw him at lunch, no weird vibes, so I've chalked up yesterday to exactly what I thought it was—a bad day.

"Hi." He steals a kiss while we're alone in the foyer, but for once that doesn't settle my nerves because of course Jude will like him. Which means I know what's coming my way later—a brotherly talking-to.

Jonathan has changed out of his black "uniform" and is in dark blue jeans and a moss-green sweater that makes his eyes shift in colors of seagrass and sage behind the gray. Rachel, who isn't privy to the variations in his closet the way I am, makes wide eyes as he enters the kitchen.

"Green," she chirps. Then she holds out the tray. "I mean, cookie?"

"Maybe later." Jonathan nods toward the back of the house. "The light is disappearing. We need to hurry up. Is he ready?"

By "he," he means my brother. Who will soon be in a calendar full of hot guys. Shirtless.

"I can go get him," Rachel offers, a picture of innocence. "Give you two a moment."

"No, no." I step away from Jonathan. "Arm length's distance," I tell Rachel, pointing at her. "At all times."

She rolls her eyes.

Like he's a boxer ready for a round, Jude comes downstairs in shorts and a robe when I call his name. He runs his hand through hair that looks unstyled but that I know he's probably spent at least thirty minutes on and bounces lightly on the balls of his feet.

"Jude, this is Jonathan. Jonathan, Jude," I say, making introductions. "Rachel you know."

"Hey, Rach." Jude gives her a small wave before shaking Jonathan's hand. "Nice to meet you, man."

Rach? The fact that he's given my friend a nickname temporarily distracts me from the fact that the two guys currently at the top of my list are meeting for the first time. I quickly put a pin in it though as Jude takes us through the house to the backyard. We have maybe twenty minutes of good light left.

"I've seen your photos," Jude says to Jonathan. "They're impressive. But I honestly have no idea how I let Holly rope me into this. I'm no model."

Jonathan looks at me with a cheeky spark in his eyes. "She can be persuasive," he says.

"All you have to do is take off your robe and stand still," Rachel says. "Nothing to it. You'll be great."

I send her a pointed glare that she ignores.

If Jude is apprehensive about posing for pictures, Morris is all about it. The goldendoodle could not be more excited to have a whole group of people with him in the backyard who might throw a ball if he only wags his tail and looks cute, which is all the time. We waste at least five minutes chasing him around before deciding that the only way to get him to be still in the photos is for Jude to hold him. The results are some pretty darn adorable pictures of my brother and his best friend hugging cheek to cheek that I know will fit perfectly into the calendar.

Only Rachel is disappointed. "You can't see his pecs," she complains quietly to me. "Morris is covering him up."

I shrug gleefully. "Too bad, so sad."

"But can I please get a copy of the photo anyway?"

"You can buy the calendar," I say, fluttering my lashes at her before I announce to the group that we're done.

We head inside, and Jude offers to put on coffee for everyone while I pull out Ava's cookie tin to add to Rachel's plate. Ava isn't home, but I know she won't mind. She's been working her way through a pastry cookbook this past week, so there's been no shortage of sweets around. I'm grateful she brings most of the batches to school or tennis.

"I can get the cups," Rachel offers next to Jude. "Just point me in the right direction."

He smiles at her. "Thanks. Up there." His robe falls half open as he points, and her eyes drift to his chest.

I'm about to get between them but pause, momentarily rendered immobile by the vibe. Because there is one between them. A strong one. Is this not just Rachel teasing?

"Okay." I finally snap to it. "Jude, why don't you go put on clothes. Rachel and I have got it."

"Party pooper," Rachel mutters under her breath.

Am I? Has the solution to Ava's moving problem and Jude's loneliness been staring me in the face this whole time? I watch my friend move around my brother's kitchen. Huh. This may require further thought once we're done here.

When the coffee is ready, we find Jude and Jonathan in jovial conversation on the living room couch.

"You didn't tell me Jonathan is a musician," Jude says. "I was just telling him about how I met Jolene at a Norah Jones concert where I was working extra as security."

I sit down next to Jonathan. "That's right. I forgot about that."

While they talk, I put on Norah's *Come Away with Me* album as a soothing backdrop to the rise and fall of our conversation. Like I suspected, Jonathan and Jude get along like biscuits and gravy, moving seamlessly between topics from music and photography to dog ownership and travel. Rachel interjects comments here and there, but I mostly observe. With this last photo session done, a new calm is settling in that makes me feel like I could sleep for several days. I think I might, once the files are off to the printer tomorrow. Jonathan will edit Jude's photos tonight, and we'll put everything together tomorrow for submission.

I go with Jonathan to his car when he leaves a little after 8:00.

"Cool guy," he says, nodding toward the house where Jude is handing Rachel her jacket. "I can see why you're close."

I nestle into him and look up. "Funny, he said the same thing about you."

"I'm glad." Jonathan kisses me lightly through a smile. "See you tomorrow?"

I'm tempted to ask why Jude's opinion of him matters. Against better judgment, it thrills me that it does. But ultimately, I lose my nerve. "Bright and early." I squeeze his hand before letting it go.

Jude is waiting for me in the kitchen when I get back inside. "So, you did it," he says with a grin. "Twelve months of photos. Are you excited?"

I sink onto a counter stool and reach for the last of Ava's cookies. "Very. And exhausted. But I'm not done yet. It's got to sell, too."

"Looks like Jonathan has come a long way since you started. I'll admit I was a little worried he was going to be that brooding force you described back then."

"No. Not anymore." A series of rapid-fire images of him play like a reel before me. Jonathan and the puppies, Jonathan bent over the keys of his grand piano, Jonathan and his dad, Jonathan feeding me French toast.

Jude points at me. "That smile is not the smile of someone who's going to be fine picking up and leaving the country in a month or two. Are you sure you know what you're doing here?"

I start to reassure him, but the brotherly way he sees into my soul stops me. I press my lips together and then slump back in my seat. "Fine. Maybe not entirely. I mean, I will go. And I will be okay. So there's no need to worry."

"And what about him?"

I wave off the question. "Jonathan will be fine. He's better than me at keeping things..." I make a downward motion with both hands extended forward, palms facing each other.

"Linear?"

"I was going to say 'neat.' Or something. He's very clear that there are things keeping him here and what they are." A little too clear. Which makes him less likely to entertain other prospects. "We've known this was the plan all along."

"Uh-huh." Jude looks skeptical. He licks his finger and presses it against some crumbs on the empty plate. "You know what I think? I think you need to talk and come up with a better plan. Life is too short. I would know. And that's all I'll say about that." He taps his palms on the counter and pushes back before he takes the cookie plate and sets it in the dishwasher.

I watch him wipe down the counter with one practiced sweep, rinse the cloth, and hang it up—the very definition of a neat man who desperately needs someone to shake him up. Because life *is* too short.

"Hey, I had an idea for your next date," I say.

"We've already been over that. One was quite enough."

I pop the last bite of the cookie in my mouth and wait until he's retrieved a dishwasher pod from under the sink. "I was thinking you could ask Rachel."

Jude stills with his hand halfway to the detergent hatch. "What?"

"She'd say yes. Something to think about." I stand. "And now I'm heading to bed, but thanks again for doing the shoot."

"Rachel who was just here Rachel?" he calls after me.

"I'll give you her number," I call back, satisfied that will knock him a little off course.

And who knows—maybe Jude was right. Maybe while I'm at it, it's time I shake things up for Jonathan and me, too.

Day of printer deadline

On Friday morning, my wake-up alarm is not as shrill as it usually is, I don't struggle getting into my fifteen-minute yoga poses, Jude's leftover coffee tastes fresher, and the red lights I hit on the way in to work change quicker than normal. There's a brightness to the air in the lobby of the building that makes me think of summer despite October being almost halfway done already, and when the security guard mutters his curt "Morn'," I surprise us both by responding with a bouncy, "It is a good morning, isn't it?"

The feeling is only magnified by the sight of my fellow interns with their heads bent over keyboards and phones. They'll still be scrambling these next two weeks as their events aren't scheduled until right before the fundraiser challenge ends, but me? I'm done with the heavy lifting.

"Drinks after work?" I ask Rachel as I shrug out of my jacket.

"You bet your sweet program liaison ass." She raises a hand to high-five me, but I leave her hanging, too aware of eyes watching. Also, I haven't won yet. Though I do admit that knowing the quality of the images we've produced, I feel one giant step closer.

"Shh," I say. "You're going to jinx it."

"No such thing." She grins.

I meet up with Jonathan in his office at lunch. We keep it professional since Jacques is at his desk, but when I pull up a chair, Jonathan gives my leg a soft squeeze before he opens his editing program. One final look-through, and then we'll zip everything and send it off.

"Do you have the list of who goes with what month so we can double-check?" Jonathan asks.

"Naturally." I open my phone and navigate to the document. "Ready?"

"Ready."

"Okay. January is Dennis and Tank. First shoot, first month. Makes cosmic sense, I think. February is Jude and Morris because they're hugging. Valentine's Day and all that. March is Bear the Newfoundland in the woods, April the fishing Samoyed."

"Aah-chstalker," Jonathan pretends a sneeze, nudging me in the side with his elbow.

"Haha. May," I continue, "is old George and his Aussie, June the golden retriever in the beachy golden sunset, July our bonus Dalmatian in the woods, and August Xander and Milton in full action, running."

"That's one of my favorites," Jonathan says. "I never did much motion photography in the past, so it was a fun challenge."

"Then I put Nick and Bo down for September, and Aroon and Cricket for October. I'm glad we got at least a few pictures where he's not licking Aroon. Thanks for sticking with it."

"So that leaves Theo and the beagle puppies for November, since Marcus and Naveem's Santa shoot is December." Jonathan clicks open the final image of the twelve. "That's it. They're all in order. Are you happy with it still? If not, now's the time to move them around."

I give it a moment's consideration, but I've sweated over this enough already. Everyone is where they should be. "Nope, I'm good. Everything looks great."

"I'm heading out for a sandwich," Jacques announces. "Anyone want anything?"

We tell him we don't, and then we're alone. I get up and look out the windows facing the hallway. There's no one around. "Come here," I tell Jonathan, beckoning him to me in the corner behind the door. If someone walked past, they would only see us if they leaned close to the glass.

He's quick to obey, and soon he has me against the wall next to the printer, one of my legs hitched up to his waist. After all we've accomplished together so far, I need to kiss him like a marathon runner needs water at the finish line. I'm not trying to make anything more than a kiss happen, though, no matter how tantalizing the thought.

He pulls away first, breathing heavily. His eyes are wild, which is a tremendous improvement to the half-vacant look he used to present while walking these halls. "Damn it, Holly, you can't get me hard at work."

I give him a cheeky smile and do a little roll with my hips against him. "I beg to differ. It's not difficult at all."

He grabs my ass to make me stop. "Someone could walk in."

I pout, though I know he's right. An office tryst would definitely ruin my appearance as a consummate professional. "Fine, I'll stand down. Let you compose yourself."

"How kind of you," he says drily, but his eyes glitter.

I return to his desk and open the manila envelope with our signed release forms. "Okay, well, since a quickie is out of the question, let's get these scanned and be done with it." I hand the stack to Jonathan, who stays conspicuously out of reach from me as if he's worried I might wrestle him to the floor.

He heads to the printer and flips through the stack before placing it in the feeding tray. Then he pauses and picks it up again. Flips through it one more time. "Um, Holly?"

I'm busy imagining various scenarios for how such a wrestling match might pan out, but his tone snaps me out of it. "Yeah?"

"There are only eleven forms here."

"What?" I get off the chair and join him. Count the pages. "That can't be right. I know we got forms signed at every photo shoot." I dig through my bag, though it's unlikely one could have slipped out of the envelope on my way here. Each time we've gotten a new signed form, I've added it to the envelope, and it's the kind that closes with tiny metal wings. "Maybe I left one at my desk?"

"You want to go check?"

Icy tendrils are slowly spreading through my rib cage. There'd be no reason for it to be at my desk. "Yeah, give me a minute."

I run down the hallway, past the elevators, and to my workspace that's as pristine as it was when I left it some forty minutes ago. No stray papers in sight.

"What's going on?" Rachel asks as I pull out drawers and get down on the floor to see if the form might have joined the dust bunny party.

I don't feel like explaining the situation until I've found the form. Then it'll be a funny anecdote and not this leaning tower of dread that might tip if I name it. "I...um...think I lost an earring," I say. "Nope, not here."

FINDING MR. JULY

"Have you checked Jonathan's pockets?" Rachel grins at her clever joke, which I'm sure I'd appreciate more were my brain not scrambling for where to look next. Unfortunately, I know I haven't taken any of the forms out of the envelope once they were put there.

"Gotta go," I tell her. "I'll talk to you later." I rush off before she can respond.

"Anything?" Jonathan asks when I return, optimism tingeing his words.

I shake my head. "I don't understand. Whose form are we missing?"

"Let's see." Jonathan sits down and starts going through the list, placing the corresponding form to the side when he finds it. "Dennis, Jude, Garrett, Samuel, George, Oliver..." When he gets to our Mr. July—Pete with the Dalmatian—he stops and thumbs through the papers again. "He's the one," he announces. "There's no form for him."

We both fall silent as if simultaneously being transported back to the woods that day when Pete and Nala walked in on our shoot with Garrett and Bear and volunteered to join the calendar on a whim.

"You did ask him to sign a form, didn't you?" I ask.

"Of course," Jonathan says right away. But then his brow creases. "At least I think so."

My stomach drops. "You think?"

Jonathan's gaze flashes to mine. "You handled most of the signatures."

I cross my arms. "You were the one interacting with him the most that day."

"But you got Garrett's signature, so you had the envelope. And I was doing the shoot."

"With Pete!"

We stare at each other as the situation sinks in. We only have until four o'clock to submit to the printer, and they won't print anything for commercial use without proof that we have the rights to the images. Arguing won't change that.

"Okay, well... I'll call Garrett," I say. "They seemed chummy, right? Maybe they've kept in touch."

"Worth a try." Jonathan's voice is clipped, and he's no longer looking at me. Instead, he's shoving the forms back into the envelope.

"What are you doing? Those still need to be scanned."

He eyes me warily. "Sure you trust me to do it?"

I huff. "What's that supposed to mean? Of course I do, and you know it."

That seems to knock the fight out of him, and his shoulders slump. "You're right. I'm sorry. I don't want to fight."

Despite my irritation, I force myself to match his softer tone. "Yeah, me neither. Please, will you scan them? I'll go call Garrett in the meantime. Hopefully, this is a blip."

"Okay."

But Garrett is a dead end.

"No, sorry," he says. "We had a good chat that day, but he was heading back to Ireland, so what good would keeping in touch have been, you know?"

I thank him and return to Jonathan, my chest threatening to cave in. He doesn't even have to ask me how it went.

"So we have no way of reaching him," he says, stating the obvious. "Then I say we use the photo anyway. Chances are he will never see the calendar, and we don't have time to find another model. It's him, or we don't have a product."

Every boring tidbit about contract law my brain has stored

away finds that moment to rise to the surface. I'm sure he's right—Pete won't know. But I will know. I'll know we'd have to lie to the printer, and I'll know I'd be opening myself up to a lawsuit should Pete be more tapped into the environmental nonprofit calendar scene than I think. It would be a risk, and that is not me. I simply can't do it.

I look at the clock on the wall and sink into Jacques's chair. It's almost two. Jonathan is right—there's no time to find another model—and yet my mind keeps working the problem as if there's a solution. There has to be. I stare, unseeingly at first, at Jonathan's framed photos on the wall—the captivating black-and-white ones I didn't know were his the first time I was here. Gradually, they come into focus. He's stuck a recent snap of Sir Leonard to the frame of one of them. Already a dear family member.

That's when it hits me.

"Jonathan!" I call.

He looks up from his computer, where it appears he's currently searching social media for our elusive model. "What?"

"You could do it. You're hot as hell, and you have a dog now. You can be in the calendar."

A silent beat turns into two and three as Jonathan blinks at me. But when he finally opens his mouth, his response is not what I want to hear. "No," he says. "No way."

My jaw slackens. "No? Why not?"

"You may have talked me into getting back to photography again for this project, but I draw the line at stepping in front of the camera."

"Because? And you'd better not be bringing back the whole pinup narrative." I cross my arms.

The muscle in his jaw ticks, and he looks away. "Sorry. But

no. There were enough photos of me circulating after the airplane incident. You'll have to find someone else."

I throw my hands out wide as a scoff deflates my lungs. "How? We are literally out of time. It would save the project."

Finally, he looks at me again. "Call the printer. Maybe they'll give you an extension over the weekend. Buy you some time."

It doesn't pass me by that he's no longer saying "we," but since I can't think of a better solution, I grab my phone and dial. All the while, the only thought spinning in my head is that for the second time in my life I've gotten close to a colleague who I thought would have my back, and for the second time, I've been wrong. Fool me twice and all that.

But maybe I'm not being fair. Modeling isn't for everyone, and I have deliberately staked no claim on what Jonathan does or doesn't do. I'm the only one with everything riding on this project.

But you hoped he'd come through for you, a voice nags in my head.

I did. And I should have known better than to rely on something as flimsy as hope.

Days until new printer deadline: 2

I am thirty-four years old. I've gone to college and law school, I've been involved in sports, I've traveled, and I've worked several jobs. I've lived some. So why do I not have more contacts in my phone? It takes less than an hour to call everyone I know (or everyone who could reasonably be expected to call back anyway) to ask them who they know who is a dog owner that might want to be my Mr. July. Since it's a Saturday, I leave lots of messages. People are busy—I know that. But every time I get voice mail, I grow more dejected. Not everyone returns calls right away, and I don't have time to wait. Not even Rachel picks up. She's at a classic car meet in Bend, Oregon, with her dad for the weekend.

My follow-ups to pet stores and puppy-training places yield nothing, and of our previous models, I only reach Robert and Ava's tennis coach, who says he might know a few people, but he can't guarantee they'll get back to him before Monday. I tell him to do what he can, but deep inside, I know it's another dead end. Robert is just back from New York and says he'll let me know Sunday if he's free, but I won't be holding my breath.

Jude and Ava are in the kitchen when I enter in search of anything chocolate for comfort. Ava is making an omelet for lunch, and it smells amazing. She has two plates out, which I take as another sign that she's no longer giving her dad the cold shoulder.

"I didn't know you were here," Ava says to me. "I would have made more food, but I thought you were staying over at Jonathan's."

That makes two of us, but I'm still having a hard time with his immediate refusal to save my project. The fact that he wouldn't even discuss it doesn't sit well with me, and since he didn't mention me coming over after our little spat, I assume he feels equally ruffled.

"That's okay. I don't need food. Something sweet to skyrocket my blood sugar will do the trick. Do we still have boxes of Girl Scout cookies somewhere?"

"No luck finding another model, then?" Jude asks.

I shake my head. "Maybe Robert, but he's more unreliable than a Pacific Northwest weather forecast. Can you please call some of your coworkers?"

"I already told you—the ones I'm close with don't have pets. Well, Lorna has two cats, but that's not what you're looking for."

"What about the ones you're not close with?"

He raises an eyebrow at my desperate question.

"I know, I know—inappropriate, crossing professional boundaries, yada, yada, yada."

"I'm sorry, Hols. I wish I knew someone, I really do," he says.

"What about you?" I ask Ava. "Any hot teachers I could reach out to?"

She sputters a laugh. "No. Jeez, you have run out of options, haven't you?"

"Damn it." I sit down, grab Jude's fork, and help myself to a bite of his omelet.

"By all means," he says, pushing his plate closer to me.

"Sorry," I say, shoving a second bite into my mouth. "When I'm stressed, I eat. You should have seen the amounts of ice cream I devoured the day I quit Heckles and Romer."

"I can have a sandwich," Jude offers.

"No." A third bite, and then I return the plate to him. "I'll find something else. Thanks, though. I'm just stuck."

"And you're sure Jonathan won't do it?" Ava asks, sitting down to join us. "Maybe he needed to sleep on it."

He did come around on working together. *With Manny's help*, a voice in my head reminds me. Somehow, I doubt our boss would be willing to exert any leverage to make Jonathan get in front of the camera. No, this one is on me.

"Are you seeing him tonight?" Jude asks.

"I don't know." This was definitely not what I had in mind when I considered shaking up our relationship a bit. "I mean, I want to."

I get up and grab a can of cola from the fridge. It's not chocolate, and I rarely drink soft drinks anymore, but I need the boost. Could it be that Ava is right and Jonathan as Mr. July is still a possibility? "I'm going to text him," I announce, setting down the barely sampled can. "Or I'll go over there."

Jude frowns. "You know, there could be another reason why he doesn't—"

Ava cuts him off. "I bet he'll come around. He's really into you."

Her suggestion manages to spark that fizziness in my belly despite what happened yesterday, so I take that as a good sign. I smile at my niece. "Let's hope so." I turn to Jude. "What were you going to say? Something about another reason?"

He pauses for a beat. "I don't know." Taps the countertop. "Could it be..."

"Spit it out."

"Fine. Maybe he doesn't want to help because if you win, he loses." Jude squints at me.

"Loses what?"

He groans. "You."

Ava gawks at her dad and turns to me.

"No." I wait for his words to settle, but they don't. They buzz about in my head like mosquitos in ambush when you've tucked in for the night. "No, that's not...He wouldn't." I swat at the words to make them stop attacking. Jonathan is not that selfish.

Jude shrugs. "It was only a thought. I'm probably wrong."

"As usual," Ava quips, but she does it with a wink that triggers some good, old father-daughter banter.

I take that opportunity to excuse myself and pull up my message thread with Jonathan. I weigh my words carefully as I type to avoid appearing confrontational. **Can I see you tonight? Will bring food.**

I don't have to wait more than a few seconds for his reply.

Please, he texts. **I'm starving.**

I smile to myself. **What are you in the mood for?**

He takes longer to respond this time, and when he does, it's with an apology. **Sorry, Sir Leonard and I are on a walk with Dad.**

As the three moving dots jiggle, I roll my eyes at the stupid twinge of jealousy that inevitably jars me at hearing of his newfound canine companion. "He's a dog," I mutter to myself. "Get a grip."

I'm up for anything. Just want to see you, comes his response. The optimist in me stirs. **Seven?** I ask.

Six, he responds.

All the better.

I have one more shot. One more shot to convince Jonathan to model for me. One more shot to finish the calendar. One more shot at the future I've pictured since I lost my old job.

I open the photos I've saved to my phone of apartments in Glasgow and start scrolling. It's so easy to picture myself there. Far from Washington. Doing good work. Popping down to the local pub for happy hour with my new colleagues who share my need for making a difference. Hiking around Loch Lomond on my days off. I'll be happy when I'm there—I know I will. Happy starting over.

I flip to the next photo, and there's Jonathan playing the piano with his band at the blues bar a couple of weeks ago. Our first date.

As I stare at the photo, something strange happens in my chest at the sight of the familiar focus he exudes. First, a tightening, heavy and dense, that makes my shoulders slump. Then a slowing of the heart into a somber rhythm. And last, the sensation of the two merging, which makes breathing hard. The feeling moves up through my throat where it lodges itself into an unnerving hurdle that makes my eyes burn.

I return to the image of a town house complete with a cheery kettle on the stove and blooming roses outside the window, but it doesn't help. A tear still breaks free and drips onto my screen.

So dumb, I tell myself. A bit of fear of the unknown.

But as soon as I flip back to the picture of Jonathan, I know that's not what's amiss.

It's the starting over. Specifically, the starting over without him.

Still dumb, my inner voice persists. And it's right. I've come too far to lose sight of my goal now.

Days until new printer deadline: 2

It's one of those perfect fall evenings when I pull into Jonathan's driveway with portabella-and-goat-cheese burgers and hand-cut fries in a paper to-go bag from my favorite place. It's completely calm, the air is crisp and chilly, and the twilight stars are already competing with the waning moon for brightness as the sun sets beyond the Olympics, leaving a cloudless sky behind.

My insides contrast starkly with the calm around me.

I tell myself it's because so much hinges on tonight, but the truth is also in the crumpled tissues I left behind in my room at home. I have feelings for Jonathan that I wish I didn't have. Feelings I both want and don't want him to know about, and that I both want and don't want him to reciprocate. Feelings I may soon have to forget about.

I inhale deeply and press my free hand to my stomach.

But not tonight. Tonight, I'll allow those feelings to guide me. Provided we can move on from yesterday's discord, that is.

Jonathan opens the door slowly when I knock as if he's not sure he should be letting me in. "Hi." He grabs Sir Leonard's collar to temper the big beast's eager greeting while I step onto the front stoop.

"Hi." I hold up the bag of food and lift my brow. "Peace offering?"

His shoulders relax, and when he's sure his canine companion is in check, he opens the door wider and steps back to allow me inside. "That's not..." He scratches the side of his head.

I kick off my boots and hand him the bag so I can give Sir Leonard some love. "That's not what?" I glance up at him as I ruffle Sir Leonard's ears.

"Necessary. A peace offering, I mean. I'm glad you're here."

I stand. "Yeah?"

He nods. Reaches for my hand.

I take it. At least he's not mad about yesterday, then. But whether that means he's thought about posing for me or not remains to be seen. "I'm glad I'm here, too. Hungry, but glad."

Finally, he smiles. I swear the way his eyes crinkle as that flash of mirth bursts forth could make even an award-winning comedian feel accomplished. It's a rare gem with magical powers. My nerves calm, my insides warm, and my mind forgets for a moment that this can't be forever. It makes me want to nestle into his arms and claim squatters' rights.

"Let's eat. Come on." He takes the stairs in five long strides, and to my surprise, Sir Leonard keeps up.

"This guy has a new lease on life all of a sudden," I say.

"He does, right? We're getting along. I think he's happy."

I dig in my bag for one of Morris's cookies that I stole from his stash. "Can he have a treat?"

Jonathan lights up. "You brought that for him? That's really sweet."

I shrug. He doesn't need to know it's to help me feel better about the less than generous thoughts I've harbored toward Sir Leonard these past few days. "So he knows I'm a friend."

Jonathan pauses for a beat but then moves around the island to set the brown paper bag down on the counter. "And is that what you are?"

The hesitant note in his voice commands my attention. It's a wolf of a question camouflaged in sheep's clothing.

Thankfully, Sir Leonard chooses that moment to finish his cookie and come looking for more. He licks my hands and bumps my leg with his nose. I squat and take hold of his face. "Are you my friend, big guy? Yes, we're such good friends," I coo. Then I join Jonathan at the counter. "He says yes."

If he finds my answer incomplete, he doesn't let on. Instead he bumps his hip to mine. "Glad you're here," he says. "I missed you last night."

I lean my head on his shoulder and within seconds he's folded me to him like I wanted earlier. "Me too."

As we eat, we avoid the topic of the calendar altogether. It's still there, a ghost lingering behind us, but in our candlelit bubble of food, wine, and casual touches, we keep it at bay as long as we can. We talk about Wayne's new square-dancing course, Jude's impending move, Ava's chances of a tennis scholarship, and Sir Leonard's improving sleep habits. We compare notes on office gossip, agree on a new restaurant to try, and squabble over what's the superior shape of a french fry. I make a good argument for waffle-cut fries I think, but then Jonathan promptly shoves a couple of hand-cut ones into my mouth, which finishes off both the conversation and the food.

The ghost moves closer.

Jonathan leans back in his seat but keeps looking at me. In the background, Bonnie Raitt's low voice croons about how love has no pride, and for a moment, I allow myself to get lost in the notes. If I could choose, we'd simply share a meal and pretend there's nothing wedged between us, but I know what's coming. There's only one topic left unaddressed, and the evening has been building toward it whether we want it to or not.

So, when the final notes of the song ring out, I brace myself before I say, "I haven't been able to find another model. Robert is my best chance—he says he might call tomorrow—but I think we both know that's not going to happen."

He nods slowly. "I was wondering."

"The timeline is too tight. I've left messages with people, but the chances of anyone coming through are—"

"Not great," he fills in.

"Right."

A new song starts—one I don't recognize. Its rhythm is faster, more upbeat, and with that as a boost, I decide I have nothing to lose.

"Look, I don't want to fight, but I have to ask you again. You're my only hope of getting the calendar done in time. Or at all for that matter. Will you please reconsider?"

Jonathan looks down at his hands, squeezing one with the other. The corner of his lip is caught between his teeth, and all of a sudden, I know he's going to say no again, which means I'll be done, and I can't let that happen.

"Do you not want me to win?" I blurt. "Is that why you won't do it?"

His head jerks back. "What kind of question is that?"

I think about Jude's suggestion that helping me isn't in Jonathan's interest. "A fair one," I say. *If you're as into me as I'm into you.*

"I think it's the opposite of fair," he says. "The only answer that doesn't make me an asshole is that of course I want you to win. We've put in all this work." He gestures around us as if our models—human and canine—are here with us.

"Then there should be no problem."

He scoffs, his head slumping to his chest. "You know it's more com—"

He swallows the word I know is on his tongue.

Complicated.

So maybe Jude was right. "If you truly want me to win, you know I can't do it without you. Please be in the calendar. For me."

"For you," he repeats. "But not for us?" He peers up at me. "No, don't answer that. I'm sorry. I knew this was the deal."

I reach over and take his hand. I can't help myself. But I also know I need to steer this conversation away from where it's ended up. Give him a different out. "If you're worried about people seeing you and judging you for modeling, we can hide your face. It's nighttime anyway so if your face was in shade or you were backlit...I don't know. You're the expert on that stuff."

Finally, he weaves his fingers through mine. "That wouldn't be very summery."

I consider this, and then I have an idea. "If it's for July, we could add in fireworks." Suddenly the vision is completely clear in my mind. It's an artsy shoot with Jonathan lit up in relief by a colorful sky, Sir Leonard seated in front of him. It would almost make a butterfly shape where dog and man are the body and the fireworks the wings.

"Hmm." Jonathan's forehead wrinkles. "Maybe up on the rooftop," he says quietly. "It would require more editing than the others. And it might look a bit out of place."

"I mean, I'd also be willing to have you pose naked on the beach, but you know…" I smirk.

"I have scruples."

"Yeah that." I study him closely as the rigidity in his face gives way to something more animated. "Does that mean you'll do it?" I ask carefully.

"Who would take this photo?"

"Me. If you let me."

He sighs. Shakes his head in a dejected shrug. I hold my breath.

"Fine," he says. "As long as my face isn't front and center."

"Really?" I gasp, jumping out of my seat.

"Really. Let's do it." He lets me pull him up, too, and when I hug him tight, he laughs, his chest rumbling against mine.

I retreat a few inches so I can see him. "Right now before you change your mind?"

He nods. "Let's get the stuff."

The temperature has dropped further when we get out onto Jonathan's deck, and the stars have competition from the lit-up skyline beyond. It doesn't take too long to set up the tripod and light stand that will create the effect Jonathan will later attribute to fireworks when editing. Even though I'll be taking the picture, I let him adjust the settings for shutter speed, f-stop, and all the other terms I've picked up while working with him. I've heard them, I know they're photography related, but that's where my knowledge ends. I also pose where he'll be standing so he can make sure the whole thing is framed right.

"Okay," he says finally. "Here's the remote. You'll make sure the light is positioned for the right effect, give me a count, and click here."

"What about Sir Leonard?"

"Don't worry about him. Whoever he was with when he was little trained him well. He'll sit when I tell him."

"Cool." I look from Jonathan to the setup and back. "I guess there's only one more thing then. Clothes off."

"Nuh-uh. Shirt only. My legs will be behind Lenny anyway?"

"Lenny? No, you can't call him that."

Jonathan pulls his black Henley over his head. "Why not? He's my dog."

"It's undignified. He's clearly a knighted noble." I scratch Sir Leonard's head. "See, he agrees with me. Besides, have you never read *Of Mice and Men*?"

Jonathan pauses. "I forgot about that. You've got a point. Damn, it's cold tonight."

"All the more reason to get on with it. Positions, please."

It's not easy to picture what the final image will look like when you're working with low light and a backdrop that will be altered later, so I focus on what I think is the most important aspects of these photos—the dog and the male form. Jonathan's face is shadowed to the point of unrecognizability, but I'd know that chest and those arms anywhere. The lamp behind him makes them glow in relief, and the small lights we've set up to draw attention to Sir Leonard create a powerful map of ridges and trails across Jonathan's torso.

He checks the progress once I've snapped a few shots. "Not too bad," he says. "Are there other poses you want to try?"

I stare at him. He's giving me creative control? All right, then. Because I love the angle of his jaw, I ask him to tilt his head toward the sky and snap another picture, but it's not as strong as I want it to be. "I wish I could tell Sir Leonard to do the same. The symmetry is off."

The dog blinks at me but doesn't move.

"Let's try something," Jonathan says. "Be ready." Then he tips his head back again and howls. Sir Leonard freezes for a split second before he, too, starts howling.

I click away, and now the results are as I imagined. "You look like a hot werewolf in this," I say, showing it to him. "I think I'm going to keep this for me even if it's not the one we pick for the calendar."

"Fair, since I have a few of you."

My cheeks flush at the mention of that day in Discovery Park. "Right."

"Anything else you want to try? I have maybe another ten minutes in me before my nipples fall off."

"And we wouldn't want that." I look through the viewfinder. Try to imagine the sky lit up in every color of the rainbow. "There is one thing."

"Yeah?"

"Usually when there are fireworks, people watch them. So I'm thinking you take off your clothes and turn your back to the camera."

"Um what?"

"Your back. To the camera." I do a circle with my finger.

His eyelids lower into an unamused glare. "Before that, Holly."

"Ah." I pretend to catch on. "Yes, so for this idea, I need you naked. Maybe you've just woken up and come outside to watch the festivities. And maybe the sheet you swept around you falls to the ground because the fireworks make you forget to hold it up."

"Oh, there's a story to go with it and everything?"

"I figure it might help you get into character." When he

doesn't move, I come out from behind the camera and approach him. "Please. No one will see your face. And I only want the top outline of your cute ass to show, not full cheek."

"Not full cheek? That's much better, then." He rolls his eyes.

I allow his features to settle before I take another step closer to him, my fingers reaching behind me for the button fastening my top at the nape of my neck. "What if I took off some of mine, too? Would that make it better?" I pull my top up and out of my jeans and then lift it over my head. The cold air makes me suck in my belly as a shiver runs through me. He wasn't joking about the temperature.

He still doesn't move, but at least the eye rolls have stopped. Sir Leonard tips his head to the side as if he's confused about this nighttime shedding of coats. *Foolish humans*, he seems to say. Maybe he's right.

I bridge the few feet still separating Jonathan and me and don't stop until I'm right in front of him. "Thoughts?" I ask.

"Not many at the moment." His gaze dips to the pink-and-black bra I'm wearing. In the light we have set up, the pink trim shimmers like pearl against the dark satin. He reaches for me, reverently tracing the lace, before running a hand up to my throat and back down again.

"Take your clothes off," I murmur.

He swallows, the shadow beneath his Adam's apple jumping as he does. "Okay."

While he sheds his jeans and boxer briefs, I return to the camera. He covers himself with his hands, and considering the temperature, I let it slide, instead focusing on the shoot.

"Turn around and look up as if you see the fireworks," I instruct him. "And let's have Sir Leonard sit next to you. I'm going to move the lights. There. Good." I snap a couple of pictures. "Your back looks really strong like this. Feel free to flex it if you can."

"Are you almost done?" He glances over his shoulder. "If not, you're going to have to take off your bra, too."

"Bargaining for time, are we?" But as I ask the question, I unsnap the hook in the back and let the garment slide down my arms. Without the thin layer of protection, my nipples instantly grow painfully tight. "A few more shots. I'm going to lower the tripod for a different angle." I do, but when I stand again, he's still watching me, eyes gleaming with want.

"I think we need to be done soon," he says, voice strained. Then he flashes me a glimpse of what's going on behind his cupped hands. "Considering the temperature, that should tell you something."

I squirm at the sight.

"I saw that," he says, covering himself again. "Let's get this over with, Holly, and let me take you to bed."

I let out a sharp breath. "Okay, okay." I grab hold of the remote. "Whenever you're ready. Don't clench."

"Easier said than done," he mutters, but he does what I ask. Even though he didn't want to model in the first place, and even though he might prefer it if I don't win, and don't move away, he's come through for me.

One glance at the last image on the screen, and I'm overwhelmed with the need to be done and to be closer to him than the camera has allowed. I drop the remote and hurry to him, wrapping my arms around him from behind. The skin between his shoulder blades is surprisingly warm against my nose, but he doesn't seem to mind the temperature difference.

I hear him tell Sir Leonard to go inside, and then he clutches my hands tightly against his chest.

"Thank you," I say over and over again between kisses along his spine, and I'm still saying it when he spins around and wraps his arms around me, too.

"Don't thank me yet," he says into my hair. "There's still a lot of work to be done."

"But not now." I move one of his hands to my breast and press into it.

"No, not now," he says gruffly.

Days until new printer deadline: 2

Jonathan sets me down at the foot of his bed, and I reluctantly release my grip around his neck. I barely noticed him picking me up and carrying me past his bookish sitting area and through the hallway. I was too busy holding on to pay attention. Too busy not letting go.

He's breathing hard, his bare chest heaving beneath my palms. Still backlit, now by the nightstand lamp, his contour glows warm orange, though his skin is still cool from the night air.

"Holly, I..." he starts, but I silence him with a look and a soft caress along his obliques that makes his abs ripple.

I know there are words to be said; they stir inside me, too. But next to them is an even greater urge to delay and treasure. "I want to touch you for a bit," I say. It's purely selfish—a chance to commit more of him to memory than the camera would allow. "Is that okay?"

He watches as I trace the outline of his pecs with my forefinger, his chin lowering in a slow nod.

I press a soft kiss to his shoulder as I begin my lap around him.

Standing at his side, I run my right hand from his chest down, while my left mimics the movement from his shoulder blades to the small of his back. He doesn't move a muscle, allowing me this odd embrace—at least for the time being. The smattering of hair down his belly offers a different textural experience than the smooth skin on his back. I note the difference, catalogue it, and then move on, my fingers inching lower but stopping short of his growing erection, veering instead right, past his small appendicitis scar and to his hip bone. I let my thumb caress the rounded ridge as I take another small step sideways.

From there, I bridge the gap to his arm, which hangs loosely at his side. A swollen vein adorns his forearm, up and across his bicep, and I follow it like it's a river on a map guiding me home. He has a birthmark near his armpit in the shape of a crescent moon and a vaccination scar a few inches from that. Two new entries in my Jonathan inventory. I'm happy to add them, and at the same time, I wish I'd found them sooner. After what he did for me tonight, I don't know if I'll have enough time to remember everything.

I force down the sudden knot forming in my throat and continue on. His shoulders, his neck, his hair. Then I run my hands down his spine and wrap my arms around him. *That's better.* I relax against him, and he sighs contentedly.

With my chest and cheek pressed to his back, I skim my nails down his torso and smile as the hairs on his arms rise.

"You're teasing me," he mumbles.

I press my lips to his right shoulder blade. Then I retreat a few inches. "A little. Do you mind?"

"Hell no." He shifts his stance slightly.

I let my hands linger on his hips. "Your skin is warming up. It was cold before from being outside."

"Both thanks to you, I believe." Voice cashmere soft.

I start moving again, this time to chart the hilly rises of his muscular ass. Each round handful gets a cheeky squeeze that makes him start.

"Hey," he says.

I step up to his left side. "Hey yourself."

His hooded eyes glimmer at me when I encircle his bicep with both hands, his muscles flexing beneath my grip. I let my hands slide downward, and when I get below his elbow, I turn his arm to expose the wrist. The gleam of the light against the thin skin there reveals a steady pulse beneath the surface. I touch it with my fingertip, fascinated by how its discreet *tap tap tap* transfers to my skin. Without thinking, I bring it to my lips to let them feel it, too, but as I do, he cradles my face in his hand and twists to bring me in front of him again.

"Enough," he whispers, voice strained. "My turn."

He tilts my face back and kisses me without urgency. *You took your time. Now I'll take mine*, his mouth seems to say. Soft lips press against mine, brushing over first the top and then the bottom. I invite him in and gasp open-mouthed against him when his palms find my breasts. They only linger a split second, though. He has a plan.

"On the bed," he says, nudging my hip. Then he adds, "If you don't mind."

I get on it as fast as I can in response and lie down on my back propped up on my elbows. I wish I had the camera, I think, as Jonathan stalks toward me. The light renders his body in gold and shadows—a mouthwatering mix of splendor and secrets—but it's his expression that has me take a mental snapshot for my records. His gaze caresses me in a way that mimics what I just did to him. Memorizing. I'm convinced my heartbeats must be visible through my rib cage as he straddles my legs and starts unbuttoning my jeans.

My eyes flutter closed when his knuckles skim the sensitive skin beneath my waistband, and my arms give out as he scoots back and yanks the rough fabric past my hips, pulling my panties along with it. His sheets are cool against my backside, soft in my eager grip. He's gentler pulling the garments over my feet, one leg at a time, and then he discards them on the floor next to the bed.

He lies down on his side next to me and runs a finger from my belly button up between my breasts and down one collarbone. "Did you ever think that day when you were stuck in the pantry closet that this would happen?"

"Ha." I tip my head left so I can see him. "Not in a million years. You?"

"No. Though that lacy tank top thing you were wearing featured prominently in my thoughts in the days following."

"Really?"

He starts drawing patterns across my forehead, prompting my eyelids closed. "Mm-hmm." Temples, cheekbones, nose, chin. "It was unexpected. Like...a sign of life. In me, I mean," he clarifies. "It had been so long since anything surprised me. Everything was a rut."

"It was a basic cami."

He traces my jawline, the shell of my ear. "Not to me. That whole morning threw me off, and at first, it annoyed me, but now I see how badly I needed it. Needed to be unsettled."

I smile. "I'm glad my top and I could be of service."

Without warning, warm heat engulfs my left nipple, making me arch off the bed. Jonathan's tongue dances over the tight bud in slow twirls while his nails draw circles around the other one. When he releases me, he keeps his left palm resting on my abdomen. "Sorry, I had to." He smiles, and then he nudges his nose along my upper arm until his chin comes to rest against my shoulder.

I push a strand of his hair away from his forehead. "Did you hear me complaining?"

"So I should do it again?" His resting hand inches closer to the rounded swell of my breast, pausing there.

I watch it, my skin aflame with anticipation. "If you want." The wobble in my voice gives me away, and he smiles.

He flips his hand to cup me. "How is this?" His thumb rests against my hard tip, gently stroking.

"Uh-huh," I manage on an exhale.

"Or like this?"

The pinch that follows brings my shoulders off the bed again. "Are you...getting back at me for the teasing earlier?" I ask when he releases me.

He withdraws his hands completely and kisses my neck before pushing himself up to sitting. "Maybe." His eyes linger on mine for a moment before wandering down my body, and I swear I feel it no less than I did his fingertips earlier. His gaze darkens as it caresses my chest, mimicking his physical attention moments ago. Then lower it goes, traversing my belly in a zigzag pattern, roaming the curves of my hips, pausing at the triangular summit of my thighs. His lips part slightly, and then he can't help himself. He bends over and places a kiss halfway below my belly button and follows it with a gentle stroke from hip to hip that sends a luscious ripple through my core.

I clench my already closed legs together tighter, and like before, he notices.

"Not yet," he says. "Soon."

I stretch my arms above my head and squirm against the soft comforter. "So mean."

He chuckles, but at least he starts touching me again, a firm stroke down my legs—to keep them still no doubt—and then he grips my ankles and urges me to flip over.

My backside isn't used to the ambient air, and that along with another caress in reverse up the back of my thighs makes my skin prickle all over.

"You're not cold, are you?" he asks.

I try to look at him over my shoulder. "No, I'm hot. You're a worse tease than I am."

"Mission accomplished, then. You're very...mm." He drags the back of his hand up my spine, one vertebra at a time. Pushes my hair out of the way so he can follow it all the way to the base of my skull before retracing his steps. "If I photographed you like this, in black and white, it would look like an exotic landscape." He nuzzles his stubbled cheek into the arched slope of my back, a warm exhale against my skin making my stomach clench tighter. "A valley to rest in." His hand returns to my ass, rounds each cheek, once, twice. "A drift of desert sand reflecting the sunlight." Then, along the back of my thighs and up between them, the briefest touch. "A hidden canyon perhaps."

A low moan escapes me.

"Photos like that would win awards..." The bed shifts as he straddles my legs. "Except there's no way I'd let anyone else see them. They'd be for me only."

I can't see what he's doing anymore, but I feel the weight of his gaze on my naked body all the same. It makes me attempt to lift my hips—an urge to get closer. Immediately, he pins them back down, but his urgency is building, too. Through the rush of blood in my ears, I hear it in his labored breathing, and I feel it in his increasingly eager touch.

If he asked me now, I'd pose however he wanted.

Finally, he extends his body on top of mine, runs his hands up my arms, and plants his lips against my neck. His hard length lodges flat against my sex, making me writhe beneath him. I can't move much, though, not with his bigger frame bracketing me, but I'll take it. For once, my brain can't focus on anything but where he'll touch me next and when that will happen.

I'm aching for him, and so ready that when he rolls off me, an involuntary "no" bursts through my lips. I want him closer, inside, not away, damn it.

"Hold on," he grunts. "I need to get a condom before I completely lose control."

Oh. I roll onto my back and wait, as patiently as I can, while he rummages through his nightstand even though my whole body is thrumming, the rhythm wild and unstoppable. Thankfully, he's quick and back on top of me before I can do something silly like get myself off.

Finally face-to-face, I wrap my arms and legs around him, pulling his mouth to mine as he shifts his hips upward, closer. *Yes, almost there.* Our kiss is frantic at first, greedy and sloppy, matched by sweaty skin and wandering hands, but it's not long before something changes. Hurried becomes gentle, urgent becomes sultry. He stills first, I think, and when he reaches up to cradle my face, I open my eyes to find him looking down at me. Intent, querying. Solemn.

"You okay?" I ask, relaxing my grip on him.

"Yes," he says. "Of course." He brushes a strand of hair off my cheek and kisses me again, softer this time and with a reverence that reaches deeper somehow.

"Good," I murmur.

"Good," he whispers back.

I relax my arms above my head again to allow him purchase against the mattress for a final adjustment between my legs, and then he slides one hand under my side and pauses there for a beat.

I don't know if it's his loud heart or mine that prologues our union, but I do know that, when he finally pushes into me, we both let out vowels encompassing more than the moment, more than our short history. I resist the urge to close my eyes, instead holding his gaze as he retreats, then slides forward again, fitting us perfectly together.

As a rhythm takes hold and pressure starts building, the lump in my throat returns. Moored to him, beneath him, the juxtaposition of awe and impending loss is overwhelming. Here, in this moment, he is everything. My buoy to cling to, the reader of my soul, a fortune teller promising the kind of life only victors earn in fairy tales.

But my subconscious refuses to completely let go of the real world where the two of us have no obvious future. I squeeze my eyes shut and tip my head back. Try to focus only on now.

He slows and reaches for one of my hands, bringing it to his lips. "Don't think," he whispers, soul-reader that he is. "Come here." He gets up on his knees and pulls me into his lap so I'm straddling him. A teasing gyration with his hips and he hits places inside me that effectively demand all my attention.

I gasp and cling to his arms to adjust. Then I try a tentative move. Another. Being in control works to home my focus, as do Jonathan's fingers digging into my hips. He's so smart, distracting me with a mission.

"You're so amazing," he says, hands roaming up and down

my sides as I start moving in earnest. The veins on his neck and shoulders are outlined in relief beneath my palms. His temples are beading with sweat.

I'm past the ability to form words, so I kiss him instead, imbuing it with all the things I cannot say. He's fast to match, and soon our lips and tongues urge an accelerating tempo. This is not a time for savoring anymore. Now it's a binge.

We hurtle toward climax entwined and gasping, free-falling over the edge as one, with our bodies rocking, shivering, and clinging. The heat radiating from my core in violent bursts knocks the air out of my lungs and restraint from my brain, and before I can stop it, that knot in my throat becomes a sob tearing out of me. It's too intense, I tell myself. That's why. I don't think Jonathan heard it, but in case he did, I bury my face in the crook of his neck to prevent any more such outbursts.

For a long moment, we merely hold each other, easing the other down from the high. Our breathing quiets, our heartbeats settle, and our skin cools, but neither of us moves. He's still inside me, and I have no idea how we're going to be able to separate and let go. Because this feels so right.

"It will be okay," he whispers in my ear, strong arms clutching me to him.

Maybe he did hear me after all. Or is he reassuring himself?

I nod against him, afraid my voice won't carry. He kisses my temple.

"Come on," he says, helping me off him. The sudden emptiness is startling, but I forget about it when he settles us in a spooning position and pulls the blanket from the foot of the bed over our wrung-out bodies.

With one arm wrapped across my stomach and the other

under my neck, he's got my whole backside covered, gradually quelling the storm inside me. Sex has never been like that for me, and I want to tell him, but how do you tell someone they're rocking your very existence and then leave the country?

We lie like that for a while, thoughts drifting but not far enough out to sea for sleep to roll in. Occasionally, his grip on me tightens, as if he's reassuring himself that I'm still there. I clutch his embracing arm in response and tuck my toes between his calves.

Eventually, I have to get up, though, or I'll regret it later, so I start the extraction process—legs first and then a scoot forward of the hips, lifting his arm.

"No," he murmurs. "Stay."

"Girl necessities," I tell him over my shoulder. Then I have a brilliant idea. "Shower with me?"

His face lights up. "As in...?"

"Water, soap, lather, rinse."

"Oh."

I yank the comforter off him and start walking away, swinging my hips. "And probably a lot more sex if you're interested."

He beats me to the bathroom.

In the past, I've never been able to sleep soundly wrapped in someone else's limbs, but when the sun comes up the next morning, it does so without my knowledge. I'm gone to the world, spent through and through, muscles and heart equally aching and needing respite. I'm vaguely aware of Jonathan occasionally getting out of bed, but he always returns, and the next time I resurface, his arm will be slung across my shoulders or I'll be using his chest as a pillow like our very first morning together eons ago.

In those hazy moments of consciousness, there are still gentle caresses, mildly suggestive embraces, and lips brushing against sleep-warm skin, but neither one of us takes it any further. Either the needs that propelled us earlier are finally satiated or, more likely, one of us simply falls back asleep before something can happen.

But at some point, I stir to find Jonathan awake, a small smile playing on his lips right in front of me.

"Pretty creepy to be watching me sleep," I mumble, turning my face into the pillow in a stretch before facing him again. The light in the room suggests it's later in the day, but I'm in for a shock when I glimpse the alarm clock on his nightstand. "Holy shit." I push up to sitting. "It's almost four o'clock. You should have woken me up."

"I just woke up myself." He wraps his arms around my waist and kisses my shoulder. "Besides, it's Sunday, and we were up all night."

His scratchy chin tickles the crook of my neck, and I laugh. "We were, weren't we?"

"Mm-hmm." He wrestles me back into the mattress and hovers over me, his gray eyes soft and attentive. "I want to stay in bed until next Sunday and then some," he says. "What do you think?"

"I wish." I reach up to touch his jaw, but my stomach chooses that moment to rumble impolitely, ruining a tender moment. "Unfortunately, I also have other human needs...."

He grins. "I can order pizza."

"Are you trying to turn me on again?"

"Is it working?"

I push at his shoulders and flip him onto his back. "Always. But without sustenance I might be forced to just lie here while you take your pleasure. No energy, you know."

"And we can't have that." He crushes me down onto his chest, hugs me close, and then whispers in my ear, "I much prefer you perky and spry."

Despite my exhaustion, his words make my body attempt to ignite dormant spots throughout, small thrills of electricity sparking before fizzling. No, I really do need food.

We eat on his couch wrapped in towels after another, quicker shower. Poor, neglected Sir Leonard zooms like a puppy around us, overjoyed at finally having company, and I feel obliged to sneak him the occasional small piece of pizza so he won't hate me for monopolizing Jonathan's time. The old boy did get fed and taken outside while I slept. It turns out that's where Jonathan had disappeared to.

The clock ticks on, the sun begins to set, and I know I need to get going to get things in order for the week. Not to mention that Jonathan has work to do on our chosen photo from last night. I wouldn't have the past twenty-four hours undone, though. Not for anything.

I'm putting my shoes on in the foyer when Jonathan rests his hands behind his head and sighs. "Ugh, I don't want you to go."

I still with my hands on my shoelace. He's just promised me he'll get the edits to the printer before he goes to bed tonight, definitely before tomorrow morning's deadline, and with that topic still at the forefront of my mind, my first thought is that he means Scotland. *He doesn't want me to go to Glasgow.* The sentiment hits me square in the chest because he's not allowed to feel that way any more than I'm allowed to want him to come with me.

"There will be way too much space in my bed," he complains, and I draw a shaky inhale that I willfully attribute to relief.

He means tonight.

I finish tying my boot and go to him. "Sir Leonard can hold my spot until next time." I grab hold of the front of the robe he's put on and pull myself up to kiss him. A quick peck.

His dark lashes dip against his cheeks before he looks up. "And there will be a next time?"

Complicated, complicated, complicated, echoes in my head. I clutch the terry fabric tighter to make it stop. "I promise."

"Okay." He rubs my shoulders. "Then you can go."

I smile. "So generous of you."

He leads me by the hand to the door. "That's me. Mr. Generous."

I open it. "I'll see you tomorrow."

He lets go. "Tomorrow."

"Don't forget…"

"The printer. I won't. And I'll send you the image for approval first."

Finally, it will be done. No more last-minute photo shoots, or bad dates, or fights about missing forms. Only him and me, for the time we have left.

He's still in the doorway when I pull into the street and speed off. And he's still in my thoughts when I fall asleep in my own bed hours later.

Day of second printer deadline

"Why do you look like you're about to break into song at any moment?" Rachel points a pencil at me during a slump in foot traffic at the business expo we're attending Monday morning. "It's not like our booth is pulling crowds."

She's right. It's been slow going today. Only a dozen people have stopped by, and it's nearing lunchtime. Not like the Chamber of Commerce event in June where we didn't sit down all day.

"I'm happy to be done with the calendar. And"—I lower my voice—"I had a really great weekend."

Her eyes widen. "Oh, so that's why. Good for you."

Two suits walk up to ask about GCL, and I take this one while Rachel hangs back. I go over our goals, our vision, our successes, and send the potential new investors off with our materials.

"That was good," Rachel says. "I think my work here is done. You're ready to fly, little bird."

"As long as the calendar sells."

"It will."

"That reminds me—I want to call the printer to verify lead

time again and that they're sending me a hard copy for approval. Do you mind if I step out for a bit?"

She tells me to go ahead, so I find a corner in the hotel lobby and settle into a low armchair. As I unlock my phone, it opens to the last message I sent to Jonathan at 7:30 this morning: **Everything go ok with the edits?** There's no response, and no read receipt. It's a little odd, but then again, I haven't checked my phone since then either. Mondays are always busy.

I pull up my contact at the printer and dial. He answers after three beeps. After the normal pleasantries, I get right to it.

"So five days puts us at Friday. Will I have a copy to sign off on by then so we can start directing people to the sales platform immediately? If everything looks good, I plan on picking up the boxes I'm hand-selling Friday afternoon."

There's a brief pause on the line. "Okay, but...Hold on a second." The line goes quiet for a long minute before he comes back. "As I thought." He clears his throat. "We don't have your files, so you've been bumped from the schedule."

His words take a moment to register. "What do you mean you don't have my files?"

"We gave you an extension, and you were supposed to send them over by eight a.m. today."

"Yes, I know that." I stand up and face the windows, my hand going to my forehead. "You should have them. He was sending them over."

"He?"

"My photographer. Oh!" A thought strikes. "M-maybe since they would have come from Jonathan Summers, not me, they got caught in a filter or something."

"I don't think—"

"Can you please check?"

He sighs. "Sure. Hang on."

While he's gone, I type out another message to Jonathan. **Issue with the printer. You did send in the files, right?** My stomach is feeling more and more liquid by the moment.

"Nope, sorry. We've got nothing."

Fuck. "Okay, well..." My brain races, trying to unscramble the mess to create a next step. "I'm not at the office at the moment, but I can head over there, get the files, and send them within the hour."

"Unfortunately, that wouldn't really make a difference. We're running other print jobs already, so the earliest I could get to yours is... Let's see... Oh, we have an opening Wednesday. With lead time that would then mean Monday the twenty-fourth."

"But that's too late!" My stomach roils beneath my hand. I think I'm going to be sick.

"I'm sorry. There's nothing I can do. Let me know what you decide." He hangs up.

The lobby spins around me, and I'm not getting enough air. *Monday, Monday, Monday*, echoes in my head. He may as well have said Christmas. I'll miss selling at both a big open-air market and a bookstore event. I bend over and stick my head between my knees as I squeeze my eyes shut. My eyes burn, and my lungs sting, but at least the nausea recedes.

What am I going to do? I'm fucked. If I don't have a product, the rules of the contest say I can't start selling, and if I can't start selling, I won't raise any money. I won't win.

I need to see Jonathan. Now.

I jog back to Rachel and give her the CliffsNotes version of what's going on.

"Yes, you go," she says. "I've got this covered."

I give her a quick hug and then I dash to my car. I'm almost to the office when a text from Jonathan comes through: Yes, I sent the stuff. What's going on?

A momentary ripple of relief skirts through me before I remember that it doesn't matter. Regardless of what Jonathan says, the printer doesn't have the files.

Since I can't text him back while driving, I'm forced to sit on all my questions until I get to work. I slam the car door shut with too much force, stab the elevator button a half dozen more times than necessary, and ignore Letitia's cheerful "Hey" in the vestibule. All I can think of is getting to Jonathan and figuring this out.

He's at his laptop, typing furiously when I enter his office, and thankfully he's alone. Jacques's chair is empty.

"The printer never got the files," I say, skipping my hellos. "I'm freaking out."

He finishes typing and scoots his chair back. "I know. I'm emailing with him. I..." He scrubs a hand over his face and sighs.

The fact that he's not approaching me, not trying to reassure me makes my chest constrict. "You did send it, right? This is an error on their end?" *Please tell me it's the printer's fault.*

"I thought I did."

My mouth falls open. "You thought you did. What's that supposed to mean?"

He finally meets my eyes. "Hear me out, okay. It's not a big deal. I'm fixing it." He gestures to his computer.

Clearly, the printer hasn't painted him the whole picture yet. "There is no 'fixing it,'" I say. "The presses are tied up with other projects until Wednesday at the earliest. That means I lose. Please tell me you didn't make me lose."

His jaws clench. "I sent the files. Or I set it to upload before I went to bed. My fucking internet—it must have failed to send."

"You didn't check?" My voice makes someone walking past the office turn and look. "Why wouldn't you—"

"I would have, but Sir Leonard kept needing to go outside with an upset stomach all night, and then I overslept and had to rush to an, um... an appointment before work so in the midst of that, it must have slipped my mind."

"It slipped..." I pace away from him a step while collecting myself but then spin back around. "It should have been the only thing on your mind!"

His features darken. "Because it's the only thing on your mind?"

"Yes! Because you promised. How could you...? What am I...? What the fuck, Jonathan? I have worked so hard."

"We," he says, voice clipped. "*We* have worked so hard. It was a simple mistake, and for what it's worth, I am very sorry."

I scoff. "Yeah, it's not worth much." I know I sound cruel, but how else can I make him understand the full impact this will have on my life?

He presses his lips together and closes his laptop.

"I don't understand," I say. "I'm sorry your dog was sick, but how did you not check it this morning?"

"Like I said, I was late for an appointment."

"But this was it. You knew how important this was." My eyes are starting to sting. How on earth did I let feelings for a coworker screw me over again? "I thought you... we... but clearly I was wrong, or this would have never—"

"It was a passport appointment," he says, interrupting me. "Mine expired, and I need one to start contesting the no-fly status." He gets up and takes a step toward me but stops. "I wanted to do it for you."

Somewhere in what he's saying I recognize the true sentiment, but of all the misguided efforts... Because of him there is no need for travel. A fresh wave of anger rolls over me. A fresh need to lash out, to hurt. "Well, it doesn't matter now, does it?" It takes every ounce of self-control not to allow the boiling ugliness inside to overflow into name-calling and blame. I want to rage at him, but who am I kidding? I'm the one who put myself in this situation, knowing better. I take a deep breath. "Whatever, it's my bad. I shouldn't have let my guard down. Big mistake. Lesson learned. Fuck." I sigh. I can't do this anymore.

He stares at me a long moment. "That's how you feel? We're a mistake?"

No, I want to yell. *No, no, no.* But instead, I gesture around the room. "It's not exactly a success, is it?"

I watch him shut down. His shoulders first, rolling in, and then his fingers curving into his palms, neck slumping, jaw clenching.

He angles his face away from me and clears his throat. "Then I'll make this easier for both of us. We're done. No more need for you to worry about me fucking up your life in any way." He sits back down and turns his back to me. "Goodbye and good luck."

I stare at his hunched figure for a beat, and then I flee before the tears can come in earnest. I don't know where to go or what to do; all I know is that I need to get away.

Not only have I lost my chance at winning the fundraiser contest today, but I've also lost the man who may well be the love of my life.

35

The rainy season rolls in with a vengeance that week. We get mist, sprinkles, and roof-smattering showers. Sideways rain, open-sky downpours, and even five minutes of hail. The low, gray clouds loom as ominously over Seattle as the upcoming winner announcement looms over me.

I finally get the calendar printing under way that Wednesday, and online sales are great once they kick off after the weekend, but with less than a week left, there's no way. Letitia's and Eric's events were both raging successes. While we won't have final numbers until Friday, it would take a small miracle for me to beat either one of them.

I avoid the design side of the office since Jonathan ended things, and he doesn't venture over this way either. I still jump every time the door to the elevator vestibule opens, but it's never him. His absence lines my lungs with lead that weighs me to my chair and chokes my air supply. I'm starting to think I'll need to soak my laptop in rice for all the tears that have dripped into its keyboard. Everyone else seems to think it's because of the printer mix-up and my waning prospects of winning, and that's fine. I don't need to add "dumped" to "loser" after my name.

"Any better today?" Rachel asks when we head downstairs to grab lunch.

"Nope." I hold the door to the café around the corner for her.

"You could still win. The calendar is selling."

"Eric sold out his Green Gala at a small fortune per envelope."

Rachel falls silent. "Okay, but Ashley hardly got any participants in her Instagram contest."

"You know that doesn't matter."

We grab our food and get a table in the corner.

"So what will you do?" she asks after swallowing her first bite.

I pick a leaf of lettuce from my wrap and examine it closely. The nonexistent plan B. "That's what I'm trying to figure out. Definitely not staying here."

Rachel lowers her sandwich to the table. "No?"

"My family is probably moving, I've nothing to fall back on professionally, and now with..." My voice breaks.

"Jonathan?" Rachel guesses.

I nod, and she hands me a wad of napkins.

"Fuck. I don't know why I'm like this," I say, dabbing at my cheeks. "It was supposed to be a bit of fun. It was fun. I never intended to fall in love with him."

"Wait, what?" Rachel lowers her voice. "You're in love with him?"

"As if you didn't already know that."

She sits back. "I really didn't. You never said. I mean, I thought you looked closer than a fling, but you made it clear it was temporary." She pauses as if replaying the past few weeks for clues. "Damn, Holly. Does he love you, too?"

"Doubt it. That goodbye came real easy for him." *Though he did make that passport appointment*, my inner voice reminds me.

"Hmm." Rachel's forehead creases.

I've wiped my tears, and now I take a big bite of my chicken Caesar wrap. "What?" I ask, my mouth full.

"Maybe you should ask him."

I cover my mouth so the crumbs won't fly as I sputter, "Like, 'Hey, Jonathan, do you love me?'"

"Yeah."

"You're high." I swallow and have a swig of water. "I promise you that wouldn't go over well. Besides, like I said, I'm not staying here anyway. Bad memories are piling up in this place. I need a fresh start. Now more than ever."

Rachel sighs. "Fine, I get it. I still think you should talk to him, though."

"To what end? So I can apologize for what I said? So he can apologize for what he did? The fact remains. Mistake or not, he made me lose this job like Chris made me lose the promotion. Oh, and my reputation." I shake my head. "I truly have a terrible way of picking them."

"But it's not the same." Rachel leans forward. "It sounds like this really was an accident. And a job is only a job. If you love him..."

"Please, can we not?"

Maybe it's my still-damp eyes or the edge in my voice, but Rachel stops short of finishing her sentence.

"Thank you," I say. "It'll be a lot easier for everyone if I can avoid him completely until my time at GCL is over. Clean breaks are less messy and all that. I'll be fine." I fold my wrap into its paper and push it aside. A sense of resolution comes over me. "No, I've got to start looking for something else. I can use you as a reference, right?"

Her expression softens. "Of course." Her phone chirps, and she glances at it.

"Thanks. And I'm sorry. This isn't how this was going to go."

"I know." She picks up her phone, her forehead wrinkling. "Um..."

"What?"

Face flushed, she looks up from her screen. "I..." Her mouth snaps closed as she looks at her message again. "This is going to sound super weird, and I promise it's not my fault, but I think your brother just asked me out." She holds the phone up for me to see.

So he finally did it.

"Obviously I'll say no. I know how you feel about that. Or maybe it's a wrong number situation?"

"It's not." I smile at my friend. "You should say yes."

"I should?"

"If you want to. I'm done interfering. Promise."

Her whole face lights up. "Really?"

"Really. You two are my favorite people. Have fun. Just remember he's still planning on moving." I push my chair back and stand. "But who knows—maybe it's meant to be?" I shrug. "I'm heading up. See you in a bit?"

She nods. "Thank you. And for what it's worth, I still think you'd make the best program liaison. No matter who wins the fundraiser."

If only it was that easy.

My plan to avoid Jonathan works fine initially. In addition to Rachel keeping me busy at GCL, I drive to Portland to get calendars from the printer, do door-to-door sales in the South Lake Union office buildings (with permission, of course), and sell at a local farmers market. I also start perusing job boards around the country, which is less than encouraging. The main problem I see when considering other jobs, nonprofit or not, is how to get past having to disclose my dishonorable ousting from Heckles & Romer. At GCL, Rachel could vouch for me because she knew Manny, but without someone like that ushering me into the hiring pool, I'll have to apply with my CV, and hard questions will inevitably be asked. Not to mention references requested.

I blame being preoccupied with my lack of options for what happens after work Thursday. I'm meeting Rachel at yet another expo first thing in the morning, so I'm bringing our large display board home to have it ready, but when I get in the driver's seat and turn the key, the car dings to let me know I've forgotten to close the trunk. Grumbling about various inconveniences, I get out again and slam it shut, whipping around in a hurry as I do so.

And then I'm stuck. The side hem of my white, flowy knit sweater lodges firmly in the steel jaws of my car. My first instinct is to yank, but when the fabric protests, I stop. I like this top. The button to open the trunk is as unresponsive as always, and the key is, naturally, in the ignition out of reach.

"Damn it," I yell, stomping my foot. This is the last thing I need.

I glance around me but see no one else nearby.

"Some help?" I call. Nothing.

I close my eyes and count to ten. Then I squat and start the extrication process. One sleeve, two sleeves, and then my head joins my limbs inside the sweater. From the outside, I must look like an egg with legs or maybe a freaky sheep cowering at the rear bumper of my car.

And that's where I am when a voice says my name.

I freeze, still hidden inside my woolen cocoon. Through the knit strands, I can make out Jonathan's shoes and legs. He's standing not two yards away, and judging by his voice, this is as unexpected for him as it is for me.

"Hi?" I say, still not moving. Of all the ways I've imagined us breaking our silence, this was never on the menu. I scan the immediate ground around me for an escape. Stories of sinkholes have always terrified me, but if ever I was going to encounter one, now would be the time. I picture an expanding fissure in the concrete, me vanishing within. *Poof!*

"What are you doing?" he asks as the ground betrays me with its unshakeable rigidity.

Merely knowing he's looking at me makes my soul sing, and I much prefer the quiet. Or so I tell myself when I can't sleep at night. "Um... taking off my sweater."

"Do you need a hand?" He steps closer.

"No," I hurry to say. I don't think I can handle proximity with him right now.

He backs off.

Slowly, I tread my arms back into the sleeves and stand to plop my head through the neck hole. And my God, if he isn't the most gorgeous prospect-ruiner of all time. He's in his signature black jeans, but the gray cowl-neck sweater is new. It makes him look infinitely huggable. The ten days we've spent apart has done nothing to quell his magnetic pull on me.

"I'm stuck," I explain, gesturing to the hem. "Again. The keys are in the ignition."

"Ah." He goes to grab them. "Lucky I came by."

"I'd almost broken free," I say as he unlocks the trunk.

He hands me back the key. "Right." Noise at the entrance of

the garage makes him turn away and then put another few feet between us.

Gray sweater aside, this version of Jonathan is painfully familiar. Taciturn, curt, standoffish. He's once again choosing to withhold his softer side from me, and it hurts more than I thought it would. Against better judgment, it makes me want to force the other side back out.

"But thanks," I say, taking care to make it as friendly as I can. I venture to meet his gaze, but he looks away. Clearly, he doesn't think this was lucky at all.

I make one more attempt. "I take it you're not going to Thursday happy hour either?"

"What?" He blinks.

"Happy hour? I'd go, but I promised Jude I'd start sorting his attic. You know, in return for him posing for the…um… calendar." The more I talk, the more his face closes up. Maybe it would have been better if I'd stayed hidden inside my sweater. Or at least not brought up the calendar.

"I've got to go," he says. "Sir Leonard has been home alone all day."

"How's the old guy doi…?"

But Jonathan is already halfway to his car, and he's not looking back.

I need to do the same. Eyes on the future.

As soon as the thought has come and gone, a notification pops up on my screen: **Two new job matches for you!** One is a poorly paid internship at a nonprofit based in Alaska and the other a receptionist job for Greenpeace in DC. I get in the car, reject both, and lean my head on the steering wheel.

"Something will come along," I whisper.

Not necessarily because I believe it, but because it has to.

36

"With how often you get stuck in things, it's almost as if Washington is demanding you stay put," Jude says when I tell him about my awkward run-in with Jonathan.

Jude is doing pull-ups on a bar in the doorway to the garage. "There'll be a lot more sunny days in Austin," was his explanation when he installed it this past weekend.

I, on the other hand, am devouring a slice of the pizza I picked up on the way home. I'm seated on the floor of the hallway, my back against the wall. The floor vent on my right spews a musty warm breeze into the air. Not sure Jude got the furnace cleaned this year.

"Ha! More like the universe is leaving nothing to chance in driving home how trapped I am."

Jude lets go of the bar and stretches his shoulders. "Hey now. I've never known you to be a defeatist. You've been unemployed before. And how about in college when you weren't sure what you were going to major in?"

"This is different," I mumble around a glob of cheese. "I'm not twenty-two anymore. There are only so many times you can start over."

"I'm not sure that's true."

"Oh yeah? Says the starting over expert?" I regret the words as soon as they're out. "Sorry, that was a low blow."

He jumps to get a hold of the bar again. "I'll let it slide, but only because you're a mess. And also not completely wrong."

"But you have a plan," I whine.

"...five, six, seven..." He counts his chin-ups and then drops back to the ground. "You could, too. Mom and Dad would love it if you came with us. And not all law firms are greedy world destroyers—you know, in case the nonprofit scene doesn't work out."

My stomach roils in revolt at the very idea, but I still nod, not wanting to get into it.

"And while you noodle on that, I know the perfect thing you can do."

"Oh?" I follow him into the kitchen.

He smiles and hands me a box of oversized garbage bags. "Attic sorting time. Anything you think we should donate—kids' clothing, toys, Grandma's old tableware, linens, whatever—goes in these bags. Here's a marker for labeling."

I snatch it from him and attempt an unamused glare.

He waltzes on upstairs unaffected.

"What if I have questions?" I call after him.

"Label a bag 'questions.' I'm going to take a shower."

Smartass. But maybe this is what I need—something mindless to focus my restless energy on.

I dig out the attic hatch key from the catch-all kitchen drawer, and then I get to work.

No one could have prepared me for the amount of stuff a family of two can collect over the course of fifteen-plus years. I've peered into Jude's attic before on the hunt for Christmas garlands and ornaments, but actually stepping off the ladder onto the boards that make up the walkway from one end of the space to the other? Terrifying.

There's a window at each gable, but at this hour, they are merely gray squares, so I'm forced to rely on the three bare lightbulbs spaced overhead and a small flashlight. The air smells like damp cardboard and lumber with faint whiffs of detergent from the winter clothes Jude always cleans before storing when the season is over.

Looking around, I decide I'm going to have to start away from the ladder and work my way back. Most of the donations will likely be among the boxes that no one has touched since they were brought up here anyway.

As carefully as I can, I tiptoe along the boards to where Ava's disassembled crib has found its resting place. On top of the slatted sides are several boxes marked "Baby," which I drag toward me before I sit crisscross on the walkway. I have one garbage bag open and ready, but one quick riffling through the first box, and I determine that the whole thing can go. It's nothing but old baby toys, many barely used. I push it to the hatch and return to my post. One box down, a million to go.

I've made it through five more boxes of baby and toddler stuff when I come across a tub labeled with Mom's handwriting. I didn't realize Jude was storing things for them, but it makes sense, as their current house is much smaller than the one they sold. I open it, thinking it'll be home decor and serving platters, but instead I find two shoeboxes labeled "Holly" and "Jude."

I stare at the cursive letters for a moment. Then I rest the flashlight on the seat of a red tricycle and pull out the box with my name. At first, the items look random and jumbled, but then I recognize the envelopes with my high school report cards, the certificates of placement from my skiing days, and a bow-and-arrow key chain that used to be attached to my backpack. There's a jewelry box that holds the team charm from my last skiing race senior year, a macrame bracelet I made in art class for Mother's Day one year, a bottle cozy with my middle school's mascot, my driver's permit card, and a headband with tulle flowers that I vaguely remember went with my first-grade ballet recital dress.

Below everything else is a plastic sandwich bag with a stack of printed photos. I pull that out and set the box down next to me. Some of the photos I've seen before—their duplicates are in the albums downstairs—but several are new to me. There's one of Jude entertaining me and my friends with a Michael Jackson impression, one of me in an all-yellow getup, posing theatrically with a hula hoop and a red ball, and a whole slew of me and my teenage crew just lounging. On blankets on the lawn, at the neighborhood pool, in front of the TV, piled into a car. Leena moved back to Finland junior year, and Cat went to college on the East Coast, so I'm not in touch with either of these girls anymore, but for a while, we were tight. Sharing dreams and secrets. As successful career women, we were going to buy houses next to each other and our husbands would become best friends.

I chuckle at the naivete of it all. Although who's to say Leena and Cat didn't do exactly that? I might be the only one who's screwed up the dream.

Before I can fall down that rabbit hole again, I dig out a clipped-together bunch of papers from the bottom of the box with a rudimentary drawing of a girl on the front. The title reads "Who is…" and then my name in stilted red crayon, "HollY."

"No way," I whisper. I'd completely forgotten about this. It was a project the teachers at my elementary school did with the students. Every year they'd have us draw pictures of our lives and answer questions about our likes, dislikes, goals, and aspirations, and for fifth-grade graduation, they presented us with this book. I flip through it, stopping at certain pages. I liked rain and watermelon, disliked green beans and chocolate.

"Weirdo," I mutter. "Who doesn't like chocolate?"

I wanted to be a princess in kindergarten, but after that I had my priorities straight. I was going to be a teacher (first grade), then a professor (second and third grade), and in fourth grade, I apparently found my calling. The word *lawyer* is written in capital letters across the page along with a surprisingly good drawing of the scales of justice. That must have been the year Dad took me to bring-your-kid-to-work day.

I stare at the page a long time. How old was I in fourth grade? Nine? Ten? And I'd already picked out the career I'd stick with for decades to come. I shake my head. So precocious. No wonder it didn't last.

But then I flip to the fifth-grade page, and the harsh judgment of Little Me goes out the window. Because to the question "What do you want to be when you grow up?" fifth-grade Holly no longer responded with "lawyer." Fifth-grade Holly simply wanted to one day be "happy."

I suck in a breath and trace the heart surrounding the word with my finger.

Happy.

A memory of waking up next to Jonathan pops into my head.

White sheets, soft light. He turns his head and smiles when he sees me there.

No.

I shrug off the image and set the boxes aside as I struggle to my feet in the cramped space. It's getting late, and my back is killing me after sitting hunched over for so long.

But before I can get the donations down the ladder, my phone rings. It's Rachel, and from the sounds of it, she's driving.

"Figured I'd interrupt your deep dive into the job boards before you run out of oxygen," she says.

I look down at my dusty jeans. "Jude beat you to it. I'm currently holding up my end of the modeling bargain by sorting through his attic."

"Oooh, anything exciting?"

"That depends. Are you into old report cards and baby toys?"

"Sounds thrilling, but no. I wanted to see if you'd be up for a coordinated costume tomorrow?"

I straighten too fast and bonk my head on a rolled-up rug tucked in the rafters. It's surprising more than it is painful. "What do you mean 'costume'?"

"It's Halloween weekend. Didn't you see Manny's email about making the event a monster bash?"

"No. And since when is Halloween considered a whole weekend? That seems excessive."

She tuts. "Don't be like that. It'll be fun."

Not sure about "fun," but maybe it wouldn't be the worst idea to dress up as some sort of masked character. Then no one will know if I fail at presenting my gracious loser face. "Fine. I'll think about it."

"Yay!"

I look down at the boxes at my feet. "Hey, Rach, what did you want to be when you were little?"

"Dolphin trainer, mechanic, or letter writer," she says without hesitating. "I had at least ten pen pals I kept up with throughout middle school."

"Does it bother you that you ended up doing something else?"

"Did I, though?" Someone honks in the background, and Rachel mutters a curse. "Man, some people have no business being on the expressway." She's quiet for another few seconds, undoubtedly maneuvering away from the bad driver. "Sorry, what was the question again? Oh right, work. So, today for example, I prepared a stakeholder release about projected earnings for the fourth quarter. Some would argue that's not too far from writing a letter. And this evening, I replaced the brakes on the Chevelle."

Ah, she's driving home from the garage. "No dolphins, though."

"Which is for the best considering my mediocre swimming skills." I hear the click of her turn signal. She must be getting closer to home. "What's this about?" she asks.

I tell her about the elementary booklet. "I guess I was hoping you'd tell me childhood aspirations are bullcrap. But clearly not."

"Sounds like little Holly reached through the space-time continuum to grab you by the collar and rattle you up a bit. So now you're wondering what will make you happy."

"What? No. I'm wondering if I should go back to practicing law. Maybe this wasn't meant to be. I feel like I tried my best, and I've got nothing to show for it."

Rachel is quiet for a moment. "You're giving up?"

"Or I'm coming to my senses."

FINDING MR. JULY

"Look, I've pulled into my garage and I'm starving, but don't do anything rash, okay? If I were you, I'd spend some serious time thinking of your fifth-grade goals instead. Fifth-grade you was smart."

We say goodbye and hang up, but later when I'm at my laptop, her words linger as I renew my nonprofit searches despite the seeming futility of the effort. Rachel thinks I'd be happier staying in this field, and she's probably right.

I don't sleep well. Ten-year-old me haunts my dreams all night, dancing frantically to Pharrell Williams's "Happy" in a colorful courtroom.

For the company event, Rachel talks me into going as Sandy from *Grease* to her Rizzo. My hair is curled, and I'm wearing all black beneath a shiny pink bomber jacket. I've also brought a pair of sunglasses, both to achieve the right attitude and to hide behind when Manny makes the announcement.

GCL has rented out the same bar in our building where we had the anniversary party six weeks ago, so as soon as I step inside, I'm flooded with memories from that night. I scan the bar for Jonathan, but unless he's in an inflatable T. rex costume, he's nowhere to be seen, and somehow I doubt that would be his choice of getup. In fact, I can't imagine him dressing up at all, which means he'll probably show up in his regular black clothes looking like...Danny Zuko.

Wait a minute—did Rachel plan this?

"Holly, over here." Ashley waves to me from one of the booths by the window. She's Cleopatra to match Eric's Caesar.

Letitia is in a gray wig and black flowy robes with a white collar. "RBG," she says when I sit down, pointing at herself. "Thought you'd get a kick out of that."

"It's good," I agree. A server comes by with a tray of complimentary champagne glasses, so I snag one and down half of it.

"Looks like someone's nervous," Callum says from behind his Batman mask.

"I think we all are." Letitia glances toward the small stage. "I wish they'd get it over with."

"That's the beauty of knowing you don't stand a chance," Ashley says, holding her hand horizontal in front of her. "See. Zero nerves."

"Next time, babe." Eric kisses her cheek. "I believe in you."

Soon the two of them have retreated into their own world, leaving Letitia, Callum, and me to entertain ourselves, but the conversation never takes off. We're opponents tonight, and as much as we've gotten along until this point, the fact that only one of us can win overshadows everything else.

I breathe a sigh of relief when Rachel finally shows up and rescues me. Not only do I prefer her company, but her costume also lends logic to mine. I let her guide me to the bar and order me a glass of wine.

Still no sign of Jonathan.

"Looking for someone?" Rachel asks when I've swiveled my head for the third time.

I have a sip of my chardonnay to avoid answering, but she is, as always, perceptive. And persistent.

"Did he tell you he'd be here?"

"I think you forget that we're still not speaking."

"He helped you in the garage the other day."

"Because he's not an asshole." I glance toward the door again.

"You want him to be here," Rachel says when I turn back to the bar. "Does that mean you're not mad at him anymore? Have you forgiven him?"

I sigh. "I don't know. Ask me again after they announce the winner." When she doesn't respond other than to lift one of her brows, I add, "I suppose I thought, since we worked on this together, we'd deal with the outcome together. I know it's stupid since there's no 'together' anymore, but I don't know—I was really hoping he'd show."

Rachel's face scrunches into a look of deepest sympathy as she pets my shoulder. "Damn, you've still got it bad."

"Do not." I look away to hide the intense blinking I'm forced to do to save my makeup.

She pulls me into a one-armed hug that only makes things worse. "Whatever you say."

The microphone squeals with feedback. It's time.

"Thank you. Thank you very much," Manny says with a Southern twang as his Elvis costume glitters in the light. "I see you, Bob." He points to the old custodian who is also dressed as the King. "Good choice, my man." He takes the microphone off the stand and grins. "Good evening, beautiful people. Oh, I just love Halloween, don't you?"

Everyone claps. I put on my sunglasses.

"Tonight is about having fun and enjoying each other's company. A chance to kick back before we enter the holiday season, which we're going to make our best ever this year, am I right?"

More applause.

"But before we can do that, we have five people in here dealing with more suspense than most of you, and I am going to put them out of their misery right this minute."

"Please don't call us up onstage this time," I mumble.

Rachel takes my hand.

"We've been crunching numbers all afternoon, and at this time, I can tell you that...we have a winner."

"Woohoo," Eric hoots from the booth.

"Yes, indeed." Manny grins. "But first let me say that you

are all winners in my book." He takes care to find us in the crowd, one at a time. "It was close, folks. Five fantastic fundraising efforts that will contribute to GCL's mission in the year to come. I am honored and privileged to have worked with you."

"Get to it," a random voice shouts from behind me at the bar. DaVon.

Everyone laughs.

"Yeah, yeah." Manny pulls a piece of paper from his back pocket and skims over it. Then he looks up again.

Rachel squeezes my hand. "You've got this."

Despite my misgivings, my heart picks up speed. Maybe there is a small chance after all.

"In fifth place, but with the biggest social media engagement of the group—Ashley."

Hoots and whistles follow. Ashley stands and takes a bow.

"Well done, and we wish you the best of luck." Manny consults his note again. "In fourth place, we've got...Callum. Almost there. Keep at it."

Callum smiles, but even from across the room, I can tell his gracious loser face could use some practice. His cheeks flush red, and he looks down. If I were him, I'd have kept my Batman mask on.

"Aw, I feel bad," Rachel whispers.

"In third place...Drumroll, please." Manny makes a sputtered noise with his lips. "This person actually raised the highest gross amount of the five but came in third once expenses were accounted for. A great learning experience for anyone in this field. Congratulations to...Eric!"

Rachel and I look at each other. Holy shit. That only leaves Letitia and me. I down the rest of my wine and scan the space for Jonathan one last time. No luck. He must be adamant not to see me.

The crowd quiets.

"And so," Manny continues, "after six weeks of intense planning and hard work, and with a net profit of a respectable sixteen thousand eight hundred thirty-six dollars, the winner of this fundraising challenge is..."

"Come on, come on, come on," Rachel chants under her breath next to me.

Manny raises a glass of champagne someone has handed him. "Our new Glasgow office program liaison—Letitia Fowler!"

The restaurant erupts in cheers and felicitations with a large faction of the room crowding around the booth where Letitia is currently crying tears of joy.

Manny taps the mic and adds, "And let's give a hand to our runner-up, Holly King. Well done, Holly. It was close!" He tips his glass in my direction.

I don't know if other people hear him over the ruckus, and it doesn't really matter. It's done. I lost. As predicted.

"Can we get a refill here?" Rachel asks the bartender. "On second thought, let's make it something stronger."

Before I know it, I have something golden over ice in front of me. I down it in one go, appreciating the burn. "Thanks," I tell her. "It's not like I didn't know it was coming."

She watches me, a concerned wrinkle between her brows. "Will you be okay?"

"Always." I jump down from my chair. "I'll be right back. I need to go congratulate Letitia."

I make my way through the crowd to where my fellow interns are holding court but hang back until most people return to their tables. Then I take off my sunglasses and put on my biggest smile, which isn't that difficult. I am happy for her. She's worked hard for this.

"So proud of you," I tell her as we embrace. "You'll do great."

"I wish we could both win," she says. "My mom is going to flip about me moving."

Callum scoots in on the bench seat to make room for me. "Have a drink with us. Might be the last time."

"No way," Ashley protests. "We have two more weeks before we're officially done."

I sit down and flag a server. "I'll still have a drink now. I'm not going to lie—I really wanted it."

"Me too," Eric says. "It was the damn catering. It ate too much of the profits."

"For me, not enough people bought wine after doing tastings," Callum says. "I overestimated."

"And I'm sure you know I missed my printer deadline," I add. "Letitia, what's your secret for being so organized and perfect?" I flutter my lashes, and they laugh.

"Seriously, I feel like I got lucky everything worked out. And I'm excited that we got so many trees planted. The Duwamish River Valley needs a lung badly, and with new cedars and firs framing the river, air quality will improve for generations to come."

"I'll toast to that." Eric raises his glass.

We do the same, joining together to celebrate Letitia's effort, and for a few moments, I manage to forget the pickle I'm in.

But then Letitia asks everyone what they plan to do next, and reality comes crashing down. When it's my turn, I tell them the first thing that comes to mind—that I have an interview lined up at a law firm in Texas. After all, it could be true if I wanted it to be.

"I knew it," Callum says. "Once you reach a certain age, it's too hard to change tracks."

Eric slaps him on the shoulder.

Ashley levels him with an icy glare. "You did not just say that."

"What?" Callum lifts his hands in defense. "I didn't say she's old. I meant she's used to a different lifestyle."

I lean in to temper the upset. "Guys, it's fine. He's not completely wrong. But it mainly has to do with my parents and my brother. I'm basically helping him raise my niece, so…" Slight exaggeration, but whatever.

The others nod along.

"You'll have to let us know how the interviews go," Letitia says. "Are you excited about it?"

"Sure." I force a smile.

"Good, that makes me feel better about winning. Leaving my family on the other hand…" She grimaces with clenched teeth.

Callum's and Letitia's words stay with me throughout the evening because the truth is that standing in front of the unknown at this point in my life does feel different than it did ten years ago. My capacity for remaining energized in the face of failure is not infinite anymore. I'm not so jaded that I don't recognize that the unknown inherently brings a chance of possibilities, but with it comes risk. A gamble. And look where that's left me—unemployed and heartbroken.

Maybe what I need is the safe option. Staying with my family. Giving the career I've spent the better part of my adult life on another chance. I'm wiser to the pitfalls now—I won't ever get involved with a coworker again. And like Jude said, not all firms are bad.

The more I think about it, the more sense it makes—to go

back to what I know, back to something I'm good at, away from Washington and Jonathan and disappointment. Why struggle with fitting a square peg into a round hole if I don't have to? Plus I'll have Jude to vouch for me in lieu of a reference from Heckles & Romer. If he explains the situation, maybe they'll listen.

So, Saturday over breakfast, I tell Jude to set up an interview with his new firm.

Ava jumps up from her seat. "You're coming with us?" She rushes me, almost knocking over my coffee. "Thank you, thank you, thank you! Then it won't be completely miserable."

I hug her back, her excitement shoring up my confidence that this is the right thing to do.

"It's not a done deal yet, though," I say, cautioning her.

Jude studies me for a long moment, looking like he's about to say something I don't want to hear, but when he finally opens his mouth, it's with a reassurance that his firm would be lucky to have me. "I'll send off an email later."

He gets a response at 10:30 Saturday evening expressing excitement about my résumé. They're happy to set up a phone meeting Tuesday.

"So soon," I say. "I didn't expect to hear back until later in the week."

"You know how it is; the law never rests."

I do know that. The prospect is suddenly more real, but I tell myself that's good. I can make this work. Idealism is not without merit, but I've always prided myself on living in the real world, which is what this is. All the signs point this way.

All the signs except maybe the single-word text waiting for me when I turn on my phone Sunday morning. It's from Jonathan, and all it says is **Sorry**.

I keep the text to myself. I want to ask Rachel if it means anything, but how is she supposed to know? Nevertheless, I read that little word too many times to count, wondering what…speculating if…hoping maybe. But I still need more than one word.

At the same time, I prepare for my interview with Jude's firm. Our call is set for 5:00 p.m. Tuesday to accommodate my workday. In the back of my mind, I note that this means the team I'll be talking to will still be in the office at 7:00 at night. I remember those days well.

It's the first time I've opened the box with my things from Heckles & Romer since I left. My diplomas and admission certificates, the bound leather law tome my parents gave me when I graduated, half-filled notepads, and a framed photo of Chris and me on Mr. Heckles's yacht. Each item I uncover stirs up memories of my attorney days, but while not all are bad, they also don't do much to boost me for the interview. I thought seeing these items would remind me of who I am, connect me with the identity I once chose for myself. Instead, they only remind me of what I used to do and how it ended. It sounds similar, but the difference is vast. Nevertheless, I tell myself that nothing says I can't do it again. I can do anything I set my mind to.

But it turns out, that's not entirely true.

The interview begins on a high note. The partners have looked into my past achievements, courtesy of the portfolio Jude provided them with. They're impressed, they say. "So, tell us why you want to work here."

I blink at the computer screen. There are three of them. Three smiling men in suits against a generic bookcase backdrop. They're younger than the partners at Heckles & Romer, but the slight pallidness of their skin is the same, speaking of irregular meals and infrequent exercise. I know exactly what they'll look like in ten years.

Yes, why do I want to work there? Somehow, I doubt "I want to be where my family is" or "I have no choice" will be acceptable answers.

"I've been looking for a smaller firm," I hear myself say. "One where my business law expertise could make a difference in the lives of regular people. My brother tells me you're expanding your services on the family business law side."

The men nod and launch into a series of rapid questions regarding my visions there. I know my responses resonate, that I am acing this interview, but the longer the call goes on, the sweatier I get. It starts in my palms and moves up to my torso until my shirt clings to my back. I'm parched, and if I wasn't on camera, I'd be guzzling from the bottle of water next to me.

"What are your long-term aspirations?" one of the men asks suddenly. "Where do you see yourself in five years? Ten?"

"We do offer a partner track," another one chimes in. "Which I assume someone with your background would be interested in."

My tongue feels like a wad of cotton as I scramble for an answer. I don't understand it—I have always had a plan. Several plans. Short-term ones and long-term ones. But right now, I'm drawing a blank. When I try to corral my thoughts into visualizing what my ideal future looks like practicing law, they skate away like quicksilver. And then I realize that if not for these men watching me, I wouldn't even be trying.

I've been guided by professional aspirations my whole life. Every one of my successes and failures has been linked to tangible achievements. I've hinged my life satisfaction on doing instead of feeling.

What do you want to be when you grow up?

"Holly? Did we lose you there?" one of the partners asks.

Happy, I think. *My long-term plan right now is to be happy.*

And going backward isn't going to achieve that. Not even the most ideal job would. I need more.

"Sorry, you're breaking up a bit," I say. "Might be the Wi-Fi. If I lose you, I—" I disconnect the call. Let out a shaky breath. A panicked giggle. Then I down the water bottle.

When it's empty, I throw it in the trash and lean back in my chair, resting both palms on my closed laptop. I only know one other person who knows this level of floundering—who's lost track of themselves and struggled with moving forward and who would fully understand my headspace. Understand me.

The one person who has given me a glimpse of happy.

I reach for my phone and dial.

"You've reached Jonathan Summers. Please leave a message at the tone."

Damn it.

I almost hang up, but then I think how much I'd hate if he did that to me, so after a brief silence, I sputter out a "Hi." I clear my throat and press the phone closer to my cheek. "I didn't expect to get your voice mail, so sorry in advance if I ramble." I get up and pace to the window in my room, take in the dimming sky. "Um, I got your text, so I assume you know how Friday went. Not great, that is. I, um, thought you'd be there. I looked for you." My fingertips brush my reflection in the pane. The glass is like ice. "I'd hoped you'd be there," I clarify in a lower voice.

Then I spin around and draw a deep breath. "Anyway, I just had this urge to call. I had an interview actually—with Jude's new law firm if you can believe it. Botched it in the end. So now, while everyone else has a direction, I don't have the faintest clue what I'm going to do. And all I could think about was how that would matter so much less if I could talk to you about it." I dig my teeth into my lower lip. "I miss you. I know I said stuff, but I know you didn't sabotage the calendar on purpose. I'm sorry if I wasn't clear on that. I'm still disappointed, of course, but Letitia deserved to win. Her plant-a-thon is going to do so much good with all those new evergreens along the Duwamish. Now, that's impressive."

On my desk, I push a binder aside to reveal the back of a copy of our calendar. A collage of the twelve photos adorns most of the page. "But I don't know," I say, more to myself than to him. "I'm proud of what we did, too. All of it." I linger on the dramatic shot of Jonathan and Sir Leonard surrounded by a shower of fireworks. Resist the urge to caress it.

"Anyway..." I blink the moisture behind my eyelids away and swallow. "That's all. Nothing important. I totally get if you don't want to talk. Just know I wish you the best."

Then I hang up, wondering if this is what closure feels like and if it's supposed to hurt this much.

39

I do email the Texas firm to apologize for the disruption to the call, and they, in turn, express continued interest in arranging a second interview, this time in person. I never even entertain the idea, and a few days later, I bow out of the process citing "other opportunities" as my reason.

Ava doesn't talk to me for several days, and Jude isn't happy with me for putting him in the awkward situation of having referred someone who failed to deliver on the hype. But since he and Rachel have finally landed on a date to get together, he's mercifully forgiving.

My phone remains silent, and if Jonathan is in the office, he's more deserving of his old nickname, The Shadow, than ever before.

But Monday morning, I arrive back from lunch to find a meeting invitation from Manny for 4:00, so like it or not, I'll have to venture past the elevators again.

"Do you know what it's about?" I ask Rachel.

She looks at my screen. "No. Could be an exit interview maybe? I wouldn't worry about it."

I don't, but I still have high school–level jitters as I enter the office space across the way. Here's the corridor where I chased after Jonathan that morning, the rec room where boundaries were crossed, his office where things went south. I approach his space slowly, inching toward the glassed wall as if I'm expecting someone to jump out and scare me, but I needn't have worried. Only Jacques is there.

Relief and disappointment fight each other for purchase inside me as I continue around the corner to where Manny's office is located, but once I get there, I'm distracted by his blinds being drawn. That's unusual.

I sit down facing the door, run my fingertips down the buttons on my shirt, and adjust the clasp to my necklace. I can't possibly be in trouble, can I? Since the announcement, I've done nothing but keep my head down and follow whatever directives Rachel has given me. Maybe she's right, and it's an exit interview.

With no sounds coming from the office, no clues to latch on to, I try to clear my mind as best I can while the minutes pass. I'm just contemplating knocking when the door finally opens, and out comes not Manny but Letitia and…Jonathan. What reason would the three of them have for a meeting? For a split second, his step falters upon seeing me, but then he turns back to face Letitia who is laughing at something Manny has said behind her. They both step into the carpeted hallway.

"We're good?" Jonathan asks Letitia.

"Absolutely." She nods. "It was the right thing to do."

"Okay, good."

"Is Holly out there?" Manny calls from inside.

"She is," Letitia confirms.

Jonathan takes a step back from the door. "I should get going. Let you guys do your thing." He looks at me again. "Hi," he says, and the richness of his voice awakens every cell-level memory inside me. I would give anything to dive into that word, swim around in it, and find out what's beneath it.

I hold his gaze as I stand. "Hi."

He inhales as if he wants to say more, but then his head dips on a turn, and he walks away. I numbly watch his back as he disappears around the corner.

"Come on in," Letitia says. She holds the door open for me so I can enter the office and follows me inside.

My head buzzes with misfiring synapses. She's in my meeting, too? Not an exit interview, then.

"Sorry for keeping you waiting," Manny says to me, gesturing to the chair next to Letitia's. "I'm sure you're wondering why I've called this meeting, and I don't plan on keeping you in suspense, so let's get to it."

"Get to what exactly?" I ask. The faint scent of Jonathan's cologne still lingers in the air around me—enough to make me antsy. Now that I've seen him and know he's nearby, anything keeping me away from him another minute seems like a waste of my time.

"There's been a...development," Letitia says next to me. "With the fundraiser."

"What kind of development?"

Manny looks at her before responding, and she nods. "We've been alerted to an issue with the plant-a-tree walk-a-thon that affects the net profit of Letitia's campaign."

I spin to look at her, but her expression is completely unruffled.

"Do you want to explain?" Manny asks her.

"Sure." She scoots forward in her seat and puts her finger on a map lying open on Manny's desk. "It's about the area where the trees are to be planted," she says. "The Duwamish River is prone to flooding, so the riverbanks don't have adequate drainage for the evergreens I planned to plant."

My gaze cuts from the map to her and Manny. "Okay?"

"Which means I need to buy a different species—and unfortunately that's going to be a lot more costly."

"Oh." I say it as if everything's now fallen into place, when in reality, I still don't see what this has got to do with me.

"I made a mistake." Letitia shrugs.

"An honest one that not many people would have caught," Manny adds.

"But someone did," I say, knowing exactly who that someone is.

Manny nods but then defers again to Letitia, who briefly reaches out to touch my arm. "This means that, after subtracting the additional expense from my campaign, I'm no longer the winner. It wouldn't be fair to you to pretend otherwise."

I blink at her, the room wobbling. I must have heard her wrong. *I won?*

"But," I say, resisting the urge to put my head between my knees, "you raised so much money, and I..."

She shakes her head. "The job in Glasgow is yours if you want it. It's what's fair. And if I'm going to be honest, when Jonathan came to me with this, my first feeling was relief. It's just my mom and me and my younger siblings, and we're super tight. I don't know what I'd do being so far away from them even if it was just for a year."

"So, congratulations, Holly." Manny grins. "I'll draw up a contract as soon as you say the word."

"I'm sorry, I can't feel my face," is all I manage.

Manny stands. "I'll take that as a yes."

Images of Glasgow apartments rise to the surface of my

mind. It's really happening? "Yes. Thank you so much. But what about you?" I ask Letitia. "Now you have nowhere to go."

"No, no," Manny says. "I already spoke to the board members, and we decided to make space for her here in Seattle. It's more of an entry-level position that can grow into something more, but she'll still stay with GCL."

I turn to her. "And you're happy with that."

"I am. Promise." She smiles. "I won't hold it against you if that's what you're worried about. I was the one who made a mistake. Actions have consequences."

They do. But so does *in*action, and now that I know my victory won't mean her demise, I can't delay any longer.

I stand abruptly. "I'm really glad this is working out, but if you don't mind, there's somewhere I need to be. Can we continue this conversation tomorrow?"

Manny nods. "I need another word with Letitia anyway. You go ahead."

I sprint down the hallway to Jonathan's office, but it still only holds Jacques. I knock on the window and push open the door. "Do you know where Jonathan went?"

"No idea." He cranes his neck to better see Jonathan's desk. "But it looks like he grabbed his stuff, so he's probably done for today. Anything I can help with?"

Damn it. He can't be far ahead of me, though. "No, but thanks." I take off again, this time to the elevators. My foot taps against the tile as I wait. *Hurry, please.*

Finally, the doors open, and the people already inside cram together to make room for me. It's the end-of-day rush, and unfortunately, that means we stop on every floor for more home-bound folks. Sweat is pooling between my breasts. I'm going to miss him. He's probably already out of the garage. If it was anyone else, I'd text them, but this time, I need to talk to him in person. I need to see his face, read his eyes, feel his energy. Otherwise, what we had might as well be only a figment of my imagination.

I'm right—I don't see his car, but since he has Sir Leonard at home, I can't imagine he's going anywhere but straight there, so that's where I set course.

A windy Seattle rushes past my car windows as I speed along Aurora Avenue. Concrete buildings, bundled-up pedestrians, graffitied underpasses, construction zones. But also vast parks, a choppy Lake Union, and rows of cute bungalows sporting both leftover jack-o'-lanterns and early holiday lights.

Jonathan's garage is open when I turn into his driveway, and he's still inside unloading equipment. He pulls up short when he sees me.

I don't check my hair or teeth in the mirror. The urgency is too great. That is, until I'm out of the car and face-to-face with him. Then the spinning world slows like a Tilt-A-Whirl running out of steam, leaving me unsteady. I first stop ten feet away but change my mind and walk another two steps closer.

For a breathtaking moment, it seems as if the wind dies down and the city noise fades around us. He's so real, standing here in front of me. Perhaps that's a strange observation, but it's what comes to mind. He's real and regarding me like he's worried I'm not.

"You got the job," he says finally.

A microburst chooses that moment to stir up a heap of dead leaves between us. The tail of it whips my hair across my face.

"I did." I sputter at the strands sticking to my lips. Tuck them back behind my ears. "I'm guessing thanks to you?"

There are so many things I want to ask. How did he know

about the trees? Why go to the trouble? But also, does him helping me today mean he wants me to leave? My heart aches anew at the possibility.

I pull my jacket closer around me, but a shiver runs through me anyway, made stronger by him stepping out of the garage toward me.

"I needed to make it right. I know I messed up." He looks down, rubbing a hand across his neck. "You don't know how sorry I am. About everything—the way I talked about the calendar in the beginning, not believing in it, downplaying the deadline, not double-checking the submission. I know I'm a screwup. Story of my life. But I am trying. Meeting you made me want to do better. It's made me want to change a lot of things, if I'm honest. And I know enough about conifers from Dad to know most of them don't thrive in waterlogged ground. But I understand if it's too little too late. I just want you to be happy." He shoves his hands into his pockets and shrugs.

That word again. *Happy.* I got the job, so I should be, right?

"I am grateful to win the job," I tell him, taking care to emphasize the choice of words. "But the happiest I've been in a long time is with you."

His eyes find mine, the gray swirling with confusion.

I pick one of my questions with care and steel myself. "Do you want me to go to Glasgow? Is that why you helped me?"

"What?"

"We knew this was complicated, especially if I won. Well, now I have. But I'm thinking that maybe things are only as complicated as we make them. So, do you want me to go? Or do you want me to stay?"

Right away, his full lips part as if he's been preparing for the question, but nothing comes out. The silence stretches infinite, invading my senses, and as the seconds go by, any hope I harbored wilts inside me. I guess that's my answer.

"That's okay," I say, backing away. "All I wanted was to say thank you. I won't bother you anymore."

But as I turn to reach for my door handle, footsteps pound the pavement behind me.

"No," Jonathan says, grasping my shoulder. "That's not what I want at all."

I look up into his beautiful face. "No?"

"In fact, I was hoping you'd come. Was hoping you'd...stay." He gulps down the last word and then brushes something invisible off his brow. His scent billows toward me, prompting a starved inhale.

I search his eyes. "If you really mean it, I will." For the first time in weeks, a genuine smile grows from deep in my core. "Who needs Scotland, right?"

"No," he says again, this time taking my hands. *Oh, his hands...* "I meant stay awhile. Here. Now. I would never ask you to give up your career for me. You'd resent me for it one day, and already knowing what that feels like, I couldn't bear more of it." He reaches for my temple and runs a featherlight caress through my hair. "Because I love you."

I blink at him. "You..."

"And if you love someone, you set them free."

Wait, what? I try to make sense of what I'm hearing. He loves me, so he wants to put an ocean between us?

"You look confused," he says.

"Um, yeah. You love me?"

A crooked grin. "You're still stuck on that bit?"

"But you want me to take the job in Glasgow?"

"It's what you've been working so hard for. To leave. Start over."

I shift my stance, putting weight first on my right side and then the left. "But you would stay here."

"Right."

"I see." I nod to myself. How do I explain this to him? "I'm sorry but I think that means we have a problem."

It's his turn to look confused. "How so?"

"Because there's no way I can go without you." When he still just blinks at me, I fling my arms around his neck, barely giving him a chance to react and catch me as I let out the truth. "Because I love you, too! So much. If you want me to go to Glasgow, we're going to have to figure out a way for you to come with me."

Two crows stir from their spot on the grass at the commotion while Jonathan blinks at me. "But the job..."

"...is just a job," I say. "I want more now." I lean back in his arms to make sure he's listening. "Don't you get it? I want you."

An explosion of light goes off behind his gray irises, a jubilant imitation of his photo spread in the calendar. "You do?"

When I nod, he crushes me to him briefly before kissing his way from the top of my head down my forehead, temple, and cheek. He cups my face and presses his lips to mine. Soft, but determined. Indulgent, but urgent. Kissing him is like coming home. A familiar adventure where my favorite flavors shock me with their ability to catch me off guard. He nips my lip harder than I'm used to as if to mark me but then immediately soothes the sting with another light kiss. I return the favor with a sharp tug on his hair that makes him let out a husky hum.

When our most pressing thirst has been quenched and we come up for breath, I steady myself against him and look up. "Did you really have a passport appointment that morning?"

"I did."

"Why?"

"Why?" He laughs. "I guess you brought out the optimist in me."

"But you can't fly."

Instead of responding, he pulls his phone from his back pocket. "Did you know you can get train tickets from Seattle to New York for under four hundred dollars?" he asks. "Boats from New York to Southampton, England, run steeper, though still perfectly doable, at about thirteen hundred, and obviously a trip like that takes significantly longer than a flight—about three days for the train and seven for the boat. Then again, I've been on longer hauls than that in the past."

I gape at him. "You've done research. But I didn't have the job until today."

"I started looking into this after you told me you'd miss me. As much as I fought it, part of me knew I'd need the option to go with you. If you asked me to, that is. My attorney thinks I have a good shot at being removed from the no-fly list."

"You have an attorney and everything?"

"Your brother hooked me up with a referral."

"He did not?"

"Good guy." Jonathan smiles. "It'll take some time, but we've started the process. No pressure, of course," he hurries to add. "It needed to be done either way, but—"

"No, of course I want you to come with me." I jostle him with my grip on his jacket. "Are you kidding me? Please, come with me. I love you. Come to Glasgow with me. We'll both start over. Together."

His expression softens, his gaze velveteen as he cups my cheek. "You asked," he says.

"I did." I rise up on my toes and kiss him again. Then another thought occurs. "What about Wayne?"

"No, my dad is not going to Glasgow," Jonathan says, matter-of-factly. Only the crinkling at the corner of his eyes betrays the joke.

I pretend to slap his chest.

"No, but seriously." Jonathan shakes his head. "The guy signed himself up for a rideshare service subscription. He probably got tired of me using him as an excuse."

"Another good guy," I say.

"And I already checked. Sir Leonard is more than welcome both on the train and on the boat. He should be able to join us no problem."

Us. The word sinks in. Suddenly there's a future for *us*.

The world around me tilts as if another microburst has decided to target me instead of the leaves on the ground. I grasp Jonathan tighter and hide my face against his chest. Let out a shuddering breath and, with it, the tension that's accumulated over the past two months. All that's left is Jonathan and me and possibilities.

"You okay?" he asks into my hair.

I take him in fully, this complex man who's both been through the wringer and seen me through mine. Who's not perfect, but perfect for me. Who's changed me for good.

"Better than okay," I say. "Now I'm happy."

Epilogue

Seven months later

"Hello?" I knock, pressing my ear to the heavy door in front of me. "Jonathan?"

There's no response, but stray notes of music reach my ears from the other side, so I try again. "Can you hear me?"

The walls of the basement in our Glasgow town house are thick and impenetrable—once having provided shelter during the Blitz—and my voice is swallowed up by the low ceiling. I know this, but the glow of my phone screen tells me it's almost 8:00. High time to get out of here.

I raise my hand to knock again, but this time, it meets air as Jonathan yanks open the door to his darkroom.

"Sorry, I had to finish fixing a couple of the photos." He kisses me on the cheek while wiping his hands on a paper towel. "Are we late?"

"Not if we leave in five." I trail him through the carpeted space that we've recently turned into a guest room–slash–movie hangout. A foldable partition separates a bed, nightstand, and desk from the communal sofa and projector screen, and as we pass it, I can't help but fluff the pillows on the bed one more time.

"Ava is going to love it," Jonathan says, coming up behind me. "I love it. And once she goes back, I'll come down here to sleep when you snore."

"I've told you it's Sir Leonard, not me."

He tuts and shakes his head. "Blaming the dog... I suppose he's responsible for the unique smells, too?"

"Very funny." I set off up the stairs, taking them two at a time. "Did everything go okay today?"

"Yes." Jonathan turns off the light behind us. "The music is helping. I'm visualizing, I'm breathing."

He's been seeing a therapist for four months to combat his claustrophobia, and it's starting to pay off. Every week, he's able to stay in there longer, and I can see how engaging with the medium manually like this is sparking his creativity. For his part-time day job as staff photographer at a well-known dog-themed magazine, everything is digital, but he likes his colleagues, and Sir Leonard is a favorite in the office whenever he tags along. Jonathan is also starting to regain his artistic reputation with his inspired photographic studies of the Highlands.

"Proud of you," I say. "But now we really need to leave."

"It's evening. Traffic shouldn't be bad."

"Traffic is always bad around the airport."

"Ah. Another reason I can't wait to be allowed on a plane again."

I toss him the car keys and grab my bag. "Would you prefer another seven days on a boat?"

He saunters over to me and corners me against the doorjamb. "I have nothing but good memories from that week." He nuzzles the skin beneath my jaw. "Big sky, wide-open ocean, good food, lazy hours in bed..."

His lips find mine, and I allow myself to get swept away, back to our New Year's journey where a whole lot of this took place. I even let him photograph me like one of those "French" girls. It seemed fitting since we were on an ocean liner. Thankfully, our journey was iceberg-free.

His hands find their way underneath my T-shirt, leaving thrills in their wandering wake. I groan, wishing we had time for more. Wishing I'd not waited to go get him until the last minute.

"We can't," I mumble against his cheek. "Jude will kill me if we're not there when Ava lands. He's been texting me nonstop."

"I know." He coaxes my lips apart one more time, our tongues meeting with a soft stroke before he pulls away, stepping back. He adjusts himself, a gesture that, paired with his flushed face and rumpled hair, makes him look like a teenager caught red-handed. It takes all my willpower not to dive straight back into his arms.

"I love you more every day," I say. "Did I tell you that already?"

He holds the front door open to let me pass. "You did, but I'll never tire of hearing it."

As Jonathan backs into the street, I click open my email to get a bit more work done since I've taken the rest of the week off to help Ava get settled. She's staying with us for the summer to give Jude and Rachel some space. At first, she wasn't thrilled to see her dad dating someone, but when he made the surprise decision to stay in Seattle two more years to let Ava finish high school, she warmed right back up. Now she and Rachel get along great.

There's an unread message from Rachel at the top titled "The gift that keeps on giving," so I open that first. She starts with updates about my brother and how she's remedying his lack of automobile know-how, and then she moves on to office gossip—who gets rowdy at happy hour, who's dating, what projects they're working on.

"Letitia is already being promoted from program assistant to associate," I say to Jonathan. "Good for her."

He hums in acknowledgment as he navigates a roundabout like he's always driven on the left side.

Finally, I get to the meat of the email, and as I read, a wide grin blooms on my lips. When I reach the end, I read it again.

"You're never going to believe this," I say to Jonathan.

"What?" He glances at me but quickly returns focus to traffic on the M8. We're getting closer to the airport, and I was right—it's pretty bad.

"They're planning another edition of the calendar for next year, and now Canberra and Brasilia want in on it, too."

"No way."

"Yeah, this thing has taken off." I gesture to my phone. "One of our Australian donors—a recreation gear retailer—has offered to fund an annual edition of it. Everything from models and photography to production and marketing. They are estimating it will net GCL well into the six figures every year by selling it globally."

"Holy shit." Jonathan laughs.

"Aaand..."

"There's more?"

"Left, left, that's our exit!"

Jonathan swerves and barely manages the turn. "Sorry, I got distracted. You were saying?"

"The board wants to auction off a framed print from the calendar—our choice—at that fancy Fourth of July gala next month. Not bad for a small pinup project, wouldn't you say?"

Above us, a giant plane descends with a gut-punching roar.

Jonathan smiles. "Not bad at all. That's awesome. So which photo do you think we should give them? The Samoyed? Or maybe the Newfoundland? They both have a lot going for them in tone and composition. If I may say so myself."

"You certainly may." I grin at him as he enters the parking lot and begins his quest for a free space. "And I'm not sure. I'll have to spend some time on that."

I keep my answer vague on purpose. For now, I'll let him think this is up for debate. But as I look around me at the vast Scottish sky, still midsummer bright with Glasgow on the horizon, I already know what my pick will be—the photo that made all of this possible. My favorite and only choice.

My Mr. July.

Acknowledgments

I cannot believe I get to express my gratitude like this a seventh time! My seventh book, entering the world in the seventh month. Feels apt. If you'd asked me seven years ago, I would have expressed doubt that even one of my books would see the light of day. What an adventure it's been, and what wonderful fellow travelers I've had the fortune to keep me company, because as much as my stories are born in the solitude of my imagination, getting them to this stage is most definitely a group effort.

Thank you first, as always, to my agent, Kimberley Cameron, for your unwavering belief in my work. It means so much.

To my whole team at Forever who have brought this book to life—Estelle Hallick, Alli Rosenthal, Caroline Green, Daniela Medina, Rebecca Holland, Mari C. Okuda, Xian Lee, Taylor Navis, Maya Chessen, Grace Fischetti, and especially my brilliant editor, Alex Logan—you guys rock! Also a huge thank-you to my cover designer, Sarah Kellogg, who knocked it out of the park with this one if you ask me!

To my treasured critique partners Megan McGee and Melissa Wiesner. I'm forever thankful for your friendship and all the gut checks, cheers, brainstorming sessions, and feedback.

When I wasn't sure where Holly and Jonathan were headed, you guys kept me on track.

To Em, Julia, Lana, Lisa, and Megan—this whole thing is twice as fun with you by my side.

Thank you to my husband for being my person and for branching out in the kitchen to make sure we had food when I juggled multiple projects at once. Second career? You never know. To my kids, just for being awesome people who make me want to do better every day. Love you so much! And a big grateful cuddle to my dog muse, Archie, for the never-ending inspiration. (Pup-spiration?)

Thank you to my parents and sisters for loving books as much as I do, and for always being supportive—with an extra shout-out to Sara for giving my books their own shelf in your bookcase. Let's hope you one day run out of space!

And finally, as always, thank you, dear booksellers, librarians, book bloggers, and readers for picking up this book when there are so many others you could have chosen. Thank you for your messages, your reposts, your reviews, and your loyalty. Your enthusiasm never fails to boost me into the next story, and in doing so, you make my day again and again. I will always strive to do the same for you!

About the Author

ANNA E. COLLINS is an award-winning Seattle-area author of contemporary romantic comedies and women's fiction. Her work has earned praise from *Kirkus, Publisher's Weekly, Booklist,* and *Library Journal,* as well as coverage in *USA Today, Woman's World,* and PopSugar, among other outlets. Once upon a time, Anna was a high school teacher in Sweden, but after moving to the US with her American husband and two children, she realized she had stories to tell. When not writing, reading, or raising teens, Anna can be found exploring other creative pursuits such as drawing and singing, as well as snuggling with her mini goldendoodle, Archie, who is a Very Good Boy.

You can find her at:
   aecollinsbooks.com
   Instagram: @aeccreates
   Facebook.com/aecollinsbooks
   X: @AEC_Writer
   TikTok: @aeccreates